KILLER LESSONS

By Erika Shearin Karres

Martin Sisters Publishing

ISBN: 978-1-62553-005-9
Editor: Brittani Wolanin
Thriller

Printed in the United States of America
Martin Sisters Publishing, LLC

DEDICATION

This book is for Liz, Deesie, Vickie, Katie, and Sarah,
with love and gratitude

Do all the good you can. (John Wesley, 1703-1791)

⁰PROLOGUE⁰

Blah-blah-blah. Because of the headmaster's long-winded greeting, the young substitute teacher who was on her first assignment got to her sunny classroom barely fifteen minutes before first period was over. She had hardly greeted the class, scanned the lesson plan, and launched into a passionate lecture when the bell rang, but the students took it all in stride. They got up, said "Bye" or "See you Monday," and emptied out into the hallway in a civilized manner.

But one girl lingered at her desk in the back, digging through her book bag, taking out her laptop, putting it back. Same thing with her folders, pens, and small Prada purse. Out of the bag, in again. She poked around in the pockets of her pleated skirt and looked under her desk, instead of swiftly heading for the next class like the other kids.

The substitute marched over. "Did you lose something?" From a poor rural background, she was nervous about working in this elite school and didn't want the girl to get marked tardy because of something that happened in her class, but the girl just shook her head. After making sure all the other kids were gone, she whispered, "I'm scared out of my mind. *Please* help me. I can't talk to anyone here but I think there's something horrible—"

Before she could finish, two of her friends raced back into the room, glared at the substitute teacher and grabbed the girl's backpack, yelling, "C'mon. You can't be late. Remember the Code of Conduct."

"I didn't say anything," the girl said, turning fiery red. She ran off just as the sun ducked behind the clouds, making the room surprisingly dark. But before the girl disappeared, she shot a last look over her shoulder at the substitute teacher. It was a pleading look, a desperate look, a look that cried out for help, just like one from a calf being taken to the butcher.

PART 1:
THE STEFFORD SCHOOL

CHAPTER 1

Qiana crawled out from under her bed and stared at the door of her jam-packed bedroom. *Oh no. Who stole my picture?* Just a few hours earlier the side facing her had held a big photo that was her most treasured possession. Now the door was bare, with nothing but a bent nail sticking out of it, surrounded by mustard-colored peeling paint flecks.

She scrabbled over to find out who had breached her special security system. No one. The thick bolt she had engaged from the inside was still in place. The key in the heavy-duty lock was still turned all the way. And the arm of the hotel-room lock bar was still on just like she'd left it at midnight.

She looked around wild-eyed. Was her imagination playing tricks on her? *And why was I sleeping under the bed? And gee, what's all that stuff I've been lying on?* Three stained wedding dresses were bunched up like she'd used them for blankets. Continuing to wrack her mind over the disappearance of her picture, she examined the dresses and her memory kicked in.

9

Late last night as she was sipping red wine for the last time, since she had vowed to stop drinking, and trying on the gowns in preparation for getting married, she got so tired. But before she could climb into bed, she tripped. Tried to get up, but then didn't and just holed up under the bed like an injured animal. Obviously at night her past still had a grip on her.

Well, now it's daytime. And where's my picture?

This certainly wasn't a good way to start the day. She rubbed her forehead, trying to erase her hangover headache and wrestled the only window there was open. Maybe the thief had crept in that way. But no, the window looked like it hadn't been opened in eons. Took forever to pry it open, during which Qiana got madder and madder. She was sure it wasn't her imagination. Someone was messing around with her. Who was it?

Never mind now, I've got too much to do. She yanked open one of her trunks and went to work. In seconds bundle after bundle of sequined halter tops, elastic mini-skirts and purple rabbit-fur jackets sailed through the open window and landed in the Dumpster in the alley below. Pitch-pitch-pitch. This was all expensive stuff and selling it at the nearby consignment shop where the wedding dresses had come from would bring in some serious cash. But the thought that some girl would end up wearing this trash was unbearable. Pitch-pitch-pitch.

One trunk down, 19 more to go. Unexpectedly Qiana felt hot tears trickling down her cheek and swiped at her cheeks. But no time now for feeling sorry for herself and worrying about who could be so cruel as to steal the photo that showed three people— her fiancé Gunner, his sister, and herself.

Onward, no time to waste. I'm going to stop child abuse.

Qiana sniffed the musty air, ruffled her short platinum curls. From habit she pinched her cheeks that were always too washed-out looking, but only once. No need to undo her latest Botox treatment.

10

A chill crept through the open window. She took a deep breath, yanked on one of Gunner's old football jerseys and looked around. *What next?* She would work all day until all her remaining stuff was respectable. That meant she'd have hardly anything left, but so what?

Zeroing in on the next trunk, she squeezed between the crates, lockboxes, and luggage crammed into her small room. The cracks in the walls and ceiling, made worse every day by the renovations going on downstairs. In one corner wood splinters, trash and cobwebs combined to look like a hand sticking out of the floor and waving, due to the swaying floor boards.

She stomped over and kicked the "hand" to smithereens. This was nothing, just another reminder of the past. *Onward I said.* Yet she kept shivering.

Just another chill, okay? While scrounging around for some leggings to put on, she checked to see just how bad the wedding gowns were messed up. Pretty bad. They all had big blood stains. *Must've cut myself when I tripped.* She was in the process of bundling them up when a hammer-like pounding on the door stopped her: *Bam-bam-bam.*

Not amused, she opened her useless locks and her housemate Honee, wearing lots of padding, yet looking amazing with her beautiful dark-honey skin, barged in. "Move it, girl," she snapped. "Time to substitute teach."

"Have you lost your mind?" Qiana snapped back. "Can't you see I'm up to my neck in stuff? Besides, someone stole my picture." She indicated the empty door.

"You sure you didn't take it to the frame shop? You talked about it."

"No, not that I can remember." But maybe Qiana did drop off the big photo there. With all the mind-boggling events that had been going on recently, she was on serious overload. Besides, even when things were totally in sync, she always feared the worst. She

11

was the kind of woman who just *knew* she had stage IV cancer of the uterus at the slightest tummy twinge. And now with all those epic changes in her life, she felt totally anxious and out-of-kilter.

"Okay, I'll call that place," Qiana said and glanced at the old-fashioned alarm clock clinging to her rickety nightstand for dear life. "No, too early, I'll do it later. But I still can't go with you. I'm hurt. Look." She brandished a foot, the source of the blood.

"What happened, girl?" Honee leaned down to check Qiana's feet. "Pah, that's nothing, just some *piddlelicious* scrapes. So what? Did the bedposts gangle up on you?"

Qiana couldn't help but smile at the way Honee talked. Whenever she couldn't think of a fancy-schmancy word, she just made one up. Another unusual thing was Honee's way of dressing. For example, instead of taking off her clothes before going to bed, Honee piled on extra layers regardless of the weather, which she knew made her seem nuts, but she couldn't help herself. She felt safer in her layers which she was now in the process of shedding, hoping maybe she could also shed some of the layers of her troubled history. That was something she shared with Qiana. Calling their past a checkered one would be the understatement of the year.

Qiana produced a yawn bigger than a hippopotamus can muster up. "Quit joking, okay?" She dug band-aids out of her purse like a dog after a bone and slapped them on her feet. "Guess I was sleepwalking again and stubbed my toes on those trunks. But honest, I had the worst dream. Picture a blood-thirsty flash mob after—"

"You, girl?"

"No, they were after my purse."

"Yippee yahoo. Why're you always toting your whole life—?"

Qiana cut her off. "Didn't I tell you the moment we met? I'm neurotic as hell to put it mildly, in addition to all my other issues."

She rubbed her left hand. Her rheumatoid arthritis, which she had since childhood and still suffered from, was supposed to be in remission but her little finger had drawn up again. "Besides, didn't we agree to just sit tight until Gunner gets back home?"

"Well, that's not till tomorrow evening, girl. Plus, today gets you out of the house. You won't have time to drag around whining and hankering after—"

"Jealous, huh?" Cocking an eye, Qiana cut Honee off again.

"Nope, not over my own brother." Gunner was Honee's half-brother. They had the same mom, a white woman, but Honee's dad was black; Gunner's white. Neither of them knew they had a sibling until a week ago when, by a kind twist of fate, all three of them had met for the first time. "But man, I miss that dude even though I just met him."

"Same here." Qiana knew it was weird how fast she'd fallen in love with Gunner but rationalized it was meant to be. After so many years of rotten luck, maybe Gunner was her reward. He looked like a baby brother of Tom Brady, but with real blond hair and pale-blue eyes. Gee, how she wished he was standing next to her now on the second floor of this rickety antique shop she had recently inherited from a childhood friend. More precisely, a fellow victim of terrible abuse. Qiana's mind drifted back to the last time she'd seen that poor girl...

Noticing Qiana gazing off over Honee's shoulder at something horrible only she could see, Honee clapped. "C'mon, let's go."

"Sorry, can't. Got way too much on my to-do list."

"It can wait, okay? Now get dressed or I sell that on eBay." Honee pointed to Qiana's gigantic Louis Vuitton bag. "What you got in there anyway?"

"Just my usual. Curling iron, hair dryer, electric tooth brush. Defibrillator just in case, you know. Plus Epinephrine for my allergies and—"

"I mean that." Honee pointed to a piece of cloth lolling out of the purse like a Chihuahua's tongue.

"That's my good luck charm."

"Bring it, girl, by all means. Now five...four...three...two…"

"All ri-i-ight," Qiana groaned. After years of living alone, suddenly having someone crammed in with her in this sardine-can space and trying to tell her what to do was tough. Of course, with Gunner gone, it made the place less creepy. Plus, she promised Gunner to take Honee in and be nice to her.

Still she couldn't suppress how she felt. "Gee." She stomped to the bathroom that was tinier than a JetBlue Airline toilet, slammed the door so hard the antiques on the first floor rattled like yard decorations on a stormy Halloween night. "Can't you do your job by yourself?"

"Better believe I can do my job by myself," Honee said, rushed to her own tiny room and speed-dressed. Without a trace of make-up, she looked stunning with her willowy figure clothed in a shirt three sizes too big and a baggy khaki skirt. Taller than Qiana, she had well-proportioned features. Her dark-honey skin always shimmered like it was kissed by the sun even though Honee never did anything to it besides wash it with soap and water.

On rare occasions, she globbed together some dry grits and Dial suds as her one beauty treatment. Back when Honee was homeless, she'd break into a vacant house and scrub herself down with the sudsy grits that always felt like sandpaper, each time hoping a few spots would come off her sorry soul as well. And maybe she'd even erase the Obama-like parenthetical wrinkles that were starting to etch themselves in around her mouth.

Now Honee had only one thing left to do—scrape the mud off her Adidas. Quick, before Qiana could notice. So far Qiana didn't seem to have a clue Honee had sneaked out during the night. The skin-crawly thing was, someone must've sneaked into the building during that time and climbed up in the unfinished ceiling. Using a fishing pole, he probably knocked the picture off the back of Qiana's door and reeled it up without her ever noticing it, curled up under the bed as she was. What probably happened was that a local piece of junk glimpsed Qiana and immediately craved something belonging to her.

Finished with the shoes, Honee whacked one on the bathroom door. "Besides which," she yelled, "all those students are sweetie-pies, even the big dudes..."

She waited for a comment from Qiana, some smart-alecky remark from the "sophisticated Northern big-city chick" trying to lord it over the "simple-minded Southern country gal." Yeah right, the reverse was the honest truth. Qiana might look cosmopoliticious but she knew navy beans. This was Honee's turf.

When nothing came other than furious tooth-brushing sounds, she went on, louder: "But this is what happened. Last Friday this little chick was just dying to tell me something. But man, what a loony day. All that stuff the office threw at me. Curriculum guides, handbooks, policies. Anyway—" riffling through her pockets she checked the margins of her crosswords "—here's her name. Logan Adams. Poor baby was scared out of her britches. Said she couldn't talk to anyone at the school but didn't have time to tell me what was wrong. So I couldn't do anything about it. But today with you as my teacher aide, I'm gonna get the bottom of it. I got to. See, if I can't even make sure one little chick that begs me for help is fine and dandy, then..."

Qiana didn't hear the rest of what Honee was saying because she skipped to the bathroom and stepped under the wheezing shower head. *This is it—the start of my new life.*

"Gunner, I love you with all my heart," she murmured to herself, remembering the last time she'd seen him, while the tepid water trickled down on her like a soft rain shower. Crazy, wasn't it, how fast they'd fallen in love? He told her he never wanted to marry anyone until the moment he saw her. Meanwhile she'd been

15

asked to marry someone a gazillion times, but each time it was just a lie to get her to cooperate. But this time it was for real. Gunner loved her and she loved him.

They'd been lounging on the old camel-backed sofa downstairs and she'd fallen asleep on Gunner's shoulder, when she jerked up. "Oh God, no!"

"What's the matter, sweetheart?" he asked. "Another bad dream about your childhood?"

"Not this time," she said, having seen in her mind's eye red flashes, as if blood vessels were bursting inside her eyes. What was that—an omen? She destined to witness what?

A blood bath?

Nope, I'm not wacky enough to believe that.

"I think it's just pre-wedding jitters," she said briskly, but her mouth felt tight, "or butterflies about my chance to finally do something I always wanted deep down. But I'm so scared and nervous I'll mess up."

"Don't worry, sweetheart, you'll do fine." Gunner rubbed her shoulders just the way she liked it and kissed her forehead. "And don't fret about the wedding either. That's why I took this gig, see, flying this big wheel to Bermuda. So I can pay the bills. Sure wish I was rich, so we could have a super deluxe—"

"But I don't want a big wedding, Gunner, I told you. Just something plain and simple. I need all the money we can save for a new computer and other office equipment. Actually I've got two goals, first get justice for what was done to me, then start my mission. No, forget about getting justice for me. It's been too long."

He kissed her lips. "Whatever you want, sweetheart. You know I'm behind you 100 percent."

She snuggled up to him as close as she could, inhaling his masculine smell. "Oh Gunner, you're a prince. Now my life is perfect." Wasn't it amazing she had finally figured out what she

16

was meant to do, plus found such a fabulous guy? Gunner knew all about her ugly past and still he loved her. Only in his embrace could she sleep like a baby on her mother's lap and no Chianti or child-like behavior needed.

As Qiana stepped out of the shower, she thought, *What do I really know about him? Maybe he's just using me.* The thought was like a worm boring itself into her heart.

But she'd been so cautious. A week ago when she first met Gunner Gates, she immediately Googled him but nothing popped up to worry her. He was just a regular guy who grew up in Red Mill, NC in a middle class family that took him in at birth. In high school he turned into a football standout, got a scholarship to the local college.

Besides that, there was nothing unusual about him except that he suddenly took up flying—just like those 9/11 hijackers. And now he worked for a private helicopter charter company out of Raleigh, NC and for some reason was super crazy about her.

Doubts crept into Qiana's mind again: *Why is he so into me? Does he have something sinister up his sleeve?*

Her skittish mind lit on something she'd read recently. After the Navy Seals eliminated Osama bin Laden, they found his journal in which he wrote, "Don't use Arabs, they arouse too much suspicion," along with instructions for more horrible mass killings.

Of course Gunner looked nothing like an Arab, just like millions of other young American men, but they couldn't all be home-grown terrorists, right? Still, she had her suspicions and—

Stop it. You're just being paranoid as usual.

Sighing, Qiana veered her thoughts back to where she was—the shabby little bathroom upstairs in a torn-up antique store in the South in Nowheresville. She toweled off, realizing her real problem was she was totally out of her comfort zone—New York City, high fashion, rich people. This rural state, this small town, this rickety junk shop were all so quaint on the surface.

17

What if there's someone nasty lurking behind the scenes? And what if that person stole my picture? But gee, why would anybody do that?

Enough! Qiana got dressed.

"Actually, Honee, I'm thrilled to come along," she said through the warped bathroom door that cracked open on its own. "I really want to help kids that are being abused and maybe someone on the faculty is after Logan. Or maybe she or one of her friends is getting blackmailed over a 'sext.' Gee, some of these girls can be so naive, don't I know it?" She frowned. "What's she look like?"

"She's cute. Looks kinda like you."

"So it's true? To an African American all blondes look alike?"

"Uh-uh, girl. That's a big fat fibulation. But about the sexting, you may be right. Logan sure was scared out of her mind over something. So today while you keep the class busy as bees, I'm gonna find out what it is. The problem is all these kids're so into sports and clubs, there's not a free moment to talk. Aiyeee—" Honee glanced at Qiana, hated what she saw and screeched like a barn owl. "Over my dead body, girl."

Qiana had sashayed from the bathroom in a low-cut, orangey cashmere top and a melt-in-your-mouth leather pencil skirt so tight she had to shoehorn herself into it. Although her forehead was creased in a frown, it didn't detract from her pretty face with the small straight nose, bee-stung lips, royal blue eyes, and pore-less skin. Her paleness was her only flaw but after she troweled on foundation and rouge, her face looked dewy, with her cheeks resembling polished apples.

Add to that her gorgeous shape that she liked to flaunt, and it was only natural that wherever she went, people snapped to like PFC's meeting a five-star general. They were most amazed by her halo of hair that looked like cotton-candy molded into luscious curls.

18

Now Qiana examined herself in a cracked mirror slouching against the wall. "But Honee, that's the only skirt I've got that's not a micro mini."

"Well, it's gotta go bye-bye, girl. You ain't—are not stepping on stage with Lady Gaga. Listen up." Using her finger to underline the words, Honee read from a thick binder entitled *The Stefford Code*: "The best results are achieved in a professional atmosphere and that begins with a staff that dresses the part.' Here you go." She frisbeed granny bloomers, a vomit-green maxi-skirt, and a poop-brown polyester top, size XXL, from Wal-Mart at Qiana.

"Yuck." Qiana touched the garments with pointy fingers as if they were contaminated with E. Coli. "Are you serious? I've got to wear that for one day at the school?"

"Yep, and don't mess it up so I can get a refund."

"Gee," a sigh from Qiana, "well... okay..." More sighing. "Have you seen my iPhone?"

"Since when am I your personal assistant?" Honee groaned as she threaded herself through the trunks and other obstacles, looking everywhere until she unearthed the device. She reached for it, then jerked back as if bitten by a snapping turtle.

"What's the matter, Honee?"

"Nothing. For a moment I was thinking it was my cell but that can't be."

Qiana gasped. "Oh no. Did whoever broke in grab your phone too? What else is missing?"

"Knock it off. There was no break-in. And my cell? I lost it looong ago. Now strap on a cotton-pickin' bra, girl. I want my kids to focus on their lessons, not your big titties."

"Better than having ping-pong balls." Qiana grinned, expecting a sarcastic remark from Honee.

Instead, Honee beamed as she ran her hand from her swan-like neck down to her 32A's. Then she winced because a stab of pain shot through her breasts, where the tissue around her bone-deep scars was still tender.

CHAPTER 2

At 13 Honee felt invincible. Finally everything was cool. She knew all the safe routes. Knew where to make a pick-up and how to deliver the packages, quiet and efficient-like. Plus, she was raking in enough cash to keep herself going—without anyone supporting her.

But one November day when it was sleeting, she took a shortcut through Luke Forest, a vast expanse of thick pine trees. That's when things went rotten fast.

As she ran through the woods, a guy sneaked up behind her, threw her down and pounced on top of her. "Hold still," he said, straddling her, his bony knees digging into her sides.

Trying to escape, she squirmed terrified on the wet ground. But she couldn't get away, with the guy's posse crowding around and yelling: "Me next, Hades! Me next!"

"Just a minute." Hades clicked a switchblade open, cut Honee's shirt apart like tissue paper and ripped it off. Desperately she clutched at the torn material to cover herself. If she'd only worn several layers of clothes, maybe she could've wrestled free before he got down to her bare skin and cut into her like a butcher.

The sight of her nakedness and her blood beading up excited the other guys even more. They pushed Hades out of the way, grabbed her arms and legs, lifted her off the ground. They ripped the rest of her clothes to shreds. Pawed, pinched and punched her. Hit her with sticks. Yanked at her skin, hair, breasts, and tried to invade her with their fingers. They forced her legs apart so violently her hip bones almost snapped. And they kept hurting her worse all the time while yelling obscene words, with Hades urging them on.

She knew she was going to die and felt so sad.

All these years I fought so hard to survive and this is how it's gonna end?

Several times she lost consciousness. Each time she came too, it was worse. The dudes duct-taped her mouth and muffled her screams while they kept mauling her. Tears streaming down her face, she withdrew into herself, waiting for it to be over. Please Lord, make it soon. *Didn't even feel the deep cuts any more. She had given up when the torture stopped suddenly. An older man came running, swinging a baseball bat and offering wads of high-dollar bills. That finally made the gang scatter...*

Quit thinking about it.

Honee shook her head, trying to erase the memory. A second later, she felt a corner of her mouth creep up in a smile because somehow even back then she'd done it—avoided the worst, a horrible death. Man, how lucky she was, always so lucky. Being taken in by this flibberty-gibberty white-bread chick was another huge stroke of luck. So now she had everything except for one thing—romance.

Staring at the peeling wallpaper with the faded flowers, Honee slid her hand from the scars up to her shoulder and down one arm, for a moment pretending it belonged to a guy that liked her enough to give her a rose. *Oh man!*

In reality, her hopes weren't that high. She didn't hope for the impossible—some good guy actually "getting her." Once she heard a girl prancing into a Dairy Queen say, "I wouldn't have him on an ice cream cone." Well, Honee sure would, but she couldn't even get that kind of dude to notice her and pat her on the head like a stray puppy.

She shook her head again. *Why're you thinking such foolish thoughts today?*

No reason. She switched gears, back to the exciting present. "Hurry up, girlfriend," she called to Qiana, skipped downstairs, and ducked into the alcove that used to be the break-room for the antique store, chuckling because she knew: The word *girlfriend* would make Qiana rev up. Both of them had been so lonesome all these years they'd give anything to have a girlfriend. Of course ideally she would've loved having a damn sister.

Lordy-lord! Can't say *damn* in the classroom. Man, so much to do to shape herself up, so much to de-floozy-ate Qiana.Honee rustled up some 3-carbs toast, zapped water in the old microwave that squatted like a roosting hen on a beat-up metal file cabinet. It housed a folder with a newspaper story about how she, Gunner, and Qiana and her parents had met. Almost implausible how it happened but they all got along fine. Now life was perfect. Nothing but smooth sailing here on out.

Clomp-clomp-clomp.

The circular staircase shook as Qiana stomped down to the first floor. Garbed in the frump outfit, she snatched up the cardboard toast and instant java and swallowed a couple Hydrocodones. "Okay, let's check into what your little Logan was so scared about."

Eyes on her handbooks, Honee sipped a mug of Lipton's and gnawed on a clump of Tide she'd dug out of a box. She liked to eat the weirdest stuff.

"I knew you'd help me," she said. "Both of us having been abused, we know the world can be a danger zone. So when I had a second on Friday, I bee-lined it to the guidance counselor. Cool dude, laid back and all, but was he ever up to his neck in little bums. So I asked the office, could I bring in a teacher aide just for one day, so I could take care of—" Honee looked up and her face crinkled like a broomstick skirt. "Didn't I tell you about how primrosish you gotta look?"

"Okay, okay." Qiana dragged an antique tea towel over her cheeks to tone down her make-up. Yanked off false eyelashes resembling giant centipedes. "Ouch. Dammit! Is that any fricking better?"

Honee's eyes raked her over from head to toe. "Some, but no more cussing. Do. You. Hear. Me? Teaching school's about being a role model, not a rap rehearsal. Now slip on your Reeboks. Everybody there wears sane shoes, not killer heels."

Tucking the last crumb into her mouth, Qiana beamed down at her platform pumps with their sky-high heels and sterling-silver ankle wraps. What a pain it was to dig through her luggage and unwrap just about all of her 100 pairs of shoes that she kept swathed in pages torn from her old diaries. Still every now and then she vented her feelings with paper and pen about what bothered her. What cut her to the quick. What broke her heart.

"Want me to go barefoot, huh? I don't own any tennis shoes."

Honee hopped up and grabbed her books. "Girl, why are you so hung up on fancy footwear?"

"It's just my style."

"Okay then, let's hustle." Honee couldn't know that in a few hours these shoes would save both of them from torture. Or worse, much worse.

These shoes would be the only thing to stand between them and the unthinkable.

CHAPTER 3

Ten miles away on the campus of Stefford School, Logan Adams came awake with a start. She ached all over from the uncomfortable position she found herself in. She was duct-taped into an old school desk. Even worse, she'd been gagged. *OMG, what's going on?*

No matter how hard tried to get her bearings, she felt confused. Desperately she listened for any sounds—nothing. She strained her eyes but couldn't see much in the dim space she was in. It was the size of a big closet and made her feel claustrophobic.

Even more horrible, she had been stripped down to her underwear. There were some black magic-marker lines drawn across the tops of her thighs and on her upper arms near her shoulders. *What kind of freakish thing is this? Who's messing around with me?*

Her tears which had been threatening since she woke up, spilled down her cheeks as she realized where she was. Locked away in that ugly old equipment shed near the football field. She'd never been in it because it stank so badly from the outside.

Inside, it stank worse. Plus it was so creepy, like ghosts were hiding behind all that junk that was too good to pitch out but not good enough to use. Broken tennis rackets, deflated footballs, and torn wrestling mats piled everywhere. And in the middle of all that crap, Logan was immobilized in that stupid old desk, marked up like some sort of chart, and hurting like crazy.

It can't possibly get any worse. But it did. Suddenly an old sweat-suit moved and a snake slithered out.

"Help!" Logan screamed but with her mouth taped shut, all she could produce was scared-out-of-her-mind squeaks, sounding like an old rocking chair set in motion by the wind. Nobody heard her except for the copperhead that wove closer like a ribbon of lava and scared Logan so bad she thought she'd faint.

Somebody help me! She pleaded in her mind. *Doesn't anybody miss me?*

Nobody came while the snake serpentined closer. But maybe it would lose interest if she pretended to be dead? Which wasn't far from the truth. Logan had just endured the worst night of her life.

The copperhead stopped three feet away, its triangular head aimed at her like an arrow from hell. That's when she realized what else she smelled—something real gross and disgusting. *Oh no, is that the smell of evil?*

That thought scared her even worse if that was possible. It meant other kids had probably been imprisoned here before and sweated like pigs. Just like Logan did now because she was sure something real *real* horrible was going on at her school. Something way weird was going on with some kids. *And now I'm caught up in it.*

She felt like she was on the edge of a vortex. Any moment she'd get sucked under and die-die-die. *Oh, if I could only talk to that new substitute teacher.*

26

Ms. Money was brand-new to the school but seemed super smart. Most likely she'd see through any smoke screens or whatever. But no doubt about it. She'd rescue Logan and check into what she was so worried about.

Ms. Money, I need you! NOW!

CHAPTER 4

Whistling through her teeth, Qiana sailed over the mud puddles in the neglected service alley that curved behind the antique shop. Helping Honee was a great idea even if it turned out Logan was just freaking out because another girl had bought the same dress for the Homecoming Dance. But no matter what was going on, Qiana would dash to the library and check the computer for any reports of local child molesters. Then make sure none of them had slithered into the school under the guise of "parent volunteer" or "assistant coach." Too often these days, unsavory characters charmed themselves into positions of leadership at a school.

Child predators, watch out. Here I come.

Bursting with nervous energy, she keyed open the faded-blue SUV hunching at the end of the alley and she and Honee climbed in. Seconds later the vehicle zoomed out of Plaza Center, a strip mall thrown up in the 1960's. Over time it had fleshed out into a big L, attracting all kinds of small businesses—from a dime store, discount pharmacy, and a bridal consignment place—from which Honee had "borrowed" the wedding gowns—to a hardware store, cafeteria, McReilly's Sports Bar and several more forgettable places, with the run-down antique shop squatting right in the middle. But not much longer: The shop was about to be reborn, with the proceeds from running it going toward Qiana's work.

Can't wait. She hit the gas even harder and the SUV raced south like a Lamborghini borrowed by a parking valet, entered a country road and cut through a forest of hardwoods that looked imported from paradise.

When they got to a section with trees leaning over the road and forming an intricate roof, Qiana said, "Wow, Honee. Doesn't this look like a cathedral?"

"Sure it does." Honee looked up from reading the *Code of Conduct* and used a bridal veil looking like a tail feather as a bookmark. She was happy to spill a few facts. "After all, this county's named after a saint. Poor guy was a martyr. Thank the Lord, folks aren't into torture anymore."

"What about that water-boarding?"

"I mean now, girl, and in this country."

At that point the SUV bounced across an old bridge with a flimsy railing and a swath of water snaking far below. "That creek down there," Honee went on, "it ends up in a pond that used to be St. Stephen's Ford 'cause a Daniel Boone trail ran across it. But over time the apostrophe got dropped, same with the school. First it was an abbey, St. Stephen at St. Stephen's Ford. Then it changed to St. Steph's Ford, then Steph Ford. And now it's the famous Stefford School."

"Gee, I thought it was Stefford all along, kind of like *The Stepford Wives?*"

"Don't even mention the word *Stepford.* I did it on Friday. Oh man, did the folks in the office go off like roadside bombs. Whole topic's taboo. The original family—"

"They're still around?"

"Nope, just an ancient dude on a feeding tube in a retirement home down in Florida. But all this land? A hundred-plus years ago it was deeded to them by the Earl of Granville."

Qiana kept stomping on the accelerator. "Amazing, Honee, how you've gotten into the history of—"

Honee cut her off. "Well, you know I wanna make a good impression. If I can get there in one piece, hint-hint." She braced herself. "Just hope and pray it leads to a permanent job, know what I mean?"

"Sure, so we can... I mean if everything works out... I mean after the wedding if the three of us can keep living together...?"

Since Honee didn't object, Qiana raced on: "In that case we'll always have at least one steady paycheck coming in, besides what Gunner makes. But honest, who would've believed it? You without a college degree snagging this cushy job?"

Honee grinned. "Yup, feels like I won the Mega Million lottery. But please don't tell anyone, I don't even have a high school diploma. Only thing I did was take a few on-line courses and teach Sunday School."

Qiana grinned too, so hard her face almost split. A second later, she knitted her brows. "Weird, isn't it? This fabulous school hiring a substitute without the proper credentials?"

Honee made a swat-a-gnat gesture. "No, not with that teacher shortage they're having at the moment. They take just about anyone that's not on the sex offender list."

"Well, that's what worries me. What if some disgusting pervert slipped in under the radar? And that's what Logan was trying to tell you? But as for you, they're lucky to get you. At least you finished junior high." Unlike Qiana, who completed only the

31

sixth grade at her orphanage in Canada before she ran away. Ran like the Devil was chasing her, not knowing she was running straight into his and his wife's arms. "Anyway, we've both got a Ph.D. from the streets, don't we?"

"Yup, summatra cum laude. You from the jungles of Chicago and New York City me, from the streets of Durham, NC. That's where I got into some skanky stuff. Not the sex biz, Qi, but dope and hooch which I hated. Tell the truth—" Honee remembered the time when she was a skinny little girl and lived alone in the woods off and on. No food, no shelter, no nothing. Later she turned into a bag lady, pan-handled and snatched old ladies' pocketbooks. None of it easy, "—every day back then was a root canal without any anesthesiatrics. But finally we changed course, both of us. No more slimy crimey stuff— Slow down, speed bumps coming up."

Qiana eased up for five seconds, then zoomed ahead again, preoccupied with doubts the size of the Rocky Mountains. *Can you really shed your past like a sweaty leotard and reinvent yourself as a good woman?*

Suddenly she felt hot and cold at the same time. It was like being stuck in front of a train, seeing it coming, and not being able to jump out of the way. Everything around her faded out except her emotions which was scary. Oh no, why did Honee beg her to come along?

Is this a trap?

Did the guy who stole her picture bribe Honee to deliver Qiana to him?

SCREECH.

Narrowly avoiding the ditch, Qiana veered back on course. She took a deep breath and decided this wasn't a trap. "Honee, you really think we're really through with the world of sleaze and crime?"

"Sure, girl, 'slong as nobody finds out about our background and you don't relapse on me."

"Relapse?"

"Yep, girl. You do, I'm gonna put you in rehab for recovering sluts. No way I'm having my brother marry a floozy, okay?" Especially not after I just escaped from a mother who made her living that way. Well, *escaped* was the wrong word. Honee had made 200 percent sure Momma would never again—

"Don't worry," Qiana broke into Honee's thoughts, "that's history. Look over there." She pointed to a sign on a brass plate on the left of the road that was twined with a rambling rose bush. *"The Stefford Spa?* Wonder how much they charge for their chemical peels and Relaxerol—?"

"Quit fretting about looking like a high-priced you-know-what all the time, I mean it. Now for the last time, slow down." Honee gave Qiana a fierce stare until the SUV decelerated, then hung her head. *Shouldn't be blabbering about Qiana's former life. Did lots of sorry stuff myself.* Honee peeked into the visor mirror to see if it showed.

Nope, no siree. She looked like she was meant for this teaching gig. It was her eyes. Radiating strength and caring, they gazed out from underneath graceful eyebrows. And whenever they fastened on somebody, that person felt like they were the only one in the world. Several times when Honee taught Sunday school she was told her fierce gaze was her best teaching tool.

Too bad all the kids at Stefford School were angels.

Still, it was good to know she could nail any goof-off with a look even today when she had dark smudges under her eyes, the result of a night on the go. They made her look older than she was. At the moment she and Qiana both looked about 27, older than Honee, younger than Qiana.

Honee punched the mirror out of the way and fingered her steel necklace, a rod she had hammered into a circle. Not David Yurman, but her own design. "This is the plan. We'll sell my creations, the antiques and other stuff at the store. That plus my substituting should bring in plenty. And then you can do your thing, okay?"

"Okay. Right after the wedding I'll turn into another Erin Brockovich. Go head to head with the big guys and gals but not over some contaminated drinking water and other environmental issues. I'll be an advocate for kids. Give them a voice and stop their pain. So what're we going to call our shop?"

"The Q Store."

Qiana chuckled. "Are you serious? You want us to sling barbecue? Can you picture me with a chef's hat, long apron and my five-inch heels?"

"Nope, girl, the 'Q' is for your name."

"No way, Honee. It's such a stupid name. What was I thinking back when I picked it out?"

When she fell, she hit herself on the back of her head so hard, she lost consciousness. When she came to, she smelled rotten eggs, vomit, and fresh urine. Slowly she remembered she'd gone in search of a telephone booth to pick out a new name but all the booths in Chicago's Southside had been vandalized.

Which she thought couldn't be true, so she checked them all, each and every one of them. That took hours and with her having nothing to eat, she felt so weak and exhausted until she fell down. That's how she smacked her head on the metal floor of the latest booth and knocked herself out.

What led up to this? After running away from her Canadian orphanage at age 12, she sneaked on a bus that was headed to the US. She had nothing—no home, no money and a name she hated. Back at the orphanage they called her Skelly, for skeleton, because she was so skinny. Or the Girl in the Box. Those were the days when she asked the universe each day, "When will the pain end?"

But never mind. I'll show them. "Them" meant anybody who had ever hurt her which was just about everybody. But first she really needed a new name.

So she went in search for a phone book and ended up lying in this disgusting booth, without the strength to get up. She felt worse than a speck of dirt and couldn't help it. She curled up and cried, hoping she'd lose consciousness again.

Even that didn't work. So she looked around for something to wipe her face and snotty nose with. That's when she noticed it—a neon-green rag stuck to her worn flip-flops. It had the word "QIANA" printed on. Not knowing this was a type of polyester that used to be popular years ago in the manufacturing of disco shirts, she smiled grimly. Why not?

On closer examination she discovered the brand name of the little rag was "Lloyd," according to the label that was so worn it was missing the last two letters and said only "Llo--." So she added a v and an e.

And Qiana Llove was born, a girl with a first name meaning "polyester, nylon, or fake silk," in other words, something plastic or a fraud, a phony, and a last name that was misspelled.

Maybe Qiana had chosen the right name after all, what with her cosmetic surgeries and tons of make-up. And her feelings so squelched and stunted years ago she always had to fake them. Frequently she reacted to a situation only after checking out other people's emotional responses and imitating them.

That was on the outside. Inside there was no faking. She always felt the same—empty, hollowed out, totally defeated—until in one crazy week she met Gunner and Honee and her biological parents, and learned about her past before the Canadian orphanage. It was as if all her life up to then had been a gray, painful, hopeless and torturous path.

Suddenly spring burst out. Her life had promise, potential. It was as if all of those astounding meetings and revelations occurred at the same time for one reason—to wake her up and turn her life around. Even though she'd always yearned for it deep down, it was something she hadn't managed to do at age 12. Because as soon as she'd picked her new name, she spiraled into an abyss of depravity.

But now? Now she'd finally do good.

Of course, personally, it was too late. She was damaged goods. But it wasn't too late for other young victims. Helping Logan Adams would be her first project if there really was something serious that bothered the girl. Qiana felt like a police dog, straining at the leash and hardly able to contain herself.

Meanwhile Honee was still taking about their shop. "But the Q Store has such a nice ring to it."

"Well, it rhymes with 'shoe store' and you know me and shoes," Qiana said. "But it leaves you out, so no. It won't work."

"But girl, the letter Q means a lot to me too. It's my middle initial."

"Really? What's it stand for?"

Nothing from Honee, she was steeped into her books again.

"Well, whatever," Qiana bounced on her seat, "but I can't wait, Honee. We'll fix up the Q Store, use the front as a shop, the back as my office. So I can track down child abusers and predators which won't be cheap. So of course we'll avoid the Stefford Spa. We'll stay continents away."

"You know what's odd?" Qiana asked as she zoomed past a series of beeches, poplars, and elms, decked out in gold, copper, and red cloaks and lining the country road. "We're the only car."

Finally Honee looked up. "That's 'cause all the kids get there so early, some at 6 AM. And after school, you've gotta chase them home with a stick."

"Gee, they're that crazy about their books?"

"Nope, it's all that other stuff. Every student's got a zillion extra-curricu— Hey, you passed it." Honee pointed back to a side-road they had overshot.

"Why didn't you warn me?" Qiana u-turned and screeched onto a gravel path, with not a pebble out of place or a hint of litter.

Seconds later, a polished marble sign greeted them: *Welcome to Stefford School. Academic Excellence Since 1960.*

Qiana slowed to a crawl and shook her head. "Wow." Directly ahead, immaculate lawn squares and walkways alternated with islands of lush crepe myrtles and blooming rosebushes. Farther away, blue-green hills undulated like well-mannered ocean waves. "Gee, somebody must've spent a fortune."

"Just wait till you see the school, girl."

"Any of the kiddies play golf?"

"Yup, plus lacrosse and polo. They're all like a young Prince William or Harry, know what I mean? Every one of their hankerings gets fulfilled."

"Well, no surprise they show up before dawn." Wonder what would've happened if Qiana had these opportunities? Her dream used to be to go to law school. But Erin Brockovich didn't have a formal law school education either. So Qiana would just have to earn a GED, then enroll in college.

At her age? Well, why not? It wouldn't have stopped Erin Brockovich.

Next to Qiana in the car, Honee was thinking about her own hurdles. To start with, wasn't easy being black—well, dark-honey colored—and having a lily-white Momma here in the South, even nowadays. The few times she and Momma ventured out in public together, folks ogled them with their eyes. They had to be asking themselves: What's this white whale doing with this pickaninny? Looks too red-neck to have adopted a baby from Africa, like Angelina Jolie and Madonna would later on.

Honee always hoped they didn't realize she was just an accident, the result of Momma's work. But if she'd had just one speck of normalcy during her early years, maybe she could've graduated from Red Mill High, gone to North Carolina Central, and married one of those fly guys with a shaved and oiled head, destined for success. Together they could've put Durham, NC back on the track to greatness. Oncet downtown was called Black Wall Street—

Now don't be saying oncet, *girl. That's gonna give you away for sure.*

As for that fly guy: *QUIT DREAMING!*

Honee drooped against the car seat. She'd never even been on a date. She felt her eyes puddle up and wiped the hot tears away. No time to feel sorry for herself. Besides, finally her life didn't suck. She had a fine future ahead. As if an iron rod had been shoved down the back of her shirt, she sat up. "Here we are."

CHAPTER 5

After hugging a bend in the road, the SUV found itself stopped by a massive fence at whose opening an ancient guard goose-stepped out of a bungalow. "Sorry, no visitors."

"Excuse me, sir." Reaching across Qiana, Honee fluttered her new ID card out the driver's side window like a winning lottery ticket. "I just started working here and this," indicating Qiana, "is my guest speaker."

The guard, who had his gray hair trimmed to perfection and his starched uniform pressed to the nth degree, mumbled into a walkie-talkie. Seeing Qiana up close, his glasses fogged up. "Um, yes. For how long, miss?"

"Just today."

He scratched something on his clipboard. "All right. Welcome to Stefford." He reached through the window to give her a hug, but Qiana jerked back. That made him break into a hacking cough that got worse instead of better.

Honee exploded out of the truck, raced around the hood, and whacked the guard on the back so hard his upper plate shot out of his mouth. Snagging it out of the air like a baseball, she gave it back. "Are you okay, sir?"

He nodded red-faced, harrumphing and spitting. Qiana pretended she hadn't noticed the flying choppers. "Amazing what tight security you have. Have you had a lot of problems?"

"Oh no, got everything under control. But it's all them papanazis. Pretend to be students, next thing you know they're over at the Spa, YouTube-ing the celebrities. Then there's another story in the *National Enquirer*. Always about that Hollywood trash. Nothing but sex sex sex and—"

"O-ka-a-a-y," Qiana stopped him. "Thanks for the scoop." And before he could try to hug her again, she peeled away from the bungalow. "What a pervert," she said to Honee. "For a second I thought he was going to grab me, drag me in his lair and show me his purple—heart. But I bet the parents eat this stuff up. Nobody can get in here that could harm their little darlings."

"Yup, that's one thing we don't have to fret about, some crazy dude busting in here and blasting away at the kids. You know what's most amazing? This school's like the UN. Blacks, whites, Hispanics, and Asians all tight as ticks. No wonder they win every sports event. And best of all, you don't have to take roll."

Qiana sped down the winding road that snaked deeper into the perfect park landscape. "You're kidding." At her orphanage school the nuns checked for absentees nonstop. And any missing kid was tracked down like a lost religious icon. That's why she had to run away at night. "You don't keep a register or a roll book or attendance sheets?"

"Well, the students sign in every morning but nobody ever looks at it. All of them show up automatic. Unless they leave. Too bad a lot of them do."

"Why?"

"There's no sinisterious reasons," Honee said. "You've heard of Fort Bragg, that big military base, haven't you? It's close, so kids come and go all the time. Families get transferred, move overseas, quit the Armed Forces. But there's no military brats, no skippers and no—"

"Then why that Supermax fence?"

"That's so nobody can sneak in. See, every kid in the state wants to come here but until they expand— Fortunately Stefford's about to go national and international." Honee brandished a fold-out page with maps, blueprints, and a list of other states. "But first more spas have to go up. They're the backers. This one here? I checked it out Friday. Man, what a deluxe place. Palm trees touching the sky, huge waterfalls, crystal pools and, you know, a big wildlife park with all kinds of exoterical— Anyway, that proves it. That old Granville dude ain't—is no Bernie Madoff."

"So that's why all this is so picture-perfect. It's nothing but a big money-making operation."

"Can you blame Earl Granville, girl? Nowadays retirement homes cost two arms and two legs. And just think how much big parcels of land are. Plus starting more super spas, putting in more private roads. All that before a single new classroom, gym, soccer field or..."

Honee couldn't stop talking about the terrific new school plans being in the works, but Qiana tuned her out. Finally her headache was gone but her little finger was hurting like Cayenne pepper rubbed into an open wound and the vision of blood kept replaying in front of her inner eye.

Honee was still talking: "...the latest facilities, equipment and technology are on board. Schools are so different now. Big screens everywhere, so teachers can broadcast their lessons from home if they have to. It's really amazing how disciplined these kids are. They go in the classroom, click on the TV and get right to work. And the parents? Man, they're all so passionate about educ—"

"Hold it." Qiana stomped on the brakes, embarrassed about the loud squeaks the SUV emitted. Belonging to Gunner, it was on its last tire tread but had to do until she could scrape up something better. "Why... didn't... you... tell... me?"

Qiana stared through the pitted windshield at the slate-gray building that suddenly loomed in front of them. It looked magnificent, this enormous ancient castle that appeared to have been transplanted from Scotland. The massive building had dozens of wings and towers, featuring all kinds of turrets, uneven roof lines, and crenellated walls. Steeped gables presided at strategic spots, along with so many stone protrusions and ledges that counting them would take all day.

Honee was tickled over Qiana's reaction. "Just wait till you see the inside, girl. Turn here." She pointed to a driveway curving up to the front entrance. "See over there by that rickety old well structure? That's the faculty parking lot and we get to use it. Yippee yay."

They muscled into an empty slot and poured out, with Honee hauling her books and Qiana her suitcase. "Gee, this looks ivy league-ish," she said. "I've never been to Harvard but that's exactly how..." Her voice trickled off as she shifted her attention from the building to the students, ranging in age from kindergarten to high school seniors.

Milling around like shoppers on opening day of a new mall, the older kids resembled cadets at the Citadel and the younger ones, toy soldiers chewing on pretzel sticks. Obviously they'd skipped breakfast at home. None of the kids wore an actual uniform, but they all had on Tommy Hilfiger, Ralph Lauren, or other preppie garb—knife-creased long pants, pressed Bermuda shorts, or khaki skirts—and polo shirts tucked in tight.

"Unreal," Qiana whispered. "No body piercings? No boys with earrings or tattoos? No girls with band-aid-size skirts and overflowing corsets?"

Even more surprising than the clothes was the kids' behavior. Even the kindergarteners studied their iPads like the latest press release of an international conference on global warming in Helsinki. Or they thumbed their BlackBerrys as if they were practicing for the speed-texting Olympics.

Hurrying up the front steps, Qiana said, "C'mon. Nobody yelling the F-word?"

Gliding along next to her, Honee beamed, her eyes like chestnuts dipped in olive oil. "Told you, didn't I? All these kids are angels. Now let's check in, then up to my room, okay?"

They stepped through the massive doors and found themselves at the end of a long line of adults.

"Hey, what's going on?" Qiana asked.

"That's the parents I was talking about, girl."

What a big bunch. Qiana couldn't help but beam too. "Excuse me, did you just move here?" she asked the woman in front of her.

"No, we live here."

"But didn't school start last month?"

"Oh, this is for next year or the year after," the mom said. "This school's so popular, you know, scores through the roof. For example, last year's senior class had a 4.76 grade average. So you have to enroll your children in pre-kindergarten or earlier. Just hope and pray my Jordan and Jonathan will make it." She flashed a snapshot of two mischievous toddlers.

"Is it tough to get in?"

"Not really. Your children just have to follow the rules. So you think I look all right?"

"You look fine, ma'am," Honee said, noticing all the parents were dressed for a country club convention. "Why did you all coordinate your wardrobes?"

The woman tittered. "At the Open House last week we met the chairlady. What a miracle worker she is. As a matter of fact, the whole faculty's extraordinary, just so professional. So none of us dare to come here looking like the Wal-Mart crowd. We want Stefford kids."

43

Qiana rolled her eyes at Honee, in regards to her own frumpy outfit as more parents chimed in: "We want bumper stickers with 'My Son Goes to Stefford'… 'My Daughter is on the Stefford Honor Roll'…" Their faces sheened with perspiration, they waved cell phones with images of children on the screens.

"They are desperate," Qiana whispered in Honee's ear. "It's like they're in the biggest competition of their lives."

"Can you blame them, girl? Public schools are pitiful nowadays. Constant fights, teachers being cussed, drive-bys every time you turn around. It's especially bad for black and Mexican kids. They get put on the street or in jail. At least these folks got this option. Mighty pricey but looks like they can afford it."

Qiana looked around the lobby. Honee hadn't exaggerated. The chess-patterned marble floor gleamed and the walls shimmered with fresh paint. Streams of light rayed down from giant chandeliers and landed on glass tables with enough fresh arrangements to rival a royal flower show. Only thing missing was a Starbucks.

"Just look at those elevators, Honee." Qiana tracked a transparent bubble floating to the ground floor where it yawned to accept a throng of happy kids. "The bell hasn't even rung and the kids're already off to class."

A man looked up from pecking at numbers on his iPhone. "Just checking to see how close my son is to being valedictorian of first grade." He chuckled but seemed serious. "Those kids are off to the labs. Any time there's a science fair in Tokyo, London or Beijing, its Stefford kids that earn all the honors. Just look at those shelves."

Qiana glanced at the collection of plaques, silver bowls, and trophies that brought the shelves on the far wall to their knees. Above them a banner proclaimed: *Today Best in the Nation. Tomorrow Best in the World.*

"What about the little kids?" she asked. "Where do they keep their spelling bee awards and coloring prizes?"

"The little ones have their own wing and for a good reason. You know kids always take it to the next level, just like with Facebook. First it was for college students, then for high school, then junior high. Next it'll be for kindergarten, just wait and see. But fortunately here they don't allow little children to get exposed to any adult stuff. That's really why we parents are so determined to "

"Excuse me," Honee cut him off. "That neon sign over there? What's that about?"

"Well, that's the payoff, I mean the acceptance roster. See where it says, 'Congrats to those universities lucky enough to—'?"

"That's crazy," Qiana broke in. "Thirty-three kids got into Harvard last year? Twenty-nine into Yale? Twenty-four into Oxford?" She shook her head. "And what's that?" She pointed to the space above the roster where constantly changing numbers in bright colors crawled across, resembling the latest stock market prices. The numbers seemed to flash like a warning signal that was counting down to a horrible event: Three...two...one—

Oh no, is something about to happen?

"That's the Stefford Counter," a woman with premature gray hair said, eager to explain. "These days you've got to keep your children busy nonstop, you know. So they have class all day, competitions and sports afterwards. Weekends it's all about saving crack babies and the homeless, plus tutoring the first-graders and going to church, synagogue, or temple. But most important is the Code of Conduct."

She took a breath. "It requires all students to act honorably all the time. So therefore those flashing numbers are their latest scholastic scores, plus all the bonus points they get for their good deeds and for abiding by the Code. But isn't this awesome? It sure makes all the kids focus on their academics and their behavior."

45

That seemed to be true for a group of boys that was passing.

"Kierkegaard's concept of destiny is—" one boy said, as another one cut in, "Excuse me for interrupting, but let's be certain to ascertain we don't omit the ideologies of Kant and Frederick Douglass."

"Man, they don't even sound like young'uns," Honee commented.

"Well, that's the award-winning debate team," the mom said. "But just wait until the bell—"

"Speaking of which," Qiana interrupted, "do you think we'll make it to the office in time? We're substituting," she explained.

"Oh my goodness." The woman got excited. "Could you please mention my Jordan and Jonathan to the chairlady? Around that corner over there, that's the faculty door. Please hurry, maybe you can catch her before class."

"We'll certainly try," Honee fibbed, having her mind on her own agenda, and rushed to a door lettered STAFF, Qiana beside her. Just then three girls swished past.

"If you concur, I propose we juxtapose Gloria Steinem and Betty Friedan," one said, "but let's not nullify Naomi Wolf's oeuvre either."

"Gee whiz." Qiana hitched her purse higher on her shoulder, tempted to root in it for paper and pen to take notes for her friend. "But thank goodness, the girls aren't held back. I was beginning to wonder if this school wasn't a throwback to the fifties. You know, everybody in their place and—"

Honee didn't let her finish. "How many times I gotta tell you, girl? There's no problems here. None." She knocked.

"But aren't you suspicious, especially after what Logan told you?"

"Come in," a voice called through the door.

CHAPTER 6

About a third the size of the lobby, the office was cut in half by a counter. In front was the start of the long line of parents. Behind it bustled three secretaries, two young and pretty, the third one neither. They were dealing admission forms and monthly statements to the parents like poker cards and accepting checks, credit-, and debit card payments. Qiana could almost hear the ching-ching, like from a casino.

Most of that money was probably already spent, she thought. The plush burgundy carpet smelled brand-new. The elaborate light fixtures, illuminating numerous unopened computer-, printer-, and copy machine boxes, glittered.

As the two young women detoured around the boxes, they passed several recessed areas crammed with accreditation certificates, awards from international education agencies, and oil portraits of previous principals and pictures of school personnel shaking hands with dignitaries, sports stars, and other celebrities. It looked like a Hall of Fame for Education.

As Qiana and Honee examined the photos, a man in a pearl-gray Armani suit and a mauve silk shirt with matching power tie strode through a back door. He had tan skin and brown eyes sparkling from behind gold-plated designer glasses. After waving to the parents, he cut through the counter by way of a swinging door. "Good morning, ladies. What can I do for you?"

Honee smiled. "Oh Dr. Reinholt, good morning. May I introduce my guest speaker? Qiana Llove."

"Ms. Money, you mentioned bringing in a guest but I had no idea it would be someone this delightful." He flashed a gleaming-teeth smile and gave Qiana a hug that felt like the initiation to a secret club. She tolerated it, not wanting something similar to what had happened with the guard to occur.

"I hope you will like it here," he said.

"I'm sure I will." Qiana said. "I never realized there were so many studious kids."

"What is even more important, Ms. Llove, all our students abide by the Stefford Code of Conduct." He spoke at a slow pace, imbuing every word with meaning. "You see, our sacred mission is to get the highest performance out of every child, morally and academically. And the younger the minds, the faster they can learn to behave and absorb even the most difficult subjects, such as advanced science. So after you talk to Ms. Money's classes, would you please stop by my office?" He winked. "So we can put you on the permanent substitute teachers' list too?"

Face bland, Qiana stared at him. She knew his type. Next time it wouldn't be just a creepy hug. It would be a suggestive pat on her backside, his hot breath on her neck.

"Sorry, Dr. Reinholt," she said, saccharine sweet, "I'm way too busy."

But that wasn't the reason Qiana didn't stop by later.

Dr. Reinholt cleared his throat. "Can you not rearrange your schedule, Ms. Llove?" He winked again. "You see, diverse viewpoints so profoundly inspire our students. And the fact is you look as if—" He paused.

I've been around the block a few times? Well, yeah.

"—you've seen quite a bit of the world. Am I correct?"

"Absolutely. I was born in Europe and was speech-impaired for years. English is actually my second, well, third language. So the way I express myself is—" Qiana wanted to say "fricking screwed-up," but for Honee's sake she said, "—quite limited."

Honee nodded. English wasn't her native language either. That was Southern country talk, spiked with some verbal concoctions of her own.

"I was raised in an orphanage in the French part of Canada," Qiana went on. Of course *raised* was the wrong word. She'd been terribly abused—the box!—but no need to get into that with this phony pony.

"I knew it." Dr. Reinholt beamed like he was auditioning for a tooth-implant commercial. "You see, my father was not born in the U.S. either."

"That guard at the gate is your—?"

"No." Dr. Reinholt chuckled. "Henry is 100 percent American. He's ex-military, but we felt obligated to hire a retired soldier. So many of our students are from Army families. My father is a bishop and remarkably fit for his age. As a matter of fact, he will be here later today to speak to one of our clubs. I hate to admit it but some of our students can get much too immersed in their work.

"That's why we try to—" he smoothed his hair like the fur of a beloved pet "—expose them to as many fascinating people as we can. Unfortunately most of our teachers are—" he lowered his voice "—such absent-minded professors or sweet little school marms utterly out of touch with—"

The old secretary stopped him: "Yoohoo, Dr. Reinholt. Phone call for you. The State Department of Education again. I transferred it to your desk."

49

"I shall see you later, ladies." With a wave and smiling again, Dr. Reinholt ambled back to his inner office. As he opened the door, Qiana glimpsed several massive book cases behind his desk. The collection they held was more than startling.

Crocodiles of all sizes had taken over the shelves. Some were stuffed toys, others were plastic. Still others were made out of glass or ceramics and intended as shot glasses, mermaid figurines, salt and pepper shakers, even clocks.

The biggest crocodiles squatted on the floor, with a huge one leaning against the headmaster's desk. Made of metal, it wore a blond wig and looked like Marilyn Monroe. Next to it, another big crocodile was carved out of wood, wore an Afro wig and had its features arranged in a scream a la Munch. And in front of the desk lay a real crocodile that had been preserved.

Qiana shivered, wondering if Dr. Reinholt had a dark side, a crazy side. Maybe that's what scared Logan. She was glad when his door clicked shut.

"Mercy me, that man," the old secretary said, bustling down the counter. "He's so naive, right down to his fancy shoes."

Qiana winced. *Fancy shoes? Oh no. Does this woman know about my background?*

Fortunately Honee steered the topic to the odd collection. "Why is Dr. Reinholt so into crocodiles, ma'am?"

"Oh, no worries," the secretary said. "That's just some silly PC mess. Dr. Reinholt's got a habit of saying, 'The crocodiles are snapping,'" when the students act up. Headmasters before him, they used to say, 'The natives are restless.' But these days you don't want to mention anything related to any ethnic group. So that's how Dr. R.'s hobby started, but mercy me. He really thinks they're looking at him for a national leadership position. The next U.S. Secretary of Education? The Nobel Peace Prize? Pshaw."

Puffing out a sigh, she turned the parade of parents over to her assistants. "His biggest problem is he trusts everyone but that's a huge mistake these days." Her left hand started rotating like a hamster wheel in motion. "See, nobody realizes it but the secretary's the heart of a school. She knows it *all*. Yes, she does. Year after year waves of kids wash through, but we secretaries stay put, strong and steadfast, just like the White House."

"What about the teachers, ma'am?" Honee asked.

"Oh sure, there's a few exceptions but so many of them? They just breeze in, lift a little finger and everyone thinks they're the greatest. And now with all that new technology, they've got it made. They skip to the lounge and plop on the couch while the kids copy down the PowerPoints in the classroom. The fact is the kids mostly teach one another and encourage the younger kids to go by the rules. Yet and still, the teachers get all the praise, the supplements. The red roses on Valentine's Day.

"But I ask you, who does all the work around here? We do, the school secretaries. Society would come to a screeching halt without us. We make zillions of copies, order thousands of textbooks, count out hundreds of locks. Write admission slips till we catch carpal tunnel syndrome and still nobody appreciates us and…"

While the secretary was running on like an air-conditioner in August, Qiana looked her over. Gee, what's with this school? She thought. First that old clown by the gate, then that phony principal, and now this crazy crone? In her early 60's, she clung for dear life to any remnants of youth. Her eyes were rimmed with black liner and hooded with blue eye shadow. Pink lipstick made her lips look like dried worms dipped into Pepto-Bismol.

Qiana felt the urge to pass on a few basic style hints, but why bother? The woman was hopeless. She wore a khaki jumper over a purple hoodie with horizontal green stripes that made her look like a pregnant barrel while her low bosom looked lumpy like bad mashed potatoes.

51

Qiana shook her head. *What is it with older women? Why don't they get an industrial-strength bra and hoist up their boobs? Or is this where they hide something?*

The secretary kept rambling on: "...the worst are those hotshots over at the Spa. They're just after the publicity they get from backing us. The whole world's trying to copy us. Some folks even have the nerve to poach our faculty and—"

"Is that what happened with Ms. Hill?" Honee cut in, trying to stanch the flow of jibber-jabber. "That's the teacher I'm subbing for," she explained to Qiana.

"All I know is she left overnight," the secretary said, her hand rotating faster. Just an email to Dr. Reinholt, how unprofessional. But lucky for us, we were able to find you, Ms. Money."

"Lucky for me too, ma'am. Now if you'd excuse—"

The hand started racing. "But what guarantee do we have we'll be lucky again? I mean after you quit?"

"I won't quit, ma'am. I promise."

The hand stalled for a moment, along with the pursed pink lips. Then: "Well, what about those recent teacher scandals? Teachers having sex with students? One boy was just eleven. What's the world coming to?"

Qiana had to suppress the urge to scream. She wanted class to start, Logan to appear, and Honee to have a talk with her. Or she'd do it herself. "You certainly don't have to worry about things like that with us," she said, gazing at her engagement ring. The diamond was smaller than a salt grain but seemed to burst with Gunner's love. She pressed it to her lips, trying to mask her fidget attack. *C'mon, let's go.*

"We're not like other schools." The secretary kept chatting away like an old-time alarm clock that's been wound up, while her hand circled like crazy. "We have the highest of standards. Of course, I only speak for the Upper School. Don't work with the little ones, but we give all children the best education, no matter how high ticket or low—"

"What's that mean?" Honee broke in, squirming worse than Qiana.

"Poor kids, underprivileged kids. Dr. Reinholt hands out scholarships like Kleenex. Now Ms. Money, are you ready?"

"Yes, ma'am!"

Finally the hand slowed down. "Okay then, best of luck to you. And here's something to keep in mind. You do good, you'll get one of these." The woman reached under the counter and produced a dangling object. "Isn't the Stefford Medal gorgeous? It's solid gold. Ms. Lisa Hill just got hers but she really deserved it, what with all her meticulous files. Hard copies of everything, and not just for her high school classes but also for the early grades. Mercy me, how she loved 'her sweet little babies,' as she called them. She really taught her heart out in her elementary and kindergarten classes. And everything was cross-referenced to a T and presented with the latest teaching principles in mind and—"

Lordy-lord, not again! "Sorry, we've got to run." Honee ducked out the door and headed for the nearest staircase, Qiana behind her.

"Wait up, ladies." Trailing them, the old chatterbox offered a plastic basket like a collection plate. "You know we don't allow cell phones in the classroom. So does either of you got one on you?"

"Nope, lost mine," Honee said, lips pinched, as Qiana handed hers over.

"And your watches? You see, we don't want our kids preoccupied with any material possessions. Besides, we have intercoms, phones, and clocks in every room. Oh, I'm so glad you're here. I haven't slept in weeks; it's all these bad outside influences, attendance fluctuations and teachers quitting. Just now a cafeteria worker's gone missing, the pretty one, Rosario."

Her rotating hand started up again, pausing only to swipe a tear off her cheek. "One last thing. Always remember the Code, and absolutely no physical contact with the students."

CHAPTER 7

"Man, what a looney biddy," Honee said after the secretary waddled off. "How can they keep her working here?"

"Well, if you've got any second thoughts," Qiana said, "just say the word and it's bye-bye Stefford. To tell the truth, I'm relieved. Until I met that crazy lady I thought this place was just too—"

Ring-ring.

"So have you made up your mind, Honee?"

"Yeah, I'm gonna stay, at least until I can question the girl." Honee found her floor, walked down the hall, and jammed a key into a door. "Look, here's my room."

"Oh wow." Qiana's eyes skipped from the shiny teacher desk to big-screen computer, color printer, elaborate phone, and copy machine all huddling by a sunny window and waiting for business. She inhaled deeply. Then like a three-year-old turned loose in O.E. Schwartz, she raced from the mint-green walls to the chalk board and white-board with colorful magic markers, with a plasma TV screen sandwiched between them, smiling the whole time. This classroom was like day and night, compared to the one in the orphanage school where Qiana had to squeeze on a wobbly bench on the days they let her. But even on her best school days she picked up splinters and had to share a grimy pencil.

Here the desks were brand-new, the supplies in abundance. The oak shelves in the back were loaded with art books, sketch pads, boxes of charcoal, colored pencils, and more magic markers. And in one corner, new file cabinets stood at attention like soldiers waiting for inspection.

Qiana opened one, expecting to find it empty. "Look, Honee. Ms. Hill left you a big present—all her lesson plans, tests, outlines, final exams."

"Are you serious?" Honee sounded dubious as she approached. "Don't you know most teachers guard their files like Greek cooks their *pastitso* recipes? Man, how lucky can I get?" She grabbed a stack of papers, flipped through it and leaned against a desk like a tired question mark.

"Is that old bag still worrying you?" Qiana asked.

"Nope, every school's got a batty old gal. It's Dr. Reinholt. Actually he's no big deal either. I bet he's gonna be tied up chasing skirts—"

"Oh no. You think he's been harassing some of the girls? You think that's what Logan was trying to tell you about?"

"I don't think so. I feel like he loves his job too much to jeopardize it. But it's all these incredible files, girl. Why would any teacher leave—?"

Ring-ring. RING.

"Yikes." Honee stashed the papers back in the cabinet, marched to the front of the room and watched as a swarm of kids poured in like a mudslide, but a polite and respectful one. Settling down took them only seconds. During that time she stood taller, as if a weight had been lifted off her. It was more than that. A blissed-out feeling enveloped her because this was *it*, the fulfillment of her dreams. To have this opportunity to make a difference in these kids' lives, wasn't that plum wonderful? She smiled over at Qiana to share her bone-deep joy.

Qiana had a warm feeling enfolding her too, her like a mist of cashmere, because for the moment, she'd gotten her neuroses under control and finally things were moving. Waiting for Honee to start her instructional spiel, she eyed the clean-cut boys, but skipped over the girls because for some reason girls always made her feel bad.

At the front of the room, Honee cleared her throat. "Good morning, class. Is everyone feeling okay?" This was a rhetorical question. She already knew the answer. The kids all smiled, sat up straight like boards, laptops open on their desks, scrubbed ears perked, and nimble fingers poised over the keyboards, just itching to tap away.

But they disagreed with her. Vehemently.

"No, Ms. Money," came a chorus, "we're not feeling okay."

The speaking in chorus was odd, but Honee had a more serious concern. If they all had on their minds whatever it was that freaked out Logan, no teaching would get done today. Then the loony secretary would hear about it, and no telling what might happen. "What's wrong, guys?"

"We feel terrific, ma'am!"

Whew. Honee chuckled. "All right then, let's get started." She introduced Qiana, then said: "Does anyone remember what I told you Friday about the pre-historic beginnings of art?"

A sea of nods.

"So what are the basic art elem—?"

"Form. Line. Tone. Color. And texture."

The chorus again, but the voices were lively and the kids' eyes shone with excitement. They were eager to learn which thrilled Honee. Wasn't teaching fun and easy as sweet potato pie? "Good job. Now let's do an experiment. This is Ms. Llove, our guest for today. Would you move front and center?"

57

Qiana scooted a stool over to where Honee pointed and sat down like a little girl in Sunday school.

"Here is what I want you to do, class. Make a sketch of our guest, just a simple drawing. But to make it more interesting, our guest will portray a different emotion every so often. Of course, she won't tell you what it is. You just have to guess and try to capture that emotion in your work. Any questions?"

There were none.

"Okay, Ms. Llove, the floor is yours."

Qiana remembered what Honee had told her to portray first—anger. This was easy. Over the years her deep-seated anger had festered in her. Now letting it come to the forefront, she hopped up and propped her hands on her hips. She was thinking about the people she hated most—the Devil and even more his demonic wife. Immediately bile shot up in her throat and a pain erupted in her stomach. Knowing that her tormentors, especially that horrible woman, had never gotten punished felt like a red-hot poker stabbing her. Involuntarily, Qiana gave an outcry that caused the kids in the front row to jerk back.

Honee was impressed. "Good job. And while you're working, class," she said, "I'm gonna—going to call you up to my desk, one by one, and conference with you. Logan Adams."

CHAPTER 8

"She's absent," a girl in the third row said. Chrissie, according to the seating chart.

Honee felt a wave of fear well up in her. Oh no, where was Logan? Had something happened to her? Honee's mind raced through what that might be. Was it maybe something drug-related? Even the best schools had a few kids that dabbled in illegal substances. Even some teachers were known to sell illegal stuff. So did the school's weed supplier hear about Logan staying after class on Friday and assume she turned him in? So he threatened her?

Or was it something worse?

Perhaps a gang like Hades' crew had lured some girls through Facebook out into the woods behind the school. Was that what Logan was trying to tell Honee on Friday? And now she was too scared to come to school?

But that couldn't be the case. With that Supermax fence around the whole campus, no intruders could breach security. Besides, the grounds were surely patrolled by an army of monitors and volunteers, trained by Henry. So the girl had to be okay.

That's what Honee hoped fervently as she waved Chrissie up. "Can I see your homework?" Then happy like a kitten with a saucer of half & half, she scanned Chrissie's notebook. "Well done," she said although the assigned report seemed to be copied straight from Wikipedia.

Chrissie frowned. "Just a 'well done,' ma'am?"

"Well, what about a 'magnificent and first-rate job'?"

"Yay, goody gumdrops. So what's 'a magnificent and first-rate job' numerically speaking, ma'am? Is it, like, a 100 or higher? Even the smallest percentile point makes your score go up."

Tap-tap-tap. Honee hit her desk with new red pen and strained to keep looking pleased. She could already tell that the myriad details of teaching would be a pain. All that record keeping, for one thing, because every mark and every check and comment had to be entered in the computer. But still, overall it was so joyful, sitting in *her* classroom, talking to *her* students. Of course, a few kids might spell trouble, like those little dudes in the way back who were only pretending to be engrossed in their work. But just wait. She'd have every student complying with the Code shortly.

"Don't worry. I'm sure by the end of the term you'll get an A."

"Oh no," Chrissie whimpered, tears spilling down her face. "I need an A-plus. It's the most important thing. It's my parents. They're only staying together because they read that a kid's grades plummet when their folks split up. So I have to make top grades in everything and act perfect, don't you understand? I really truly have to, so they'll stay together."

Poor little chick. Honee handed her a Kleenex. "Okay, I hear you. Now tell me about Logan's absence."

"Well," Chrissie sniffled, "today's like the first time she's ever been out but her folks went to New Zealand. Yesterday or today, I forget. Anyway, Logan said she'd spend all week with me.

So when she didn't show, I called her but she never answered. Guess she went with her parents after all."

"But you aren't sure? Logan might just be home alone and—?"

"No, ma'am. She'd never stay home alone. Her folks wouldn't let her. What with Josh and—"

"Josh?"

"That's her hot boyfriend. He's our quarterback. All the girls like drool over—"

Honee was getting impatient: "So where do you think she is?" *Was Logan with that boy? Were they both skipping today?*

"I don't know. Maybe she tried to call me? My BlackBerry goes down sometimes. Josh would know, he's here. Guess I'll ask him at lunch but the Jocks have study hall then."

"Don't you think you should tell the office?"

"I will, ma'am, but not now. I can't miss any work." Another flood of tears threatened like a funnel cloud.

"Okay. But before I let you go, tell me. Has Logan been worried about something recently?"

"Not that I know of, ma'am."

"All right, back to your seat." As Chrissie hustled to her desk, Honee kept wondering about what had happened to Logan. *She was so scared on Friday, now she's absent?* A sense of foreboding gripped Honee. Was the girl hurt? Was she lying somewhere, unable to call for help?

Honee felt on edge. Obviously hanging around Qiana had rubbed off on her as far as being neurotic was concerned. She had to get a grip. *It's gotta be something minor.* Maybe Josh broke up with Logan and the poor chick was hiding out in her closet, boo-hooing her heart out. What to do? Honee's hand skated through her handbooks like Apolo Ohno: "Report any student out more than three days to Guidance."

61

Okay, that's what Honee would do today, never mind the three-day rule.

"Psst, ma'am. Can I be next?"

Before Honee could respond, a bean pole with acned skin loped up and whisked a bulging notebook and a dozen folders from a suitcase on rollers, like a lawyer.

"Look, Ms. Money, what I did. I printed out your lecture from Friday. Filed the hard copies in triplicate. Made note cards with bullet points. And my mom, she gave me a quiz. ASK ME!"

"Shhhh." Trying to calm the boy down was like trying to pacify a basket of cocker spaniel pups. "Ask you what, Jefferson?"

"About some painters. Like that Dutch artist Vermeer. Also called Jan Van Der Meer Van Delft. Born Oct. 31, 1632, in Delft. Died Dec. 15, 1675. Is mostly known for landscaping, architectural visas and general studs."

"Oh, you mean he did landscapes, vistas and genre studies?"

The boy gave a panicked shriek. "Who's *he*?"

"Vermeer."

"Sorry, ma'am." A chuckle, followed by a gnawing on fingernails already chewed down to the quick. "I thought it was a woman. Please don't hold it against me. Here's my extra credit." Jefferson unfolded an accordion-like poster that buried Honee's desk. "It's a timeline of all the art movements in the world from the earliest times until now. What do you think?"

"This is...," wracking her brain, Honee tried to scrape up a truly spectacular adjective, "...very..."

But the awful thing she'd been dreading happened. Her mind froze up like an overloaded computer. *Now it's all gonna come out—who I really am, just a no-count street person trying to pass herself off as somebody respectable.* Then all these nice kids would hold their noses and scoot away from her just like back when.

CHAPTER 9

Sitting on the steps of a tin trailer that hunkered on a patch of dirt in the middle of the woods, Honee scratched in the sand with a stick. She was looking for chiggers. Little critters always had so much fun, the way they flitted around, not that Honee could see them well. They were tinier than ants, than ticks before they sucked your blood and swole up. Tinier than the lice Honee had, according to the teacher who screamed at her that morning: "Go home and don't come back until you're rid of the nits."

But how was Honee supposed to do that? Seven years old, she had no way to get her hands on any louse shampoo. Didn't even have any regular shampoo or soap. Honee used the woods to pee, but on the rare times Momma let her in the bathroom, she wouldn't let her touch the soap.

"Too expensive to waste on you, Honee Trash. You're nasty."

Honee knew she was nasty. Whenever she glanced at the mirror, she scowled at the skinny little gal with the knotty, nappy, lint-specked braids. No wonder the other kids threw gum at her hair. Even worse were her rags. They were so awful the other kids *refused to sit next to her: "Teacher, she stinks like she messed up her pants."*

Jolting back to the present, Honee noticed Jefferson was still waiting for her to praise his gigantic poster. And still no words from her. She sniffed her forearm and flicked her eyes at her clean outfit. The antique store had a bathroom and a washing machine—both huge luxuries to her.

In the past laundry was always tough. Momma used to waddle around in a ratty robe when she was alone. But when customers came, she draped herself in the gaudy veils she had dry-cleaned while Honee had to wash her clothes in a creek. But she had only one outfit. Waiting around shivering while her clothes dried on a bush was okay in summer. But in the fall and winter, she had to go to a "laundromat." That was any K-mart, Wal-Mart, or dime store. She'd wait until a woman herded a bunch of kids in and followed. While the woman picked through the discount racks, Honee grabbed a few shirts and pants, and when the woman hustled her brood to the fitting rooms, Honee tagged along.

The clerk always only counted the items a customer took to try on. Once inside a cubicle, Honee exchanged her filthy clothes with clean ones, then returned the correct number of items, her stinking ones hidden among the new ones. Of course she could get away with this only once at a particular store, but there were always others.

Now in the sunny classroom, Jefferson eyed her suspiciously. "You were saying, ma'am?"

I'm so stupid carouselled around in Honee's mind. What good were all those synonyms, antonyms, roots and fixes, pre and sub, she had memorized? *Stupid, stupid.*

Her lips must've moved. "Ma'am, did you say my work is *stupendou*s?"

"Yes, Jefferson. Your work is super-duper stupendous."

"So can you give me a 150? See, I already know everything about art. And that includes the famous General Janice Vermeer with her Visa Card. Plus, I'm going to volunteer at an old folks' home. Collect some of their drawings, add some doodles by Blago, Kim Jong Un, maybe even some by bin Laden's or Qadafi's wives and publish them. That way I'll get written up in the *New York Times* and—"

"Why're you gonna—going to all that trouble?"

"Don't you know the Ivies? They want brilliant but well-rounded students. It's a rat race but all the kids're into it. The seniors are the worst cut-throats. Wait a minute, ma'am. Are you trying to ruin my GPA?"

CHAPTER 10

Not far from the back of the school in the old shack, Logan kept her eyes glued to the snake. She was scared out of her mind but the gag prevented her from screaming. So she did it in her mind: *Mommy! Daddy! Why'd you have to go on vacation?*

If her folks hadn't left town, they'd have missed Logan last night and the whole state would be beating the bushes by now. They'd have called in the FBI. Or the Navy Seals. Or the Royal Dutch Marines, like in that Natalee Holloway case years ago.

Logan was supposed to stay at her best friend's house during her folks' absence but Chrissie was such a ditz. When Logan didn't come over, she probably thought Logan's parents had postponed their trip. But why hadn't she called or texted?

Probably had. Logan remembered her BlackBerry being snatched from her. She fought so hard to keep it she broke her nails. But they'll grow again in time for Homecoming—

Ohmigod! Is that why this happened? She and Josh were the most popular couple at Stefford and would be crowned King and

Queen for sure. So was somebody mega pissed? Is that why those magic-marker lines were drawn on her? Or was this part of a weird hazing ritual? The Jills, the most popular sorority, had just sent her an e-vite. Were they testing her?

Most likely this was a test for Josh. The football team always cooked up new treasure hunts. So was she being held captive until Josh figured out where she'd been stashed?

Another thought hit Logan: *Is it because I broke a rule?* There were a gazillion of them, plus random drug tests, and she'd been tested three days ago. Logan had never done drugs but she and Josh had gotten too close.

But why didn't the office read me the riot act? Or set up a parent conference? And why did this have to happen just when I was about to confide in that new substitute?

Logan just had to tell her about her scary feeling that something awful was going on. When did it start?

It was the day that new boy Angelo talked to her. And from then on Logan paid attention to *all* her classmates and noticed something weird. Probably nothing, but venting her suspicions and fears to Ms. Money would help because Ms. Money was so *real*. And so pretty, like Halle Berry. Even better, she was an iron woman. One look at her eyes made it clear she was tougher than the toughest drill sergeant at Parris Island where Logan's brother was stationed.

Oh Tommy. How I miss you. They got along so fab. Both of them being adopted was a special bond and their parents were the best. Too bad they were far away right now and Tommy was on maneuvers in a swamp in Louisiana. That's why Logan felt she had nobody except Ms. Money.

Oh no! The copperhead was moving again, its head taking aim at Logan's ankles. The poisonous fangs were bared, the fatal bite only a split-second away.

MS. MONEY!

CHAPTER 11

In her sunny classroom not that far away from the shed, Honee asked, "What're you talking about, Jefferson?"

"You give me an A-minus. Most teachers aren't like our faculty chair lady, you know. She's so nice and—" The boy stopped, intrigued by what was happening at the front of the classroom. Qiana was in the process of changing poses. She pulled the piece of cloth out of her purse that turned out to be a rag doll. She hugged it, trying to portray happiness—her next assignment.

But it didn't work. On the contrary: Her face scrunched up, her lips trembled. Tears flooded her cheeks, making a girl in the front row whisper, "Look, guys. She's losing it."

All the magic markers paused in mid-air and a graveyard silence embraced the room. Aware of the sudden stillness, Qiana crammed Annie out of sight, praying the kids' eyes would stop lasering her. Otherwise, they'd dig out the ugly truth.

Can't let that happen for Honee's sake. So Qiana just had to cough up a cheery expression. She thought of all the happiness ahead but her future seemed diaphanous like a wisp of gauze. So she scoured her past in her mind.

Sitting on a grassy patch behind a tall building that even decades after World War II, hadn't been rebuilt since this was the poorest section of Munich, she knew she wasn't supposed to go outside. Her mother always said, "Never leave the room when I'm not here."

But on this day she did. The sun must've known it was her birthday and winked so bright through the high window in their basement. And the sky was so blue and beautiful that Qiana just had to take a look. Her whole life was underground, mildew-gray, and smelling like death. Qiana was always starved for color, fresh air and any sign of hope. So she tiptoed up the crumbling stone stairs, ran to a clothes line and jumped between the sheets flapping in the breeze.

And then she saw it—a field of little red lollipops bobbing in the breeze. Clover in bloom.

Now many years later at the front of the classroom, Qiana pretended to be four years old again. Back then she scrambled out of her make-believe tent and collected some rocks. Pretending it was her birthday party, she picked up some sticks and offered them to the rocks. "Would you like some cake?"

Oh, if she'd only stopped then and run back to the basement, the tragic events would've never—

Don't think about what came afterwards. Qiana felt a determined smile that started out grim and then softened, light up her face. Amazed by her transformation, the students settled back down and black magic markers squeaked over sheets of paper again.

A peek at the wall clock and Qiana smiled even more. *Only 33 more hours until Gunner gets home.* Great, she could do this—keep going until then, especially since "sadness" was up next. That was easy. All she had to do was pull out the bunch of papers her stilettos had been wrapped in and read what she wrote in second grade: 2 *day ile do it. Make mi self pritty. Or elz!!!*

Monday was always crying day at the grossly understaffed orphanage. So every weekend she prettied herself up and inhaled hope with every breath. Because that's when the people came who wanted to adopt a child. *Maybe today I'll get picked.*

"Smile," Sister Gertrude barked as she inspected the children, while fingering a calculator. When a child got chosen, the new parents always inked a big check.

Qiana used to hop up at five, if she wasn't in the box, and tried her best to copy the other kids who all glued on grins like those the first-graders carved into pumpkins on Halloween. But her smile was always a grimace, with her pathetic eyes telling the truth. She was malnourished and a runt who got pushed around. The other kids called her *Skelly from Hell* for a good reason. She resembled a skeleton and the box she was so often kept in was hell.

To look less skeletal, she'd stuff a pillow under her shirt because she was nothing but bones under skin so transparent her veins cast a blue tinge on it. Worse was her shivering like a baby stork trapped in a storm. Her hands were icicles, her nails indigo-colored, her little finger a hook. And her hair so pale she looked like an albino.

But did she give up? No, never. She bunched toilet paper into her mouth to plump up her cheeks. Slapped them until they looked like swollen beets. Painted her hair yellow and scraped it down over her face to hide the fact she used masking tape to lift the corners of her lips.

Still, the visitors rushed past her like she was a mangy puppy. Which meant on Monday mornings Qiana always cried her heart out. Nobody had liked her enough to give her a try. Of course, she knew what was wrong. She was too ugly. So night after night she wracked her brain about how to get pretty, but the only thing she could think of was to run away.

71

Even that she botched the first time. *Dumb fool.* She thought masking tape, when layered and twisted, would make a rope and hold her as she stole out of the second-story window.

She just turned seven when she broke her legs—compound fractures on both of them.

Now years later, Qiana was sad, remembering how bad it hurt, having to drag her bum legs around. The casts made them weigh a ton but the nuns made her weed the fields of string beans and peas anyway. Days and days of slave labor, weeks of being miserable in the broiling sun. And later it got worse. So much worse.

When will the pain end?

Now! Payback time! Too late for her but not for this bunch of kids. Quickly Qiana examined the faces of the students but saw nothing that hinted of any abuse.

But what about Logan? Qiana had overheard Chrissie tell Honee she didn't know where the girl was. *Oh no, did someone on the staff approach her inappropriately? And that's why she's skipping school today?*

Meanwhile over at her desk by the sun-splashed window, Honee was still wondering what to do with the giant poster. Maybe she could sell it and some of the other kids' stuff at the Q Store.

A voice floated up. "Ma'am, can I be next? I got so many extra points to get."

"Me too."

Honee groaned. "Guys, hold your polo ponies. Whoever doesn't get called on today will definitely get called on tomorr—"

"But that's so not fair. Kids you call on tomorrow get more time."

"Right. Just didn't realize how much grades—"

"Grades're our life, ma'am."

"Chill, guys. I'm not strict so you can all count on good—"

"Oh no, not the *best*?"

"Correction. You're all going to get the most outstanding, perfect, supreme, utmost, ultra and utterly divine grades. Do. You. Understand?"

Nods all around, but not one smile. "And tomorrow," Honee went on, "I will give you all a handout. It's going to list the penalty for plagiarization and exactly how much each assignment counts. And that includes class particip—"

"Me. Me. Me." An ocean of hands rose like a killer wave. "Call on me. How am I ever gonna get 500 percent for class participation?"

***

"Can you believe it? Two boys from the back of the room actually thanked me," Qiana said after the bell rang and the last student left. "But gee, I feel stiffer than a granite slab from all that posing." She stretched and eyed her hand that had ink smears. "So that's why those rascals insisted on shaking hands but I'm disappointed. These kids aren't brilliant. They're just parrots begging for extra credit. That Code of Conduct doesn't seem to be working."

"Yeah, girl. Soon as I opened my grade book, the kids turned into barracudas. But the worst is behind us. We survived first period, right?"

"Right. So do we have a few minutes between—?"

"Afraid not, there's more rules."

"Well, did you at least find out what Logan's problem is?"

"Nope, Chrissie didn't know a thing. Or if she knew something, she didn't tell."

"That doesn't sound good." Qiana noticed that the sun had ducked behind a cloud, steeping the bright classroom into gloom and shivered. "Think, Honee. What exactly did Logan tell you? Who's after her?" With girls there was always the fear of some sexual predator targeting them.

Honee frowned. "She didn't mention anything specific, just that something awful was going on. But next time I see her, I'll get the whole story." She flipped through her handbooks. "Okay, here it is. 'During class change, teachers will stand by their doors and supervise the hall traffic.' But today we got an assembly, so we do get a break. Okay, let's do it."

Honee stood by her door and pointed to another one at the back of the room. "Could you take that command post back there, Qi? So when Reinholt napoleons the halls, he's gonna give me some brownie points. Man, I'm getting to be worse than the kids."

Glad she didn't have that to worry about Qiana strolled to the back door, trailing what looked like the tail of a kite. "Just look what else your little sweetie-pies did to me." As she bent down to remove the toilet paper, she noticed something wedged under the back door. "Come here a minute, Honee."

Striding down the hall, Honee could feel her frustration ebb off. Maybe her first period class was unusually GPA-crazy but her later classes wouldn't be. She examined the small disk Qiana had found. It was brown-splotched and scratched, exposing a dark core.

"That looks like that pendant Ms. Looney dangled in our face. See those initials? It's gotta be Ms. Hill's."

"Yeah right," Qiana chuckled, "solid gold? My a...bs. And just look at those stains. Don't they look like blood?"

Honee sniffed the pendant. "It's probably rust. I reckon Reinholt's a real cheapskate except when it comes to his own duds and haircuts. So when Ms. Hill found out the Stefford Medal was fake, she pitched it. So let's just take it down to Guidance. Gotta talk to the counselor anyway. I can't help it, I feel like Logan's in trouble."

"I agree." Qiana nodded. "And what about this stuff? Should we take it along too?" Crammed behind a bookcase she had found a stack of papers that turned out to be copies of Ms. Hill's teaching

74

certificate, college diplomas and glowing job evaluations from previous schools.

"Wonder who went through Ms. Hill's files," Honee said. "Bet it was those same pranksters. Man, this isn't acting honorable. Wait a minute, have I got something stuck to my back?"

"No," Qiana said, then frowned. "But someone drew a bull's eye on your shirt with black magic marker."

"Man, just wait till I catch those rascals." Honee inked half a dozen small bull's eyes on the front and the sleeves of her blouse. "Now it looks like a design. Okay, let's go."

***

"This blows my mind," Qiana whispered to Honee as they stepped into the lobby of the Guidance Department. Hawaiian-style pink and orange blossoms bloomed everywhere in terra-cotta planters. Not a dead leaf in sight. The reason had to be the vapor that swirled in a controlled cloud, providing constant water droplets. Even more amazing was the powerful perfume.

There was only one negative—the crowd. Dozens of black and Mexican boys packed every available inch. But what a different bunch from other kids this was. Beneath the perfume, Honee couldn't help but sniff the familiar street smells. Not a hint of soap or shampoo.

Had they been expelled from public school? Or were they runaways or drop-outs? With their torn T's, saggy jeans and matted hair, they might even be on a field trip from Juvie. But the excited way they pawed through the college catalogs and yearbooks that sat around showed there was hope for them. All it would take was one teacher to motivate them.

Honee rocked on her feet. That's what she was born for.

"Shee—," a boy yelled. Realizing where he was, he amended it to "—shoot. Can't wait to come here. Act like Barack."

"Me too. I'm dying to attend Stefford School."

Qiana smiled, picturing all these street kids cleaned-up. Marching to class and studying like crazy. What if they didn't get in?

"Excuse me, do you have an enrollment cap?" she asked the middle-aged woman with beige hair and a flawless complexion who perched at the reception desk. Her eyebrows, eyes, and lips matched her hair color, providing almost no contrast to her skin, as if she wanted to fade away completely unnoticed, while her front teeth overlapped like children leaning into each other and sharing secrets.

JoBelle Edwards, Guidance Secretary, according to a sign. Well, at least she wasn't a show-off. Even her voice was soft and unassuming.

"Yes, our limit is 1,000 students. And before you ask, we've got a third white, a third black or Latino, and a third Asian or multi-ethnic kids. But we're always open to accepting new youngsters, especially," JoBelle's voice lowered, "minorities."

Honee drew closer. "Why's that, ma'am?"

"Because Dr. Reinholt is a product of the slums himself. His father used to minister in Harlem, so naturally he's got a soft spot for..." With a glance at the boys who kept erupting like a bubbling cauldron, JoBelle dusted non-existent dandruff off the shoulders of her navy-blue dress. Brush-brush. "But if anyone can shape *them* into productive members of society, he can."

"Has it ever backfired?" Honee asked, her voice low too. "How many of these kids turn out to be rotten apples?"

Brush-brush. JoBelle dusted off her immaculate dress again. "Not a one of them. Once even the toughest street kids meet our faculty chairwoman it's like a miracle. We practice tough love but they really appreciate it—finally finding a home."

"For real, ma'am? Not even the worst hoodlings—hoodlums act up?"

"That's right. I've been here for years and keep a record of all infractions. And not once have I ever sent a demerit letter to the parent or guardian of a *lost* kid."

Qiana was curious too. "Has that always been the case?"

"Oh no, only since Dr. Reinholt took over. He's the one that got Stefford on the map. This used to be an abbey, you know. There's still an old chapel but now everything's being redone. Our latest project is a new polo field and tennis courts. And best of all, a club house for the Jills.

"Of course, all our girls are darling but the Jills are future Supreme Court, U.S. Cabinet, and governor material. Maybe even the first woman in the White House."

"So the Jills are considered the best club?" Qiana asked.

"Not considered." JoBelle's colorless face sported a few pinpricks of pink. "They are. Always neck and neck with the Jacks, except they take the Stefford Code very seriously and never pull any pranks. Much too busy being on the homecoming court and doing their good deeds. And from what I hear, it's to-die-for, their new meeting place. It's right next to the chapel and—"

"Don't the guys resent it?" Honee broke in.

"Oh no. The Jacks have their own hang-out and it's even better, not that I'd know. Too much to do, new kids in and out all the time."

"So everybody's got their own pad and posse?"

The pink dots on JoBelle's face flamed scarlet. "No, ma'am! We definitely don't have any of those. But yes, all our students join a group, and all teachers and staff sponsor one. Me, for example, I'm in charge of the ITC, the Inter-Team Council. That's a powerful group, made up of sports captains and club presidents only. What Dr. Reinholt did was brilliant. He took the peer pressure concept and made it a good thing. That means the kids themselves police their classmates."

"Police?"

"I mean they help the other kids to follow the Code, so we rarely have discipline problems. Now what can I do for you?"

"Is the head counselor in?" Honee asked.

Brush-brush-brush. JoBelle consulted an appointment book. "Yes, and I think he can spare you a few minutes. Have a seat." She pointed to a loveseat where the street boys fell all over themselves to make room for Qiana and Honee.

"Thanks, guys." Honee sat down and started thumbing through one of the gold-embossed annuals.

Qiana sat next to her. "What's going on?" she whispered. "There's hardly any non-white kids pictured."

Honee sighed. "Poor kids, they never show on picture day. Me, for instance? I always scrammed whenever a camera was in sight."

"I see," Qiana said and riffled through the faculty section of the book, stopping at the picture of a pretty young teacher. "That's Ms. Hill. Wonder why she looks so scared."

"Maybe because it was her first year at this elite school, been quaking in my Adidas myself all morning."

"Don't worry, Honee. You're doing great. But what about these graduation photos? They don't represent all the kids either."

"C'mon, Qi. Wake up and smell the world's armpit. Caps and gowns? You can't touch them without pecuniarous resources. So if you're dirt poor—"

"But what a shame," Qiana cut in. "To do all this work and then be left out at graduation? You know what?" she felt excitement pop up in her like tulips in April. "How about if we pay for the graduation stuff some of these kids can't afford? Of course first we've got to deal with those wedding gowns. Get them dry-cleaned, pay a rental fee, and somehow admit you "borrowed" them. What were we think—?"

"Ladies," JoBelle Edwards broke in, "Dr. Davis can see you now. Go right in."

"Thank you." Qiana shoved the Stefford yearbooks aside like they were dirt. These would be the last editions to feature only the rich students, mostly white. "C'mon, Honee. Let's straighten out what's wrong around here."

This school definitely wasn't as perfect as it seemed. Qiana could sense something ugly being covered up by all that perfume and the emphasis on the Code. But why worry? Most likely it was just her being neurotic again. And Logan had just overslept, that was all there was to it.

CHAPTER 12

From the back Dr. Davis, who was looking out the window, appeared to be a burned-out teacher ready for retirement and not a guidance counselor. Of medium height, he had a lean but unmuscular body that was stooped. And with his fringe of salt-and-pepper hair, he looked over the hill.

But when he turned around, his unlined face and intense eyes indicated his true age—early forties. In fact, he looked as if he were on the fast track to a huge discovery.

Honee had met him before, but not Qiana who raised her eyebrows. *What an odd choice for a guidance counselor.* But maybe his unusual intensity was exactly what was needed to get those street kids to comply with the rules.

Another unusual thing was Dr. Davis' clothes. He sported a vintage tweed jacket with leather patches over a tie-dyed t-shirt whose breast pocket bulged. Gee, did he have a smart-phone in there? During school hours?

Finally realizing he had company, Dr. Davis led his visitors to a formal seating area in the back of the room. That's when Qiana noticed his unusual bald spot. It was shaped like an hourglass.

They passed an alcove with colorful bean bags and stocked with teen magazines, videos, Gameboys, and Wiis. One side of the alcove covered with DVD players and flat-screen TVs, the other side, with vending machines and buckets full of quarters.

"Lucky rascals," Honee commented, "the kids that get to see you."

Dr. Davis turned to her. "That's our stress-free zone. Even our best students can get so hyper over nothing."

Qiana sank into one of the armchairs to which Dr. Davis pointed. "You're right. These kids are out of control."

He blinked, his eyebrows tilting up. "Excuse me?"

"Well, I've only seen one of her classes so far." Qiana indicated Honee who slid into a matching chair. "But gee, they were worse than Las Vegas card sharks."

"*WHAT?*"

Dr. Davis jumped to a desk with so many cumulative folders and charts waiting to be input that his computer looked defeated. Producing paper and pen, he was ready to take names. "Names please. You caught some kids playing cards? That's completely unacceptable according to the Code."

"Oh no, nothing like that," Honee said. "They're just so grade emanciated."

He looked puzzled. "Uh, you mean grade hungry? So they got you." Sinking into a love seat across from the two women, he gave a one-sided grin. "Sorry, Ms. Money, I should've warned you on Friday. No excuse, except I never got around to it. But our kids give all new teachers the *treatment,* as we call it. Nothing personal, but they can spot a greenhorn from miles away. So they go, 'Boo-hoo, just look at us poor babies. We have such *awful* academic pressures.'"

"They sure made it sound real," Honee admitted sheepishly.

"Well, that's just the minus side of being young Einsteins—" Dr. Davis stopped. "I must be losing my mind, so many lost kids to save. Could we start over?" He hopped up, his hand out to Qiana. "Hi, I'm Dr. Ricky Davis."

"Qiana Llove. Glad to meet you." She liked his firm handshake and didn't hold it against him that it took him so long to acknowledge her. Poor guy was more overworked than a cashier at Filene's during the annual bridal gown sale.

"Oh now I remember. You're the sub for our latest substitute or a guest speaker, right?"

He turned to Honee. "By the way, Ms. Money, may I congratulate you? The kids couldn't stop singing your praises. I already mentioned it to Dr. Reinholt."

"Man, that was nice of you."

"And now we get another pretty young teacher? How lucky can we get?"

Qiana cleared her throat. "Sorry, Dr. Davis, I'm just here for today."

He looked disappointed, then grinned with both sides of his mouth. "Still, Ms. Llove, let me welcome you to our close-knit family. And please call me Ricky. But no need to mention it. I know I'm a thorn in Dr. Reinholt's side."

Qiana felt heat flash from her neck to her face. Ricky must've noticed her staring at his un-Stefford-like attire. "I've been meaning to ask. Why's there such a strict dress code?"

"It's just the world according to Reinholt, you know. He loves the Code of Conduct. As for what we wear, he wants the faculty to look like the 'authority,'" he made air quotes, "to simplify things when we infiltrate—"

"*Infiltrate?*" Honee's hand flew up. "You're making it sound like the kids are the enemy. What's really going on behind all this goody-goody acting?"

"Nothing, trust me," Ricky said, looking like he regretted using the word *infiltrate*. "Of course, all our kids can act silly. It's to be expected that a few break a little rule now and then. But obedience and compliance are huge here. That makes it so easy to lead them to excellence and naturally that striving for greatness filters down. For example, get the seniors to discuss an earthquake in a foreign country, next thing you know the second-graders are collecting funds for a new school there."

"I don't get it. Don't you separate the little young'uns from the big kids?"

"Of course we do, Ms. Money. We have entirely separate wings for lower, middle, and upper school students but most of them twitter, but only after school. All electronic devices are banned during school hours, as you know. However the end result is amazing. You have no idea how brilliant our combined projects and volunteering—"

"Aren't you worried it's all fake?" Qiana cut in.

A pulse jumped at Ricky's temple like a bug wanting out. "*Fake?*"

"Well, for example, this one kid," Honee said. "He crowed like a rooster about his fancy volunteer project but his motive is pure selfish."

"Sure that happens. But by the time they're seniors—"

"I don't teach any seniors."

"Well then, that explains it, Ms. Money."

"Honee, okay? That close-knit family—?"

"Okay, Honee. But look, if you teach nothing but underclassmen, you see only the partial products. But how gratifying to see them all turn into perfect gentlemen and ladies at the end. By the way, have you heard about our first branch school? Won't be long now before we'll have a major presence in each and every—"

84

Qiana didn't let him finish. "Could Honee and I make a little contribution too before long? How's the fund raising going?"

"Not bad. Last month the kids raised close to fifty thou—"

"Man, how in the world—?"

Ricky stretched like a well-fed cat. Obviously they'd come to his favorite topic. "It's all due to our club competitions. We don't hawk Girl Scout cookies, toilet paper, or band turkeys. No, our students have to use their gray matter. So some invented new water-saving devices, others wrote songs and sold tons of CD's."

"Gee, these well-behaved little geniuses are entrepreneurs too?"

"Yes, Qiana, but here's the difference. They don't do it for themselves. It's so some underprivileged kids can come here."

"Like those little hoodlums out there?"

"Yes, but don't call them hoodlums, Honee. They're just kids nobody's ever taken any time with and all in desperate need of financial aid. See, that's the real reason most teachers work here, myself included. I don't dig all this window dressing shit, sorry." But Ricky didn't sound sorry. "I drive a clunker, wear thrift shop stuff, as you see. To tell the truth, you have no idea how tough it is for teachers. Year after year you work for less than peanuts while all these Wall Street folks rake in million-dollar bonuses. They take private jets, luxury junkets to the Bahamas, skiing in Kitzbuhel. But teachers slave every damn day just to eke out a pitiful—" He stopped. "Fortunately here we do okay, so I can underwrite quite a few scholarships."

"Oh, man," Honee inched forward until she perched on the edge of her chair, "you do that? Really?"

"Why shouldn't I? A lot of our underprivileged kids still use an outhouse or they're illegals. Three families to a one-bedroom pad. Dads in jail, moms on crack and looking for trade. Anything, no matter how disgusting, for a buck."

Oh no. Honee bounced back like she'd been knocked in the teeth. Did Ricky know about her sordid background?

"So that's where I put my dough," Ricky went on breezily, "where it can do some good, okay? Otherwise this country's going straight to hell. But I'm lucky, I found my calling and that's saving human strays."

"Man, that's awesome." Honee composed herself and offered a neutral expression. "You're a hero, Ricky, you know that?"

"No, just doing my duty." He chewed his lips like gristle. "See, not long ago I was a bum myself. My old man was the town drunk and my mother? She abandoned me when I was just one day old. Can you believe it?"

Qiana made a horrified sound. "Oh no. No."

"It's true and let me tell you, that set me up for all kinds of trouble." Ricky dropped his head.

Qiana could tell he was crying. She felt like joining in. She hugged her purse, wanting to pull the rag doll out. Hug it, kiss it, but too late, much too late. She sagged into herself, feeling a morass of misery trying to swamp her.

In contrast, Honee was tickled. What a relief to find someone at Stefford School with his own skanky past. Meant she wasn't the only piece of trash on the faculty. She gave Ricky a hug. "I went through a similar mess. In my case, it was Momma that drank and did bad stuff. That led me to also... Well, anyway, I never even met my dad which is something I plan to remnificate just as soon as—"

"Guys, guys," Qiana interjected, dropped her purse on the floor and straightened up, "if you're having a pity party, don't leave me out. A total lunatic robbed me of my folks who had the worst lives you can imagine. Gee, so much pain, so much agony for years and years.

"Unbelievable, but when they were little, they were kidnapped together from some Dachau concentration camp inmates. Never even knew they were Jewish. They were raised by

Nazis, can you imagine? Fortunately, I was finally reunited with them."

She hitched in air as she pictured her heart-broken parents over the years. Most likely they thought of her every day and paused to mark her milestones: her birthdays, Christmases, finishing first grade, her dance recitals and volleyball games. In their minds they celebrated her great report cards, watched her grow up into a moody teenage girl, and then into a smart-as-a-whip college student. All that without her ever being there. And all along they prayed with every breath that their daughter wasn't dead. That she would be safe and that they would be reunited some day. *Please God, please.*

Then a miracle: last week it happened. She met her mother and her father.

And that was the true turning point in Qiana's life—when she had seen her parents' faces flood with immense joy over finally being reunited with their long-lost daughter only in the very next instant to have their ecstatic expression change into one of crushing disappointment because they realized what Qiana had become. How she made her money as a sleazy parasite, slutting around, and sinking deeper and deeper into the morass of immorality each year. Yes, Qiana watched with her own eyes how her parents' biggest joy turned into their worst nightmare in an instant. She had felt their shock and overwhelming pain.

So right then and there she knew she had to make sure her parents' horrible suffering hadn't been in vain. She just had to amount to something worthy of their love. From now on, she would do good.

And that starts with helping Logan.

As if robbed of the ability to speak, Ricky was watching Qiana whose facial expression must have been reflecting first her feelings of deep shame, then her fervent hope for redemption, and finally her eagerness to do good.

"You know what," he finally said, "it's crazy but I think I read your story in the *Red Mill Register.*"

Qiana gulped. "Yes, that was me. The long separation from my parents was terrible but the astonishing news is it all ended up okay. And even more astonishing she—" Qiana's thumb pointed to Honee "—also benefited. She just lost her mom but finally met her half-brother who is now my fiancé. I know it's all so mind-boggling, all those big things happening practically at the same time. And as for my parents? They're fine now too. In fact, they're on a trip to New Zealand."

"That's the reason we came to see you," Honee said.

Ricky swiped at his eyes. "You know what, ladies? Stories like yours give me hope. My dad's dead but maybe some day I'll get to see my mom again." Another swipe. "Okay, so you two didn't just drop in for a visit? Damn, must be losing my sex appeal, now what about New Zealand?"

"Sorry it took us so long to get to the point but it's about Logan Adams. I think she's in trouble."

"No, Honee, not her. She's one of our most popular—"

Honee cut him off. "Well, on Friday she asked me in a scared whisper if she could talk to me about something awful going on and today she didn't show. And her best friend has no idea where she is."

"That doesn't sound good at all. Let's just hope she's home with the cramps." Ricky groaned. "You know teenage girls and all their drama…"

Honee shook her head. "I really think it's something worse. Anyway, her folks're on vacation right now, coincidentally in New Zealand too. But I'm pretty sure she didn't go with them."

"Dammit." Ricky smacked his armrest in frustration. "Why didn't she come to me? All students know they can come over to my place in an emergency. It's just a mobile home but camouflaged. Wouldn't want the trustees to see a trailer on this perfect campus, would we? Originally I didn't plan to go into guidance, so during the odd free moment, I work on my pet project back there."

No wonder Ricky resembled a scholar on the verge of a huge discovery, the way his eyes blazed again.

"Which is what, if you don't mind telling us?" Honee asked.

"Oh, it's no secret. I want to find a cure for non-Hodgkin's." Ricky dug in his breast pocket, producing a cell phone and a thumb drive. "Here's my research. See, I once had a brother, Honee, just like you. Actually two, but both died a miserable death as teenagers due to that disease." He pressed both his temples where blood vessels pulsed, trying to out-duel one another. "Dammit, why am I bringing up all that sob-story stuff today?"

Before either of the women could answer, he did: "Maybe it's because you two are kindred spirits and that's rare around here. Our faculty chair, she's the worst. Teaching's her *whole* life." Checking a wall clock, he hopped up. "Sorry, guys, gotta NASCAR. About this time's usually when the sermon ends."

"Gee, Dr. Reinholt's a minister too?"

"No Qiana, but Slick Willy loves lecturing about the rules and I'm always up next. Excuse me." Ricky yanked a white button-down shirt out of a closet, slipped it on and looped a red-and-blue striped tie around his neck like a noose. "Show time ladies. What do you think?"

Honee whistled. "Looking good dude."

"Now that slave driver can't fire my ass for not dressing along party lines."

"Is that what happened to Ms. Hill?"

"Maybe. Or maybe she broke some other rule. Ms. Hill was the super nervous type, you know. Always so scared she'd break the Code."

89

Honee searched her pockets. "That's the other reason we came to see you. We found Ms. Hill's medallion. See these brownish spots?"

Qiana knew it was a crazy thought but uttered it anyway: "What if it's her blood?"

Ricky gave a dismissive wave. "Poor thing probably just got a paper cut, what with all her meticulous files. She kept hard copies of *everything*, including every fart Reinholt made, haha. But seriously, suddenly she was in a bat-out-of-hell hurry to get out of here. Probably eloped to Vegas. She really had the worst case of biological clock ticking I've ever run across. Excuse me again." Back in the closet, Ricky wheeled out a tea cart squeaking under a mountain of trophies.

"All this is for the progress made last week. It's amazing how well *Herr* Reinholt's student management plan works. When he instituted the Code, we made enormous strides. To my knowledge, there's never been a more successful program." He steered the cart through the door. "See you guys later, okay?"

"Please don't forget about Logan," Honee called after him.

"I won't but you know girls, don't you? Last second she probably hopped on the plane with her folks. I'm sure there's an e-mail in my inbox from her with lots of LOL's. I bet Logan's having the best time in her life right now."

CHAPTER 13

Logan was in fact having the worst time in her life. The heat in the shed was so bad even the copperhead seemed to feel it. It curled up in the hollow she had scraped out with her shoes in despair.

So now she didn't dare move her feet, not a fraction, not that she could. Besides her arms and body, her legs were taped to the desk. Pretending to be dead was the only thing she could think of, which wasn't far from the truth. Actually death would be a relief from the razor-sharp pains slicing through her.

Earlier, she had wriggled and strained almost to death trying to break free. But the tape didn't give, not even the piece that was slapped on Logan's mouth, no matter how hard she worked her aching jaws. And now her situation was 200 percent impossible. She had to hold perfectly still, so the snake wouldn't bite her. So she had to breathe shallow.

They scared Logan, these dying-baby gulps of air. What if she didn't get enough oxygen in her lungs?

Then it got even worse. A spider with a figure-eight pattern scurried down a thread in front of the girl's eyes. And another one rappelled down and a bunch more. Before long, cobwebs seemed to knit themselves around Logan. She couldn't see them but felt like she was getting smothered.

Please God, get me outta here! Logan prayed with every fiber in her. *I didn't do anything wrong besides getting involved with Josh.*

Does that have to cost me my life?

And WTF, where is Josh?

What about Ms. Money? Didn't she notice I wasn't in class this morning?

Well, maybe she did, but teachers were told to wait three days before turning in any absentees. Logan knew she couldn't last that long. Maybe if she tried to get her mind on something other than her circumstances? Could she cling to something mentally until—

Until what?

There was no rescue on the horizon. Nobody knew where she was. Nobody would come and get her out. *I'm as good as dead.*

CHAPTER 14

Whistling, Ricky careened the trophy trolley to the auditorium and disappeared inside. As the two young women were about to squeeze in behind him, they heard: "Hey there, Ms. Money, Ms. Llove. I've been like looking all over for you."

Turning around, Honee and Qiana saw a girl in a hot pink polo shirt skipping in their direction. "No one told us," Honee said. "Who're you?"

"Gibson, president of the student body, I'm here to show you around."

"That's mighty nice of you." Honee smiled and Qiana couldn't help herself—she smiled too. Teenage girls always made her anxious, but this one was so cute. Her strawberry-blond hair, brushed back in a ponytail, swung like the tail of a cantering horse and her eyes sparkled. Her pleated skirt, probably size zero, exposed slim but muscular legs encased in hot pink knee socks. Matching tennis shoes completed her outfit.

"Gee, are you a cheerleader too?"

"Well yeah. Let's study—hey. Let's study—yay. Go-o-o, Stefford!" Gibson clapped, catapulted into the air, and executed a perfect split. After landing like a dandelion seed, she dropped her eyes and turned the color of her socks. "Actually not that I deserve it, but I'm head."

"Way to go, girl."

"Thanks, Ms. Money, but it's like a lot of work. But what could I do? We're taught to be compliant." The girl bounced on the balls of her feet. "Wouldn't be so bad but with all my club duties?"

"What's your club?" Qiana asked but could already guess.

"The Jills."

"Why aren't you at the assembly? Aren't they going to announce—"

"Oh, that silly stuff." More bouncing. "Fighting tooth and nail over some dumb points? Sorry, didn't mean dumb. I meant immature."

"Then why do you wear—?"

"Our club colors? That's our uniform. Can't get away with what Ricky—Dr. Davis—gets away with. Ready?"

"Can we see the whole school?" Qiana asked.

"Sorry, I don't think—" Gibson sprouted a frown. "The Upper School alone is huge. And the lower schools are housed in other ginormous parts. This place is bigger than Atlanta. Follow me."

Gibson crossed the lobby at a fast pace, forcing Qiana and Honee to hop to it. "Here's the office, the command center. You met *Herr* Dr. Reinholt, right?" She swept her hands around. "And next door's the library. Have you seen that already?"

"No, girl, we ain't—haven't."

"Then c'mon." Skirt swishing, Gibson trotted Qiana and Honee into a huge room. Book-lined walls climbed two stories but there wasn't a hint of the musty smell usually associated with old tomes and newspapers. "That's because most of our holdings're

94

underground," the girl explained over her shoulder. "To keep them safe in case of another disaster like 9/11."

Another sweep of her hands that were perfectly manicured. Did the girl sneak over to the Spa during lunch? Qiana sure hoped so.

"This used to be an old abbey," Gibson went on. "They renovated all the crypts into storage space for the literary collections. I've never been down there but it gives me the creeps just thinking about what might still be there. Like skulls and other bones from those dead monks, and maggots and worms, plus a vise with razor-sharp teeth. One wrong move and—" Gibson snapped her fingers "—you're trapped."

"*Trapped?*" Qiana asked with a shiver, her eyes on a table with new desktop computers. She'd use one of them shortly to research potential child predators in the area. Then she'd check them against the staff, the list of volunteers, and the visitors. "What're you talking about?"

"I'm just saying." Gibson circled a shiny table.

Honee was riffling through the *Oxford English Dictionary* looking for new adjectives. "A vise with razor-sharp teeth? Wasn't stuff like that used before Columbus?"

"Isn't Columbus the capital of Ohio, ma'am?"

"Now girl, don't get your geography all mixed up with your history."

"Fiddlesticks, I love history." Gibson chewed on a strand of hair, her eyelid twitching. "Okay. Christopher Columbus, 1451 to 1506. Italian navigator. Opened up the New World— Honestly I don't get it. How can they call it the New World when it was eons ago?"

"Reckon it was new back then." Honee slithered a page from a tattered thesaurus into her pocket while trying to understand what was going on. Was this girl putting on an act or was she really this discombobulated?

"But isn't Columbus a city in western Georgia?" Gibson executed another flawless split, another feather-light landing. "But which Georgia? The one here in the Colonies? I mean the Etats Unis? Or the one that used to be Russia? Sorry I'm like *so* dumb." She bit her lips.

"Now don't be so harsh on yourself, girl," Honee said. "You can't know everything."

Qiana also felt sorry for Gibson. "Yeah, just chillax."

Gibson sniffled. "But don't you get it, ladies? We can't relax, we've got to like study nonstop."

"Don't you ever just chill with your girlfriends?" Qiana asked, not that she had ever chilled with a girlfriend. She never had one, except maybe now she did. Or maybe she didn't. She didn't really know Honee, didn't really trust her because she'd only known her a week and she was so full of quirks. Plus, her past was sketchy, similar to her own in some ways, and Qiana didn't even trust herself. So how could she trust another ex-low- or sleazy-lifer?

Qiana had the sensation of an icicle sliding down her back. Had Honee lured her here on Dr. Reinholt's orders? So he could assault her, and then turn her over to Henry for disposal? Her shoulders tensed, her stomach churned. She glanced around but saw nothing threatening. *Never mind. Just crazy me having more crazy thoughts. What else is new?*

"No, ma'am," Gibson told Qiana. "Every moment we have is scheduled. We've got to have a private secretary just to keep up with our agenda, haha." But there was nothing funny in the girl's voice and her eyelid twitched again like a trapped butterfly. "It worries me tons, you know, that with all that stress we're losing our soul. That's why I'm really *not* sorry I forget all these facts. Means I'm still a human being and not a—"

"Robot?" Qiana suggested. "Or a trained seal?"

96

"An iPad walking. You know, touch an app and it all spills out. But I don't want to be a machine or device. Oh no, shouldn't have said that. *Herr* Dr. Reinholt will flat-out kill me."

"Why do you call him *Herr*?" Qiana knew why Ricky did, in reference to the Prussian taskmaster that Dr. Reinholt appeared to be. Personally she thought Dr. R. was much worse than a micromanager with a penchant for pretty females. He was sleazy, maybe even dangerous. His crocodile collection alone was a sign something was off. But she was curious to learn what the girl thought of the headmaster.

"That's because his *hair* is always perfect like Donald Trump's. But I'm just supposed to give you the grand tour, not run my mouth." Gibson dragged a smile on her face, skipped back into the hall and scampered up the closest staircase to the top of the building, Qiana and Honee hustling after her.

"Here's where the foreign language classrooms are. Did you know some students study Shakespeare in Aramanian? And a bunch of them are into Kashmirish or whatever they speak at the Bangor Air Force Base next to all those *stan* countries. Some kids even speak Bavarian and Barbarian. Can you believe it?"

Hearing that, Qiana stopped in her tracks. She might've laughed out loud if her parents hadn't grown up in Bavaria where the Dachau Concentration Camp was, from which they were kidnapped as babies. She winced remembering what pain she'd caused them recently at their long-hoped-for reunion when it was so obvious what she had turned into.

But now finally her ugly past was behind her.

Yet being born in Bavaria, she knew Bavarian was a German dialect and Barbarian wasn't a language. But why make poor little Gibson feel worse by correcting her? "Really?"

"Yes, really. We're always on the cutting edge." Swishing down the hall, the girl pointed out more classrooms. "Isn't one of these rooms yours, Ms. Money? From what I hear you're the best substitute. On to the next wing, ladies."

Again trailing the girl, Qiana and Honee hustled down a connecting corridor so glossy it mirrored the overhead lights. Qiana started skipping like a little girl, then felt like she had hit a wall. "What's that?" she asked, feeling dizzy. Both she and Honee flung their hands up to their noses. It was either that or pass out on the spot.

The sight of the two substitutes pinching their nostrils for dear life made Gibson giggle. She jabbed a button, and a double glass door on the left swung open like a hospital entrance.

"Here's our famous Science Department. We offer everything from anatromy to aster-physicals and mini—"

"I mean that smell." Qiana gagged and Honee shivered as if she'd spied something too repulsive for words.

"Oh, that's from the labs. You won't believe what's kept up here. Mice, frogs, and all sorts of creepy crawlies like hissing cockroaches from South America."

With Qiana and Honee breathing through their mouths, they checked out the long hall. Just like in the first wing, all the classrooms were locked, but Honee and Qiana could peek through the glass-paneled doors. Microscopes hooked up to computers, stainless-steel counters and sinks, and storage cabinets packed with jars of lumpy growths stared back at them. A few containers were filled with animal eyeballs, if Honee wasn't mistaken.

She shuddered. "Girl, this is incredible," she said, yet itching to get as far away from this wing as possible because she could picture litters of blind kittens cowering somewhere. No food, no water, their mama cats mutilated. Man, what gruesome experiments were these kids into? A terrifying thought hit her: Did Logan take it upon herself to explore the origin of those eyeballs? Was that why she was so scared?

Gibson didn't seem bothered by anything displayed in the science rooms. "You guys want to look at some actual research?" She unlocked a small office and prodded a computer to life.

Hesitating, Honee stepped into the small room, afraid of what might appear on the screen: images of injured pets or dead ones. She braced herself, ready to stop any animal torture immediately. Never mind it might cost her this cushy gig.

Qiana was wondering if they'd see pictures of Dr. R. in the act of assaulting Rosario, or of Henry exposing the boys to pornography. *Please don't let it be something dealing with Logan.*

Gibson noticed the women's mounting unease but misinterpreted it. "Don't worry, ladies. I'm not breaking the Code of Conduct. This is my boyfriend's work, he doesn't mind." As a file opened up, she read out loud: "One mystery to be solved is the potential existence of connectivity between the gunky plaques of beta-amyloid protein and the abnormal stringy tangles of protein in animal's brains that have been damaged by old age. However, one possibly efficacious solution might be discovered through a thorough examination of a large number of common house pets that died of old age..."

Whew! No mention of any mutilated kittens, only scientific words and columns of numbers. Honee sighed out from relief; Qiana did too. Nothing about Logan, nothing about Dr. R. That didn't mean the guy was clean. He probably preached the rules until he was blue in the face. Yet behind the scenes he sexually harassed Ms. Hill until she fled in tears, then he started in on Rosario. And now he was looking for another victim—Qiana.

Sexual addiction? Yeah right. That's what he'd probably claim once he was exposed, just like so many sleazy men did these days. "Couldn't help myself, blah-blah-blah. Didn't take my meds, blah-blah-blah..." What a poor excuse, Qiana thought, but some parents might actually buy it until Qiana would set them straight.

The fact was that many school principals considered their teachers their personal harem. Since they didn't make much money, they felt entitled to pick and choose from among the staff. Maybe Slick Willy was even into threesomes, involving a voluptuous blonde and a gorgeous young honey-skinned—

Gibson cut Qiana's thoughts off. "That's just one study, ladies." She dashed back into the hall, the two young women following. "Other kids do HIV research and, you know, all sorts of taxidermy stuff with beetles. And ohmigod, how they all love messing with transplants."

Honee froze. *"Transplants?"*

"Not human transplants, just more boring stuff. Like they take a twig from a peach tree and graft it on a pear tree."

Honee let her breath out all the way. "I bet in a few years we'll read all about the latest Nobel Prize winners graduating from Stefford."

"That's exactly what Dr. R's counting on. C'mon." The girl blazed the way to a down staircase.

"Can't we go to the next wing up here?" Qiana grumbled. Her lack of sleep was catching up with her.

"Sorry, ma'am, the third wing's still under construction." Waving the two women forward, Gibson stopped at the entrance to yet another enormous hallway. "See?"

Looking through a giant locked grate, Qiana saw doors dangling from crooked frames and scarred desks sagging on top of one another. Dented student lockers—ripped off the wall—crouched on the floor and dust and debris blanketed everything.

So back to the second wing. As they hurried downstairs, the bell rang. "Lunch already?" Qiana was elated.

"Yes, ma'am."

"I'm not hungry," Honee retched out, trying to clear her throat of the dust she'd inhaled upstairs at the construction site.

"And I'm on a diet. So how about just a protein bar and some high-test java? I mean super high test?" Qiana said, with a wink. She knew she had to stop drinking but what's wrong with a little sip for old time's sakes?

"Yeah girl, can't we just grab something at the gym?" Honee always wondered if she couldn't have played basketball in high school.

"Sorry, ma'am, I don't think—"

Qiana cut in, "Even better, can we see your club?" After that she'd start her research in the library. There was work to do.

"Ma'am, I'd love to take you over there," Gibson said, "but I don't want Ms. Taylor to kill me. Plus, we got exams tomorrow. That's why this afternoon's no good either. Everybody's like gonna race home and study, and the teachers make up their big tests. So on to the cafeteria."

Here Qiana and Honee were in for another surprise. A modern dining room more suitable for a private club than a school yawned in front of them. It had space for hundreds of kids, but so far only a few had tiptoed in, not to eat—but to entertain the faculty. Chrissie was playing Beethoven on a grand piano with Jefferson turning the pages. Next to them, a student chamber quartet was setting up.

"Died and gone to Elysioso," Honee whispered to Qiana, for once not repulsed by real food. She watched an army of waiters bustle around a huge buffet table with an ice sculpture, proclaiming: *Stefford School # 1.* Next to it was a chocolate sheet cake with white icing: Always Follow the Code.

On other tables snuggled shrimp the size of link sausages, oysters on the half shell, lox and cream cheese, tuna and chicken salad, and all sorts of fancy cold cuts. On another big table, hot entrees and scrumptious desserts acted like first-graders trying to get attention.

"Diet-schmiet," Qiana said. "Can you sew me into my wedding gown, Honee?"

Gibson squealed. "Oh, oh, are you getting married? That's all I want, not go insane over some silly points." Her eyelid twitched again like a blinking traffic light.

Poor little girl, Qiana thought; so young and already such a nervous wreck. Hope she doesn't have a nervous breakdown. Her next thoughts were even worse: Is that what happened to Logan? Did something happen to her that was so horrible she didn't know what to do except run away?

No! Always thinking the worst did no good. "Yes, Gibson, I'm getting married real soon. It's only about—," Qiana gazed at the wall clock, "—30 more hours until my fiancé—"

Honee broke in. "Do we just go over there and help our—?"

"No, Ms. Money, wait."

A heavy lady streamed toward them like a Disney cruise liner bound for Paradise Island. "That's Mrs. Taylor," Gibson whispered. "She's the real powerhouse behind—"

"Hel-lo there," the heavy lady sang before Gibson could finish. Chubby hands shot out and before Qiana and Honee could blink, she had hugged them to her bosom. "Delighted to meet you both." Releasing them, Mrs. Taylor gave them the once-over, her eyes narrowing as they came to rest on Qiana's stilettos.

"Um, Mrs. T., this is—" Gibson's face washed hot-pink as if she'd been caught making a huge mistake.

"I know who these lovely young ladies are." The faculty chairwoman was even shorter and more rotund up close, which she unsuccessfully tried to hide in her loose shirt and maxi skirt, allowing only a glimpse of her snow-white Keds.

But as far as her age was concerned, Mrs. Taylor did nothing to hide it. She wore her thin gray hair raked back, revealing a pink scalp and scads of wrinkles, especially around her eyes and mouth. Obviously they were etched in from laughing. "You two are our latest substitutes."

102

There was something familiar in her voice. Qiana thought it sounded like Aunt Bea's from the old *Andy Griffith Show* reruns.

"Yes, yes," Mrs. Taylor laughed, "this makes my day, my week, my year."

What a relief to find someone so grandmotherly and proud of it, and so sweet. Qiana felt an aura of warmth emanating from the older woman.

"Pleased to meet you too, ma'am," Honee said.

"But I'm only here for today," said Qiana.

Mrs. Taylor laughed again. "I know, nothing gets past me." She looked at Gibson, "You're dismissed. Follow me, ladies." Mrs. Taylor plowed to an oblong table where a dozen other teachers were already digging into their salads. They were all dressed similarly—dark pants, white shirts and regimental ties for the men; below-the-knee skirts, blouses, and scarves for the women. Most of them sported medallions.

After heaving herself on a chair at the head of the table, Mrs. Taylor dabbed her glistening forehead. "Hot flashes, can you believe it? But at my age I love them. Saves on heating bills in the winter, hahaha." She patted the empty seats on either side. "Sit, sit."

As soon as Honee and Qiana had been served their iced tea, she said, "Let me introduce you but today we'll just go by departments. Later on we'll get to the individual teacher names and their rate of efficacy."

"What's that?" Qiana asked, setting down a polished knife in which she'd been ogling herself, with an irritated clunk. How long would it take to get over her stupid vanity? Suddenly a sense of panic overtook her. *Is something horrible happening to Logan right now?* She felt like jumping up and yelling, "Call the police!"

Mrs. Taylor grabbed Qiana's forearm, anchoring her back to her seat.

"Stay put, I don't need a cold wash cloth. And about that efficacy rate? That's their students' achievement scores, combined with their club points, good-deed bonus points and Code compliance rate. Our teachers get merit bonuses based on pupil net outcomes. Not enough, of course. Teachers are always at the bottom of—"

Abruptly she changed the topic, her eyes sweeping around. "Faculty members, these two young ladies just joined us. Please treat them well, at least for the first few days. We don't want to scare them off." She laughed.

A polite chuckle traveled around the big table like the ball on a roulette wheel.

"Let's begin. Math?"

A man with a bulldog face raised his hand like a student.

"History?"

A thin black woman with big teeth, perching at the other end, waved as if she'd burned her hand.

"Athletics?"

A tall muscular man with an al-Qaeda beard looked up and nodded. Chewing furiously, he was in the process of forking a shrimp into his mouth. But one look at Honee, and he dunked the morsel into his water glass.

"Former NFL player. Wish he'd shave, don't you?" Mrs. Taylor whispered. "What kind of example is he setting?"

"English Department?"

She looked around the table again, then patted her chest. "That's me, of course." With a chuckle she continued to introduce the rest of the departments.

"Is there a connection between the students' polo shirts and the teachers' scarves?" Qiana asked, scrutinizing the faculty. Was one of them the reason for Logan's absence?

Mrs. Taylor clapped. "A-plus, Ms. Llove. Yes, our staff is proud of sponsoring their teams and clubs. Only too bad about the computer department, isn't it?" Her thumb twitched at the latest arrival, an Asian woman with hair in a page-boy cut. "All the top colors were snapped up when she came on board."

Honee and Qiana tried not to stare at the teacher's vomity-looking scarf.

"She wanted red but that belongs to our Science Club. But you're in luck, ladies. The art department's color is a lovely purple. Drop by my room tomorrow and I'll give you—"

"Sorry, I won't be here."

"Now Ms. Llove. You don't know how often I've heard that. Next thing you know, you'll stay on forever, just like me. That's the thing about teaching. It pays so little it enslaves you just like share croppers. They get hooked by a boss who lets them charge the necessities. Then by the time payday comes, they've already spent their wages and can't quit.

"Exactly like that, teachers always hope to make a killing but never do. Of course, it's quite different here. We have such wonderful opportunities if we but seize them." She flexed her hands that looked sinewy under their chubbiness. "I always say, the sky is the limit, and not even that. Now let's get a bite."

Mrs. Taylor hoisted herself up and bee-lined for the lavish spread. "*Tempus fugit,* ladies. Time flies. You really must refuel. One never knows when suddenly out of the blue one needs every bit of strength and energy, right?"

Qiana and Honee nodded half-heartedly.

CHAPTER 15

Back in the classroom, Qiana felt so stuffed she flopped down on a chair. "Wow, Honee. That kind of meal would've bankrupted us anywhere else if we weren't already more broke than the US Treasury. Just don't let me nod off and drool."

But as soon as the next wave of students flowed in, Qiana perked up and poured her renewed energy into portraying the range of emotions Honee wanted. This time it was so much easier and the remaining classes purred along like a Mercedes Maybach.

Only too bad these kids were also super grade-conscious and constantly tried to finagle Honee into giving them a quadrillion extra points. But by then she was used to it. They were just trying to test her. A few of them tried other annoying little things— planting thumb tacks on her seat, unplugging her computer, pilfering the ball out of the mouse—just more silly stuff. But no worries. She flipped through the Code of Conduct book to see what punishment might be appropriate.

Besides those pesky minor irritations, nothing interfered with Honee's lessons and the afternoon whooshed by like a bullet train. Still, what a relief when the final bell trilled.

"Tada. This concludes my brief but brilliant stint as substitute teacher," Qiana announced, watching Honee grab all her handbooks, some of Ms. Hill's files and three fat college texts.

"Man, it's gonna be a long night. Want to swing by the gym on the way out, Qiana? I've seen enough of their academics and rules but nothing about their sports program."

Qiana wiggled her eyebrows. "I think that coach guy is crazy about you."

"Stay out of my business," Honee snapped but her eyes danced.

"Just admit it. You're dying to catch him coming out of the shower. Picture all those rippling muscles and—"

"Shut up, girl, I mean it. But maybe we can get the scoop on Logan over there. I won't be able to concentrate on my work until we find her. Besides, maybe we can catch Gibson doing her cheerleading thing. I think the poor chick's totally misplaced."

"Did you notice her tic attacks?"

"Sure I did. Lord-awful stress can do that. Don't I know it?" Honee said. At some point she had ended up on the street and lived off trash. But when she couldn't scrape up any moldy leftovers, she ate un-eatable junk that after a while tasted pretty good. And before long she developed a condition called *pica* that made her crave dirt, wood, chalk, clay, even plastic. Of course, she had read up on her eating disorder. It was associated with poverty, neglect, mental problems—all true in her case.

Now she was trying to get a grip on her eating disorder. Wasn't easy, just like Qiana's wine-guzzling wasn't easy to stop, nor her whining or her pill popping or her floozy acting...

Plenty to work on for both of us.

108

On their way to the gym, the two women passed the entrance to the science wing again. Honee raised her head and sniffed the air like a housewife expecting her mother-in-law.

"Is that formaldehyde getting to you again?" Qiana asked.

"Nope, girl, this smell is worse. It's like from being scared out of their mind."

"Let's just hope the lab animals are kept in humane conditions. You think we ought to check?"

"Not now, girl, okay? I'm beyond beat." But Honee kept sniffing. "You know what? I think I smell weed."

"Gee, wouldn't be the first time today. I picked up something similar in Ricky's office."

"Me too, girl, but I was thinking it was from those street kids. Can I tell you what the best part of my day was? It was seeing Ricky care so much about those little bums."

"I agree, that was heart-warming. But wouldn't it be shocking if Ricky was into drugs himself? Maybe that's the reason Ricky's on Dr. Reinholt's sh— *hit* list."

"Sure, maybe Dr. R. picked Ricky off the street and cleaned him up to serve as a role model for the little hoodlums. 'See what you can achieve if you pull yourself up by your boot straps?' Like, I bet, he's planning on using me to light the fire under any African American slackers."

"Well, if that's his plan, good for him." So maybe the headmaster wasn't all bad. It was just that Qiana was *uber*-suspicious. Neuroses did that. You saw the boogieman in every corner. And every itch had you quaking in fear of a flesh-eating disease. But now things were different. She had helped Honee out. Next was making sure Logan was okay, and then stop child abuse.

Psyched up, she bounced down the hall. "Yay Honee, you'll be a terrific role model and Ricky's a great role model too. I saw his diplomas, what super credentials. Guess what his middle name is? Ta-ta-ta, drum roll. It's *Granville.*"

"Really, Qi? He's kin to that sweet old dude down in the Florida nursing home?"

"Well, maybe his mother's maiden name was Granville. But she was the black sheep in the family and—"

"Hold it." Honee whipped up a hand which forced her to balance her stacks of books and papers with a knee. "Lord, would you look at that?"

Without thinking, they had wandered to the construction site where the big metal grate was now pushed back. "Man, that's crazy," Honee said. "Everybody knows kids're mighty curious. One of them just might've—" She dropped her things and wrestled through the opening. "Let's take a look."

Perching her Louis Vuitton on top of Honee's stuff, Qiana shook her head. "Complete idiots, whoever did this." She panzered her way through the gap too.

Getting more steamed with every step, the two young women fast-tracked down the long hall. Leaning doors, heaps of rubble, and stacks of old desks tried to block their way, but Qiana and Honee weren't deterred. Soon the smell of marijuana was a thick cloud and a boom box throbbed in the distance.

Honee raised a fist. "Man-oh-man, just wait till we carry this to Dr. R. He's gonna have a heart attack."

"Better have an ambulance— Watch it," Qiana screamed. In front of them and half covered by linoleum, canyoned a hole. Shocked, they stared into the belly of the abbey. At first glance nothing but darkness loomed but soon a few details emerged: Buckling pipes, strips of metal sharp enough to slice off a body part, and rusty wires coiling down to the floors below.

"Girl, that could've been ugly. Bet it's the shaft for another elevator but why does it look like a trap?"

"C'mon, Honee. It's nothing but a sloppy construction site. As they say, paranoia can destroya."

110

"But why ain't—isn't this hole taped off, girl? Or marked with some cones or something? Oh no, you think that's where Logan—?"

"No way," Qiana said, but only to calm Honee down. She was worried too. This abyss could've swallowed any number of students who might be lying unconscious at the bottom. Qiana nudged a small rock over the edge of the hole. It bounced off somewhere below, sounding ominous. A smell of a crypt being opened wafted up.

"Logan," she screamed, "Logan!" afraid of what she might hear in response. "Are you down there?"

No weak call for help, not a peep. "See, Honee? Nothing. So stop worrying—"

"Ms. Hill?" Honee yelled. "Rosario?... *Rosario?*"

Qiana exhaled audibly. "Stop it. We're just wasting time. Ms. Hill's probably interviewing lawyers right now wanting to sue Dr. Sleazebag for making advances. And Rosario got homesick and went back to Ecuador. And Logan? She's home munching popcorn and watching her soaps."

"She'd better be," Honee pressed out between thinned lips, "or I'm gonna give up. Because it would mean I'm Honee Trash after all, just like Momma always said. Just not any damn good, excuse me. If I can't even make sure one little chick that came to me for help is okay, then what kind of an abysmalacious failure am I?"

"Stop it, Honee. You're not a failure. That girl's fine, just *fine.*" Behind her back Qiana crossed her fingers. "She's probably over in the gym palling around with Gibson. So let's put up a great big sign and—"

"Nope, let's make those construction fools do it." Honee charged farther down the hall, determined to read somebody the riot act. Qiana wondered if she'd head-butt the first construction

111

guy she came across or throttle him with her bare hands. Afraid of what might happen, she took off after Honee.

Finally the two young women made it to the end of the wing where the music was earsplitting. By then Honee was cursing like a dozen sailors whose shore leave was cancelled.

Qiana was furious too. *This is wasting so much time.* Her life's work was waiting. In the real world, away from this deluxe school, there were so many abused kids who desperately needed help. From what she had read, child abuse of the type she had experienced was being reported up to 80,000 times a year, but the number of unreported cases was many times that because most kids were too afraid to tell.

She never reported what happened to her either, never told anyone about it, except for just hinting at it to Gunner and to Honee.

So was that the reason for Logan being scared? Was she afraid of being assaulted or did she have a girlfriend with similar fears?

Only one way to find out—find the girl! *Now.*

Gee, why couldn't those dumb construction workers have kept their partying under wraps until Qiana and Honee left the building?

Frustrated and irritated and worried and out of breath, Qiana reached around Honee and yanked open the door to a lecture hall that had escaped the renovation work so far.

Then she felt broadsided. *Oh no! How horrible!*

PART 2:
THE STEFFORD POND

CHAPTER 16

Logan tried so hard not to freak out completely. Aware of the increasing danger of the snake and the spiders, she felt sweat slicking her body and the stench of her fear clogging her nostrils. That must be what death smelled like—her death, which seemed imminent.

Oh my God, what can I do? Nothing.

But if I don't do something, I'll go crazy.

So why don't you fasten your mind on something else? Like school, for instance? Which for the most part was fine. Tough, of course, what with tons of homework, but the kids were nice, most of them. And the teachers were okay too, most of them.

Except for that new substitute teacher. Ms. Money was terrific, the way she seemed to really care. If Logan could only text her: SOS HELP ME

Ridiculous to pin her hopes on that teacher rookie that Logan had only talked to once but what's that saying? Never underestimate the power of a teacher. She definitely didn't underestimate Ms. Money.

But even she didn't have supernatural powers. So how could she know where Logan was? The fact was, nobody knew. And not knowing why this happened and why she was marked up with those black lines made it so much worse. But Logan's wracking her brain helped. And thinking about school helped even more. So she kept visualizing first period. Then second and third—both canceled today because of the assembly. Then came lunch, fourth period, fifth and sixth....

Desperately clinging to her class schedule in her mind, the girl managed to hold on, minute after excruciating minute, hour after excruciating hour. In spite of that, her agony increased until Logan just couldn't stand it any longer. But finally after the last bell a ray of hope.

Suddenly Logan could hear voices outside the equipment shed, an ocean of wonderful voices. That was nothing unusual. School just let out and throngs of students poured out of the buildings. Because so many were stressed out, they hung around campus. And a few always walked around the back of the school to decompress. That's why Logan could hear these voices that got louder as their owners headed toward the old shed.

Excited, she sucked in a breath. *Oh, oh.* This was three girls from her Honors Trig class. If she could only get their attention.

But how? Desperately Logan tried to think. Never mind that copperhead or those spiders now. She sucked dusty air and tried to scream. But the whimpers that trickled out of her parched throat sounded like a baby bird getting strangled, not like a desperate call for help.

The girls kept on chatting like they were on the way to a Taylor Swift concert.

"Logan's like so slack," Geena said. "First chance she gets, she ditches school. Bet she's getting a French pedi at the Spa."

116

"Can you blame her with her folks out of town? She'll show up for cheerleading practice though."

"Yeah, Logan would never miss a chance to see her sweetie. You want my opinion? I find it totally disgusting, all that PDA."

"Guys, I'm in here. Help! *Help!*"

But the girls didn't hear her mewling. Moments later, they passed the shed and the slap-slap of their shoes echoed off. Before long, their voices were like ocean waves ebbing. Then came a horrible sound: Tap-tap-tap. The girls were skipping down the bleachers like five-year-olds while Logan was imprisoned so close by. Nothing but faint echoes now, then nothing at all…

Gone. Her friends were *gone.*

Completely devastated, she sagged into herself worse than before. Her surroundings became a pitch-black tunnel, with the light at the end shrinking.

It's over. I'll never get to see my friends again. Never have another class. Good-bye Mommy, Daddy, Tommy.

Bye Josh, I love you forever.

MS. MONEY!

CHAPTER 17

Hoping their eyes were playing tricks on them, Qiana and Honee inched into the big room that was bathed in subdued light. Then they stopped because the ugly scene in front of them was real.

What about the Stefford Code? Qiana thought. These kids acted as if they'd never even heard of it. A bunch of them were prancing around in the lewdest dance steps imaginable. Worse was, the girls were topless and the boys wore only shorts. Even worse, as another raunchy song blasted from the sound system, several kids puffed on home-made cigarettes. She held her breath, trying not to inhale while trying to calm down and figure out what was going on.

Next to her, Honee was visibly shaking. "So that's where those clouds of weed are from. Ain't—isn't the construction guys."

There were no adults in the room, only all these out-of-control kids. Shocked, she shook her head, trying to understand why these kids felt so free to guzzle liquor and wash down what looked like prescription pills by the Ziplocs full.

There were more awful sights. In one corner half a dozen kids hunched on a mattress and shot drugs in their arms. In another corner, another group snuffed white powder up their noses and a third bunch heated up something in spoons poised over burning lighters. Honee was furious enough to scream. What a sham that Code of Conduct was. These kids didn't act honorably. But usually kids didn't go totally wacky on their own, unless someone let them, or even encouraged them. Who was that?

Honee glanced at Qiana who was equally furious, her attention on a pyramid of tangled bodies that looked like a human octopus while yet another explicit rap song blared, trying to overpower the room that reeked of alcohol, marijuana, and all kinds of body fluids.

Honee couldn't take it any longer. "Quit it! Right now!" She stomped on the floor to draw attention but the music drowned her out. As she lunged to the light switch, she touched something nailed to the wall that felt furry—a dead cat that had a dog's leg grafted on. Even in the dimness she could see the poor animal had been blinded and taxidermied.

Qiana noticed the same thing and retched. "No lights," she hissed at Honee. "The state they're in, no telling what they'll do to us."

Remembering the collection of animal eyes in the science wing, Honee balled her hands. She couldn't wait to expose whoever allowed this mass orgy and unthinkable cruelty. Maybe these disgusting goings-on were what Logan had stumbled on. No wonder she was so scared. "C'mon, let's get Dr. Reinholt's lazy butt up here before anyone sees us."

Racing back down the long hall, the two women looked over their shoulder to make sure no one was following. *Hurry, hurry.*

But too late.

"Yo teachers." Three muscular boys in black polo shirts stepped out of a bathroom behind them, swinging table legs. "Wait up. We won't hurt you. Promise."

Yeah right. Qiana—with Honee right behind—increased her pace. Probably on drugs or with enough alcohol in them to make them dangerous, the boys would grab her and Honee, if they didn't manage to get away.

She started sprinting, dangerous because of all that junk lying around. Still, the boys gained on them. Frantic, Qiana looked for a place to hide but none of the classrooms were any good. She and Honee would only get trapped. This was the third floor, so jumping out a window was out of the question. And now up ahead, the big connecting hallway teemed with even more boys.

Honee also realized their impossible situation. She dived behind a pile of sheet rock and yanked Qiana down with her. Holding their breaths, they peeked out. Both groups of boys were slowing down but how they lapped it up—their relentless closing in from both directions.

"Got it made now, dudes," one boy yelled, bashing a door until its glass panel shattered into a million shards and rained on the floor.

Qiana's heart almost stopped. *Oh God, what's this?* A bone-marrow deep fear had gripped her, causing her mind to make a big leap. *Is this another Kristallnacht when broken glass was everywhere in Germany as a sign of unspeakable mass murder soon to come?* That horrible event had occurred decades ago but maybe these kids liked re-enacting shocking historical events. She felt like such an idiot. Until now, she'd always been so wrapped up in her own problems. Then suddenly in a whirlwind of events she met her parents and felt ashamed to her core over her disgusting past. At the same time she met Gunner who swept her up in a hazy glow of love and befriended Honee. So with all these changes, she hadn't time to think things through.

121

But now she thought about the fact that her parents were Jewish. That meant she was Jewish too, right? She was ecstatic over having roots. Gee, she wasn't just a neurotic tumbleweed anymore that had been abused over and over.

Yet Qiana was also scared to death because what did she know about being Jewish? *Nothing.* She'd have to learn a lot and couldn't wait to do it. But in the present environment, being Jewish might put her in horrible danger. Maybe it was a crazy thought, but was Herr Dr. Reinholt a neo-Nazi? Was Henry in cahoots with him? Was that cat—and dog—torture just a warm-up act by the kids?

Would she and Honee be next?

"Yippee yay. Can't get any better," another boy yelled just then. We grab the subs. Strip them down and show them a good time, know what I mean? Then we do what we have to."

Whew. Qiana thought that sounded like the bragging of typical oversexed teenage boys and not like Dr. Reinholt had anything to do with it. So were the boys were after her and Honee so they could assault them?

Seconds later, the answer: "No, dudes. Let's make some cash off of them as long as we can, okay? Put them on exhibit, like at the State Fair, like a two-headed horse, and charge admission. Chess Club's way down in points. How about we contact them and the other loser clubs?"

Another *whew*. Now Qiana understood. The kids were after them to one-up the other clubs and get the most points. Not good, but not nearly as bad as if Dr. Reinholt were the mastermind. These were just wild kids. And maybe in order to surpass their classmates, they tossed out all the rules and went crazy.

Why didn't anyone on the faculty get suspicious? Or was that why Ms. Hill left? Did she complain about the kids' insane projects and was forced out? Or was Logan going blow the whistle and the kids had gotten wind of it? And that's why she didn't come to school today?

No matter, it was urgent that the two young women get to the bottom of it.

"Let's move, Honee," Qiana whispered as the boys kept closing in from both sides. It sounded as if they were banging on trash cans. Dust balls rose in puffs, rocks sailed through the air and glass shards sleeted down like after a car bombing in Afghanistan.

Frantic, they scrambled to the crater into which Honee had almost fallen earlier. "Let's get down to a lower floor, girl," she hissed.

"Are you nuts? I can't—"

A series of thwacks cut Qiana off. The boys had found their earlier hiding place and whacked the sheetrock until it exploded. Qiana ducked as Honee scampered down a buckled pipe. Somewhere below, she jumped sideways and was on solid ground again. "Come on down, girlfriend."

"No, no."

But there was no other way out. So sucking in dust, Qiana embraced the pipe like it was Gunner, clamped her eyes shut and inched down, holding her breath and waiting for the pipe to snap and pitch her into the abyss.

The pipe swayed like a tree during a tornado. Qiana flickered her eyes open to see Honee pointing overhead. She reached back up, pulled the linoleum piece over the hole and in almost-darkness fumbled her way down a few more feet of pipe. Finally, she grabbed Honee's hand and jumped, but missed the spot on the second floor she'd been aiming for.

And stepped into nothingness.

"Got you," Honee groaned through clenched teeth. At the last moment she had managed to grab Qiana by the arms and yank her to safety.

Qiana collapsed like a plastic bag, her heart fluttering. She tried to calm down, slow her breathing. "Thanks... for... saving... my... butt."

"No problematico." Still breathing hard herself, Honee scanned the floor from one end to the other. Now they were one level below the crazy boys. "Oh Lord, not again," she groaned. "I'm so sick and tired of this mess."

Unfortunately she hadn't imagined it. In the distance where this floor, like the one above, joined a connecting corridor that offered the only escape route, another big bunch of boys loomed, this one wearing green polos but acting no different than the kids upstairs.

"Can't stay here." Fueled by whatever little adrenaline she had left, Qiana catapulted to the other end of the hall. Maybe there was an exit down there, a staircase, a fire escape. But there were only more abandoned classrooms in various stages of demolition, with another huge lecture hall at the end. This one empty, thank goodness.

Qiana and Honee scurried from window to window like frightened kittens and clawed at them. Jumping from the second floor wouldn't be as bad as jumping from the third, but all the windows were sealed like mausoleums.

Trapped. Meanwhile the ruckus in the hall escalated. The green polos carried chains, cloth pieces, spray cans, and an axe. Qiana could imagine what would happen: They'd spray the women with something, truss them, hood them, drag them off.

What's that axe for?

"Clang, clang!" the chains clamored.

"Hey, are we gonna teach the Jacks a lesson or what?" a green shirt yelled.

"Yup, we can buy another soccer victory," another one yelled. "Undefeated again this year. A perfect season."

They boys were only two rooms away. Then one.

Then just a few more steps.

CHAPTER 18

Logan was still imprisoned in the shed. Still taped to the desk and surrounded by a deadly snake and black widow spiders. Still unable to get help from anyone. She was so weak she was about to collapse but at the last moment she had a feeling of release. Free, she was free. She raced across the football field toward Josh who just scored the winning touch-down.

What a moment of bliss. The most important game of the season was over. All the kids swarmed down from the bleachers and mobbed the team. And right in the middle was Josh but he had eyes only for her.

"Oh Josh," Logan breathed, "I'm so proud of you."

"And I'm so proud of you." He swung her around. "I love you, Logan. *I love you—*"

"No, wait. Put me down." Better tell him right away what she'd been through. Together they'd find Ms. Money. "Listen, Josh, someone drew some magic marker lines on me. I think that means something awful's about to—"

"Don't worry, sweetheart. We'll deal with it."

"But what if it's something *real* awful?"

Waiting for his answer, Logan watched Josh open his mouth but no words came. That's when, with a gut-slamming finality, she realized she'd just had a wonderful dream that her tortured body had manufactured to ease her into what would come next—her last moments on Earth.

And then her dream morphed into reality.

Again Logan heard voices. Not girls' voices. This time it was two male voices, and one belonged to Josh. She assumed the guys were about to start football practice down on the field and for some reason Josh had taken a detour past the shed. Did he sense her presence?

Logan got so excited, hearing Josh's voice get louder. The other voice was deeper, older. Somebody was walking with Josh—Coach al-Said. A former Carolina Panthers player, he had more muscles than a young Arnold Schwarzenegger. Yay. Between the two of them they'd knock this shed to smithereens.

Filled with renewed hope, Logan listened to the approaching voices with all her heart. With her whole life on the line.

"When was the last time you saw her?" Coach asked.

"Last night after that sports clinic," Josh said. "We ate at the Golden Corral. Afterwards, the cheerleaders got back on the activity bus but I wanted to talk to Logan. So I told their adviser I'd make sure Logan got a ride home. But she already had one lined up with one of the chaperons."

"Which one?"

"Sorry, Coach, I don't remember." Logan could hear the regret in Josh's voice. "But as soon as we finished talking—"

"Smooching, you mean? How often have I got to tell you not to let your hormones—?"

"Sorry, Coach. Anyway, Logan hopped in one of the faculty cars."

"Which one?"

"I said I don't remember. Parking lot was kinda dark but it was a teacher's car. That I know."

"How?"

"'Cause it had this bumper sticker. 'I Proudly Teach at Stefford, School of Champs.'"

"Anybody can get hold of a bumper sticker."

"I know, Coach, but Logan's smart. She'd never get in the car with just anybody."

"What a mess." Coach sighed so loud Logan could hear it. "Josh, what do you know really about that girl?"

"I know I love her. And she loves me. We plan on getting married soon."

Hearing this public declaration of Josh's love for her made Logan's heart go thump-thump so loud it had to be audible through the thin shed walls. But to make extra sure, she squeezed out her most pitiful squeaks yet.

Finally her terrible ordeal was over. Now she was just waiting to be rescued. *Thank you, God.*

CHAPTER 19

CLANG!

The boys were so close Qiana could feel their chain-banging reverberate through her. Crouching under a desk, she shook like in the advanced stage of Parkinson's and her little finger had drawn up like a dry root. Was her rheumatoid arthritis back?

"Can't stay here," she said for a second time, grabbed a brick and launched it like a spear through the open door. It pinged into a locker down the hall and drew the searchers' attention. As the boys raced off, she wrestled a movable chalk board aside, revealing a narrow door through which the two women squeezed.

"Boys' bathroom upstairs, so made sense." Qiana was breathing like a mountain climber in the Andes.

They bolted the door from the inside and scanned the tiny girls' room: Where was a hidden broom closet? A secret compartment? A loose section of the wall?

No luck. The ceiling, walls and floor were solid stone. And the toilet stalls offered nothing but ancient commodes. Trying to think, Honee raked her hands through her hair and glimpsed into the mottled mirror over the sink. Lord, what a mangy-looking gray face stared back at her, like she'd been caught in the Twin Towers aftermath on 9/11. Furious, she chomped on a piece of chalk.

Qiana stepped to the mirror too. Never had she looked worse: Chewing gum and other gunk in her hair. Her face paler than the porcelain sinks, ink splotches on her torn outfit. Forget getting a refund from Wal-Mart.

Only her ankle-wrap stilettos still looked like an ad in *Vogue*, but what good was that? Well, maybe she could beat back one or two guys with them, but not that big bunch.

Eating the chalk revived Honee. "Let's get out of here, girl."

Which was urgent. From the sounds of it, the green shirts were back. Any second, they'd find the door and pour in like a horde of marauders. Well, maybe the kids were just playing. Teenage pranks could easily get out of hand. She gnawed on her nails. Poor cat, poor other animals, poor misguided kids.

What's happened to Logan? And where's Mrs. Taylor, the rest of the faculty? Dr. R.? Coach? The construction crew?

Clearly no adults were around, only all these wild kids. She jumped to the tiny window, the only one there was and wrenched it open.

"Lord, can't we get a break?"

Peering over Honee's shoulder, Qiana felt equally discouraged. There were so many kids in the front yard of the school. Some were texting or tweeting, others spoke into walkie-talkies. But this window was their only chance.

But how could it work? This was the second story but each floor was huge. And even if the women landed unharmed, the students would grab them.

"Me first," Qiana said in a quivering voice. "Maybe I can break your fall."

"Have you lost your mind? You're the bride. Outta my way."
Honee threaded one long leg through the narrow window and
compressed the rest of her agile body through. Perching on the
window sill, she looked around and got ready to lower herself
down the wall as far as she could. Then she'd let go and with any
luck, end up in the flower beds. Hopefully they'd cushion her fall
and the kids wouldn't be that bad.

Her nerves like guitar strings, Qiana begged,
"Please...don't...get...hurt." Her voice quivered even more because
she had a bad feeling. It was just too good to be true that she
finally had a girlfriend. So of course she'd lose her.

As Qiana imagined her friend lying hurt in the rosebushes and
the kids pouncing on her, Honee did something unexpected. And
crazy.

Instead of jumping down, Honee wiggled around on the
window sill and scrabbled up on her feet while clutching the wall.
When she stood erect, she rose on tiptoes, reached as far as she
could, and vaulted *up*.

Stunned, Qiana poked her head out the window. Honee was
dangling from a stone rim that formed an accent line around the
building's façade, about eight feet above. A split-second later, she
chin-upped herself all the way and perched on the rim.

"C'mon, girlfriend," she urged Qiana just as the boys reached
the bathroom and yelled: "Open the damn door." The sounds of
several kicks ensued.

Qiana trembled as if she had palsy.

The door suddenly looked flimsy: "Hey dudes," someone
yelled, "let's get a ram."

Envisioning the kids stepping back, running a bench against
the door and breaking through, she trembled even more. *Gunner.*

Nobody had ever loved Qiana before. Nobody had ever come
close to making her feel like she could let her hair down. Only

Gunner, and maybe Honee, understood her. And maybe some day she'd muster up enough courage and tell them *everything.*

"Hey, you in there! For the last time, open the damn door or we'll kick it in!"

The screaming snapped Qiana out of her immobility. Hands shaking, she rolled up her skirt and clutched the outside edge of the window. Squished her upper body through. Hunching on the window sill, she contorted her legs through the opening and teeter-tottered on the sill, her back to the world. Whimpering, she next unfolded herself like a wooden measuring tape and trembled up the wall as far as possible, her hands scrabbling for something to hold on.

There was nothing.

But stretching even more, Qiana found Honee's ankle and clutched it like a lifeline. So she see-sawed on the window sill until she latched on to Honee's other foot, rose on tiptoes and hopped up. No good.

But after a few more false starts, she jumped high enough to grab the stone rim above but her legs still flopped in the air. She felt weighted down like wearing a lead apron when getting her teeth x-rayed and was slipping. Even worse, she was dragging Honee off the ledge. Finally one of her heels found a crack in the wall that she used as a foothold. That's how she scraped a foot over the ledge, struggled the rest of her body up and slumped like a rag pile on the strip of stone.

"Hold... on... to... me...." she squeaked.

Honee held her tighter than her books earlier, wanting so bad to make this nightmare go poof but she couldn't.

CRASH! Below them inside the building, the boys had axed their way through the bathroom door.

The kids took out their anger over not finding the two women on the toilets, sinks, mirrors, making it sound as if the world were exploding

"Don't worry, we're okay now," Honee whispered as both of them huddled on the high ledge, the sounds of destruction ebbing off.

Qiana waited for her heart to stop racing. "Gee, Stefford School seemed like such a dream and now this. What do you think's going on?"

"All that studying, girl. It's cracked those kids like eggshells. They're so into their silly points they don't care how they get them."

Qiana nodded, looked around and froze. "Oh God, what if I fall?"

Honee tightened her grip on Qiana's shoulders. "You won't, just be careful. But looks like most of them have given up."

The campus did look deserted now. "I bet all the good little boys and girls went home to memorize the wikipedia," Qiana said, pressing herself against the wall. Each time she leaned forward, she felt dizzy and sick to her stomach.

"Yup. Only kids that stayed behind is that Sodom and Gomorrah bunch and their posse," Honee said. "But we did it, we got away. Only too bad they locked the window and barricaded it. I heard them."

Still, the two women were okay for the moment. Breathing the flowery aroma wafting up, Qiana started to feel more comfortable with every passing second. Actually, the stone rim was quite roomy. So relaxing a little, she let her eyes meander over the gorgeous campus, zeroing in on a brook that circled one side of the huge property. "Oh, is that the creek you were talking about, Honee?"

"Yup, that's the border between the school and the Spa."

"Looks pretty," Qiana said, admiring the modern buildings that clustered around a renovated old southern mansion which must be the ancestral home of that sweet old guy, Earl Granville. It was gorgeous. Even the botanical gardens with their tropical trees and dark lagoons that spread out around the buildings looked gorgeous. They reminded her of the San Diego Zoo where she'd been at a lavish fund-raiser once.

Honee rolled up her sleeves. "Wonder how they manage it— keeping out these mini Cameron Crazies. That's what they're called over at Duke University, you know, brilliant students that can go too far. But don't you think we'd better scoot? Any moment some kids might come back. One look up and they'll spot us like *this*."

As she snapped her fingers, Qiana noticed that the skin on her friend's muscular arms was pebbled with goose bumps.

Why? Did Honee sense danger beyond their high perch?

Gee, what else could be a threat to them?

Honee stood up and took a few steps. "C'mon, girl."

Behind her on the ledge, Qiana took a few steps too, gaining confidence. Not bad really, she could do this. "Look, Honee," pointing to a spot below, "there's our SUV. Don't you wish we could rappel down and zoom out of he-e-re?" Her voice cracked because falling in love with Gunner and growing fond of Honee— sort of, off and on—had made her vulnerable. And once you let yourself feel, it was like being skinned alive.

"Yup yippee, girl. All we need's a way down."

They inched to the end of the massive building where several stone pieces projected out of the façade, giving them plenty to grab on as they negotiated the corner where the ledge continued. Halfway down this wall that took them farther away from the front of the school, they sat down again.

"Yay, we're through being a bull's eye." Qiana waved like from the Queen Elizabeth II leaving the New York Harbor.

"What're you doing, girl?"

"Hoping someone from the Spa sees us and—"

"Nope, Qi, don't draw attention. Never know who else might be looking."

"Okay." Qiana concentrated on the scenery again, picture-perfect even back here, except far to the right where a pond stretched out. Connected to the creek, it resembled a balloon on a string. Only too bad the water was brown and stagnant, but once it must've been beautiful. There was still a platform with a rotting pole in the middle. From up here it looked like a toothpick stuck in a cracker.

"You think the monks used to skinny-dip down there?" Qiana asked with a chuckle, and then grew serious. "Oh no. You think maybe Logan went near it and—?" She shook her head. "No, doesn't look deep enough. And with that nasty swamp around it, I doubt seriously any girl would get anywhere close. Wonder why they haven't gotten rid of it?"

"See all that stuff over there?" Honee pointed to the right of the football field where an old shed hunched as if it were ashamed. Nearby a pile of construction supplies leaned like the Tower of Pisa. "I bet soon as they finish the third wing, they're gonna put a state-of-the-art Olympic pool in place of the pond."

"But why didn't they run a fence around that eyesore? Or at least get rid of that old platform?" Qiana asked with a shiver. "A bunch of water moccasins is probably sunning themselves on it right now, like brats on the grill. Gee, what a nuisance."

More floral-scented air billowed up and the sun turned into an orange disk, tingeing the sky in wondrous color. "It's beautiful up here," Qiana said, "but I'm so ready to get down and track down Logan. Make sure she's fine."

"Wonder how far away she lives."

"Hopefully close by, Honce. I really can't wait to talk to her; even if it turns out she's just getting bullied. Which is terrible and something I want to tackle too, plus all the other kinds of child abuse." Qiana knew what the signs were: failing grades, skipping school, seductiveness, delinquency, suicide attempts.

137

"But after that it's home," Qiana went on. "A hot shower, chicken soup and crackers and a stiff one—"

"But Gunner won't get back until—"

"Get your mind out of the gutter, Honee. You know for someone claiming to be a virgin—"

"But I am a virgin, girl." That horrible assault years ago didn't count. "Never even kissed a guy."

Qiana looked unconvinced. "Yeah right. How's that even possible?"

"Well, I spent my teenage years decked out as a guy. And any dude getting fresh got punched in the mug. Had some close calls but eventually I got these cool brass knuckles. See, I used to go by the name of Hun, like Attila, but that wasn't cause I'm a stone cold killer." Honee gulped. Not stone cold, not back then, but the end result was the same, wasn't it? "It was because of my stare."

"I'm sorry, Honee. What you've had to go through, but I'll make it up to you. Actually I was talking about some whiskey which was stupid. Told you, I'm through with alcohol. Now let's get to a phone and— Look," Qiana craned her head to the left where she heard traffic sounds, "over there by the gate."

Barely visible through the trees, three cars were creeping toward the guard house. The cars stopped. Maybe the drivers had forgotten their IDs and Henry was giving them a hard time. Then the cars started moving again and snaked along the scenic drive up to the front of the school.

"Yoo-hoo," Honee yelled, and then stopped. "Mightn't be any teachers or parents."

"Right, this looks like just more—" Qiana clipped her sentence short as an orange jeep angled into the faculty parking lot below while the other cars continued around the far side of the big building. The jeep spewed out a new bunch of boys.

Were these some of the good ones? Qiana flattened herself on the ledge just like Honee. They weren't directly above the boys,

138

but if one of them glanced up and in the direction of the football field, he'd spot them. Fortunately the boys were busy getting into a huddle as if planning their next play in football. "You sure?" one boy asked, pointing to Qiana's SUV.

"Sure I'm sure," another boy said. "That's the Suburban of the subs."

"Neato. Let's sell it on Stefford e-Bay, guys, so we can get the cash— Hey, stop it, jerk. What're you doing to our wheels?"

A scuffle broke out as a third boy pulled out a switchblade and slashed at a tire like a cook at a Japanese restaurant. "Just making sure those subs got no way in hell to escape."

Hearing Honee groan, Qiana whispered, "Don't worry, I've got a spare."

As soon as the boys left, she hopped up. Stepping around Honee like there was all the room in the world, she stomped along the ledge to the next corner and snapped around it like an eel.

"Wait up, girl." Honee sprinted after Qiana. "Don't charge ahead like a rhino in a—"

"Why not? I'm going to find a way down. *Right now*."

"But girl, this is the oldest—"

Clunk! A piece of the ledge in front of Qiana clattered to the ground, leaving a gap of about four feet. Panicked, she wheeled around to hustle back to their earlier spot. As she was waiting for Honee to turn around too, an entire section of the ledge behind them melted away.

They froze, waiting for the noise of the stone pieces hitting the ground to attract the tire-slashing guys. Fortunately it didn't. Still, how scary to be stuck on this crumbling high ledge. Qiana wrung her hands. How long before the part they were standing on would drop away too? Already a crack meandered along the seam where it abutted the old building.

"You know what? I've got better things to do than play hide and seek with these little creeps." She flung herself over the gap and sprinted on until she came to a big retaining wall, extending far beyond the rim of the ledge.

Honee was shocked. Oh man, how could Qiana leap like a mountain goat in those killer heels? She must have ankles of steel. Honee wouldn't be able to walk half a step with shoes like these, let alone jump with them. Even with her Adidas on, she thought the gap was too wide to negotiate.

But when she heard more stone pieces cracking behind her, she had no choice but try to sail across the gap too that kept getting bigger.

She didn't make it.

But as she fell, her fingertips made contact with the spot on the other side that her tennis shoes had aimed for. By then Qiana raced back, knelt down and grabbed Honee's wrists. Groaning like a woman giving birth, she held on until Honee could scrabble up on the ledge that kept disintegrating and sinking like pieces of lead. Completely drained, both women finally slumped against the retaining wall.

"Thanks, girlfriend." Honee's breath came in ragged spurts. She examined the massive wall, noticed its dark mirror-smooth surface, and butted her forehead against it. Impossible. There was no way to climb down it or up. They were stuck.

CHAPTER 20

Logan got tired of waiting. But there was still no sign Josh or Coach had any idea she was in the old shed. But she knew couldn't let this chance pass her by. It might be her last one.

So here goes. She swung her legs with all her might. They didn't move an inch but her feet did a little, just enough to kick at the snake. Yet never mind the consequences now. Her rescuers were *this* close.

Coach was still talking: "High school kids getting married? What a crock. Don't throw away your future, you hear me?"

A moment of silence, then: "Way I see it, boy, it's simple. You screwed up worse than Jason White during that big game against the Trojans. Didn't I show you that old video? Yeah, sure. You'd put Logan on the bus last night, she'd be all right. But now we're gonna have the cops crawling all over."

"Why?" *Poor Josh.* He sounded so worried. Wouldn't he be happy when he found Logan only a few feet away.

"Because she's gone missing, that's why. Well, maybe she's just getting a new hairdo but the upshot is—"

No, I'm right here. Can't you hear me?

The good news was Josh and Coach stopped walking. Had they heard something?

Yes?

Yes! Fresh hope flooded Logan like an active sprinkler. Any moment they'd come real close and investigate and then—

Oh, now—? Now—?

So far they didn't pound on the shed, didn't rattle the door, trying to get in. But that's only because Coach continued to give Josh a talking-to.

"—this is interrupting our whole game plan. Who can keep their mind on practice? You sure won't and we got that—"

Enough! All that chit-chatting while she was *this* close to death. So Logan did the only thing she could—go completely crazy. She bucked and bounced like a herd of colts trying to break out of a corral. Nonstop she twisted, wrenched, and yanked around, trying to jerk the desk loose, make it tumble over and produce a real loud noise.

Finally with a last spurt of energy, she managed to torque the desk unstuck and fling it sideways to the floor, herself with it.

SPLATTT.

The noise was so loud the copperhead shot out of sight and the spiders laddered to the ceiling. Logan was thrilled even though she'd struck her head on a metal piece from a broken basketball goal.

Of course she felt the pain and the blood oozing out of a wound above her ear, but it was worth it. Any second, her rescuers would spring into action. *Any second.*

"—big game coming up," Coach said while Logan was desperately listening for the sound of the door splintering, the wall being ripped apart, the roof being yanked off.

Oh now? *Now—?*

Nothing happened, except for the coach continuing to talk but farther away like he and Josh had started walking again. Like they were on their way down to the football field.

"Wonder who the hell's crammed more crap in this shed?" Coach said, clearly in a sour mood. He must've heard the noise and commotion but had no idea what caused them. "Tell you what, Josh. First thing tomorrow we're gonna burn this shack down. Be sure to get me some gasoline and matches. Now on to practice, boy, and I'm warning you. You show any lack of focus, you can kiss your position good-bye. You're never gonna be another Eli Manning. Do. You. Understa…?"

His voice faded like a transistor radio with a dying battery. Then nothing again, no more voices.

As a result of the fall, the tape had loosened but Logan was still attached to the desk as she writhed on the floor, bleeding profusely. Her burning eyes squeezed shut. *Oh my God!* All this effort, all this pain for nothing? Now if she didn't bleed out or die from snake poison or spider bites, she'd burn to death—in a fire started with the help of Josh.

Her dying would be horribly painful. Even worse would be Josh's discovery of her charred bones. It would ruin him. Worrying about that, Logan felt herself fading more and more. When she next dragged open her eyes, probably for the last time, she saw in the dimness two fiery bits of coal.

Are those sparks from the fire?

No, silly goose. Relief flooded her. *It's not tomorrow yet.* Then she felt punched in the stomach for she hadn't imagined it. There really were sparks, two small burning pieces of coal—little eyes that stared at her, sizing her up. The smell of her blood had attracted a rat that chittered.

It sounded like a death knell.

143

First the rat was just a moving shadow that tripped closer—a couple inches forward, a couple inches back. But before long, the forward darting became longer, the backward moving shorter. Then the shadow materialized completely and revealed its aim—Logan's face.

She tried to play dead. But how long can you play dead when rat whiskers brush against your cheek? Petrified, she lifted her head and shook it, trying to scare the rodent away but her efforts did nothing. Then came lapping sounds, like from a kitten slurping milk. The rat was slurping up her blood that had seeped on the floor.

Oh no. When the blood was gone, would the rat attack Logan's face?

By then she couldn't put any coherent thoughts together any more. All the girl could do was echo: *Please God. Please Ms. Money.* There was no one else she felt a connection to. She felt so scared and parched and starved beyond anything she could've ever imagined. When was the last time she ate?

At that sports clinic, almost 24 hours ago. Logan had helped herself to the buffet but only like a hummingbird. Now she wished she'd chowed down like a pig. She was *so* hungry.

Hungry-hungry kept going around in her mind and made her think of that new boy again. When she ran into him at her locker after school, he hustled her out of the building. "Out, Lo-gan! Out!"

"What's wrong, Angelo?"

"Bad, mucho bad here."

"Oh no. Are the other kids mean to you?"

"No, they just loco, but not bad."

"What about the teachers?"

"Teachers okay too. Is the building. Building hungry. Eat all my friends."

CHAPTER 21

Still stuck on the high ledge with no way down, the Qiana grabbed Honee by the arms. "Stop hitting your head against that wall before you damage your brain."

When Honee stopped but only reluctantly, she went on, "Let's sit down and consider our options."

Honee was breathing hard. "What options, girl? We're stuck between the second and third floor of this wacky school with no way down. Wish I'd never seen—"

Qiana snapped, "Honee, don't let a few crazy kids ruin your dream." Wondering where they were, she looked around. They were stuck above the back campus where not much had been renovated except for the gym right below them that was connected to the main building by a walkway. Behind it to the left, the football field hadn't been upgraded yet either but to the right no renovations were needed. There were just vast stretches of dark-green woods covering rolling hills as far as the eye could see.

And in the distance through those woods peeked a white spire.

Honee saw it too. "Hallelujah." She lowered herself down on the ledge next to the impossible retaining wall and rubbed her forehead that looked bruised. "Look girl, that's the Stefford Chapel. Nearby is the Jills' pad. They've gotta have a phone and a ride."

"Yes, I can see something metallic."

"Sure, Qi. How else could those Barbie dolls get there? So here's the plan. We get cleaned up over there and— Nope, even better. That trailer, see it behind all that building junk?"

"Oh, that must be Ricky's place. Okay, let's leave the Barbies out of it."

"Yup, I think I can see Ricky's clunker. We can't find him, I'm just gonna hot-wire that heap and—"

"You can do that, Honee?"

"Sure, did it plenty times back when I was a courier. Small-time, but even when I was twelve, I always got the job done."

Twelve? Qiana felt her face catch on fire. She knew what she was doing at that age. For a moment the memories flooding back made her eyes squeeze shut. "So how do we get down?"

"Can you climb on my shoulders, girl? Bust a window on the third floor and—"

"—fall right into the arms of those crazies? No way, Honee. There's probably still a few around."

Honee's eyes that had been roving around landed on the gym below. "You're right, girl. See that bunch poking in those trashcans? Man, these kids are like bloodhounds on steroids."

Bloodhounds? Qiana shivered even though sweat beads had popped out on her face. Oh no, was her past finally catching up with her? "Maybe we better wait till it gets dark."

"Nope, out of the question. I gotta get down *now.* Find Logan. Make some killer lesson plans with goals and objectives, inviting lectures, intriguing instructional activities. Pretests, retests. I don't have time to dilly-dally." She felt anger rise in her. Her hands fisting, she tried to hit herself on the back. When that proved too difficult, she pounded on her chest. She was totally fed up. How often can you get your hopes up, only to have them dashed? Becoming a substitute teacher had seemed like such a wonderful thing. Now it was a nightmare.

"I hate it too, being stuck up here. It's horrible." With a groan, Qiana collapsed next to Honee on the ledge and picked up a glass sliver. She pulled her feet up and started working on her scarred toes.

Honee stopped pounding on her chest. "Hey, what're you doing, girl?"

"Getting rid of those dirty Band-Aids."

"Liar! You're cutting yourself. Lord, girl, knock it off." A pause, then: "This morning when your feet were all bloody? Wasn't any sleepwalking either, right? That was you doing it deliberate, right?"

"So what?" Qiana whispered, glad to see fresh blood spurting from between her toes. She grimaced and grinned at the same time as she drove the shard deeper. Sure it hurt but this localized pain was something she could deal with. It was nothing like all this frustration, this mounting despair, this feeling of powerlessness. All the guilt, the shame, the long-repressed anger...

The worst was knowing it could never be made right. Too late for revenge.

"You're hurting yourself, girl. That's what. You're self-mutilating. Quit it right now, you hear me?"

"Pah. This from someone that bumps her head on the wall like crazy? You beat yourself on your back and chest too. Don't even try to deny it, Honee."

Dropping her arms, Honee sagged against the slick black wall. "Well, that's different. I got us in this mess, so it's all my fault. So therefore I gotta punish— but you— Why?"

"Don't worry, I'm no vampire. It's just... Well, let me ask you something. Did you ever have a perfect moment? A moment when you felt like you could touch the sky and make everything better?" Qiana leaned back and closed her eyes. "I had one a long time ago. And all that posing today made me remember. See, everybody's got one perfect moment and everybody always wants it back. What about you, Honee? Did you ever have a perfect moment?"

"Sure did, girl." Honee shifted closer to Qiana, pried the glass piece out of her hand and flung it far away. "There was this big tree in the woods, not far from Momma's trailer. It had all these low branches."

"What kind of tree?"

"I don't know. Don't laugh. I was about three or four and, you know, I called it *Daddy*. What I did was sit on the roots, pull the branches around me like arms and pretend like I was sitting on my Daddy's lap. And that he was reading me a story. I found a Bible and read it to myself."

"Oh wow, Honee. You could read that early?"

"Nope, I couldn't. Still can't—not well. Sure, words, definitions, sentences, I pick them up easy, you know, but not a whole book unless I have weeks. Never learned to read without moving my lips."

Qiana nodded. "I noticed. So about your perfect moment?"

"Well, I'd sit there cozy-like on the lap of my Daddy tree and babble something. Made up my own language, you know. Probably held the Bible upside down but that was my perfect time, feeling a big strong male was there for me, protecting me. Man-oh-man, was I happy."

"Cute. I can picture it, Honee. Then what happened?"

148

"Momma had the tree cut down. And that was the end of it."

"Gee, I bet you were furious. What did you do?"

"Nothing, Qi. What could I do?" Honee shrank into herself. "Remember I was just a little gal, poor and all alone. Back to your perfect moment. What happened?"

Qiana said, "My perfect moment... well, it segued into my worst—" She knocked on her forehead: "Hello, anybody home? Gee, why didn't I see it before? Question is, do I dare?"

Alarmed, Honee asked, "Dare what, girl?"

Qiana jabbed her forefinger at a spot below. "Jump down on that—that blue thing down there at the end of the walkway. I think what happened is part of the roof broke off during a hurricane or something. And that's why that big tarp was put up. To keep the kiddies nice and dry."

Bending down, she inspected as best she could the sturdy cover that was tacked up about 20 feet below. The size of a large beach towel, it was secured to the surrounding poles with big metal bolts and looked solid and able to hold just about any weight.

Honee shook her head. "Now girl, don't do nothing fool—"

A knot of boys, emerging from the main building, made her stop.

"Got every classroom checked out," one boy bragged, his voice floating up, "and every hallway posted. Only place hasn't been gone over with a fine-tooth comb—"

"—is the main office," another boy said. "Which is the shits. Those subs get their hands on a phone, we're toast."

"That's covered too." A third boy. "Dr. Reinholt's daffy secretary? She's still here, so we're having a study-in. Got two dozen kids stationed in the lobby, pretending to cram their asses off. Even ordered them some pizza, the old biddy did."

"She have any idea what's up?"

Wanting to find out what the secretary knew about the chase, Qiana cupped her ears, but the students disappeared under the tarp and into the gym. Yet time was crucial. If the two women waited any longer, more boys would probably converge back here. *One look up and it's all over.*

Qiana unstrapped her stilettos, tossed them into a bush. She hiked her skirt up to her waist and tucked it in her granny panties. Before her fears could get the best of her, she faced the building and lowered herself from the ledge until she dangled by her fingertips. Holding her breath, she pushed off from the wall and dropped like a piano. The tarp bounced like a trampoline but held. Qiana scrambled to the ground. "Come on down, Honee."

After Honee carried out the same crazy jump, they hid in the shrubbery. Qiana found her Manolos and kissed them with tears in her eyes.

More boys were on the way. "Don't you just love it?" one hooted. "This is way better than any computer games."

"Yeah," another boy said. "First club nabs them wins for sure."

Just a few feet away, Qiana and Honee shrank deeper into the shrubs, their stomachs rumbling. Qiana pressed her hand on her midsection and picked thorns off her forearms. "Can you believe it?" she whispered when the boys were gone. "Now I'll have to wear a burqa at the wedding. 'Skelly from Hell,' the other orphans used to say, 'get back in your box.'"

"What box?" Honee asked as she dug around for a clump of clay. When Qiana clammed up, she went on, "Don't worry, you're gonna look dynamite as a bride." *After I'm done making you respectable, girl.*

"Thanks." Qiana peeked into a gym window. "Yay, seven-thirty. So only about 22 more hours till Gunner gets home. Now let's sneak over to Ricky's place and—"

Another bunch of boys jostled out of the main building. "Guys, I can just about smell them," one said.

Yikes. Qiana made herself as tiny as she could, but even she could smell herself.

"Me too." Another kid. "So after we turn the gym inside out, let's check the Counselor's crib, okay?"

"You think they're hiding under his trailer?"

"Gonna find out. Bet your nuts on it."

Honee gave a muted scream of frustration after boys disappeared. "That leaves what, the SUV? Slap that spare on and outta here?"

"Yes, that's the quickest way," Qiana said, weighing the pros and cons. With so many kids on the rear campus now, the front of the building should be okay. Or maybe they could get the secretary's attention if she wasn't in cahoots with these crazy kids. What did she know? But never mind. There was still Henry, unless he was mixed up in this too.

"First let's make sure the kids stay put." Honee peeled off her filthy blouse. Her body was slick with sweat that stained the leather halter-top she always wore. She bunched the blouse into a ball. "Where should I throw this, girl?"

"One second." Qiana squeezed her toes until fresh blood bubbled up like tomato juice and smeared it on the shirt. "Okay. Now the kids will think one of us is hurt. And with their walkie-talkies and texting, won't be long before all of them run back here. C'mon." She peeked through the glass-paneled door of the gym, Honee beside her.

A huge lobby, wall-papered with certificates, stretched before them. Numerous glass-fronted display cases showed off the bigger prizes—pewter cups and crystal bowls proclaiming the Stefford kids to be the regional, state, and national champs in an amazing number of sports.

Even more amazing was the big chalice in the middle of the lobby. Ringed by dozens of boys, it was engraved with the names of various clubs, along with the year they won the Stefford School

151

Competition. And above it, a banner dangled from the ceiling: *The American Ideal*.

"Look at those heathens, dancing around the golden calf," Honee said.

"And not a coach in sight. Where are the people that are supposed to supervise them?"

"Don't you remember, girl? Their big test is tomorrow. So everybody normal went home. It's only these loonies that stayed back."

"You think the secretary knows about it, Honee? Or that lady in Guidance or—?"

But this wasn't the time to consider who might know something about these outrageous goings-on. Too much was happening. Inside the gym, the boys started dancing around the chalice, clapping and chanting, Jefferson among them: "Catch those traitors. Now, not later. No reason for high treason. You break the Code, that's all she wrote—"

Honee gulped. "What're they talking about? They're breaking every rule in the Stefford Code and they call us traitors?"

"Obviously they've got their own code. And they call us traitors because we're going to stop them. But don't worry, we'll find Logan soon. Then get to the bottom of everything, including that gross experiment with that cat and—"

"Us against them. Hunt 'em, catch 'em. Chase them, snatch 'em. Rub-a-dub-dub. Good-bye subs."

As the boys moved faster, a few started touching themselves, furtive at first. Turning red, Jefferson stepped away only to be yanked back in place by a bigger boy. Jefferson looked like he wanted to be anywhere but where he was—in this circle of boys that seemed to be caught up in a frenzy.

"Man, somebody wrecked these kids bad."

"Only one way to find out who did. We've got to call the authorities and the sooner the better. Keep your fingers crossed."

Qiana cracked the gym door and flung the bloody cloth wad underhandedly. It landed in a corner. So far none of the boys noticed.

Deep breaths. Then Qiana and Honee raced to the corner of the main building, dived around it and leapt down an outside stairwell. Too bad the door leading to the building's basement was locked but this was a good place to regroup.

"Looks deserted," Honee whispered when they finally sneaked to the faculty parking lot. They unlocked the back of the SUV and dragged out the spare when the campus-wide loudspeaker system pierced the air.

It was the old secretary:

"Attention, anyone still in the building. Two lab animals just got loose. They were last sighted in the gym. Everyone still on campus, please help find them. There's a big reward."

Immediately several students popped up like cardboard figures on a shooting range at various points of the grounds. Shouting to each other, they moved at a trot but fortunately away from the front of the school.

"They're the animals," Honee muttered. She ripped the jack and other tools out of the SUV, raised it off the ground and unscrewed the lugs on the flat tire. Qiana turned into a NASCAR pit crew. First she Frisbeed a work-out top she kept in the backseat at Honee who yanked it on and brushed her hands when she was done. "Let's roll, girl."

They hopped into the SUV and rocketed off, gravel spraying like water from a fire hydrant. The sun had disappeared and shadows floated across campus. So maybe no one from the office would notice it wasn't any students that were leaving.

The SUV barreled down the winding road toward the guard house, with Qiana stomping on the gas. "Listen, Honce. If the gate's shut, I'll just smash through it, okay?"

"Okay, gonna brace myself." Honee propped her knees against the dash and laughed. "Yippee yahoo. Gate's wide open and no sign of Henry."

Just then a young man in uniform stepped out of the small building and waved.

"Sorry, pal." Qiana accelerated the SUV even more, making the tires howl like wolves but that didn't deter him. He stepped into the middle of the driveway and raised his hand. Pop-pop-pop.

"Gee, what's he trying to do? Shoot us?"

Honee noticed his uniform was open, allowing a swatch of polo shirt to peek out. "Oh Lord, that's no guard. That's a student. See his red—?"

"Get down, get down. God help us." Qiana was frantic because the shots just kept coming. She reached over to make sure Honee had dived under the dashboard and squonched down as low as she could herself and still able to peer through the windshield. It was spider-webbed with a hole in the middle where a bullet had hit. Fortunately, it missed them both.

But the science student wasn't done yet. As Qiana tried desperately to stay the course and drive straight at him, hoping the boy would jump out of the way at the last minute, more gun shots: Pop-pop-pop.

Not aimed at Qiana this time, nor at Honee who was completely out of sight, the bullets hit the motor. As a result, the steering stopped functioning and the SUV swerved, uncontrollable. Horrified, she stomped on the brakes. There was a grinding noise—steel rubbing against steel—and the tires seemed to smoke as the smell of hot oil spilling and rubber burning filled the air. With both young women screaming at the top of their lungs, the SUV veered right and smacked into a tree. *Crash!*

Qiana heard the impact noise. She gasped from shock and pain that was bad, but not that bad. The crash had deployed the airbag on the driver's side, though not completely. Still, she felt

154

squashed and slumped in her seat, immobilized, eyes closed. Dazed. Out of it.

Seconds later, she snapped to and felt sore all over. Everywhere there was dust, some sort of powder, and her little finger felt like a bomb had exploded in it. But that was about it.

"Honee? Are you all right?" Qiana's voice wobbled with worry. "Honee?"

No answer. Frightened, she pulled the lever moving the seat back to make more room. She pawed under the dash on the passenger side where Honee was balled up. "Say something, Honee. *Please*. Are you hurt?"

Honee was only dazed. "No... I'm... okay..." She inched up on her seat, trying to make it around the airbag, that was in her way too, and all those dust clouds. "I'm mannihilated pretty good but otherwise— Oh no! Sweet Jesus."

CHAPTER 22

"What's the matter?" Qiana asked, her eyes sweeping out her window at the shooter who had moved to a meadow farther away. He held both arms in the air like he'd won the Publishers Clearing House Sweepstakes. Then he reloaded his pistol, eyed the SUV, took another shot. Pop!

When nothing stirred, he stopped shooting, picked his walkie-talkie off the ground, wiped it like a silver belt buckle, and started talking.

Qiana flinched, knowing what would come next. All the kids would come running, not that there was a chance of escaping before then. The gate was out of the question, with the shooter keeping his eyes on it. And the fence was too high to climb. But no time to worry about that. For the moment just being alive was enough. It seemed like a miracle neither Qiana nor Honee had been grazed by a bullet or gotten hurt worse.

Honee kept groaning. "Oh Jesus!"

"What's the matter?" Qiana asked again, this time snapping like a rubber band. "I don't mean to grouch but I'm still in shock. Kinda groggy but so relieved. What is it?"

"Your face... It's...all...swole..." Honee's voice was mouse-like. Twisting, she climbed into the back seat and reaching forward, touched Qiana's cheek like it was blown glass. "You're hurt, girl. And all my fault."

"What? Where?" Horrified, Qiana ran her fingertips over her forehead, her cheek bones, and down to her chin, trying to find something sharp-edged. Not another broken bone, but she couldn't find anything wrong. "I'm all right." She raised her shoulders, flexed hands and feet and looked in the mirror.

She unearthed an emergency lipstick in the glove and tossed it back, unused. "Feels like I got a trillion bruises, Honee, but that's about it. I'm all shook up, worse than Elvis, but by no means down and out, okay?" She was trying to lift the gloom that permeated the SUV like swamp gas from the pond.

"Oh no, girl... You're getting... a black eye... And your chin—it's all puffy... And those scratches from earlier—"

"That's nothing." Still, Qiana trailed shaky fingers over her face a second time and checked her whole body that felt like she'd been holding a jackhammer all day. But nothing was wrong that she couldn't conceal with foundation and— She froze. In her side-view mirror several polo shirts came into view, galloping like wild ponies. "Looks like we got bigger worries."

Honee broke down crying. "Don't... mean... the kids... My... promise... Didn't... keep... it."

Where's a Kleenex or a paper towel? Qiana stuck her arm into the backseat. "Here, use my sleeve and tell me what's going on."

Honee used the back of her hand instead. "Before Gunner left...took me aside, he did... Made me adjuriate... to not let

158

nothing... happen... to... you.... And now-ow-ow... Gonna be... no wedding... It's... over..."

"I know it looks bad, Honee, but those bozos won't get their hands on us, okay?"

But Qiana wasn't convinced herself. She could see what was happening in her side-view mirror. A huge crowd was thronging around the fake guard. First the kids gaped at the SUV that was some distance away and watched it like a bootlegged DVD. They must think the passengers were either unconscious or dead, but nobody 911-ed an ambulance. Maybe later the kids would come over to investigate and drag the two women out of the wreck. Stash them somewhere, like in the construction wing or that old shed, and then do something horrible to them. The women had seen too much, knew too much, and weren't going to shut up about it. And the kids knew it.

After a few moments the boys started to rake leaves, twigs, and branches together. What were they planning to do? Make a bonfire to celebrate the capture of the substitutes? Well, maybe if the kids got into that, Qiana and Honee could figure out a way to escape.

Thinking about this possibility, Qiana inhaled and wished she hadn't. The air was still pungent with wrecked automobile fumes that made her chest ache. "Listen, Honee. You didn't know this place would turn into a nuthouse once all the good kids and teachers left. Besides, Gunner isn't your only kin. What about me?"

Honee sniffled. "You'da been my sister-in-law if... "

"Not *if*, understand?" Qiana wrestled out from under the deflated airbag and squeezed over to the passenger side where she was more comfortable. "I've made up my mind. This weekend or the next or the next, it's going happen. The wedding. Wonder where Henry is."

He was nowhere to be seen. Maybe he'd gone into hiding, not wanting to get in the middle of what some kids were doing— rolling a chair out of the guard house and hurling it on the flickering fire. Hopping up and down, they screamed like they'd won a national championship. Budweiser cans made the rounds. Even a few girls came staggering. Behind them, a marching band swept up, their instruments shining in the flickering light of the fire.

As the flames grew, a few kids hurtled over them, thrilled when they got singed. Their shrieks were arrowed in all directions while deeper shadows spread over the campus. Must be after eight or nine PM, but what difference did that make? Qiana felt exhausted, watching the fiery tongues lick into the sky. After the metal ticks from the ruined motor stopped and the band took a break, the only noise in the SUV was her friend's crying.

"I really thought I was more to you than a sister-in-law," Qiana said softly.

Honee sucked in a breath. "Want the honest truth? First time I saw you, I plum hated your guts. Then I developed a liking for you. First time in my life I had me somebody, Gunner and you. And now… Thanksgiving was always the worst."

Hunching in the airbag dust, Qiana realized again how impossible their situation was. There seemed to be a hundred crazy kids milling around. But maybe by the time Honee finished talking, she'd figure out a way to sneak off. "Go on."

"Well, me and the other bag ladies, girl? We used to huddle under our cardboard blankets and dream about the perfect holiday, know what I mean?"

"About having a place to go home to?"

"Nope, Qi, never aimed that high. We always dreamed about the L&W."

"The cafeteria at Red Mill Plaza?"

160

"Yup. We'd be watching all these nice folks parade in there on turkey day and chow down. Whole families."

"That doesn't sound so hot to me."

"Girl, you're on the street, that's about as high as you dare get your hopes up. The L&W. And another thing, Florida."

"That I can see. I've been to Miami, the Fontainebleu, the W, South Beach. So you dreamed about a Florida vacation?"

"Yep, but not like a family going to Disney World. We'd always be talking about hitching a ride down there and wearing new visor chapeauses. It's so hot down there, you know. And going to the races."

"The horse races?"

"Nope, the greyhound races. We'd always mull over what we'd do when we got to be 50 and had *nobody*. We'd picture ourselves as loony old biddies wearing fanny packs. Saving up a few bucks from panhandling. Going to the dog races and winning a big stake..."

Odd, how Honee's rambling on had a positive effect. Momentarily it focused Qiana's attention away from the crazy kids and their impossible situation. "What were you going to do with the winnings?"

"Come back up here to North Carolina. And invite all the homeless folks to an L&W feast. Man, with all the trimmings."

"That's touching, Honee, but let me tell you something. You're never going to be alone again for as long as I live. And about that holiday meal? Let's be sure to include it in our budget."

"What budget, girl? The Q Store won't happen now. These kids, they're gonna ruin everything. Nothing's changed, you know. Nobody ever gave a flip about me but I really thought I finally got me somebody that—"

"Loves you?"

"Hell yeah, excuse me. But I don't even know the word." Honee dropped her head into her hands. "*Love*? Is there such a thing? And, you know, am I *lovable*?"

"This is so weird," Qiana said. "Just last week I was asking myself the same questions, but now I know love is real. It's like this old definition. 'Love's like a stiletto. It lifts you up and makes you feel wonderful.'"

"Forget it, girl. I'm never gonna part with my Adidas."

"You don't have to. Come here." Turning to the backseat, Qiana picked paint chips, plaster bits, and cobwebs out of Honee's curls. "Just always know one thing, Honee. You are very lovable."

Honee raised her head and peeked out from under her lashes like from under a thatched roof. "Says who?"

"Me. It's like Shakespeare says, 'Care I for the limb, the thews, the stature, bulk, and big assemblance of a man? *Give me his spirit.*' You and I, we're so alike. We've got the same spirit and I just found true love, okay?"

"Huh?" Honee gave a tremulous smile. "I'm your spirit sister now? Any voodoo come with that? Why don't you twitch your nose and genie us outta here?"

"Sure wish I could." Reaching over the back of the seat, Qiana hugged Honee awkwardly.

"Thanks, girl." Honee wiped her face, then broke down again, this time crying like a nursery full of newborns.

"What's wrong now?" Qiana barked, her attention reverting back to the kids. The marching band had set their instruments aside and formed a gigantic conga line that wove around a large area and the fire. From the looks of it, the dancing would occupy the kids for some time. So still nothing to do but wait, just like waiting for the start of a late period. She stretched impatiently, ready to bolt the moment she spied a way out.

"Another thing… been weighing… on me."

Gee, this wasn't the time for dark revelations. But if Honee had done something awful too, Qiana wasn't the only bastard. "What's that?"

"Never funeralized Momma. Didn't do anything to mark her passing. I'm such a pile of—"

"Stop it, Honee. The police haven't even released her remains."

"But see, I decided to not even bother once they do. Just gonna let the cops dump her in the trash."

"So?"

"Can't do it, girl." Fresh tears cascaded down Honee's face. "I'm... such... a... wimp... For... instance...last... night... snuck... out... Hiked ... over... to... where it happened... the trailer fire. That's why... my shoes... so muddy... Plan was to... spit on... the burned-out shell... Pee on it... and worse... But... couldn't... do... it..."

"So that's why you didn't hear me having that nightmare. That's why those valleys under your eyes... But good for you, Honee. That proves it."

"What?"

"That you're not trash, Honee. So just do some little memorial thing to honor—"

"*Her*? Over my dead body."

"No, Honee, to honor you. Accidentally or on purpose, your mom made you strong. And smart. And beautiful. And yet so tender-hearted."

"Girl, you couldn't be wronger!" *What I am is stone-cold hearted. And meaner than a rattlesnake.*

"Look at it this way, Honee. Maybe your mom was abused herself. So just plant a little tree, then let her go," Qiana said, feeling her stomach turn. What a fraud she was, telling Honee to let go when she never did. *For years I've carried my guilt and shame around with me like an incubus. That's what's been eating*

163

at me, not just my bad life and my unfulfilled wish for revenge, but what I did before—

Honee sighed. "You're right. Once when Momma was drunk as a skunk again, she babbled about her old man after her, you know, when she was but nine."

"See there? So just lay your mom to rest. Be sure, that 'after life's fitful fever, she sleeps well.' That's from Macbeth."

"Man, how'd you ever get into Shakespeare?"

"One day I just picked up a book. I read all kinds of stuff."

"Kinda like me getting into my puzzles? See, girl, sometimes when I had no place to stay, there I'd be wrapped in Piggly-Wiggly grocery sacks under the overpass."

"Doing the *New York Times* crossword?"

"Girl, you're homeless, the days're incredibly long. And nights, they're the worst. So I busied myself with newspapers from the Dumpster and a pencil. You got no idea what a fine weapon a pencil is. Better than a can of corn rolled in a sock."

"I started reading a lot when I first went on the street," Qiana said. "I had to do a bunch of porn flicks. That was so bo-o-oring, all that waiting around between, you know—"

Honee gave a hiccup-py giggle. "Really?"

"Well yeah, those flicks were pretty realistic. The male actors had to show they got turned on by Goddess Qiana, my neon name. So when they went too far, we had to wait around and I read. Makes me sick to my stomach thinking about it now." She shuddered. "How could I have done that? Anyway, Honee, let's buck up." Qiana stretched and crept around in the wrecked car, looking for a way out.

"*Buck up*? Did you know to black folk *buck* means a handsome hunk? A dude in the prime of his manhood? But," Honee's voice wilted again, "gave up on finding me one long ago. I'm Honee Trash, you know, forever unlovable and unkiss—"

164

"Stop saying that. There's someone perfect just waiting for you, Honee." Qiana had no idea how right she was. Honee would find her soul mate even before Gunner came back from Bermuda. "But let me tell you something about the relationship thing. It won't solve all your problems." *Not if you've got tons and tons of baggage. Can't leave it at the Good-Will Store either. It always follows you.*

"Don't tell me, girl. Something wrong with you and Gunner?"

"No, we're perfect together. But do you think we'll ever... see... him... again...?" By then Qiana had tried every door and window. But unfortunately the crash had impacted the frame of the SUV to such an extent that none of them budged. And if she broke a window, the kids would come running.

From anger, frustration and exhaustion, she had tears trickling down her cheeks. She felt like she was suffocating. She wanted out of the SUV. Get some Oxys, some ice packs, a stiff drink— Her tears grew into a flood. She knew that in order to clean up her life she had to give up pills and alcohol but didn't know if she had the strength. Face it, she was just a wimp, a crybaby. Why was life so hard when all she wanted from now on was do good?

"Hush, girl." Honee's fingers raked through Qiana's hair and combed out the debris from the construction site and the leaves from those bushes. "Can I ask you something kind of personal?"

Qiana shrugged. "Sure." *As long as it's not about my rag doll.*

It wasn't. "Girl, why ain't—isn't there a single dark root in your platinum hair?"

"That's because I was real blond as a child."

"I mean now, Qi."

"You mean my snowy roots? Well, that's real too. I was completely gray—white—by the time I was 19. I told you I had rheumatoid arthritis ever since I was a baby. So maybe that's the reason for my premature aging but I don't think so. This is how I explain it to myself. Everything takes a soul toll. And since I lived such a disgusting—"

"Lord, girl," Honee broke in, "no more Shakespeare. Please."

"No, this is me. But I've got to face it, I could've made a different choice. Those early years? I was a victim but later I could've turned my back on the sleaze biz. But I went from bad to worse. So it wasn't just my illness and my bad childhood and all that abuse I suffered. It's what I turned into."

"You turned into a righteous chick."

"No, Honee, that's just a façade, just like this school."

"Begging to differ, girl. You got guts and yet you're a doll."

Doll? Qiana flinched like she'd been jabbed with an ice pick. Frantically she searched for her purse which she'd left in the building.

"Wasn't your fault those scumbags abused you," Honee went on.

"But don't you understand? Sure, I was terribly abused as a child but one day I had a chance."

"So you had the chance to kill one of your abusers and didn't? Big fat deal. By then you were so squashed down in the dirt, baby. You didn't know you could strike back."

Qiana rubbed her gnarled little finger. Unwanted, a memory came to her, like a pop-up ad on the computer. It was about the people who ruined her. The Devil was terrible but always straightforward, but his wife was evil beyond words. She pretended to be her savior and then—

Qiana hurt so bad she started rocking. What she wouldn't give to get back at that demon woman but it happened so many years ago. By now she had probably changed her identity, retired to Cancun, and was living it up in a luxury condo. Even the place where it all happened had been razed long ago. She had googled it. "But I did strike back, Honee," she whispered, tears dripping down her face.

166

"Yippee yay, girl. You got revenge on those a-holes?"

Qiana sighed. "Not on them. They both got away... On myself."

"Poor baby. You tried to kill yourself?"

"Not tried, Honee. I did."

"Quit riddling me. What exactly did you do?"

Qiana folded her arms. "I don't want to talk about it. But believe me, it was awful. So of course it took a toll on my body. My arthritis is supposed to be in remission but any day it might flare up again, who knows? But it's definitely all connected, my rotten life and my health issues."

Honee raised her eyebrows. "Sorry, I had no idea." Of course, she'd noticed Qiana rubbing her little finger lots of times but thought it was just a nervous habit.

"Do you mind?" she asked. When Qiana didn't say no, she grabbed Qiana's hand and massaged it, starting with the little finger that felt like a chicken bone wrapped in Saran wrap. *Mighty creepy.* Honee thought she was holding the hand of a 100-year-old woman. *But we all got our burdens. Me, I got the worst and it was all my fault.*

"Never thought about it," she went on, "but you're right, girl. I had a choice too. Coulda flown the coop much earlier. Gotten me a job at Burger King. And before the fire I really could've done something but too late now."

Qiana whispered, "Yes, much too late. The nuns always talked about Hell. But I thought they were talking about *after* we die, not *before.*"

"But now," Honee said brightly, "we've both come to our senses and can make up for everything, at least try to, right?"

"Right. I'm going to stop child abuse—" Suddenly Qiana had a vision of a terrified girl huddling in a dark space. "What're we doing running our mouths? We've got to get out of here and find Logan." Qiana focused on what was going on outside the car

167

again. The conga line had disintegrated and the band had swept off, but a lot of the kids were still feeding the bonfire. Some heaved in tree limbs from outside the fence. Others swung from branches until they broke and dragged them over.

Gee, what'll happen when the fire dies?

But no time to worry about that. Qiana scrabbled around inside the SUV again, ending up at the back door. "Let's try one more time for Logan's sake." She waited for Honee to squeeze in beside her, gritted her teeth and twisted the handle. "Ready, set, go! We're coming, Logan." Both young women kicked the stuck door like pro footballers with a contract renewal coming up.

A tortured pop. *Finally.* Qiana lifted the door just enough to scrape through and squatted behind the car. *Where to now?* The gate was out of the question as was the fence. Too many polos with flashlights were still scuttling along it in search of more fire wood.

"Main building's out too," Honee whispered. Most likely a few students were still in there, plus the secretary who couldn't be trusted. The gym and Ricky's trailer were no good either. Judging by the number of kids milling around the crackling fire, it was obvious a few students were still prowling around on the back campus.

"Only one place left." Qiana scratched her head. She felt utterly filthy, as if her sleazy past had deposited stains on her on top of all the dirt she'd picked up during the chase. How she yearned to wash her hands and face, jump in the shower. Drink something, eat something. Most of all, get to a phone. But very soon. *Hold on, Logan.* "I'm sure Gibson's club will welcome us with open arms."

"And I bet those Barbies know exactly where Logan is, girl, and what's bugging her."

168

CHAPTER 23

Seconds later Qiana and Honee circled the main building, while avoiding the brightly lit-up front yard. The walkways were also illuminated but offered plenty of shadows which allowed the two women to dash from one dark spot to another and then skirt the athletic complex as well.

Honee set a brisk pace, with Qiana gasping behind her, her feet numb, but her shoes held up. She'd gild them but first she had to get out of here in one piece. Their horrible predicament wasn't over yet. As soon as the kids ran out of firewood, they'd check the SUV, find the back door unlatched—

Must be now. An uproar in the distance, like from spectators disgusted with the outcome of a Super Bowl game. Their escape wasn't a secret any longer.

So, faster. *Faster.*

Honee flat-out ran and Qiana tried her best to keep up. Her knees turning buttery, she started stumbling, but finally: "Look." She pointed to the woods that hugged the farthest corners of the campus while on the main grounds the kids were going on a rampage.

"I see it." Honee high-fived Qiana. Holding hands, they plowed through the dense trees and there it was—the chapel. It looked like an angels' retreat with ornate windows that transmitted soft light like candles. On one side, half a dozen BMW's and Mercedes-Benzes preened like in a show room. Gibson and her friends were here. What a relief, just a few more steps. Qiana counted down: "Three, two, one."

The chapel door creaked like the bones of an old man, allowing the women to totter into a simple but awe-inspiring house of worship where major renovation had been done. Up close, the ruby and gold stained-glass windows all featured the same saint; his arms open as if he wanted to embrace the substitute teachers. And the smell of incense and holy water was like a heavenly cloak.

Honee locked the door, jiggled it like a stuck gate. It stayed shut. Qiana threw kisses at the stained glass. "Thanks for saving our butts, Saint Stephen."

They staggered to an archway leading to a hall that ended in another door. Honee knocked and the door snicked open. "Yes?" a pretty girl asked.

It wasn't Logan.

"Excuse us, we need help," Qiana said. Of course, that should be obvious from their looks. They were all banged up and covered in dirt.

The girl smiled. "Come in. I'm Cindee with two e's."

The two women stepped into a medium-sized room and Qiana almost squealed. An old-fashioned phone perched on an end table. Another pretty girl was chatting on it.

Honee elbowed Qiana. "We did it, didn't we? So let's chill for a minute."

That's what this room was meant for. It looked like a suite in the Miami Ritz-Carlton, where one of Qiana's customers used to whisk her to. *Ancient history. Ancient disgusting history.* It was embarrassing to think about it.

Quickly she focused on her surroundings: yellow chintz drapes, matching upholstered chairs. Cozy love seats clustering around a huge entertainment center with a giant flat-screen TV. Flowers with pink and purple blossoms draped the side tables but left room for trays of finger sandwiches and silver bowls brimming with peaches, pears and cherries. There was also a minibar. Maybe if she'd get something to eat and drink, Qiana's anxiety that kept rising to choking intensity would ease up. As usual, these girls made her feel bad.

In contrast, Honee relaxed quickly. The girls made her smile with their perky all-American looks, reminding her of Katie Couric. Only their hair colors and skin tones varied.

Besides Cindee, there were six other girls, all swathed in silk teddies and matching robes that whispered when they moved. Expensive jewelry made them sparkle like fireworks. Obviously they'd been in the process of giving one another manicures, pedicures and facials. But as soon as they saw Qiana and Honee, they all froze like rabbits sniffing danger. "Sorry, we had no idea we'd have guests," Cindee said, her smile flagging.

"You all go right ahead," Honee said. "I'm a new substitute teacher and this is—"

"Your teacher's aide. I know, I saw you in the cafeteria." Cindee's smile rose again. "Everybody was like talking about you two fabulous subs."

"Thanks. Anyway, everything went great but after school—" Honee wondered just how to explain the horrible nightmare that had unfolded. But there was no need for these sweeties to find out what ugly things their classmates were into, "—something went down and then—"

"Oh no," all the girls looked shocked. "What exactly—?"

171

"We had a little accident," Qiana supplied, also deciding not to mention the other kids. The psychological break-down, temporary psychosis, or whatever it was that caused them to go so crazy would best be explained by Dr. Davis, not by the brand-new substitutes. "Could we use your phone?"

"Sure, just a sec." Cindee invited the women to sit and help themselves to the refreshments. "Carlye, hang up."

"Naw—no, girl, let her finish."

"But she's been talking to her boyfriend for ages, Ms. Money." Cindee rolled her eyes. "I mean, how many times can you go over what type orchid you want for the Homecoming Dance?"

Qiana smiled which took some effort, what with her face so dirty it felt like a death mask. "Could I wash my hands?"

After that, she plowed her fingers through her mop of hair. "By the way, did Logan ever make it to school today?" she asked.

"No, ma'am. But with her folks gone, she probably went to visit her grandma or her aunt in Virginia."

Qiana felt stupid. Neither she nor Honee had considered that possibility. It would've been a good explanation for Logan's absence from school today, except for the fact that the girl was so scared on Friday.

Well, as soon as we put this nutty school in the rearview mirror, we'll check into it.

"What're you guys watching?" Qiana asked.

Cindee looked sheepish. "You must think we're babies, but this evening we're into *The Princess Diaries II.* Tomorrow it's *Cinderella Story.* See, no textbooks anywhere, only coloring books and comics." She flushed. "Oh no, did Mrs. Taylor send you? Are you going to report us for breaking the Code?"

"Absolutely not," Honee said with a smile as wide as the flat-screen TV. "Besides, nothing but hitting the books can push kids your age over the edge."

Qiana nodded. Maybe if those crazy boys had skipped class once a month and gone down to Myrtle Beach, they wouldn't have cracked like pumpkins dropped from a balcony.

Honee washed her hands too, wishing she had some grits. She tapped the spigot with her fingertips, palmed a piece of soap. *How much longer before Carlye hangs up?*

A few feet away, lounging in a cushy chair, Qiana eyed the crystal glass Cindee gave her with the words: "Would you like some champagne?"

"Yes. I mean *no*, thank you," she said. "I have a question. How come you Jills are so privileged?"

"Oh, that's all due to Gibson."

"She's here? Really? So what is she doing? Using a tanning booth or having a body contouring session?" Qiana laughed, but it wouldn't have surprised her. From the looks of it, no expense had been spared in this girls club. "Or does she have a gym back there with Brad Pitt as her personal trainer?"

Cindee turned pink. "Of course not, ma'am. She's doing her term paper and it's not even due till next year. Let me see if she's got a minute."

The girl crossed to the floor-length drapes and rrrtched a section of them back, revealing the opening to a much larger space. Was this where the monks used to eat their Spartan grub? Honee wondered. This place sure had plenty of history and any other time, she would've been fascinated by it, but not now. She was itching to locate Logan, and get her tired fanny home.

Gibson emerged, beaming like a 5,000-watt lamp. "Ladies, how nice to see you again." A frown replaced her smile as she looked the two young women up and down. "Goodness gracious, are you all right?"

"We are now," Qiana said, "thanks to your hospitality."

Even better, Carlye had hung up. "Thanks again," Honee said, "but now we gotta—"

173

"I know what," Gibson cut her off, beaming again. "Let's make you honorary Jills."

"That's sweet," Qiana said, "but we *really* have to go."

"Can't you stay just a *little* longer?" Gibson looked hopeful and crushed at the same time while Qiana marveled at the girl's chameleon-like quality, the way she could switch from one facial expression to another in a nano second. "*Please?*"

And when Qiana and Honee hesitated, the girl broke into the biggest smile yet. "Goody gum drops. Let me welcome you to—" she curtsied "—something totally cool. Stefford School's own Abu Ghraib."

Bless her little heart. Honee felt so sorry for Gibson. Maybe she had ADD or some other learning disorder. Poor thing didn't know the difference between *abbey* and *Abu Ghraib.* Or maybe she just misspoke.

"What's the name of this place again?" she asked after a beat of silence during which she suppressed her chuckle urge but a teacher should never make fun of a student.

"It's St. Stephen's Chapel, ma'am. Hard to believe, I know, but it was nothing but a pile of rubble until me and my clique got our hands on it. Tada." Gibson showed off her French-manicured nails, like illustrations to a book report. "And behind the chapel is still a way old cemetery called the Abbot's Grave."

Is that why the girl called it *Abu Ghraib*?

"According to rumor, the old abbot's supposed to be buried there. And every so often he like haunts the grounds," Gibson went on with a shiver. "But he never comes here, not to my knowledge. Can I give you both a quick tour?"

Gee, not now. But Qiana also felt sorry for the confused girl who looked like a five-year old begging for her first bike. It would be cruel to say no. Besides, the other girls were already crowding in behind Qiana and Honee to see the latest improvements themselves. Had Gibson just redone another part of the building? "If you insist."

"You won't regret it, ladies. Promise. I was just working on a special project. Look." Gibson stepped back, allowing the other girls to surge forward even more, with Qiana and Honee advancing like on the crest of a tide.

What a disappointment. There was nothing much to see in this backroom although the walls were papered with an expensive ivy print and the sofas and chairs lining the walls were upholstered in a matching fabric. Otherwise the space wasn't anywhere near completion. It was a huge bedroom and study combination, but only two bed frames were set up. And they were old and rust-chewed, like straight out of the Dumpster.

'Maybe they're genuine antiquitaries,' Honee thought. *But where's the mattresses, pillows, and bedspreads?* And while the ornamental desks serving as nightstands boasted sleek laptops, after seeing the plush front room, this room was a let-down. Actually it was an ugly, depressing space, the kind that makes you shudder. Was evil hiding under the wall paper?

"Ni-i-ice," she said, hiding her feelings. She looked around and silently went *yep*. Besides a bathroom, there was no other door, so the tour would take only seconds. They'd peek into the garden tub, ooh and aah over the marble sinks and gold-plated fixtures, then scat. "Could somebody call us a cab?"

Gibson told Cindee to do it, and turned to Qiana: "What do you think of our dorm?"

"Lo-o-ve it," Qiana said, feeling the hair in the back of her neck stand up. "But have you thought of doing the beds in a contrast color? You're the artist, Honee. What do you think?"

"Tell you what, girls. I'll be glad to come up with a hot new color scheme for you all. This matchy-matchy decor is so old-fash—"

175

Honee's voice sheared off because three girls had jumped her and wrestled her to the floor. At first she was too flabbergasted to resist. *They know what I did.* A second later she realized the girls knew nothing about her. "Quit it," she shouted and swung her elbows. Kicked her legs and fought back just as hard as she could. "Right now, you hear me?"

The girls didn't even pause. Their faces shining like their jewelry, they made her lie flat on the floor and pinned her wrists and ankles.

Watching Honee being attacked, Qiana felt like she'd landed on Mars. She shook her head to clear her mind but nothing changed. "What're you doing?" She waded in to help Honee but before she could take her next breath, she too was forced to the floor, stretched out, clamped down.

"Guys," she sputtered, "c'mon. We didn't mean to criticize your taste. You can decorate any way— Ouch." One girl had slapped her so hard Qiana's teeth rattled. Another one punched her in her chest, making her gasp. She let out air but only in spurts. Her ribs were aching, which re-awakened her pains from the accident.

"What the hell's going on?" she screamed, realizing what this was—revenge. *They know what I've done. Know instinctively, like an animal can sense if a person's harmed its kind before.* Oh no, now the truth will come out. It'll reflect badly on Honee. Maybe even cost her her job, how horrible. But when Qiana thought about it more, she stopped blaming herself. This had nothing to do with her.

"Quit it. Remember the Code," Honee shouted again but the girls still didn't listen. There was nothing about them resembling Katie Couric any more. Their true character had emerged and it was scary. Once they had the two women laid out like planks of wood, the girls stared down at them, panting, their faces red like plums.

176

What made them so vicious? Qiana wondered, writhing as hard as she could and lashing out with her arms and legs. She kicked at the girls with her stilettos but was easily outmatched, so she let herself go limp.

Arms folded, Gibson stood back and watched what was going on. But when Honee reared up and bit a girl in the arm, Gibson kicked Honee in the ribs.

"Dang it, girls," Honee exploded. "Have you all gone crazy?"

"No, ma'am." Gibson planted herself on a spot between the two women, so she could look down at both of them with a flick of her eyes. "It's you two fakey broads that's gone crazy. Or you will be soon." She kicked Honee again, even harder.

The thump of the girl's shoe connecting with Honee's body made Qiana wince from sympathy. She could hear her friend gulp. *What a tough cookie*. Qiana was proud of Honee even as she herself kept wincing because the girls who pinned her down were equally brutal. One girl even placed her naked foot on Qiana's throat, feather-light so far, like a bird's wing. But whenever Qiana moved, the pressure increased. Any moment her voice box could be crushed.

"Why're you doing this?" Qiana croaked. "What did we do to you, Gibson?"

The girl knelt down, her face hovering a foot above Qiana's. "You still don't get it?"

"Is this supposed to be a joke?" Qiana still had a spark of hope that that's what this was—just a joke, a prank gone too far. Okay then, she'd crawl, scarf down dog food. Eat hissing cockroaches. Their taxi had to be close by now.

What if Cindee didn't call one?

How horrible to think about it, but the fact was, most of these girls were older. So maybe whatever awful psychological problems the boys developed had spread to them too. Hoping she was wrong, Qiana shook her head, which increased the pressure on her larynx. *"Argh."*

As if wanting to take in every detail of Qiana's suffering, Gibson's face zoomed inches close and Qiana's spirits plunged like an elevator with the cables cut. There wasn't the slightest trace of mischief on the girl's face. She gave another dazzling smile but it didn't reach her eyes any longer. Maybe it never had.

"You know what?" Gibson sounded disgusted. "You guys're fricking hopeless." She hopped up and with a wave eased the pressure on Qiana's throat.

"What… do... you... mean…?" Qiana hoped she could keep the girl talking while fear ate through her like fire through an old apartment building on Chicago's South Side. It dawned on her, and not for the first time, how dangerous their situation was. Nobody knew where they were.

"Don't you know anything? The Jacks are ahead at the moment."

Just got to humor these crazy chicks, Qiana thought. "Can we sit up so we can talk about that?"

"Sure, why not?" Gibson's hand whipped up, a signal for the other girls to help Qiana and Honee into a sitting position but held on to them.

Whew. "Now I get it," Qiana said, sighing out. "You want to use us in that epic points race. Well, I've got a plan that's guaranteed to flush the Jacks down the toilet."

"Let's hear it, Bottle-Blondie."

Honee, who'd been following the conversation, suddenly remembered who she was—a substitute teacher. *So show me some respect.* She cleared her throat, imbuing her voice with authority. "Under no circumstances can the Jacks be first. You Jills deserve to be number one, always. That's why we'll be thrilled to help you all just as soon as you let us get up."

178

Qiana was glad Honee was taking charge. And it might actually work—buttering up these crazy girls like toasted English muffins. Maybe that's all they really wanted, just some praise, some compliments. But being so stressed out, they'd gone over the edge.

Gibson ignored Honee. "I said let's hear it, Bottle-Blondie."

"How about if we pay you guys however much—" Qiana started.

Gibson stomped on the floor. "You think I'm stupid? I read all about you in the *Red Mill Herald.* You're both like totally broke."

"But my fiancé's coming home tomorrow evening with a huge paycheck."

"Too late. The final point totals come out at lunch."

"Well, I've got several other hot ideas and so does Ms. Money. Can we get up now?"

"You gals want to get more comfy? Club members, where's your manners?"

Holding her breath, Qiana was anxiously waiting to be released from the girls' grips. Their clutching fingers had felt like snake fangs but it was a nightmare averted. She could already envision herself dialing 911 on the sly.

But to her dismay, she was dragged like a duffel bag to a bed frame and laid inside it. And before she could scramble off, her hands were roped to the head board, her feet to the foot board. Now spread-eagled, she was worse off than before. The rope bit into her skin and cut off her circulation. She could barely raise her head to see what was happening to Honee.

Oh God, no!

The girls slammed Honee into the second bed frame and lassoed her to it so brutally she formed an X. Qiana almost felt Honee's pain as a cloud of girls' sweat wafted over. Maybe all the

179

girls were expecting their periods, maybe that's why they were acting so crazy. "Dammit, Gibson, what's going on?"

Gibson checked the ropes. "Plenty but it's all good." She dismissed the other girls except for a pretty Asian girl. "Allie, you got first shift. Sit over there and watch them like a hawk."

"Do I have to, Gibson? I don't like hurting—"

"Hop to it or else."

"Okay, okay." Allie stalked to the front room, came back with a stack of magazines and plopped on the sofa.

Three feet away, tied into an old bed frame and almost fainting from pain, Honee managed to rear up a little. "Hey, what about the Stefford Code of Conduct?" she rasped out. "You know that's not how you're supposed to act."

"You're right, ma'am. We shouldn't be dragging it out."

Honee collapsed back into her bed frame, her mind spinning like a whirly-gig. Were Gibson and her friends crazier than those crazy boys? And what caused their craziness? It didn't matter what the reason was. Honee had been pissed before, now she exploded: "Girl, why don't you get to the point?"

"The point is I read all kinds of bull about you two broads, like you were heroes in Red Mill. So I Googled you and found out you're nobodies. Of course, Ms. Hill had to go bye-bye first, so you two could come on board."

"Girl, you made her quit?"

"Well, she was a traitor too, Ms. Money. Except she wasn't a retard like you two."

Listening to Gibson, Qiana realized that screaming at the girl or pleading with her would accomplish nothing. "You're right, Gibson. We really are nobodies and if you want to call us traitors, feel free. But please let us go. I promise you we won't say a word."

"Of course you won't. We got like a gazillion gags."

"Gee, there's no need for gags."

"Well, we wouldn't want anyone to hear you screaming your heads off once we get into the water-boarding and the branding irons, whatever's first on the agenda. Look," shoving a chair aside, Gibson revealed an old fireplace with implements resting against it like pickets, "I just scrubbed everything with Brillo and polished the stones."

"The stones?"

"Well yeah, Ms. Llove. Didn't you know Saint Stephen was stoned to death? But don't worry, we've got a better system."

Qiana cringed, imagining her skull being punched in like a melon or worse. "But who can hear us out here?" She desperately hoped somebody would. Maybe there was someone out there. Maybe Henry—

Gibson dashed Qiana's hopes. "Nobody can hear you. But after we're through with you guys, we're going to move you to the labs. The Science Club always pays good money for new guinea pigs. But first the Jacks might get a shot at you, those sex maniacs. Really haven't decided what I'll do before I charge you with high treason."

"What're you talking about? You'll never get away with it, whatever you mean. My fiancé—"

"Won't be back in time, you just confirmed it. Now do you get it?"

"What I get is you speak Barbarian real well," Qiana said in an icy voice.

Gibson giggled. "Fooled you, Jew bitch, didn't I? You're just lucky your parents weren't gassed in Dachau before you were born, you slut. But now they're far away."

She turned to Honee who was seething silently. "And you, uppity nigger gal? You've got nobody. You're just trash, but no worries. I already emailed in your resignation. And your wrecked truck? We're gonna push it off the bridge. Let's see now, did I forget anything? One second." She crossed to Qiana's bed frame

181

and cranked a lever several times. With a screech, it moved the head board farther away, yanking Qiana's arms almost out of their sockets.

White-hot pain sliced through her. Tears shot into her eyes and gushed sideways down her face. Her stomach was cramping, her heart pounding.

"That's what you get for lying, okay? Promising me cash when you're broker than your SUV. Apologize or I'll do it worse."

Qiana couldn't say anything. She had to bite her lips just to keep from screaming.

"Oh, you'll do it soon enough. Don't you love working out? Well, this is gonna give all your joints a work-out. Yours too, Ms. Phony Art Teacher, trying to show off with those silly words that don't even exist. Sure don't want you *exclusiated*, tee-hee."

With an exaggerated oomph, Gibson cranked Honee's head board back a few notches too. That made Honee feel as if her arms and legs were tied to the rear bumpers of trucks going in opposite directions. Tears streamed into her eyes and overflowed. Worse than the pain was her feeling of total powerlessness.

Finally Qiana managed to whisper, "Still... haven't... said...Why... are... you... torturing...?"

"Isn't it obvious? I want to soften you guys up. Dregs of humanity, you should be thrilled to participate in my research. 'Prisoner Abuse from the Middle Ages to the War in Iraq' is the topic of my term paper, with an emphasis on old English methods. Years ago, they really knew how to torture somebody and traitors got the full treatment, *before* and *after* they croaked.

"I did mention the tunnels, didn't I? That's where we found these cool racks. Honest, I was so afraid I was overdoing it earlier with my dumb bunny act. I'm the valedictorian and editor of the newspaper and yearbook. And I star in all the drama productions. These racks here," Gibson tapped her forehead and her voice spilled out like from a machine, "they were medieval torture

182

instruments. The worst sinners were laid into the frame and their wrists and ankles tied to a mechanism that moved in the opposite direction until their bones got ripped—"

"Hey Gibson," Cindee poked her head into the room, "you just got texted. Emergency War Council meeting in five."

"Fiddle sticks, I mean dammit. Just when I was getting into it. Guess everybody's realized you two flew the coop. And now they want to get together and strategize. Well, all right."

That dazzling cheerleader smile again. "Allie, check your watch. Every five minutes, turn these levers. Righty-tighty. And be sure to record everything. I need a detailed description of their facial expressions, body language and crocodile tears. When I get back, I'll take over and mark them up with the Magic Marker.

"Meantime you guys," Gibson sailed different-colored polo shirts like straw hats at the other girls who now wore Seven jeans, "infiltrate the other clubs. Find out the latest buzz. It's so dark, I'm sure y'all can blend in. Oh, and one more thing." Gibson tossed a switchblade at Allie. "Feel free to use it but just skin them a little, okay?"

"Wait, Gibson. Is that what happened to Logan?" Honee squeezed out. "Did you hurt her too?"

"No, ma'am, she's just a lost and lowly junior. Ciao, babies." Hurried footsteps sounded and a door slammed, leaving the two women alone with Allie.

Strange, no mention of Logan's visiting her relatives now but at the moment Qiana couldn't consider what that meant. She hurt too much. Even when she concentrated on counting the ivy leaves on the wallpaper—five, thirteen, 26, 51, 78—her pain was excruciating. She tried to loosen her ropes but they only tightened like leather straps getting twisted. The odor of her fear clogged her nostrils. She was dripping cold sweat like crazy. "You okay, Honee?" she whispered.

Allie looked over. "Guys, Gibson didn't say you could have a convo."

Grunting an affirmative toward Qiana, Honee said, "Girl, aren't you supposed to take notes?"

"Yikes, almost forgot." Her face a pale mask, Allie clicked a laptop open, hit a few keys like a child on a piano. "Could you repeat those moans and stuff, ma'am?"

Honee gave a groan loud enough to wake the ghost of the abbot.

"Good job. And what exactly did you say?"

"What I said was," Honee rasped out, "it's not fair, you having to hang with us while all the other chicks are out having fun."

"Way true, ma'am," click-click-click, "but it's all my fault."

"What'd you do, girl?"

"Made an A-minus."

"Ain't—is no reason to make you do this slave work."

"Think so too, Ms. Money. 'Specially not when I'm, like, trying to read."

"What're you reading?" Qiana asked, her voice turning saccharine.

Somehow she just had to get this girl, who didn't seem as hardened as Gibson, on their side. And the topic of reading might work because Allie's face lit up like the White House Christmas tree. "Oh, all about the coolest fashions. Like Armani and Donatella Versace... Chanel and Prada... Dior and YSL... Vera Wang and Gucci."

"Oh wow. You love clothes? Me too." A spark of hope caught in Qiana. Maybe if she kept the girl chatting along, she'd forget all about Gibson's instructions.

Honee realized what Qiana was trying to do. "You dig purses too, Allie?" she asked, not caring a pork rind about them. Her Adidas was all she ever needed. Travel unencumbered to better burn up the road. And look where it had gotten her. She tasted something vile.

"Yeah, love them. Anything New York City, ma'am. Fifth Avenue, you know? Like where all those incredible shops—"

"They sure are incredible," Qiana jumped in. "I lived in Manhattan before I came here."

Unfortunately her plan wasn't working. After checking her watch, Allie said, "For reals? Well, just a couple more minutes before I've got to adjust your frames, sorry. But I've always been wondering. Are the shoe stores in the Big Apple really under lock and key? Shoes are my passion. But I heard they're so expensive up there they have armed guards and Brink's hummers."

"You're right, Allie. Those NYC designer shops are locked up tighter than Fort Knox. And those prices? Unbelievable. My shoes? They cost over $1,500."

"Really truly?" Allie tiptoed over to Qiana. "Of course I spotted them right away in the cafeteria."

"See, what exquisite taste you have?"

Allie's cheeks glowed over the compliment, a development Qiana was glad to see. "Don't tell anyone, but I know a place right here in North Carolina where you can score those same brands for 90 percent off. We're going to open our own store soon, so we have all these connections."

"Don't tell her," Honee snarled right on cue. "It's top secret."

"But why not? She's going to get the name out of me anyway just as soon as she cranks—"

"Right, ma'am, and that's in less than a minute. So dish and I'll turn it real gentle, okay?"

Qiana felt her spark of hope growing. "Thanks, Allie, but here's the problem. How do you even know you'd like shoes like mine? I mean they look way different on every foot."

"Yeah man, on me they look sick," Honee said. "But on you, girl? Who knows?"

"Only one way to find out, Allie." Qiana sounded like a lawyer summing up a case. "You've got to try them on. Right now, before Gibson gets back."

"But ma'am, I'm not supposed to."

"Well, I noticed Gibson ogling them," Honee said. "So maybe you better let her have them. Ain't she the queen bee around here?"

A short silence, then Allie: "Guess it won't hurt to try on one shoe." She knelt on the floor, unstrapped one of Qiana's sky-high pumps and manipulated it until she held it in her hand while the rope remained fastened around Qiana's ankle. Not at all what she'd been hoping for. With a sick feeling she watched the girl yank off one of her Mary Janes, peel away a sock like an orange rind, and slip into the stiletto.

A moment later, Allie clomped around like a little girl in her mother's party shoes. "Awesome. Oh, this is like something by Michelangelo Buonarotti, 1475-1564. Italian sculptor, painter, architect and poet of the Renaissance. That's what? A mall?"

"Whatever you say, Allie, but I'm amazed. Gee, you're not only the prettiest girl at Stefford School, you're also the smartest."

"Promise you're telling the truth, Ms. Llove? Pinkie promise?"

"Pinkie promise."

Clomp. Clomp. Clomp. "You want to hear more about Michael Jordan? I mean Michael Douglas? I mean whoever I was—"

"No, that was great, Allie. Extra credit. But just wait till you get that ankle wrap on right. No, not with that chain twisted. Come over here, let me help— Gee, I'm afraid you have to untie one of my hands. Just for a second, okay?"

Brandishing the switchblade, Allie clomped over to Qiana. "Please don't try anything. Or I'll cut you, I have to."

Honee chortled. "Get real, girl. What can *she* try? She's nothing but a girlie girl. But me? Damn straight I'd try something."

"Shut up." On purpose, Qiana volleyed her pent-up anger at Honee. "You're just jealous. Your feet are gunboats, size 13 and a half. I'm going to help Allie get the total effect of these Manolos and you can't stop me."

On pins and needles, she prayed for a break.

Please God. For Honee's sake. And for Logan. Poor thing's in trouble, I can feel it.

Hands shaking, Allie unknotted the rope around Qiana's right wrist. Finally Qiana's arm was loose. She flexed it, getting a little feeling back. "Okay, let's have that shoe." When Allie handed it over, Qiana grabbed it. Moving forward and upward at the same time next, she whacked the girl on the head with the stiletto heel.

Allie burst into screams, collapsed and curled into a ball. Blood oozed from a gash on her scalp, matting her hair. Grabbing the switchblade, Qiana twisted sideways to reach her other wrist. Sliced through the restraints there—cut, cut. She freed her ankles, flew over to Honee's rack and went to work there.

"'Bout time." Honee wriggled her fingers, feet, toes. Massaged her wrists like a physical therapist on Speed. "I'll tell you one thing. Never gonna bitch about your shoes again." She dragged Allie who was all right except for a superficial wound to the bathroom like a roll of carpet and tied her with the ropes. Qiana helped lower the girl into the marble tub, placed a towel on the gash, and weighed it down with a gilded soap dish.

"Lie still, Allie. Somebody's going to come shortly."

"But Ms. Llove...Gibson...will take it...out on me..." Sobs interrupted Allie's muffled voice. "Make... me... her... worst... slave...and—"

"Nope, girl, that's all over with."

187

"No, Ms. Money... She's gonna... grab you again... Do you... like... Ms. Hill... She broke... the Code... Turned into a...traitor, so therefore—"

"We're no traitors."

"You're... about to... tattle... Same thing... But anyway... never… wanted… to... be… part… of... this…." Allie's sobbing rose and fell like the tide. "And now… I... won't... get... those... fa-ab... sho—shoes…"

"Don't worry. I'll send you the latest hot-hot style, size 8, right?" Qiana said. "Just as soon as this insanity is over. Deal, Allie?"

The two women took off like bullets, raced through the club. Back to the chapel. Their immediate surroundings, visible through the big door they cracked, looked like a relaxation video—pleasantly shocking, after what they had just gone through. When they got to the edge of the woods, they paused to breathe out the smell of fear and body odor and fill their lungs with the fragrant scent of leaves and pine needles. Lush undergrowth hugged their legs, assuring them all was fine.

But peeking out over the back campus, they had another shock, a most unpleasant one. The vast nightscape was pierced by hundreds of lightning bugs—flashlights that turned the school grounds into an enemy camp. The crazy boys, now fortified by the crazy girls, were still out there searching for the substitute teachers.

Of course, the Jills only pretended to help. They knew where Qiana and Honee were, but not much longer. Already the two women were on the move again but where to?

They looked everywhere, hoping desperately to discover an escape route.

"Gee, those little creeps are like a dirty bomb, they're all over." Qiana massaged her little finger that throbbed like a nerve hit by the dentist's drill.

Next to her in the brush, Honee rubbed her rib cage where the girls had kicked her. Still hurt like bone splinters piercing her lungs. "Main building and the gym are out." Both structures were lit up, with kids wandering in and out and shouting like during a treasure hunt that was finally netting results.

Did they find her purse? Qiana wondered. It contained her list of to-dos before the wedding but all that seemed so remote, like from another life. She felt like screaming.

Honee was equally livid. "Gunner only knew, he'd chopper out here and haul all these kids off to a mental institution."

"What about Dr. Reinholt and the teachers?" Qiana asked. "They all need to be locked up too and that includes the secretary. Sure hope this craziness hasn't spread to the little kids too. Wait a minute." She raced back to the Jills' club and back. "That phone had no dial tone, can you believe it? Whole thing was an act."

"Lordy-lord, what loonies. What time it is?"

"About 10:30. I checked Allie's watch. So only about—"

"Don't say it, girl. Do. Not."

"I'm only trying to give us hope."

"Well, that's one thing I don't need." That's all Honee had ever had—truckloads of hope. She lived off it for years. Each morning she fed herself a dose of hope. Another one at lunch and a third one at dinner, if gnawing on old Tupperware could be called dinner. Now her imaginary hope chest was like an inner tube leaking air. "We need help, not hope. We need to get out of here and find Logan. Why does this whole place have to be fenced in?"

"To keep the little psychos away from the general population, don't you think? Gee, this isn't Stefford School. It's the Stefford Zoo."

"Yep, they ought to charge admission but maybe there's a hole in the fence somewhere. Maybe behind that pond. C'mon, let's—" Honee gasped. "Oh Lord."

Peeking around an oak, Qiana gasped too. Gibson and her clique were coming back, cart-wheeling and doing back flips. Happy voices floated over like low-flying kites:

"Hey, big plans down the toilet. Yay. Hunky hubby, down the tubby. Only wedding bells will be from hell. That's what you get for being tattletales."

Qiana shuddered.

"What're we going to do?" Unless they thought of something quick, the Jills would take Qiana and Honee prisoners again, and this time the torture would be even worse. Already much closer, the girls bounced around Gibson who shone a flashlight on a scrap of paper: "Nine AM, hair appointment. Cut and color. Golden highlights. Yeah, right!"

They all burst out laughing. "Only appointment they have is with us." Gibson drop-kicked something. "Touchdown!"

Watching her rag doll arc through the night air, Qiana felt the pain of a dozen box cutters slice through her. *It's really all over now.*

"I said c'mon." Honee tugged Qiana back into the woods. They back-tracked to the chapel and ran to the cemetery where the biggest grave marker provided the only hiding place. They hunkered behind it. Now as long as nobody looked back here, they were safe.

Surveying the area, Honee realized they weren't that far from the big fence. A section of it winked like old silver from the other side of the pond and the marshy bog around it. But before she could point that out to Qiana, the girls' shouts got louder.

Qiana whimpered, "Oh God, what now?"

"Now we take a bath but not the kind I want." Honee made a snorting sound. She had tried to think of another way out. If they were only back in the school, maybe they could climb down the construction shaft. Find an entrance to the tunnels and discover an exit. But no such luck, this pond was their only option. From the

190

other side it was only a few yards to the fence. And then they'd just have to see.

"I can't swim," Qiana blurted out.

"Doesn't look that deep. C'mon." Honee took off running and flung herself in the murky water.

"No way," Qiana muttered. Yet her fear of discovery won out. She sprinted across the short distance too, and then regretted it. The edge of the pond was nothing but scum and the water inky and stagnant in the dim light. And that smell? Worse than a cesspool.

She imagined leeches glomming on to her calves and sucking her blood, and water moccasins slithering between her thighs. No telling what other creepy things eeled along in this soup that looked toxic.

A bull frog croaked like a shot, not happy its territory was being invaded. The mud gurgled like it had many mouths. But no matter how hard Qiana prayed, there was no other option.

She ripped off her Manolos, fastened them around her neck like a fox fur. Stuck a toe in the water. It was warm like pee. She dipped a foot in and retched. The foul odor forced her to breathe through her mouth.

When she finally worked up enough courage to step in with both feet, they recoiled at the way the bottom of the pond felt—all slippery and alive. She sank up to her ankles in goo and had to struggle to catch up with Honee who hissed over her shoulder like a compressor, "Let's hide behind the platform."

"No way. I bet there's snakes."

Honee didn't even slow down, so Qiana had to slog through the syrup too. It was tough. The bottom of the pond sucked at her feet. But when she realized that even at its deepest point the water came no higher than Honee's chest, she felt better. Suddenly she ducked way down, with only her nose and eyes still peeking out. Accidentally she swallowed some water that must be a haven for disease, but what else could she do?

191

The boys had arrived at the cemetery.

CHAPTER 24

"Dudes, they were here," one of them yelled as if he'd found a gold nugget. "Look at that depression behind the big stone." In seconds, more kids ran to the Abbot's Grave and scanned the ground.

Not far away and almost submerged in the water, Qiana kept sliding ahead when Honee suddenly veered over to a clump of cattails making this part of the pond look like it had a Mohawk. Qiana raced to catch up with her, while looking over her shoulder at the boys who were getting closer.

"Cool," a boy yelled as he knelt at the edge of the pond. Fortunately it was so marshy there the imprint of the women's feet had to be gone by now. "Kind of like *CSI*, isn't it?"

"Right, guys, got them trapped now." Another boy squatted down and peered at the mud.

"Wanna bet, they're right here in the pond?"

Qiana and Honee ducked even lower in their nest of reeds and Honee globbed a handful of algae on Qiana's hair to make it less noticeable. Then they clung to each other, hoping the kids would move in another direction.

Instead, more crowded around. "Hey y'all, should we get our paint ball gear? Or that archery stuff? Shoot them like Dick Cheney?"

"No, let's videotape it for YouTube. Surviving Stefford, okay? Except they won't. They broke the Code and you all know what that means. So let's make alliances. Yoo-hoo, girls, over here."

"Just so long as they don't fly the coop this time. You sure the juice is on in the fence?"

"Yup, on super high, and don't sweat. Got kids stationed all up and down it."

Slowly the Jills sauntered over. "Guys, don't tell us," Gibson said. "You actually found a trace?"

"Yeah, they're here. We two-hundred-percent know it."

"You think maybe they're hiding under that?" a girl asked, staring at the pond like it was a giant plasma screen. Qiana and Honee turned to see what the girl meant—the platform. Looking like a weathered raft, it had overhanging sides that almost touched the water, providing plenty of space underneath for concealment.

"Well hell, guys," Gibson swung the rag doll like a lasso, "I don't wanna get all wet and filthy dirty for nothing. So let's get some portable spotlights from the drama department. Then draw straws as to who's gonna investigate out there, okay?"

"Great idea." Half a dozen kids raced back to the school. Gibson, her clique, and most of the boys stayed behind. "You better make sure the Jills get the credit," she said, pointing a finger at a tall boy as headlights beamed over the pond. A black Lincoln Town Car rolled up, stopped, and the driver's side door opened.

Tears of relief in their eyes, Qiana and Honee rose out of the water like swamp creatures. Finally someone who'd help them.

CHAPTER 25

Before they could get that person's attention, a voice wafted across: "Children, what're you doing back here at this time of night?"

The students tucked in polo shirts, hitched up pants. Only then did they mob around the arrival. "Mrs. Taylor, oh Mrs. Taylor. Our favorite teacher."

"Just wait until you see my exam tomorrow." She unfolded herself out of the car. "That's the reason I stayed late, to add the finishing touches, hahaha. All the other departments, including Guidance and the library, closed hours ago. Now tell me. What're you doing back here?"

Bowing, one of the boys said, "Sorry, ma'am, it's all your fault. You taught us the meaning of excellence. You drilled the Code into us: *Always act honorably*. You definitely made us outstanding students."

Outstanding monsters, Qiana thought. She clutched Honee who whispered, "We're okay now, girl."

"Yes indeed, Mrs. T.," another boy said, "none of us never knew the meaning of *ideal* until you…"

"Young man, don't use a double negative."

"Sorry, ma'am, *ever*. But I'll never forget you. When I become president I'll still remember you. You taught us to always—no, split infinitive!—always to strive for utter nobility. Thank you."

"My goodness, that's nice to hear. Very few teachers ever get thanked." For a moment Mrs. Taylor seemed overcome with emotion and swiped at her eyes. "Come here, my little darlings. You make me so proud." She gathered as many kids as she could in a group hug, breaking all kinds of rules. "Stop stalling. Why are you really back here at this hour?"

Qiana hugged Honee who was grinning. They moved toward the edge of the pond. *Hang tight, Logan. We're on the way, baby.*

"It's—um—for practice." Gibson curtseyed to Mrs. Taylor. "We're rehearsing a play to—um—surprise you."

"What play?"

"*Julius Caesar*? We're going to make it into a musical."

"No, you don't. That's a tragedy." Mrs. Taylor took a few steps and looked the students over like a copied final exam. "It sounds fishy. And where's Josh? He'd be perfect for the role of—"

"But Mrs. T., we're not putting on *Romeo and Juliet*," Gibson said and the other students laughed.

"Besides, he's too busy trying to find Logan," another girl said. "Last I heard he was going through her locker to see if she left a note. She's probably home, waiting for her zit attack to quit. I mean, her skin blemishes to vanish. So she can face her hottie again. I mean her beau."

"Yes, such a sweet young couple, but both juniors. They still have to make many adjustments. Now Gibson, let's have the truth."

Gibson flinched and turned fiery red, from what Qiana and Honee could see. Halfway to dry land, they paused to watch

Gibson digging in the mud with the tip of her shoe, like looking for a lost class ring.

Finally! The substitutes held slimy hands. Now Gibson would have to own up to her lies, but for the moment she was still trying to postpone the inevitable. "Well, Mrs. Taylor, um—"

Suddenly her words cascaded. "We really are rehearsing, Mrs. T. Here are the lights." Fortunately for her, several students trudged up with gigantic kliegs. "It's for our senior project. We're transposing this tragedy to modern times. Right, classmates?"

The other students nodded furiously but Mrs. Taylor remained skeptical. "I really find it hard to believe—"

"It's true, ma'am," a boy said. "We were just about to do the night scene."

"What night scene?"

"The one from *Midsummer Night's Dream*, I mean *Julius Caesar*. C'mon Gibson, let's give Mrs. Taylor a preview." He touched his temple and started pacing as if lost in thought. Gibson sank to her knees, wrapped her arms around his legs, and gazed up at him like he was Zac Efron. "Oh Brutus my Lord!"

The boy placed his hand on top of her head. "Portia, what mean you? Wherefore rise you now? It is not for your health thus to commit your—"

"Bravo," Mrs. Taylor cut in, "definitely extra credit. You students are the finest group I've ever taught. With just a little more practice... Let me think... All right. Can you meet with me tomorrow morning during study hall? We'll have a glorious dress rehearsal but now it's time to go home."

"Yes, ma'am. Whatever you say, ma'am." Several voices poured like Karo syrup. "You're fabulous, Mrs. Taylor, you know that? The most awesome teacher."

A dozen kids grabbed the big lights and carted them off. "Bye, Mrs. T. We love you, Mrs. T. See you tomorrow, Mrs. T."

Waving good-bye in return, she zeroed in on the tall boy. "Wait a minute, young man. What are you doing with that pistol?"

At last! Qiana heaved out from the bottom of her lungs. The boy who had been caught red-handed looked just like the one who shot at them earlier. Obviously he'd ditched the guard uniform but liked being armed. That was good news for Qiana and Honee. Again they were moving to the edge of the pond, excited at the prospect of getting chauffeured home. While Gibson had managed to lie her way out of this situation, this boy hadn't been able to. A couple of steps later, the young women stopped again, wanting to hear what the tall boy had to say.

"Ma'am, that's not a real gun," he said, head at half-mast. "It's just a toy."

"My goodness. Were you planning to substitute it for the dagger in *Julius Caesar*? If so, it would be a travesty. Now put it up and let's all go home." Mrs. Taylor waited for the kids to start moving toward the buildings and from there to the student parking lot.

"One thing puzzles me," she said, looking at the various polo shirts. "I can see the Jills and the Jacks being back here. And the Drama Club, English Club, and Art Club for the props and so forth. The Journalism Club to capture the event for the yearbook, the Computer Club for Facebook and the programs. The ITC for leadership. But what are you Science Club students doing back here?" She propped her hands on her hips. "I want the truth, Ian. Remember, the Code."

A big boy with tiny glasses and orange hair shuffled back to the teacher. He was trailed by several buddies. "Okay, Mrs. T., the total truth."

"Yes, Ian?"

Thank God, Qiana thought. It had taken her long enough but finally the teacher was getting to the truth.

"We shouldn't have done it, ma'am," one of Ian's friends whined. "We're so ashamed."

They sure ought to be, Honee thought, still undetected in the pond but only for a few more seconds.

"We were right in the middle of our best experiment, Mrs. T. It's all about stopping the aging process in animals. Eventually we hope to expand our focus. You see, we want to keep you forever young and beautiful and inspiring many more Stefford kids."

"Aren't you sweet?"

"Thank you, ma'am, but it's huge, our latest experiment. And then it happened." The boy sounded crest-fallen. "They escaped and we lost—"

"Here we are." Qiana waved with both hands. Luckily her voice didn't carry.

"—our most important research animals. They slipped out of their cage."

"Oh no, you poor children, after all that hard work." Mrs. Taylor fluffed his hair like apron ruffles. "I'm sorry. Now do you have to start all over again?"

"Yes, ma'am. But the worst thing is, if our specimens get away, somebody else will catch them. Then they'll benefit from our efforts."

"No, that's unacceptable. What sort of animals were they?"

"Rats, I think—"

"*You don't know?* Young man, are you trying to pull the wool over my eyes?"

"Of course, they were rats," Ian injected, "but very rare and extremely valuable ones. They definitely can't fall into someone else's hands. We'd much rather see them dead. Look, Mrs. Taylor," he held up a handful of syringes, "we've got the tranquilizers. All we need is to find them."

Hearing that, Qiana whipped her hands out of the air like she'd touched fire and ducked deep into the water, Honee beside her. If they emerged now, the boys would most likely subdue them. High-fiving behind the broad back of their teacher, they gave every indication that they'd drug her too if she didn't believe them. But Mrs. Taylor accepted their lie.

"Now, children, don't take it so hard." She patted Ian on the shoulder.

"Well, we do have the fence on and the gate's been notified," he said. "But that's the *real* reason we were back here. Just think. What if those rats make it over to the Spa? Then some of their doctors will pick up where we left off and cash in."

"Don't worry, children. That won't happen, I promise. Follow me."

Still hiding not far away in the murky water, Qiana and Honee were amazed at the boys' lying capabilities. How easy it was for them to fabricate a plausible-sounding story, just like making a paperclip chain. And they were even more amazed at Mrs. Taylor's gullibility. Poor thing believed everything.

She marched the boys to another branch of the creek that was out of sight.

"Now children," her voice carried, "pull these boards over and step across, but be very careful. Okay, now grab this and lift. Up, all the way up."

Qiana and Honee couldn't see what the teacher told the boys to lift but could hear them grunting. A series of squeaks ensued like from a huge rusty iron gate being yanked up.

"C'mon, use some elbow grease but don't tear that mesh cover." More grunting, then an ear-splitting screech like from another big metal divider being wrenched out of the way and opening a closed-off passage. "All right, there you go. That'll take care of your problem, children. No rat will make it across the pond alive now. I'll guarantee it."

"Mrs. T, thank you. Thank you." The boys, their gullible teacher in their midst, appeared in Qiana's and Honee's field of vision again. They strolled back to the Lincoln Town Car that was bathed in a lone spotlight the other kids had forgotten.

Mrs. Taylor snicked the back door open. "Hop in, everybody. I'll give you a ride."

"For real, ma'am?" As Qiana and Honee watched in shock, one boy kissed the teacher. "You saved us, ma'am. Yes, you did."

"You know I'll do anything for you, my young geniuses." The motor cranked on and the Lincoln started moving.

Seeing the car zoom off, Qiana felt like gagging. Incredible how Mrs. Taylor broke the rules whenever it suited her and was she ever clueless. And she probably wasn't the only dummy on the faculty. Maybe even Dr. Reinholt was completely ignorant. Most likely he had no idea his precious Code was a joke. Gee, was he in for an eye-opener.

"Girl, let's hustle before everything gets tsunami'ed," Honee said, assuming Mrs. Taylor's goal had been to raise the water level, making it more likely for the "rats" to drown. So far it hadn't increased much and the two women made it to the platform without any trouble. Ducking under it, they heaved out all the way. No snakes, only a few squashed Miller Lite cans, cigarette butts, and condoms bobbing without a care. But now completely hidden, Qiana and Honee felt safe for the first time in what felt like ages. They peeped through the cracks in the floatable deck like soldiers through redoubts, trying to keep up with the car as it circled the back campus and was gone.

"Whewee." Honee peeled off a piece of wood and chewed it like a pack of Lance crackers. "To pee or not to pee? See, I can do Shakespeare too, girl."

"Go right ahead." Qiana was thrilled, even though they were still stuck in the pond but at least no more crazy kids around. Now the night sounds coming from every direction were just the normal ones. A few insomniac fish jumped, myriad tree frogs made their calls, and bats swooped out of nowhere like rags in a gust, curious about the spotlight. But even the awful stench wasn't so horrible anymore.

A minute later, the lights dimmed out in the main building. The chapel spire loomed in total darkness too. And Ricky's trailer was a black box hunkering down for the night. With all the scaffolding and construction equipment around, it resembled an abstract sculpture. No Henry Moore, but still.

Farther away across the creek and its tributaries, white specks winked out one by one. The Stefford Spa was also shutting down for the night. Finally everything was peaceful. The whole world seemed asleep in this, the most enchanting part of rural North Carolina.

After all the tight spots they'd been in, Qiana couldn't savor the relaxed feeling enough. Soaking in an aromatic bubble bath at a famous resort couldn't eclipse this. "How about this Eau de Swamp, Honee?" She giggled. "What do you think? Should we bottle it and sell it at the Q Store?"

"Great idea, girl. We're gonna make a mint."

"Bet it's way after midnight." Qiana felt revived like after a nap as she ducked out from under the platform.

"Maybe even later, girl," Honee said. "So let's climb up on top, take a breather. Then outta here. Let's just hope we find Logan safe and sound at her house."

"One thing for sure," Qiana said, "we won't rest until we find her even if it means contacting all her relatives."

"The office is bound to have that info, girl. So we'll dial like crazy, okay?"

"Okay." Qiana scaled the wooden planks, looked around and whopped the air like a volley ball. "This is fantastic, the little maniacs are really all gone." She wrung slimy water out of her skirt, sat down and thought about what came next—getting back on land. Breaking into the office, contacting Logan's relatives until they found the girl, then calling a stretch Hummer, stocked with

Cristalle— *No, silly. A diet coke and a regular cab will do just fine.*

"Yeah, man, let the bon tempests roularay." Splashing like a baby in a plastic Wal-Mart pool, Honee scrambled up on the shaky planks too and sat down. "Yippee-yahoo. We'll track Logan down shortly. And tomorrow afternoon Gunner's gonna get his butt home, then we can make some wedd—"

As if stung by a hornet she jumped into a standing position and her voice changed. It sounded scared. "Lord, what's that?"

Odd. Honee wasn't the scared type. "What're you talking about?" But just to be on the safe side, Qiana jumped up too, her throat constricting. She didn't know why. She didn't hear anything even though she listened with every fiber of her being. Still nothing: No more frogs croaking, no fish jumping, no owls hooting. There wasn't any movement either. No field mice scurrying, no moths flitting. Not a single bat fluttering around like before. There was just this eerie stillness.

It dawned on her that's what Honee had noticed. It was as if something sinister had arrived on campus and with one swoop, snuffed out all signs of life. Qiana felt a mounting fear race through her veins. "Yikes, that's creepy. What do you think it is?"

"Probably noth—" Honee's voice stopped working because there was *something* out there. It had targeted the two women and was stealing closer.

Qiana felt her skin pebble as she tried to see what it was. It was nothing on land but the sluggish water surrounding the platform had sprung to life. Numerous pieces of bark were swimming in their direction. Water rippled from the bark pieces that kept advancing, silent and stealthy, like heat-seeking missiles on a killing assignment.

And at the front of the bark pieces were pairs of fiery marbles—eyes.

"Oh God." Qiana blinked, hoping it was an illusion. Any moment the stagnant pool would be smooth and inert again and she could go back to her rejoicing.

Wrong. The fast-approaching threat was a Hydra-like creature that wrapped around the platform. Then the biggest pair of fiery marbles shot out of the water like a geyser, revealing a head and body the size of a Mini Cooper. The monster arched into the air and thundered down on the platform. *Crack.* A large section of wood splintered away, leaving the little island reduced by half and making the remainder of the platform a death trap.

Qiana screamed, horrified that such a creature could exist. The screaming excited the mammoth beast. A second head rose like a volcanic eruption from hell. What would come next was obvious. The monster would annihilate the rest of the platform and close in for the kill.

Qiana started moaning. Questions assailed her like blows from a claw hammer: Who wants me dead? And why? And why does Honee have to die so horribly too?

Then who's going to find Logan?

CHAPTER 26

In the old shed not far away, Logan felt close to death too. What little energy she had mustered had drizzled away like water from a cupped hand. Too bad, the rat knew it. It had come back but not alone. A dozen rats were now darting around and waiting for one of them to make the first assault on a live body. On Logan, who knew she had to hold them off—somehow.

Please God! Please Ms. Money!

The thought of the rats chewing on Logan while she was still alive was too horrible. *Let me die first.* She forced herself to move, twitch and growl—ridiculous. Only faint grunts scratched out of her parched throat but so far, the rats were still a little cowed.

Move. Twitch. Growl.

Of course if the rats got hungry enough that wouldn't stop them. They'd swarm all over Logan's face. The worst case scenario would be having her eyeballs attacked—

The worst case scenario? When did she hear that phrase?

Recently. It was last week when she'd swung by the construction wing on her way to a student council meeting. She overheard strange voices coming from one of those old classrooms.

"Not to worry," a man said. Was it one of the workers or a delivery guy? She couldn't tell. "There's no worst case scenario."

"But what if somebody finds out and blabs?" Another man. "Somebody from the outside, like a nosy substitute teacher?"

"Don't worry, nobody's gonna catch on. Not until we're ready to split."

"But just in case, then what?"

"We'll leave it up to the kids to deal with it. If that doesn't do it, we'll pull the trigger."

"Ridiculous. How can one gun or two do the job?"

"Idiot. I mean we trip the wire on our way out. Gonna be doomsday, buddy. Worse than 9/11 and right here in the idyllic backwoods of North Carolina."

Preoccupied with her plans for the meeting, Logan had dismissed the conversation. Now she wished she'd run straight to the office—

Oh no! The rats were less than an inch away from her face.

Move. Twitch. Growl. Do whatever you can to keep them from sinking their teeth into your cheeks or chin or nose. Logan tried to as her frantic feelings spiked. Again she thought about what she'd overheard. *Doomsday?* What were those men talking about? Were they home-grown terrorists, ready to blow up... what?

The school!

Oh my God. Now she absolutely couldn't die before she told Ms. Money about this but how could she? She was imprisoned, fading fast and in awful pain that made her muscles contract. So hour after hour she spasmed while slipping in and out of consciousness.

When Logan came to again, she felt several rats running across her face to get at whatever traces of blood were left. The problem was every time she lifted her head to scare the rodents

206

away, more blood oozed from her wound. That was good. Kept the rodents busy.

But bad too because she was losing so much blood.

Oh no. Logan realized she was nursing the rats like a lactating mom. So far her blood was their meal, but before long they'd get bolder. Bite her, gnaw on her flesh.

Angelo's voice replayed in her mind: *Stefford School mucho hungry... Eat all my friends.*

A shocking realization hit Logan then like that bucket of Gatorade the guys always doused Coach with after a victory. And her shriveled stomach clenched in a death cramp. Now she got it.

So that's why she'd been captured.

MS. MONEY MS. MONEY MS. MONEY

CHAPTER 27

Trapped in the pond, Qiana shrieked, her heart pounding so hard she thought her chest would explode. She stepped to the middle of the platform. "Oh God, there's seven pairs of eyes!"

By then Honee had gotten over her first shock. "Didn't I tell you about that exotic wildlife at the Spa?" she said. "That's what pulling up that gate was all about, girl. Not to flood the pond but to release this—whatever it is. Of course, Mrs. Taylor didn't know we were here." She tried to sound fearless, but Qiana could hear her friend's voice quivering and feel her shaking like a malaria patient.

Qiana was shaking worse. "What a nightmare, what should we do?"

"Let's hope that beast loses interest. But looks like we're gonna have to stay put till morning. That's when somebody's gotta come, girl. Maybe Coach or a janitor or—"

"Are you insane? I can't spend all night out here."

"Girl, would you rather end up in the jaws of—"

"But Honee, we don't even have room enough to sit." Qiana shrieked again as one head rose out of the water and opened its maw, displaying yards of saw-like teeth.

Trying desperately to stay out of the creature's reach, Qiana and Honee stepped to the other side of the platform only to hear a click-click behind them. Another section of the beast was snapping at them back there, barely missing Qiana's ankle.

"Help! Help!" Scared out of her mind, she jumped back to the pole and pushed against it so hard it cleaved her back like a sword. Honee did the same on the other side. Back to back, with only the pole between them, they rose on tiptoes to make their feet less accessible. Still they were in dreadful danger.

The creature seemed to sense the two women were trapped and acted like a playful cat. It skirted the swaying platform, gnawed at the splintered wood, and snapped air, waiting for one of the women to step closer to the edge.

"What should we do, Honee?" Qiana asked again, her voice trembling.

Honee had no answer.

"Help!" Qiana screamed again, grabbed one of her stilettos and whacked the nearest crocodile head like crazy but made no impact on the armor-like skin. "Somebody help us. Help! Help!"

No one heard her, no one came. The campus was as deserted as a distant planet, with the two or three lights still on at the Spa as remote as stars. The two young women were on their own with their fate sealed. Once its razor-sharp teeth connected with their legs, the beast would drag its prey off the platform. Too horrible to think what would come next.

Honee grabbed the other stiletto and started lashing out insanely too. "The eyes, girl. Go for the eyes."

"I'm trying." Holding on to the pole, Qiana leaned over the water, her arm with the Manolo turning into a pickaxe. It swung down again and again, whacking whatever part of the creature was closest. It was so hard. To keep going, she turned into an ancient stone hewer in her mind. Pictured lashes raining down on her whenever she slowed up. This was the image that kept her hacking away at the creature that seemed amused and made snorting sounds.

Honee whipped at the creature from the other side of the platform, her grunts of exertion rivaling those of Serena Williams during Wimbledon but also without success. Suddenly she screamed, "Take that, Tank!" and hit the reptile even harder. "And that."

Tank was the local bully who always picked on the smallest kids. Never satisfied until at least one child broke down, he liked to grab little girls, especially black ones, and smack them silly.

But Honee was smart and always stayed out of his way except one time when Momma was expecting company again. She prided herself on making the best mint juleps in the South but it took the ice trays in the Kelvinator forever to produce a few piddly cubes. So Honee to the rescue.

"Run over to the Kwickee Mart and get me a bag of ice." Momma shoved Honee out of the tin trailer so hard she forgot about sneaking to the store the back way. She used the sidewalk like everybody else. On the way home, Tank, three times her size, was waiting for her.

She tried to duck past him but he grabbed her by the arm. Grinning, he wrung it out like a piece of laundry, one beefy hand twisting in one direction, the other in the opposite.

"Leave me alone or you'll be sorry," she warned, fighting the urge to cry and making herself look taller and tougher than she was. She was just a skinny little girl with dark-honey skin.

"Yeah right." Tank chuckled as he wrenched her arm so hard her skin tore and her bones were on the verge of splintering.

"Quit it," she screamed.

"Why don't you make me? Huh-huh."

211

Honee was glad she didn't cry. Didn't want to give him the satisfaction. Yet suddenly she did—as loud as possible. With a smirk, he released her and she ran away, yelling, "Just wait."

"For what?" He guffawed. "You don't have nobody looking out for you, little trash bitch."

He was right. Honee had nobody. Momma was a grossly obese Marilyn Monroe type, that hardly ever snailed out of her trailer. She didn't have a brother or sister or anyone else who could stand up for her. She raced home, her arm throbbing, the ice melting. *I'm just no good, like Momma says. And I'm late, might as well get ready for a good licking. But Momma just did her nails. She won't want to mess them up.*

Of course, Momma was furious when Honee handed her the dripping bag. "Gonna deal with you later."

Waiting for her punishment, Honee broke off some willow branches. Picturing how Momma would do it, she beat herself on her back and chest with the branches, using her good arm. She was furious with Tank but he wasn't here. So what could she do except take it out on herself?

Now transferring the bully's face onto the horrible huge creature in front of her, Honee screamed again, "Take that, Tank, and that!" while lashing out with every fiber in her. So far the frantic bashing kept the ugly monster at bay but wouldn't, not for long. Sure, once or twice after a particularly hard hit, one head dipped back in the water but another one always popped out of the water and attacked the raft. And when that one tired, a third creature clawed at the boards, and gouged out new gashes, trying to get a toehold.

The odor of rotting plants, fish, and animal guts wafted up. It was the smell of death. And the dying would be excruciating. The creature would plunge its fangs into the women, tear them to ribbons of blood.

212

"Help! Somebody! Help!" Qiana and Honee screamed again at the top of their lungs, still chopping away like wood splitters out of control. But their efforts got the beast only more determined to devour at least one of them.

In no time Qiana was shaking from fatigue. Her breath came in pieces, like confetti. "I'm scared. I'm cold. I'm cranky. I'm sick. I want to find Logan and go home. *Gunner!*"

"I know, girl." Honee felt the same way, just so desperate. *Why do I have to die before I ever lived? Before I ever loved? Never even had a guy give me a flower. Plus, Logan's waiting for us to rescue her.* With every whack, she felt weaker. "I really can't go on."

After a few minutes, Qiana was too exhausted to fight. Even standing up was difficult. She reached behind her back to hold Honee around the waist and keep her from falling, but Honee said, "Let go. What's the use?"

"No, don't give up. We're the Navy Seals Team Chicks." Qiana's voice was hoarse. "We've got to find Logan and—"

"Don't... think...we... gonna... see… the… sun… rise... girl."

"Are you insane? All we've got to do is hang on till somebody comes." But Qiana also doubted they'd last that long without at least one of them ending up dead. The beast knew it too, lying suspended in the water and waiting. "You know what? We need a break. Turn around and wrap your arms around the pole and me."

"What's the use?" Honee said again. A split second later she hugged both the pole and Qiana who braced herself.

"Now put your legs around my waist and your head on my shoulder like you're riding piggyback." Reaching behind her, Qiana stuck her hands under Honee's backside and heaved her up.

"Got you," she squeezed out, almost caving in under Honee's weight. But at least one pair of feet was now out of harm's way. So if Qiana could just keep from crumpling... But wishful thinking was all that was. Sure, the pole helped, but Honee was heavy like a backpack of bricks. Plus she kept sliding down, so Qiana had to constantly jack her up again. Sheer agony.

Honee realized the strain she was putting on her friend. "Let me down."

"No, Honee, rest a few minutes."

"Am not about to break your back."

"Quiet!" *Why didn't Honee just shut up?* Took energy to talk and Qiana had less than zero.

"Only if you trade with me in a minute, girl."

"Are you sick? I weigh tons more than you. Now save your breath."

"'Kay." Honee's head came to rest on Qiana's shoulder. Soft breathing followed.

"Nighty-night… little... sis...." Qiana was barely able to push the words out between her clenched teeth. She was shaking and staggering. Maybe she ought to say bye-bye. And after a few more minutes, Qiana's whole body rebelled. It wasn't just her shoulders that ached terribly. The pole was killing her spine and her thighs quivered nonstop. Her arms that she stuck under Honee's butt as support were numb. She also worried about being immobilized. If the monster mounted a new attack now, she'd be in no position to defend herself or Honee. She was nailed to one spot, like with a spike.

For the time being, the monster continued to float around the platform, bumping it every now and then to establish its ownership rights, that was all.

Can we really last till morning?

The answer came quickly. Not a chance. Qiana's stomach took this moment to stage a revolt. She felt nauseous and had dry heaves. *Dammit, why can't somebody come?* Even one of the little creeps would've been a welcome sight. Maybe they weren't as nuts as Qiana remembered.

214

"Help... somebody... Help..."

Her weakening cries were in vain. The rear campus remained a no-man's land. It was eerie back here, lonely, forgotten. The other side of the moon. Because of the enormous physical strain, Qiana's mind started playing tricks on her. The events from earlier got fuzzy as she tried to will her nausea away. Worse was, pain bolted through her like non-stop lightning strikes, affecting every part of her body.

Please God. Don't let me collapse. Don't let Honee get hurt. I'm the evil one, not her.

But no matter how hard Qiana tried to tough it out, she felt limper than a dishrag and long suppressed memories ambushed her. With the blink of an eye she slipped back to an earlier time that was impossible too.

Chicago: After she got in the car with the stranger, she warmed herself on the heater, almost burning her icicle of a little finger on the blast of warmth. But after going through a drive-through, the man drove to a motel. "Hate eating in the car, don't you, girlie?"

In the cozy room, he let her have a bite. Yum. How she gulped it down. Then he snatched her hamburger away. "First you've gotta kiss me, okay?" Once she did, he gave her another little bite. "Now kiss me here and here...."

When she didn't do what he told her, he slapped her. He was strong, she was weak. Then worse came, much worse. Oh God! How bad Qiana hurt. How hard she cried because she hated what she was beaten into doing. In the end she survived by letting herself float mentally to the ceiling. And watching from a distance what first that one guy, later many others, did to her skinny little body...

Now trapped on the tiny platform in the pond and groaning under Honee's weight, Qiana could recall the horror like it was yesterday. She could remember the musty smell of the motel room,

215

all traces of fresh air having fled long ago. She could see that beige carpet again, the peeling wallpaper with the goofy fish print. She used to count the turquoise fish—each and every one of them—hoping by the time she counted them all, it was over.

Now she could feel again that lumpy mattress like a fist boring in her back. Feel again those horrible pains ripping through her, like somebody was sawing her apart with a dull knife. The agony and injustice back then didn't just hurt her body. They shattered her soul, like a mirror hammered into a million pieces. She could picture the slivers sawing at her insides year after year.

No wonder she had such a hollow feeling all the time. Suddenly a giant wave of long-suppressed hurt flooded her as she tapped into the reservoir of anger and pain from so long, combined with the enormous pain at hand and swallowed her. *It really is over now.* Qiana slid down the pole, inch by inch closer to disaster.

"My turn." Honee hopped off Qiana's back and roused her. Back to the horrible present. Qiana hitched her weary body back up the pole until she stood erect, her face gushing with tears.

In contrast, Honee channeled Kelly Ripa. "Hey girl, it worked. I feel better." She turned around, planted her feet on the platform and bent forward, her slim back to Qiana, who was glad a little feeling was creeping back into her arms and legs. At least she hadn't collapsed all the way. "Don't even think about it, Honee."

"Your turn, girl. I mean it."

"You've got no idea how heavy—"

"You don't get on my back right now, girl, I'm gonna vaulterate in the pond."

"No, don't say that." Gee, why did Honee have to be so stubborn? Even worse, she had moved to the edge of the platform. "Honee, get back!"

"Then hop to it, big sis."

Realizing she had no choice, Qiana climbed on Honee's back and tried to make herself light as a powder puff. Impossible. But

216

with her remaining strength, which was nil, she clung to the pole to try to take some of the weight off her friend. Still, Honee oomphed and bent over double. On top of everything else, it was getting much colder and started drizzling. "You okay, Honee?"

"Mighty fine."

That was a lie. Qiana felt the tremors racing through her friend's body like something trapped that wanted out. Honee must be close to breaking down or having her heart give out. But it did feel good to be off her feet for a second. Qiana fast-counted to hundred. "Time to switch again."

"Not yet, girl."

"But I feel better." Qiana oozed down on the platform and it was Honee's turn again to be carried like a little girl after a long hike. And that's how the two young women spent the next miserable hours, alternately weaving and groaning under the load of each other.

Seconds crept like minutes, minutes like hours, hours like days, terrible never-ending awful days. Before long, they felt equally horrible whether they were the carrier or the carried. But during all that time the monster never left the platform. The rain had no mercy either. It turned into a down-pour, drenching the women. Their teeth chattered. Even though they were freezing, they got so drowsy they felt like collapsing into sleep and never waking up again.

Qiana and Honee stopped talking. Praying silently, they let their tears flow like wide-open spigots. Made no sense to put on an Oscar-worthy facade of courage. Qiana could hear Honee's teeth clicking in accompaniment to hers. She was so afraid she'd pitch her friend, who clung on her back again at the moment like a cement tumor, into the water.

Well, maybe both of them would topple in: Plop, plop. Not a bad idea. Bound to be warmer in there. Wouldn't it be better than suffering on this platform piece that had turned slippery like the pole for eons, and then get devoured by the beast anyway?

After an eternity of misery it seemed to get lighter in the distance. Between the dark rain clouds, patchy pearl-gray streaked the sky like brush strokes from a blind-folded painter. But maybe it was just a figment of Qiana's hope. She didn't know what was real anymore. Everything was blurry in her mind. All tangled up.

Her life seemed to unwind forward like a movie reel. She could picture herself kissing Gunner at the end of the wedding ceremony. Wearing a 20-dollar dress from the consignment shop, she couldn't wait for their honeymoon, but not in a deluxe resort in Hawaii—in a run-down campground at Kerr Lake. But even that little get-away would never happen now. Despair overwhelmed her. She'd never see Gunner again. Sadly she remembered a recent afternoon when they were snuggling on the old sofa on the first floor of the antique store.

Instead of dozing off as she was about to, Gunner sat up straight and stared at her.

"Why don't you close your eyes and rest a little?" she asked him.

"Can't," he said. "I don't want to miss a single minute admiring you. You're the most gorgeous woman on earth, outside and in—"

"Stop it, Gunner," she cut him off and straightened up. "You don't know anything about me. You don't know any of the ugly—"

"Hush, sweetheart. I know you've been through a lot and that's one reason I'm so crazy about you. You're tough, you know." His handsome lips came close and he kissed her, starting with her forehead and moving down to her closed eyes, her nose, mouth, chin. Quick little kisses, dabbed here and there, like a shower of rose petals. "Just remember, all that ugly stuff is long gone. You've heard of re-birthing, haven't you, that healing treatment where they detox your body? Well, after we're married,

Qiana, I'm gonna detox your heart and soul. Oh yeah, I'm gonna make you whole again."

"How?" *she whispered, desperately hoping he'd be able to erase all the horrible stuff in her life. All the unbelievably tragic events. They had started* long *before Chicago. Chicago was just a flash point—*

At that moment the movie reel of her life that played in her mind went backwards. In an instant Qiana saw herself again as a frightened little girl, gagging as yet another strange guy grabbed her roughly by the hair. Staring at the wall paper, counting silently, "One fish, two, three, four, 9... 35... 167... 204..."

Never mind. What good is reviewing your life or looking to the future when you're as good as dead?

Because Qiana's legs had buckled like rusted-out gutters, making Honee glide down her back that felt broken. That didn't matter any more either, nothing did. There was just no way to stop this unthinkable horror. *Oh no. Who's going to track down Logan now?*

Before I die, I've got to tell Honee something. Instantly, words spewed from Qiana's mouth: "Don't hate me, Honee. I've done something I'm so ashamed to tell—"

"Me too," Honee flung out, "Please girl, promise you won't hate my guts."

"No, me first. It's about Annie. What happened was—"

"No, me first. It's about Momma. Man, I'm such a rotten person, much worse than she ever was. See, what I did was—"

Honee's leg grazed the edge of the platform which was what the monster had been waiting for. With a splash it shot out of the water, all its heads snapping. All its limbs scrabbling to get on top of the wooden square. The creature veered off, but this time it kept coming and made horrible sounds as it closed in on Honee's legs with their elegant ankles.

Qiana's heart stopped. *No, not Honee!* She could've been a ballet dancer, a supermodel, an actress. A great artist and philanthropist, if she only had the money. Oh, she was such a wonderful, talented human being with so much to offer. Qiana had run across all kinds of gorgeous girls during her "career," many of them smart too, many of them with big hearts. But Honee topped them all.

Too late. The reptile snapped down on Honee's slim foot.

CHAPTER 28

Finally Logan knew why she was kidnapped. It wasn't a prank or a mean trick by the Jacks or the Jills or the ITC.

It was much worse, so much worse.

She remembered hearing some seniors whisper about their latest research but clam up whenever she approached. She knew a few of them were into experimenting with all kinds of drugs while others worked on weird critters. She'd seen them graft grass hopper legs on stag beetles, a salamander tail on a lizard—crazy insane stuff like that.

A few students went beyond that type of thing. It was no big deal for them to cut up live pigs, remove their hearts and implant mechanical ones. Take puppies and sew bags of drugs under their loose skin at home, then ask clueless Mrs. Taylor if they could bring their pets to school. *Pretty please, ma'am.* Still other kids bragged about their success in genetic alterations, done with the help of their science teacher. But what if, behind the teacher's back, some kids had gone crazy and created a monster? And this creature had a huge appetite?

And nothing could satisfy it but human flesh?

Was that what Angelo tried to warn her about? He was smart, as smart as the other kids or more so, except he was wrong. It wasn't the old school building that was starving and constantly had to be fed. It was that mutant beast the kids had bred.

All made sense now. That's why new kids enrolled all the time. One day they were here, the next gone, just like Angelo. Ever since he warned Logan, she hadn't seen him. Obviously as soon as someone suspected something, they were removed.

Now she'd been snatched, maybe because someone overheard Angelo trying to warn her or because they thought she told Ms. Money about it. And that's why she was stashed away in the equipment shed.

Oh no. What's gonna happen when that monster gets hungry again?

MS. MONEY!

CHAPTER 29

At the last second, Qiana yanked Honee out of harm's way, grunting like a Sumo wrestler. Then her knees felt like tires blowing out and every bone in her turned to mush as black lace encroached on her field of vision. So she just had to let go of Honee as another part of the beast clawed itself up and it became a contest as to which part of the beast would score first.

The two young women scrabbled screaming from one side of the platform to the other as the little island dipped deeper into the water, putting them in danger everywhere. All around them thronged many beasts, their jaws moving like scissors. Bellows issued like from the depths of hell.

Qiana was barely able to see but wherever she looked, lethal armored tails swished in a frenzy. She rocked the boards, hoping to dislodge the creatures. Instead, the remaining planks broke apart. That's when the two young women went completely berserk. In the struggle, the stilettos slid off. Now they had nothing to fight with any more. *Won't it be better to dive in the water than hang around waiting for that first horrible bite?* Honee thought. Maybe she could draw the monster away from Qiana. She stepped to the edge

Guessing Honee's intention, Qiana threw herself at her friend and pulled her back but it was just a feeble gesture, like a tug on the sleeve from a corpse.

"Don't!" she screamed, trying to keep Honee from sacrificing herself, but she couldn't talk any more. What came out was just gibberish. The biggest reptile took this opportunity to lunge at Qiana when the sound of an outdoor motor burst the air.

"Over here," Qiana screamed. It came out as "Ov-va-va-a-a—hu-hu-hu-eer-eer." *Oh, this has to be Henry, a yardman, someone from the Spa.* She was almost insane from relief over the motor noise that rose from the direction of the creek and grew louder as the boat entered the pond. The creature heard it too. All its heads swung around to see what was coming and the claws relaxed. A kick by Qiana sent the monster off the platform.

"Ricky!" Honee recognized the man at the helm and screamed too. It came out as "Rick-k-k-ee-ee!" Hearing her, the counselor churned up the muddy water, causing a roar that made the Hydra slink back into the depths.

"Holy cow. What're you guys doing out here?" He cut off the motor. Wearing a yellow rain slicker and wide-brimmed hat, he was smoking a cigarette. He pulled along the platform piece, on which the two women huddled, shivering from bone-rattling chills. In silence, they toppled into the boat and hunched under the coat he handed over.

When Honee could form intelligible words again, she sputtered, "Lord... got... trapped... Couldn't... get... off... because—"

Ricky wouldn't let her finish. "That's awful. Are you ladies all right?" Concern tingeing his voice, he looked worried.

"We'll... be... okay... after... a... hot... shower," Qiana hacked out like an old woman who had smoked all her life. "Thank God... you came... A second later—"

"Don't even say it, you poor babies. I heard some lab animals escaped last night but had no idea it was some of that tropical wildlife from the Spa."

"Gee, that wasn't any tropical wildlife. That was a huge monster, like from a scary movie."

"Well, I know for a fact they have a two-headed crocodile over there. Plus a bunch of little ones. Lawsuit, ladies. My advice is to get yourselves the best damn legal team in the country. Gloria Allred or—"

"Law suit?"

"Hell yeah, Qiana. I want you to sue those idiots over there that brought such dangerous creatures up here from Miami. It's outrageous. Something tragic could've—"

"Would've, for sure, you hadn't come. Man-oh-man, we can't thank you enough."

"No problem, Honee. I'm glad I came. But honest, I couldn't believe my eyes. What a nightmare." Ricky started the motor and maneuvered the flatboat as close to the shore as a shave. "Sometimes I get up early and jog in the direction of Red Mill. Just five miles to clear my head, you know, get rid of all that stress. But this morning it was raining. That made the water level go up, so I decided on a boat ride. Let me help you." He offered a hand as the two women staggered out of the boat.

Qiana looked around, frantic. She found what she was searching for and brushed it off, a useless gesture. The doll fell apart into squishy rags.

"What's that about?" Ricky asked.

Qiana said nothing, she couldn't, so overwhelmed with relief that it was silly. The doll was beyond repair and yet.... Just clutching the slimy tatters made her feel better.

225

"That was part of our lesson plan." Honee retied her dripping Adidas, wrapped the coat around Qiana and herself, linked arms with her. After a few seconds of stomping their feet and shivering—brrrr!—they took off running to the school. It turned out to be stumbling and weaving like drunks, but they didn't care. Both of them felt like they'd just returned from imprisonment in Siberia.

"This way, ladies," Ricky pointed to his trailer, "before you catch your death. It's nothing fancy but it'll do. I'm afraid you have hypothermia."

"I could kill for a hot shower," Qiana said, "and some dry clothes."

"Don't worry, I'll scrape up something. You're heroes, both of you, you know that? What happened?"

"Your students went totally bananas," Honee said.

The counselor chuckled. "Isn't that a bit harsh? Granted, they can be mischievous, even wild on occa—"

"No, this was much worse," Qiana cut him off. "They acted like robots gone insane, completely out of their minds; didn't even pretend to go by the Code. They're either real psychos or rotten to the core and that includes the girls, at least some of them."

"Are you kidding me?"

"No, Ricky, they've cracked like eggshells. You should've seen them last night. First we discovered some outrageous things in the third wing; then we got tortured and chased all over. That's why we got stuck in that pond and almost—"

"But Qiana, didn't you say some crocodi—?"

"You got a hearing problem?" Honee lashed out. "It was your students that chased us until we ended up in the pond. And before that, they shot at us and I think they hurt that old guy at the gate. Plus I think they did something to that missing cafeteria worker. Anyway, they all acted like out-of-control gang bangers. And this one chick, Gibson? She's responsible for Ms. Hill's disappearance.

226

It sounds crazy, but she tied us to some instruments of torture and—"

"Oh no. You think maybe she was imitating a rerun of the *Fear Factor* and just got carried—?"

"No, Ricky," Qiana said. "These kids went far beyond imitating a TV show. There's something seriously wrong with them. They're sick."

The counselor shook his head. "I can't believe it. Really, I'm shocked and just as sorry as can be. I really feel like I should've prevented it. If I'd only known..." He led the shivering women around the scaffolding to his trailer. Parked next to it was a cherry-red Porsche, covered with a tarp.

"Might as well come clean to you guys. That's Dr. Reinholt's new convertible. Slick Willy keeps it back here out of sight and you know why? He doesn't want any of the kids to develop a taste for ostentatiousness, he says. Yet he's so into conspicuous consumption himself. So you think that's what happened? The kids realized what a liar, a fraud he is. That's why they took their anger out on—? This way, ladies." He stepped around a pile of tool boxes, pipes, and wires. "Sorry, renovation crews aren't what they used to be."

Offering his hand for support, he helped Qiana and Honee navigate around more construction materials and past a manhole, then up three steps to a door he unlocked.

"Guess it finally happened, ladies. Dr. Reinholt's brilliant ideas have backfired—big time. Actually I've always been afraid of that. Can't tell you how many times I told him you can't fool kids forever and too much stress—"

He paused. "You see, Einstein kids can deal with work overload but the average students? They can only take so much before they snap. Add to that all that American Ideal shit and constantly harping on the Code, well, that's like pouring gasoline on a fire."

By then Honee had calmed down. None of this was the counselor's fault. "You think the kids just got burned out?"

"Sure, that's got to be part of it. In you go." Ricky pushed the door back, letting the two women enter first.

The little kitchen of the trailer was all done in white and aqua, with just the basics, but good enough for a simple lifestyle. The air was thick with smoke however, and the trashcan next to the Formica table and chairs cascaded with cigarette butts, pizza boxes, and crushed beer cans. There was no sign of any research going on, but most likely Ricky kept his work in a bedroom.

"Sorry about the mess, ladies. I stayed over at my girlfriend's last night. But there're a couple construction guys that knock themselves out, so I let them chill in here. Nobody's around now, so make yourselves at home. Down there—" he pointed to a hallway running the length of the trailer like an afterthought, "—is the bathroom. Stocked with towels I liberated from the Spa, haha. Meanwhile I'll rustle you up some breakfast. Bacon and scrambled eggs all right? I make a mean cup of coffee."

"Thanks," Qiana said, "but no food. My stomach's still in such a knot. Coffee's fine for me but do you have any tea? Honee could really use some."

True. Honee was crumpling against the wall, a picture of exhaustion. Must be the after-effect of all she'd been through, she thought. Plus, her bad life finally exacting its toll. She just couldn't get warm. Maybe she'd caught the flu or needed an IV in her arm.

"Got it covered, ladies. You go right ahead." Ricky's chin jerked in the direction of the hall. "Coffee and tea with lemon, okay? Nothing but the best at Stefford School."

"Yeah, yeah, yeah," Honee mumbled and took a few steps, bracing herself against the wall.

"There should be plenty hot water." Ricky started bustling at the stove like a young housewife. "And afterwards, you guys can grab a long nap. Just leave the rest to me. First I'm going to alert

228

the sheriff and have that dangerous pond seen to. Then once you give me some names, we'll start dealing with the kids. We'll track down the worst head cases. Go on a fact-finding mission and dispel all the rumors. Oh, and that new football coach? Will he ever have a fit. See, that's another guy that's full of it. He's been pushing our boys to the brink. No wonder they got nasty."

"Nasty's the wrong word." Honee's voice was full of life again. "These kids were beyond vicious. Their code seems to be to act as horrible as they can. And whoever put them up to it, they're the real bastards. But you know what? Qiana and me, we're in their business now." Letting go of the wall, she fisted her hands. "Yeah, man, soon as we bounce back, we're gonna unmask them. Have them lick dust like a serpent, like the Bible says. And then we squash them."

Ricky ran water into a carafe and got out china cups and saucers. "Sounds like a plan. We've got to find the mastermind immediately but don't worry, kids love to blab. Not all, but some. So about how many were involved?"

"Maybe a hundred but all seniors, I think," Qiana said.

"Dammit, that's even worse. I was hoping some little freshmen nerds rebelled against the Stefford Code, got drunk and ran amok. Still, a hundred kids, that's only ten percent. Of course, no telling how many others knew about it. One more thing. I'd better make sure Dr. Reinholt gets nabbed before he comes to work. He's gotta be up to his neck in this. Plus, I've got to track down more counselors to help the rest of the student body deal with this bizarre—"

He scratched his head. "There're probably just a couple ringleaders. Most likely the rest of the kids just got sucked in by peer pressure— Careful." Ricky jumped over to Qiana whose knees were wimping out. "Sit down, will you?"

"No, I'm okay but what about the teachers? Don't you think some of them are mixed up in this too?"

"Trust me, Qiana. Whoever knew even one iota about this insanity gets kicked out on their fat ass. And their teaching license gets revoked, I'll see to it. I'm so grateful, ladies. If you hadn't told me…" Ricky left the rest unsaid as both women finally managed to pull themselves together enough to teeter down the hall.

"You first," Honee said as they entered the small bathroom.

"No, you first." Qiana felt another tidal wave of exhaustion engulf her and sank to the floor. Eyes closed, she curled up in a ball, one hand rooting under her top and landing on the soggy lump she'd tucked there. *Saved you this time, Annie, but what good is that?*

Honee undressed behind the plastic shower curtain with the smiley faces. Hearing the running water, Qiana walked her hands up the wall until she stood erect. She knew she looked like death heated up in the microwave, but so what? She was alive, Honee was alive. Next was making sure Logan was fine too. *What time is it?*

To find out, she dragged back down the narrow hall. *Oh joy.* There by the kitchen entrance, a wall clock tick-tocked. *7 AM.*

Now a short nap while Ricky took care of everything, but he'd better call a long-time substitute for Honee, Qiana wouldn't let her friend teach at Stefford School again until all this insanity was rooted out. Perhaps in a few weeks or months, this horror story would turn into just another wild and crazy adventure they'd talk about. Most likely they'd have another newspaper story to store in that beat-up metal cabinet in the Q Store. Onward.

At the end of the hall, Qiana paused and beamed. Just a couple of feet away now, Ricky was leaning against the kitchen counter, his back to her as he tapped in numbers on his cell phone. Gee, what a good guy, already setting the wheels of justice in motion.

He didn't notice Qiana enter the kitchen but obviously hadn't wasted any time. On the counter perched a wicker tray with

230

napkins folded into little swans and a vase with pink carnations. What a sweet gesture, intended to make the horrible events of the night fade fast.

"Good morning," Ricky said into the phone, turning sideways. His profile held an expression she hadn't seen before. It looked predatory. "Do I have a big surprise for you," he went on. "Yes, both of them and right in the palm of my hand, Mother."

PART 3:
THE STEFFORD SPA

CHAPTER 30

It had been the worst night in Logan's life. Still attached to the tumbled-over desk in the shed, she had recurring fainting spells that stretched for hours. But even during the darkest times, she roused once or twice to hear noises. First she thought it was just more kids. But no, it was only the echoes of her classmates in her mind.

Then she heard a sound that was much closer—tiny feet scurrying. They belonged to those rats that gave excited squeals as they scrabbled over her face and dug under her head, lapping up whatever blood drops were left. So far no rat attacked Logan. They just nibbled at her matted hair until she twisted her head away and groaned through her gag, hoping to sound like a tiger.

She sounded like a flea. Then she froze because any moment she expected needle-sharp teeth to sink into her cheek. Her fear made her hold her breath which made her black out again. So she wasn't sure if she was awake or dreaming when she heard sounds again, human ones this time. Some people were yelling outside the shed, but Logan thought she must be hallucinating.

Because why did it sound like two young women?

Oh my God. One of them sounded exactly like that new substitute teacher.

That had to be a dream. But how the existence of these voices, or even just her delusional mind conjuring them up, infused the girl with hope.

Is Ms. Money looking for me?

But why else would she be back here in at this hour?

Logan thought it was about three or four o'clock in the morning. No more light crept through the cracks, but she knew exactly where those voices came from—the pond behind the football field. Then Logan couldn't help it. She started worrying about Ms. Money. Did she and a friend get stuck in the mud back there? Did they think Logan had fallen in?

Yay! From the pond it wasn't far to the shed.

Logan clung to this comforting thought with all her being: *Yesss! Beautiful and fierce Ms. Money is out there searching for me.* She could picture Ms. Money in front of the class and a wonderful calm settled over the girl like a baby blanket. Because somehow it seemed like Ms. Money was looking directly at Logan. Suddenly it pipelined to the girl what made this substitute teacher so special. She seemed determined to make life fair for kids. And if she had a helper, like it sounded from the voices, she'd really do it. There was just such a righteous vibe about Ms. Money.

So of course Ms. Money will find me.

Even more important: not even the worst monster could win out over the new substitute and her friend who had to be a tough chick too. Ms. Money wouldn't hang with any shrinking violet. *So okay, Ms. Money will find me.*

But would it be in time?

236

CHAPTER 31

Mother?

Qiana felt like a fist had rammed her in the gut. Before Ricky could notice, she shrank back into the hall like a turtle into its shell, her mind spinning with questions: *Who's he talking to? Is this his partner? His only one?*

She slipped inside the bathroom. Done with her shower, Honee was draped with towels. The leather halter top she always wore had protected her torso, but the rest of her body was an assembly of scrapes and bruises. Peeking under the towels, she said, "Man, I feel ashy." In the medicine cabinet behind the mirror she discovered some Nivea, dabbed it on, and noticed Qiana's shocked expression. "What's up, girl?"

Before Qiana could answer, she added, "Just remember, we can't rest long. We've gotta get back to finding Logan. Just this second I got an awful feeling—it's not just duty anymore. Now it's a crusade."

"I just hope and pray the poor girl isn't caught up in this horrible mess." Quickly Qiana filled Honee in on what Ricky had said.

"What?" Honee's head rocked back. "You mean Ricky's behind this awful—?"

"Sounds like it, doesn't it? And I bet that crazy secretary is his mom."

"But what's their incentive, girl?"

"Money, what else? With this school doing such great business and so many others springing up, they've got a gold mine. While the kids are running amok, nobody's keeping track of the finances."

"So Ricky's jibber-jabbering about helping the trash kids was nothing but a big fat lie?"

"Afraid so, Honee. Didn't you see that Porsche? Nobody who works in education can afford one of those on a school salary. So this was their deal, I think. Whip the kids into a competitive frenzy of huge proportions and let them act out their worst fantasies. Like we've already seen, that Code is just for show. Nobody pays attention to it. Meanwhile Ricky and his pals skim whatever they want off the top. Just think how much cold hard cash they have already if they're taking only ten percent."

"But that's outrageous. Lord, I bet tricky Ricky washed out in his original field. Couldn't hack it at the Spa either, so he hopped over here. That scum bucket. Man, he's gotta be the mastermind."

"I agree. Excuse me." Qiana jumped in the shower too. In three minutes and shaking like a poodle, she emerged from the curtain and toweled herself dry, paying no attention to her own scratches and bruises. "I think there're four of them. Dr. Reinholt, that al-Qaeda coach, Ricky, and Ms. Crazy Hand. Bet they're all billionaires."

238

"Well, that's easy to find out. Cops, they can check on their bank—" Honee stopped. The trailer was bouncing from energetic steps coming down the hall.

"Room service, ladies," Ricky crooned. "Tea for two and two for—"

"Could you please set it somewhere?" Qiana asked, shaking a fist. How she'd like to punch him in the face.

"How about the nightstand?" A door squeaked open.

"Thanks, Ricky." Honee made her voice sound like Gibson's when she was being good. "You're sooo sweet."

"And then could you ple-e-ease let us sleep till after lunch?" Qiana, in a Splenda-tone of voice.

"Don't worry, ladies. I won't disturb you until this evening. Lucky for me, I already found a replacement for you, Honee. Now sleep tight, y'all."

A second later, they heard him bounce back to the kitchen and dipped into the bedroom that was also devoid of any sign of research going on. "What a lying piece of you know what," Qiana whispered, heading for the tray. They slurped the scalding liquids, burning their throats but never mind. They had bigger worries: How to get out of here and notify the cops. And make sure none of the four masterminds got tipped off and none of the guilty kids got away.

And most urgent: find Logan.

What about that monster in the pond?

Wiping her lips that felt blistered, Honee collapsed on the double bed that took up most of the room and noticed several photo albums hidden on top of a locked wardrobe. While waiting for Qiana to finish her coffee, she flipped through them. Most pages showed school functions and staff groupings but quite a few featured three men with similar faces and hair loss patterns. "Look, girl. There's Ricky with his brothers and all in the prime of health.

Wonder if they know what a malevolencier he is. Now what? Can't streak out of here, can we?"

Qiana was busy rearranging the bed with pillows and blankets, so it looked like two people were sleeping in it. "No, let's just wait till that crook scrams."

They heard a door slam, a key turn.

"Now what, girl? Should we jump in that Porsche? Put Stefford in the rearview mirror?"

"Gee, don't you remember what happened to us at the guard booth?"

"So what can we do? Man, this closet lock's impossible. Already tried it, so no clean clothes, Qi. What about we use these sheets as togas? Act like we're part of that Shakespeare rehearsal?"

"Yeah right, Honee. They'd spot us in a minute. Just because we now know who the masterminds are doesn't mean the kids don't still have their cult mentality." While Qiana was talking, she riffled through the nightstand by the window but found nothing useful. When she dived under the bed however, she discovered something in a big black plastic bag.

Is that Ricky's research material?

Or something else? Something horrible?

The smell curling out of the plastic bag was nauseating but there was nothing horrible in it. It was just a make-shift laundry basket.

"Thank God, no dead animals." Qiana dropped the reeking work clothes she had dug out and brushed off her hands. "Gee, this stuff's filthy. Maybe we should just do like we told Ricky. Sleep for a few hours and then—" She changed her tone of voice. "Can I tell you something, Honee? I had a terrible feeling all day yesterday. Please forgive me, but first I thought you were a member of the Southern Mafia that had me in the crosshairs. And that's why you lured me here into a trap. Of course, now I know it was just me being neurotic again."

240

"Maybe not, girl. Don't mean about me, but did you notice somebody tailing you? I mean besides the usual bunch of droolers? I really think one of them had the crustaciousness to sneak into our place night before last and—" Honee stopped because she looked out the tiny window. "Man-oh-man. Can it get any worse? Now the whole student body's out there."

"Maybe Mrs. Taylor got permission to have an audience for her dress rehearsal," Qiana said. "Or maybe everyone just wants to have study hall outside." The weather was certainly perfect now: nothing but blue skies.

Fortunately all the kids stayed far away from the pond that had been cordoned off with huge barricades and traffic cones. Now they looked different. More than half of them were decked out in wigs and togas, but all of them acted normal as if nothing out of the ordinary had happened the night before. They found their favorite spots like at the beach, spread out on the grass, and started studying.

But after a few seconds, some of the older boys glanced around, only to sit up straight when Ricky appeared, a stack of cumulative folders tucked under his arms.

"Would you look at that scam artist or should I call him a freaky pervert? Don't tell me he didn't know about that orgy and stuff. Probably started the whole thing." Disgusted, Qiana shook her head, imagining what had just happened. Ricky had filled in his mother, Dr. Reinholt, and Coach. Now he was on his way to the trailer to check on his captives.

Along the way, he meandered from one group of senior guys to another, pretending to encourage them. In reality, he gave them a thumbs-up to indicate he had caught the two "rats." That's why every group he passed broke into grins.

A couple of boys pulled out syringes behind his back and flashed them around. Maybe they planned to storm the trailer later and help themselves to the two women. Qiana couldn't see how

Ricky could control them all. Most of them were taller than he was, and there were so many of them but maybe that's exactly what he wanted.

"We've got to get out of here," she said, then went, "Oomph." Honee had slammed a pile of stinking clothes at her midsection. They dressed in a hurry, making grossed-out faces. But there was nothing else to do but turn the dirty jockey shorts and T-shirts inside out. Slip them on, step into grungy overalls. They stuck their feet into sweat-stained wool socks and Qiana found some brogans as Honee wrestled her squishy Adidas back on. There were even some greasy visor caps and Honee came across a pair of sunglasses and tossed them at Qiana.

"C'mon, girl. Let's track down those construction dudes and use one of their cell phones. Can't all be in Ricky's back pocket."

"But how're we going to get past those crazy preppies?"

"We'll sneak out the kitchen door. It faces the other way. Man, I know it's too much to hope for, but maybe Ricky left his cell."

"Are we cursed, or what?" Honee smacked the kitchen counter like a fly convention, disappointed because Ricky hadn't left his phone. Riffling through his blazer that hung over a chair, she found several things but no phone. But at least no students were visible through the glass-paned door that unlocked from the inside.

Easing the door, with the lock on, shut behind them, the two women tiptoed outside—tough to do with those nail-studded boots and soggy tennis shoes. But that was the least of their worries. Remembering their horrible night, they froze at the bottom of the steps and eyed the strip of land separating them from the pond.

There was nothing there besides lush patches of grass. And with the big barricades encircling it, even the pond looked harmless now like a shallow body of stagnant water with the remains of the platform swaying in the middle. Scum islands floated past, dragonflies balleted across the surface. Birds trilled and flitted against a Carolina-blue sky. There wasn't a sign of any crocodiles.

But over by the clump of reeds lurked big shadows.

"Girl, don't have a connip—" Barely in time Honee jerked Qiana behind a stack of lumber. The approaching noise indicated Ricky was on the way, some seniors with him. They didn't go in the trailer, just rattled the door knob.

Ricky was all jazzed up. "Don't worry, guys. We're gonna take care of them and this time for good."

"Why can't we kneecap them?" one boy wheedled. "Or handicap them some other way?"

"Because you want to have fun with them, not hurt them, before it's over, right? So just ask for a pass to Guidance after your exams. But be polite. Remember the Code. We sure don't want old lady Taylor to suspect something."

"Oh man, she won't," another boy said, laughing. "Old bag's so into her Othello and Macbeth, she doesn't question anything. Once she caught me swallowing some uppers. I told her it was breath mints and she believed me."

Another rattle of the doorknob. Then satisfied, Ricky disappeared back around the trailer, the boys following him like sleepwalkers.

After counting to ten, Honee, grim-faced, popped up from the wood pile, an iron rod in her hand. "Let's boogie." She shoved the sleeves of her overalls up, stuck the rod into an opening in the manhole cover and wrestled it loose.

"Bound to connect to those tunnels, don't you think? So maybe we can make it over to that open shaft in the third wing." She wedged the cover aside and scurried down the rungs of a narrow ladder.

Snatching a flashlight from a tool box, Qiana switched it on and crept into the hole too. It lit up under the beam but was still scary. "I'm scared," she whispered panicky, but Honee dragged her farther down to a stone niche and inched the manhole cover back in place.

"Let's just hope they don't check on us again for several hours, girl."

"Whatever... you say...." Qiana cowered into a ball and shut her eyes, feeling the world closing in. Smothering her, crushing her. She couldn't breathe, couldn't think. Could barely whisper. "I'm *really* scared."

"Stay put. I'm gonna prevestigate." Honee hopped down the last metal rungs and found herself in an underground universe made up of dripping tunnels with a network of pipes and wires running overhead. *What's that all about?*

Next to her breathing baby breaths, Qiana took a peek, her eyes adapting to the gloominess. *Oh no, it's worse than I thought.* Her flashlight illuminated what looked like a haunted house on Halloween. Shadows and mist patches floated everywhere like torn tissues. And all that spookiness was underlined by the scrabbling of small animals.

"Real rats and lots of them," Honee said, smelling an odor of fear and panic again, just like in the science wing. "You think the lab animals are kept down here?"

Qiana was too petrified to say anything.

"Gonna try it this way." Pointing the iron rod, Honee attempted to stand up—impossible, but she could waddle like a duck. "Right back, girl, okay?"

"No. Don't. Leave. Me... *Mutti!*" That's what Qiana used to call her German mother as a child. But too late. Honee was already moving deeper into the ghostly underground terrain stretching before her.

CHAPTER 32

Ms. Money will find me.

This thought, reverberating with ever more certainty, was on Logan's mind when the shed door was suddenly wrenched open. Several manly grunts followed, then a flurry of movement. Logan vaguely saw some human forms before being blind-folded, ripped from the confinement of the desk and dragged out into the fresh air.

Ah, morning. But she couldn't rejoice. She was slung over someone's shoulder and carried off like a picnic blanket. Since her gag hadn't been removed, she couldn't ask what was going on. And now she couldn't see anything.

But never mind. Ms. Money will find me.

So the she didn't resist, even when she was tossed in the trunk of a car like a bunch of newspapers meant for recycling. The car started and drove for many miles, it seemed. Maybe they were in another state already. Logan felt groggy and out of it. Yet she didn't get that totally hopeless feeling any more because she was sure Ms. Money and another fearless female were hot on her trail. Maybe even close.

It was like magic. As long as Logan thought about her potential rescuers, she could barely feel her aches or her thirst and gnawing hunger, or the cut on her head or the scratches from those rats. Or the new pains from all that bumping around in the trunk that smelled of oil and old tires. Must be an older model car, like the one Henry drove. She remembered reading that if you got kidnapped, you should focus on every little detail.

But why? Logan giggled, crazy as it was, because she envisioned in vivid detail just how Ms. Money would rescue her soon. She almost felt sorry for the morons that thought they'd get away with this insane prank. Yeah, her kidnapping and imprisonment would be *nothing* compared to what would happen to those punks. Probably thought nobody was on to them as they were driving down to Florida, where they'd release her in a swamp. Strip her completely, leer at her. Grab her breasts, her crotch, mark her up some more. Then tell her she'd have to find her way back to Stefford School all by herself.

Again Angelo's voice jumped to the foreground of Logan's mind: *Stefford School building... eat all my friends...*

Oh no. How could she have forgotten? This wasn't some antics of her classmates. This was about that horrible monster the kids had engineered. She was being delivered to its lair. Why? Because the beast was hungry for more human flesh—her flesh.

Thinking about it made Logan's heart go thump-thump in overdrive, but the moment the car came to a halt, she stopped freaking out. *No way will Ms. Money let that happen.*

Even when Logan was dragged into a building, taken by elevator to another floor, flung on a cot and tied to the railing, she kept clinging to the wonderful vision of Ms. Money and her friend riding up like the sheriff in an old western. Knocking the creeps out with a few punches. Taking aim at the monster and shooting it dead with a laser gun. Of course Logan knew she was mixing up reality with fantasy but didn't care. Her mind was made up. She'd be saved real soon.

Even when Logan heard some people discuss what to do with her, she thought: *Just wait. Ms. Money's gonna get your butts thrown in jail.* Maybe even put on death row if what Logan feared was correct: That this was the same bunch that had something to do with Ms. Hill's and Rosario's disappearance. Oh yeah. Ms. Money wouldn't rest until the guilty parties got exactly what they deserved.

Next Logan felt a wave of disappointment. *Besides the death penalty what is there? The law doesn't permit someone to be fed to a monster.* But it wasn't fair to just kill somebody who was so evil.

Wasn't there a penalty worse than death?

CHAPTER 33

"Honee, come back here." The thought of being left behind at the tunnel entrance was more than Qiana could bear. It was much more than the physical aloneness. It was a feeling of utter abandonment just like what happened to her as a child. Years ago, on the run from a stalker, Mutti had stuck her in a huge box that was dark as tar, hoping to hide her child. But her plan backfired. She hadn't seen her mother again until decades later.

Everybody always leaves me.

Because I am bad!

She remembered the understaffed orphanage. The worst kids, the psychotic ones, got sent to the gardener who had yellow barbwire teeth and his own method for dealing with the little trouble makers.

What if Gunner never comes back from Bermuda?

Sobbing, Qiana scrambled off the shelf, felt between her legs to see if she'd peed in her dirty overalls. Back when the nuns used to hand her over to the gardener, her first reaction always was to pee in fear like a scared puppy.

Her pants were still dry, so maybe this wouldn't be so bad. Besides, she felt Logan was in trouble, so Qiana had to get moving. She sucked in the stale air, clunked into the darkness too, and Velcroed herself to Honee.

Crouch-walking deeper into the tunnel, the two young women shuffled past spaces filled with metal scraps. Is that where those racks came from? Honee wondered. Echoes of agony seemed to cling to the spaces, like ghosts wanting to jump the women as they hustled on.

When they came to a spot where the tunnel split into two sections, they stopped to catch their breath even though Honee wished they hadn't. The air was beyond nauseating with a rotten-meat smell, like from carcasses left to rot.

"Girl, you think this goes to the school?" She pointed left, but only silence from Qiana who felt too queasy to talk. Her throat had closed from fright because she knew any moment the ancient tunnels would collapse. Squash them both to death and nobody would ever find them.

Maybe Gunner will come back. He'll land at the private airport in Red Mill and whistle while waiting for us to come pick him up. He'll be loaded with presents. A leopard-print bikini, a box of chocolates and a diamond heart pendant from Trimingham's for me. Crossword puzzle books, dictionaries and rolls of wire for Honee, to make hoop earrings out of.

But we won't be there, we'll never be there. He'll wait and wait and go crazy looking for us. But the Stefford School office will lie: "Those pretty young substitutes? They went home with all the other teachers. Haven't seen or heard from either of them since. Just an e-mail from Ms. Money saying she quit..."

Gunner would devote the rest of his life to searching for them, but in vain. Years from now, someone might accidentally come across their pale bones. It would be another Chandra Levy case, except this time it would be *two* young women gone missing—missing forever. Qiana could picture Gunner over the years turning into a gray-haired drunk with hollow eyes. *Meanwhile what's going to happen to Logan?*

"Just a tad longer, girl," Honee said, trying to snap Qiana out of her gloom. " But you know what? What if the kids're back in the building?" Honee was talking to herself. Qiana was just a quivering figure, one hand gripping Honee's overalls, the other digging into Honee's arm. Worse was, Qiana was hyperventilating.

When Honee trained the flashlight on her face, Qiana looked bloodless, her lips seamed. *Yikes, the city chick is shutting down.* "Now girlfriend," she patted her on the back, "don't you remember? We're the Q Chicks, female warriors out to get the crooks."

Qiana still didn't say anything.

"Just gotta get out of here, girl. Then we're gonna call the cops and find Logan, okay?" Honee took the right tunnel and kept moving, hunched over, for what seemed another endless stretch but probably was just a few hundred yards.

Qiana stayed glued to her. The uncomfortable position made Honee's legs cramp and her back ache to the point of breaking. Fortunately the tunnel expanded again, offering another choice of paths. So far still no signs of any animal enclosures, but the dripping increased. Drip, drip, drip.

"Maybe this goes to the Spa." Honee's voice brimmed with hope. "Wouldn't that be something? We dial up the law and join Logan in the whirlpool or the cold water plunge, in case she skipped school to pamper herself."

Still no comment from Qiana. But faster now they kept moving, with Honee continuing in front. "Yup, we gotta be close. There's bound to be an exit at the Spa."

They passed another series of eerie chambers, silent as robbed tombs, and got to another split. By then Honee had lost all sense of direction and Qiana was still no help. She just zombied along like a trailer, eyes closed, lips moving, soundless: "Gunner. Logan. Logan. Gunner."

"Help me out, girl. Left or right?"

Only mewling from Qiana, so Honee took the right branch again which seemed a good choice. This tunnel was better kept, with the overhead wiring brand-new. Almost no water drops landed on their heads though they must be directly under the creek. They trudged on, trying not to inhale deeply because the cleansing effect of their hot showers had long worn off. Now they really stank.

Honee held nose while Qiana kept breathing through her mouth in rapid intakes as if her lungs were failing. Otherwise silence except for the footfalls of Qiana's boots and the squish-squish of Honee's Adidas. Even the rats had fled.

"Not much farther, I can feel it." But unfortunately Honee had picked the wrong way.

The next stretch of tunnel had collapsed and was impassable. "Lordy-Lord," Honee groaned, "all this for nothing?"

A whisper wafted out of Qiana: "Air." Clinging to Honee, she trembled a finger to a metal shaft bisecting the tunnel overhead.

"Yep yippee, we're breathing okay. There's gotta be a source of air." Honee touched the big shaft. "You think it's an air-conditioning duct?" Excited, she felt along it until she came to a ridge, hefted the rod and hit it until one section sprang loose, opening a gap wide enough for someone to pancake through. Poking a hand in, Honee felt a draft like from the ventilation system of a plant. "You think this goes to the Spa?"

Nothing from Qiana again.

"Worth a try." Honee clambered up into the shaft. "You stay here."

But no matter how hard she tried to pry Qiana's clammy fingers off her overalls, she got nowhere. "C'mon then." Honee crawled deeper into the shaft, the flashlight tucked in her waistband to light up the path ahead.

Qiana bumped along behind her. But whenever Honee stopped, she felt a hand clamp on her calf in a death grip, one finger stabbing like a syringe.

The two young women scootched along inside the shaft that curved upwards. Before long they had to brace themselves against the chilly metal surface but they knew they were getting close to an exit. A prick of light winked in the distance.

"Thank you, Lord." Honee felt a big smile coming on. She could already picture herself lounging by the pool with Logan, chewing ice cubes and munching on cocktail umbrellas and palm bark. "Almost there, girl."

She was right. Before long, the light in the distance looked like a sun sending rays in all directions. Honee's knees got scraped from her frantic crawling but she couldn't wait to confront those four crooks. Find Logan and deal with those crazy kids.

"Hallelujah." Just a dozen feet in front of her now was light, beautiful light. It fell through a metal screen that must be an outlet of some sort. But even if the screen was nailed shut, she'd yell through it until somebody showed—a maid, a janitor, a high-dollar guest. Maybe even a celebrity like Kanye West, Will Smith, or Cee Lo Green. Wouldn't that be a hoot?

Like on the last lap of an Olympic swim meet, she flung herself forward so fast she thumped her head on the screen. Then she looked through it, again and again, as if she couldn't believe her eyes.

Qiana crept close too, grabbed Honee's shoulder and rattled it like a stuck door. She found her voice again. "Where. Are. We?"

Now it was Honee who couldn't say anything, she just kept staring down at something in shock.

Had they arrived high up a wall somewhere? Qiana wondered. *And was the view down there just too fabulous for words?*

No, it must be something else because she felt Honee's body turn rigid and cold, colder than ice, than death.

But the shaft wasn't that bad, so what made Honee shiver?

Was it the view below? Or did something stir up horrible memories?

One time after Momma whipped her again, Honee had enough. Time to run away. It was February but she packed nothing. Just tore into the woods in her jeans and t-shirt and kept running until she collapsed. She managed to crawl under a lean-to at the edge of a clearing and dozed off.

When she woke up, a snow storm was raging around her. It was one of those freaky weather things that happens in North Carolina every now and then.

She peeked out under lashes almost frozen shut and felt like she'd been punched in the face. Because all around her was a cruel landscape—white and forbidding in the blizzard, with the leafless trees in the distance glaring at her like henchmen.

She hadn't known cold weather could hurt so much. This was worse that any beating and increased in intensity. Her cheeks felt swollen and achy, her arms and legs, frostbitten. Every inch of her skin that was exposed burned. Inside her, everything felt frozen. Her muscles stopped working, her lungs had almost no air.

Raising her head a few inches, she saw the snow gale turning into a white vortex. It kept gusting and sculpted so much snow and ice around her that she looked like a white corpse. Worse was, during the night the lean-to had blown away, leaving only part of the roof as a shield for her head.

Man, this was awful bad. Honee knew she was lying at death's door. But feeble weak as she was, it would be easy. Just let herself drowse back to sleep and never wake up. That would take

254

care of her pains and her overwhelming thirst and hunger. Yep, all she had to do was lie still like a dead roach bug. Let the twirling flakes cover her even more until she completely disappeared in the winter landscape.

A second away from slipping off for good, her legs and arms spasmed. That caused her to kick and pummel the ground under her so hard she broke through to a hole. Suddenly she felt something warm lying under her. Had she punched down into a lair of some sort?

On its own, her arm moved. Her hand rooted around under her and brought up what it found: Just more snow.

She must be hallucinating because it was warm and fuzzy this bundle of snow. It felt like a small pillow. Nope, it was a small animal, maybe a sleeping rabbit. Barely breathing, she dragged it up to her face and laid it across her neck like a fur wrap. Felt its blessed warmth and the animal's slow heart beat.

Before long, the baby rabbit moved, not exactly waking up but scratching as it instinctively twitched to get away. That's all it took for Honee to emerge from dying. There was a thread of life in her yet and it asserted itself.

Without a conscious thought, she opened her mouth and bit into the fur ball as hard as she could. Shaking her head, she kept biting down until something warm spilled out, the rabbit's blood. It spurted over her face, yet she didn't relax her jaws, only bit harder and harder until the quivering animal lay still. Then she swallowed the chunk of raw meat in her mouth, pelt and all. Ripped off another chunk and ate it too and sucked up the blood.

With every chew, she felt the ice in her melting and her body creeping back to life. For a long time she gnawed on a rabbit's foot, disgusted with what she'd done but also gratified. She wanted to live so badly.

That was the coldest she'd ever been in her life.

255

Until now. Clenching her teeth and remembering how she barely survived back then, Honee felt like in a trance.

Qiana nudged her. "We did it, didn't we?"

"Oh Lord, girl." Slowly Honee swiveled her head back and forth as if she wanted to clear her mind of a horrible vision. She inched back, jerked around. The flashlight, tucked in her overalls' neckline, turned with her and allowed Qiana to see her friend's face. It looked thunder-struck but had a fierce determination written on it. As if she'd just had a terrible shock but wasn't deterred.

Dear God, what's down there?

"Move." Squeezing past Honee, Qiana pressed her face to the screen-like grate and took a look. The huge room below was set up like a high school science lab, with dozens of students milling around. Even more sat at numerous lab tables, but there were no bugs or butterflies being examined. No mice or rats running in mazes or frogs being dissected. The animals the teenagers worked on were the most magnificent specimens of lions, tigers and leopards. Strapped down, they had been cut open like pigs as their hearts were being replaced with mechanical ones that looked like the kids had constructed them.

More outrageous animal cruelty was going on in a corner. A boa constrictor was in the process of having big bird's wings grafted on. Next to it in a cage, an orangutan had suffered a quadruple amputation while nearby, a horse was getting a leg transplant from a zebra that was still alive and writhing in pain.

The view of all these brutal and bizarre experiments was nauseating. No wonder Honee was in shock. Qiana was shocked too as she moved farther along on the inside of the shaft. Then she felt like a boulder dropped out of the sky and landed on her. Gasping, she hugged herself, trying not to fall apart completely because there was another grate. And the view it offered was worse. It made even her eyeballs hurt, as if they too were offended by the horrible scene below.

Oh God! She felt like she was being tortured. It was the worst agony she could feel, reminding her of all the agony she suffered as a little girl.

She hadn't done anything wrong except run away from her Canadian orphanage where she'd been horribly mistreated. After that, she mingled with an American family with half a dozen kids and crossed the border into the US by riding on a bus and ending up in Chicago.

After that she almost starved to death until a salesman bought her some food, but he turned out to be a pedophile. Before long and with his sadistic wife urging him on, he brought in some other sleazy guy he met in a bar and bragged to about having a little girl as toy. The other fellow wanted to see the toy and soon little Qiana got sold like a slab of beef.

In the end the men discussed profit sharing like she was a business venture. They turned her into a 12-year-old sex slave. Strange men in and out at all hours. When she went on a hunger strike, they forced oily meals down her throat. When she vomited the greasy food, the wife stuck a tube down her throat like she was a goose being fattened up and poured milk shakes down, making her balloon up. When Qiana complained of the pain, the woman poured whiskey down her throat. Did so every time she gave a peep. That's what made Qiana a teenage alcoholic.

She still had trouble with liquor even though she vowed to stop drinking. However right now she could've killed for a sip—to take the edge off this horrible new view she could see through the second screen. Down there was another science lab, this one for middle schoolers.

Oh, so many animal cages stacked on top of one another, but not a sound from them. Qiana felt goose bumps break out all over. There were only the lingering echoes of incredible pain and unspeakable cruelty. The high-ceilinged room below was bathed in bright lights, illuminating the packed shelves that surrounded a swimming pool sunk into the middle of the room. The tiles lining both its inside and outside looked ancient but well kept as if they belonged to the Biltmore Estate indoor pool.

But they were dirt-streaked, with the water drained and in its place crowded a dozen kids in rags, like puppies in a tank. And the stacked-up cages held kids as well, all trapped like lab critters.

No flat boxes here, but Qiana knew exactly how these kids felt in their cages. She gritted her teeth, she was seething. *Let them out!* she screamed silently. *Let me out!* Most likely those poor kids would never be all right. Just look at her, the neurotic mess she still was even after all these years. Just physically, some of these kids would never ever be all right either because they had been blinded. *Is that where those eyeballs are from?*

Continuing to watch the horrific scene below, Qiana shook from outrage. She felt so sorry for these victims. Most of them seemed comatose, either from starvation or from being tranquilized. In contrast, the newly caught specimens still had a lot of life in them. But any kid trying to jump out of the pool was kicked back down by the pre-teen boys and girls in red polos that solemnly stood guard.

Bile erupted in Qiana's throat and threatened to choke her. She hit her head against the screen. *No. No.* Her tears came in a tsunami, burning her face like a caustic fluid. Her eyes kept protesting and her mind also refused to accept this science lab of evil.

What a horrible nightmare. Obviously the red polo-ed kids were members of the Lower School Science Club—cute and smart and from mostly white middle class homes. In contrast, the caged specimens were mostly Hispanic and African-American. But clearly they were all trash kids or kids just too smart to get sucked

258

into that American Ideal contest. Or maybe just curious kids who managed to unmask the perpetrators.

Qiana's mind was spinning like crazy. *How could something this horrific happen in this country? Why didn't anyone notice what was going on?*

Maybe the presence of the wild animals could be explained by the high school kids' pretending to volunteer in the Spa's wild life areas, then squirreling a few of them down here. But what about all these captured kids?

Why no Amber Alerts? Why wasn't the whole country in an uproar over that many missing youngsters?

Because most, if not all, were ghost students that had never been added to the Stefford School rolls in the first place, she thought. Most likely these kids started out hanging around the streets in Durham, Burlington, or Raleigh, North Carolina. In New York City, Los Angeles or Detroit, neglected kids were called throwaways. Here in the South they were just kids nobody gave a damn about until Ricky lured them to Stefford School with the promise of a shiny future. Then they were spirited down here and used as human guinea pigs by their classmates who were so crazy and grade greedy, they didn't care how they got straight A plusses in science.

And this horrible school encouraged it.

Qiana felt her heartbeat become irregular. She must be close to going into cardiac arrest. How she wanted to scream until her vocal chords ruptured. Instead, she plunged into a catatonic silence, for there were even more shocking things.

At the end of the indoor pool were several long tables set up where the subjects of the latest experiments were hooked up to all sorts of instruments. Even more shocking, directly below her, about twenty-five feet down the wall; a modern operating theater gleamed with chrome fixtures and high-tech equipment. Computer screens winked the latest in machinery emitted chirps like birds

259

and IV lines dangled from roller stands like athletic socks on a clothes line. It looked like a modern healing station, in the midst of which two men, with half a dozen young kids milling around, were scrubbing up and preparing for surgery.

Qiana blinked rapidly, hoping to make this scene vanish. But it remained exactly what it was—a small operating theater.

The person to be operated on was a pretty girl that looked like a doll, about 100 lbs., 5'1" or 5'2". She wore nothing but a bra and panties and had odd black Magic Marker lines drawn on her. Having received local anesthesia only, she didn't appear to be totally out of it and bucked against her restraints that made it clear she was about to have an invasive procedure performed against her will.

"Let me out of here," she cried, looked around and recognized someone. "Angelo!"

Qiana couldn't stand to watch and turned away. *It's too much.* Her vision blurring, she slumped into herself. That poor girl down there reminded her of herself. Of course, she was several years younger when it happened to her, but still, what was this?

A twisted replay of Qiana's pitiful life?

Staged by whom? And why?

Wasn't it enough to have lived through it once?

Pulling herself together a little, she pressed her face against the screen again and looked back down. By that time Honee appeared by her side. "Logan?" she whispered, giving a throaty sound and breathing shallow, like she was on top of Mount McKinley and couldn't get enough oxygen into her lungs. Then she was sure. "Logan!"

"Ms. Money! Ms. Money! Ms. Money!"

Had the girl noticed the substitute teacher's face behind the screen high up on the wall, or was she hallucinating? Qiana couldn't tell but was glad Logan was clinging to Honee's name like a life-saving rope. What a relief, the search was over, Logan had been found. Now they just had to get her out of there and stop all those atrocities.

But how?

While she was wracking her brain, she saw a man bending over the girl. "Shut up or we'll gag you again. Lock you in a cage."

"Why?" Logan cried.

"Don't you know? You've got a juicy embryo in the oven. Which the kids want to harvest and implant in a monkey before you get punished for high treason."

"Why? I didn't do anything."

"You blabbed to the new substitute. The other kids saw you."

"No, I didn't. Josh! HELP—" Logan let out a blood-curdling scream that cut off when the second man slapped a piece of tape over her mouth. He sat on a stool and rolled it between the girl's legs that were strapped to stirrups. Both men were middle-aged and had odd-shaped bald spots. Ricky's brothers, and both healthy as could be.

But it was the girl that held the two women's attention the most. How heart-breaking to see her eyes so frantic and staring at the ceiling with every fiber of her being. Honee couldn't imagine what awful things might be going through the little chick's mind. Surely she knew the men weren't going let her go after this. With the middle school kids guiding their arms, they had begun sticking an instrument between her legs, invading her cruelly.

Qiana thought she knew what was going through Logan's mind. Horrible images she couldn't keep at bay flooded her. She scurried back a few feet and threw up, tasting scum water mixed with coffee and bile. Seeing the cages was bad enough but seeing the poor girl reminded her of her own abortions—all seven of them. As a teenager, she'd been forced into having them in a back alley.

Actually it was six. First time Qiana got pregnant she was only 12 and a half. Didn't even know it, only that she was gaining

261

weight, which meant nothing. The salesman's wife force-fed her all the time. But one day when she'd gotten real fat, she—

Can't think about that now. Qiana flung off the strings of spit dangling from her lips and looked back down at Logan. Poor thing, her face was wet with tears, her ponytail undone, her hair in curls from all the humidity down there. And oh, those dark blue eyes that telegraphed she was in such agony and pleading for help.

To Qiana it seemed as if she was looking at herself years ago. Remembering how much she'd suffered during all those primitive abortions, performed by a gum-chewing nurse's aide wielding a melon scooper, she thought she'd pass out. Then she felt her heart jump but not in a death spasm, but in a leap of joy. Yes! That girl down there held the key to Qiana's future. She had to live if Qiana was to ever find an ounce of peace. Maybe by saving Logan, Qiana could pay her debt to society.

God, when you save a life, does it make up for taking one?

Qiana knew she had to try. But she also knew if she or Honee gave the slightest sign of their whereabouts, the science club kids would chase them again, this time the older and the younger ones. They'd catch the substitutes, drag them down to the labs and perform similar insane experiments on them. She felt enraged over the prospect and yet as powerless as a broken electric line.

What to do?

Close by, Honee felt equally powerless. An overwhelming rage boiled up in her and swept her back in time.

One day Honee was waiting outside the tin trailer where Momma entertained one of her many "boyfriends," as she did every day. Didn't even know their names, Momma never did, and always was ugly hateful before they showed. And even more ugly hateful after the Johns scrammed. Socking Honee Trash with her fist was her favorite way to let off steam. Punch-punch.

"Know what?" Momma used to say. *"One good thing about your dirty hide is I can beat you much as I want and leave no marks."*

Wrong, Momma. Marks had been left, plenty marks, big and deep ones. They were etched on Honee's mind and heart and soul, even if nobody ever got to see them. Nobody had ever erased them although Qiana was trying. Of course, she didn't know *everything.* Didn't know what Honee had done to Momma in retaliazation. Let's face it; Honee wasn't that nice light-skinned black woman. She was a fraud and evil, sly, revengerful.

One example: Right before the trailer fire, Momma called her three times, each time more urgent. And each time she left a desperate message, but Honee stopped listening after the first few words. Sure wasn't gonna visit Momma until she was good and ready. Momma made her trash. So Honee was gonna prove to Momma she wasn't, but only on her own terms. Wasn't ever gonna jump and come running again when Momma whistled.

But what if Momma called because she was plum desperate? What if she was being threatened by some real maggots? What if she knew she'd be killed and was begging for Honee to rescue her?

Momma suffered from agoraphobia. Meant she was scared to leave the trailer. She had everything delivered, from groceries to dry-cleaning. Only Honee could ever get her out of that place and that was by blind-folding her and leading her by the hand. Once Momma was in the mall, she was fine. Just couldn't handle being out in the open.

So Honee knew Momma couldn't leave the trailer without her daughter's help. Yet Honee did *nothing*. Just turned a cold shoulder and laughed. Tee-hee. Yep, she ignored Momma's desperate pleas to hell and back.

As a result Momma burned to death. Which meant Honee caused her Momma's death, not by some act but by failing to act, just like that slime ball Ricky. He wasn't down there in those

263

insane science labs, personally turning the kids into disgusting sadists and horrendous criminals, but he knew what was going on.

Lord, when you save a life, does it make up for taking one?

But no matter what, she'd try her best to save Logan and the rest of those poor kids down there, including the poor animals. Throwing caution to the wind, she raised her fist to pound on the screen and yell. Never mind she'd put herself and Qiana in danger. At that moment a door opened below. A new specimen was being dragged into the science labs, kicking and screaming—a tall and muscular boy in shorts. He looked stunned but kept lashing out. His much smaller captors had their hands full wrestling him to the holding tank, at which point he looked around. "LOGAN."

A storm of punches silenced him and sent him sprawling to the tiles. A water hose washed him into the pool. He landed on top of some kids with open wounds, all of them screaming now.

Watching this horrible scene, Honee changed her mind. Yelling and pounding on the screen wasn't going to work—too dangerous. First she had to think but couldn't, seething with anger and frustration as she was. But physically she was coiled for action. Didn't she always take justice into her own hands even back when Tank terrorized her?

The day of the melting bag of ice, Honee decided to end Tank's reign of terror. There was only one way—kill him dead. As she wondered what to use for a weapon, she laid the willow switches Momma had broken on her on the ground, like she was about to make a broom. Even though she hurt bad from the beating, she tied the switches in the middle with a piece of string and added some sticks at the top.

Now the bundle looked like a person, a female. She found some old Q-tips, dipped them in mud, bent them and glued them on to make them look like eyes, lips, a nose. Look world, here's my big "sister." *Don't got one, so I made myself one.*

264

Later that day after football practice when the boys were strutting home, Tank trailing and as always on the look-out for a little kid to torment, Honee hid behind a fence, out for revengerence. When Tank bounced along feeling on top of the world, she shoved the broom through the pickets and directly in his way. Startled, he got his feet tangled up and smacked to the sidewalk where a piece of stone cracked his kneecap. Besides becoming the laughingstock of his teammates, he suffered permanent damage and walked with a limp from then on. Goodbye, sports. That was worse than killing him.

From then on, Honee was nick-named Q-tip, *which she took as a compliment.*

Honee Q-tip Money. Even better, Honee Q Money.

Let the word go out: Don't mess with me and my sister!

Before she could spring into action now, Honee first had to hold up Qiana who seemed gripped by a dizzy spell. It was from seeing Logan in such agony, overlaid by seeing herself years ago in a similar situation and not being able to do anything about it. Even worse was—

Her vision dimmed to black, but not before she took in the portrait hanging on the opposite wall of the Stefford Science Labs. It showed a woman in a gold brocade gown and mink stole. Dripping with diamonds, she looked like an empress from a royal house—the old Granville clan.

The picture jolted Qiana out of her dizziness while her mind zigzagged like a bumper car: *Logan's alive and I was wrong. The nuns were good people, just very too short on help, and careless and naive.* They really should've kept an eye on the gardener. She always hated them for the way she was treated as a child in Canada, but all nuns couldn't be blamed for that.

No time for all that pondering. Qiana had to save that girl down there. She wrested herself free from Honee's arms, u-turned and scooted back down the air-conditioning shaft like an animal in

265

flight. When she got to the hole in the shaft, she lowered herself into the underground labyrinth.

"Slow down, girl." Breathless, Honee catapulted after Qiana. "You don't know where you going."

"Know exactly where I'm going. I'm going to get justice for Logan and all those other poor kids, those animals. Those criminals have got to be stopped—now."

"But you might take the wrong—"

"No, marked every damn corner with an X. Wasn't too out of it for that."

In seconds, the two women helter-skeltered back to the first fork in the tunnel. This time they headed in the opposite direction, toward the school. Before long and heaving from exertion, they thought they were close when they stumbled over a log. With the light from the flashlight they saw what it was—a body. Oh no, old Henry, poor guy.

Someone had killed him and stuffed him into the tunnel. From the way he looked, he had put up quite a fight. Saddened by his violent ending, Honee tried to think of something to say, a prayer, something... the 23rd Psalm: "The Lord is my shepherd. I shall not want..."

The two young women heaved the body out of the way and moved on until they found themselves up against a wooden barrier. The kids or whoever was behind all these horrible things had closed off the exit in the basement wall of the construction wing. But this didn't stop the two women.

Using her iron rod, Honee channeled her anger into prying the plywood loose. She squeezed through the gap, flew up a ladder and was gone. But when Qiana tried to do the same thing, a muscled arm shot out of nowhere, clamped around her waist like a forceps, and yanked off into the semi-darkness.

"Gal, you're even prettier than that picture," a man who looked like a member of the construction crew hissed.

266

"You stole it? Give it back—right now."

"I didn't keep it, just took a look and sent it on," he said as he wrestled with her overalls that gave under his impatient tugging. "Now don't make a peep. Or the rest of the guys will want in on the action. Know what I mean?"

Qiana could envision what would happen. She'd get raped and killed, while Honee had no idea. Overwhelming sadness doused her. She felt so sorry for herself and even more so for her parents. *They just found me only to lose me again.* Even worse, they only saw what she had turned into which was the worst a woman can become. *They never saw the real me, the good me with my life all turned around.* They were cheated, horribly punished and tortured over and over. Surely they'd blame themselves for the rest of their lives, maybe even consider killing themselves.

And Honee? Qiana's death would most likely plunge her back into a life on the streets. And Gunner? He'd be completely destroyed too—

Wait a minute. While her mind was overcome by deep sadness, Qiana's body and soul weren't conceding anything yet. Her heart slammed against her ribcage, her muscles tensed, making her feel like she was a spring ready to uncoil. She exploded into a fighting mode, dug her heels into the tunnel floor and lashed out with every last ounce of her strength. She raked her nails down the man's stubble cheeks, punched and kicked him wherever she could.

But no good.

The man was so much stronger and bigger. And so brutal and impervious to pain.

He didn't flinch at the bloody ruts Qiana gouged in his face. He snapped one big hand around her neck like a dog collar and squeezed and clamped the other one over her face like a hockey mask, reminding her of the chicken wire that had been fastened over the confinement box in which she was so often imprisoned as a child.

The orphanage had three buildings, the first one for the good kids, the second one for the handicapped ones. And a third one, a small garden shed far back in the yard, was used for the incorrigible and schizophrenic kids. It had regular cots and a table and chairs, and meals were delivered daily. But because of the severe shortage of nuns, the gardener was in charge back there. He was a horrible man with grotesquely broken teeth and his own system of dealing with the brats as he called them.

Now with the spread-out fingers the brutal man pressed over her face, Qiana was shocked back into the present, the section of the tunnel in which the construction worker held her trapped. Her temporarily restricted vision reminded her of how many women and girls in other parts of the world had to live every day. Wearing burquas, they could look at their surroundings only through slits. Most likely it gave them the impression that they were someone's property, like horses that had blinders on and couldn't see everything. Just like that, people who had someone restrict their vision were never free to see the whole world. They were enslaved.

At this moment, Qiana felt just like that. Deprived of her freedom, restrained and half-blind, she was at this man's mercy and hated it with every fiber of her being. She had already suffered so many years of injustice. All that abuse, all those degrading things she had experienced later, all those beatings—

No more. She wrenched the big fingers off her face and fought back like an insane woman until the man flashed a knife. "Be a good gal or else."

Still she didn't stop. She kept lashing out at him even harder until he stuck the tip of the blade under her chin and applied pressure. She felt a sharp sting, then the pain of a deeper cut. And then—

Smack! Noticing Qiana wasn't behind her, Honee had plunged back down the ladder and saw what was going on. She gave an animal scream, swung her leg with the water-logged Adidas like a pendulum and whacked Qiana's attacker in the head so hard he tottered before dropping like a pole.

"Whew, Honee." Qiana breathed out, back to the living. She'd break down later. Sob her heart out but not now, too much to do. She wiped the dripping blood off her chin. Then the two young women tied up the guy—arms and legs—with his belt and Henry's. Stuffed a sock in his mouth. Expelling grunts, they heaved him next to the dead security guard in the tunnel that they quickly hammered shut again.

Finally back on the ladder. They scrambled like ferrets up to the next level and found themselves in a wing of the school they hadn't seen before. A sunny hallway beckoned with a wonderful pine scent. Sucking the fresh aroma into their lungs, they raced down the hall and took in the cheerful atmosphere.

This part of the school seemed meant for little kids. Everything was brand-new but scaled down. A sign said: Stefford Kindergarten and Elementary School.

Thank goodness, this is a normal learning environment, Qiana thought. There wasn't a hint of anything amiss, not one trace of anything horrible. All the classrooms were neatly set up but empty. Obviously the children and teachers were on the playground for recess. Of course, on rainy days they could have fun inside. There were large flat-screen TV's to watch *Sesame Street* or a SpongeBob movie. Next to them, stackable boxes burst with the latest toys. There was also a mini gym, a puppet studio, an art room with small easels. Oh, anything a child could ever want.

After the horrific events in the Spa's basement and the tunnels, Qiana and Honee couldn't believe what a wonderful change this was. Everything looked so cheerful, even the kids' projects that made it clear they'd been crafted by happy little hands. Dozens of smiling dolls, cute purses, pretty hand-tooled belts and place mats were on display. Also woven baskets, pot holders, book marks, paper dolls, and lots of finger-paintings. And each little item was shown off with pride, even the clumsiest attempts from little kids who'd never be artists or craftsmen.

For a few seconds, the two women paused, hoping and praying this cheerful atmosphere would chase away some of the horrific images.

Honee breathed out audibly. "Leastways the little kids're all right. Man, I was scared out of my mind the whole school was wrecked."

"Yes, thank goodness, at least one segment of Stefford School hasn't gone completely insane," Qiana said, rushed and tense.

Already the two young women were moving again. So far, no sign of any little kids, but they couldn't be far away. In the miniature kitchen, snacks were waiting on trays and it was obvious the children had prepared them. A lot of sandwich triangles were lopsided, but all looked appetizing. Nearby a sink was filled with small plates and pots and pans. That meant the youngest Stefford kids ate here and had no interaction with the crazy older kids at all.

Thank God. The evil hadn't touched them and never would because Qiana and Honee would stop it shortly.

Grateful for at least that much normalcy, the two young women tore through classroom room after classroom room, looking for a phone when they heard it. *Rat-a-tat!* The little kids were assembled in a small arena, wearing miniature black robes and carrying miniature band instruments on which they played a wobbly tune sounding like a dirge. Too bad there wasn't an adult around. The teachers must've slipped out to get a latte or chai tea from the main cafeteria. In the interim the little kids were playing dress-up.

But any second the teachers would be back and the two women could enlist their help which was crucial. Every passing second more horrible things could happen in the science labs. Logan could get hurt worse, more kids could get maimed and—

"Hey there, ladies!"

One of the little boys greeted them and waved and Honee and Qiana waved back. That made a little girl carrying a teddy bear high-step over. She was so small the stuffed animal towered over her.

"What you all been doing?" she asked. "You look so...messy."

"Sorry about that. We..." But Honee wasn't about to tell the children what horrific crimes they had uncovered at the Spa.

"...worked in the garden," Qiana filled in quickly.

"Oh, were you doing sci-en—" Teddy-bear girl, about five years old, could hardly get the word out "—ti-fic work?" A few more well-scrubbed children ran over, eyes wide. "Like the big kids get to do?" Their practice session forgotten, they marched toward them.

"Yes," Qiana said. "Where's a phone?"

"In the teachers' lounge. Want to see our new puppy? It's on the way. C'mon." Teddy-bear girl grabbed Honee's hand and led her down the hall, with the other little kids following. Some of them stumbled but picked themselves up as they entered the academic part of the elementary school. Posters with spelling words smiled at them and flashcards with numerical equations, chemical symbols, and phrases in Spanish, French, Italian and Chinese danced from mobiles overhead.

Wow. Honee wished she could examine everything but not now. Every second counted. Man, was it frustrating to be slowed down by these babies.

Her little guide stopped at a glassed-in porch. "There he is." She pointed to a gray fur ball hiding behind a doghouse. "Can we go in and pet Puppy?"

"No, sorry." Qiana was tense with urgency. "We're in a big hurry."

The children looked crushed. A few of them seemed to pick up on her on-edge feeling and clustered around. "I need a hug, I'm scared, I want to go home," the smallest one whimpered, on the verge of crying, and raised her hands.

"Me too. Me too."

Quickly she hugged as many little kids as she could, inhaling their powder and baby shampoo smells. Tears shot into her eyes because this was such an innocent aroma and so different from what she'd seen in the science labs from hell.

Honee hugged a bunch of little children too, not realizing what they were doing—wrapping the two women with nylon twine. Standing on tiptoes, they passed the spools round and round, starting with the women's ankles and ending up with their arms and shoulders. Then they shoved them into the porch that was decked out with all sorts of high-tech equipment.

"What's going on?" Qiana asked in shock, finding herself tied up in a bundle just like Honee. A kick by several cute little boys, and both women were sprawling on the stone floor.

CHAPTER 34

In the blink of an eye, they were anchored to metal hooks sticking out of the floor. More hooks studded the ceiling.

"What're you doing?" Qiana screamed while Honee was trying to wrestle herself free from the hundreds of threads—to no avail.

Teddy bear girl lit a cigarette and started smoking. "This is *our* sci-en-ti-fic work, ladies. We're re-search-ing Puppy's in-stinct-u-al re-ac-tion, before, you know, we have to— But don't worry, the camera's going to record—"

A piercing bell. "Sorry, got to go. Our science teacher's got a new lesson for us." The little girl put out her cigarette and turned on a CD player, emitting a voice that sounded familiar.

"Lord, who's your science teacher?"

"Ian."

"But isn't he a student?" Qiana asked. "How can he—?"

"He just tapes our lessons and forwards them, you know. We turn on the TV and do what he tells us. It's real easy except for the yucky stuff we have to do at the end. That's kinda tough. But we always get A-plus and gold stars. See you later." The kids clapped and marched off in formation. One little boy with orange streaks in his brown hair ran back and patted Qiana's chest: "Nice tits, ma'am. Too bad." Then he was gone too.

For a few seconds, the two young women lay on the cold floor utterly shocked. They were unable to get up, unable to move any part of their body except the head. What was going on?

Qiana broke the silence. "Come back here, kids," she yelled, feeling anger and frustration burn in every cell of her body. "We don't have time to—"

"Girl, I think that's a wolf."

"What're you talking about?" Qiana asked, straining against the nylon twines but no good. The harder she tried to rip them apart, the deeper they cut into her skin. With a scream she collapsed, her stomach spewing acid into her throat, her head pounding like it would explode. That's what the gray animal seemed to have been waiting for. Slinking over, it sniffed at her legs and licked her skin.

Noticing the thick coat and the head with the blue eyes and sharp teeth, Qiana shuddered. Screaming for help was useless. The kids were long gone, and that CD was playing so loud it would drown out even the loudest yells. And there was no way out of the nylon ropes. So playing dead was her only option.

Awful, but they'd just have to wait until the little kids came back and released them. There was still no sign of any adults. Obviously the little kids ran the Elementary School by themselves. And without proper supervision, they had latched on to this crazy "science project," or whatever it was. Qiana didn't know what to do except to close her eyes and hold as still as possible, so the wolf would leave her alone.

As she did, she remembered. This wasn't the first time she was painfully, cruelly, mercilessly tied up.

274

One day during the early days of her captivity at the Kozee Inn, the salesman passed out drunk and she sneaked out of the room. From first-hand experience she knew how unhelpful the house-wives were in Chicago. And running down the busy road like an out-of-control Toyota would only get her picked up again, most likely by another Satan.

She ducked into the office that was decked out in a cheerful western theme with cactuses and blue and white gingham curtains. Cowboy hats graced the walls, a saddle perched on a rocking chair, and an old lasso coiled around a lamp. A young woman, wearing a tassel shirt and jeans, was obsessively dusting the clean counter with the fake cactuses. "Yes?"

"Please help me," Qiana said, waiting for the motel clerk to turn around, then was shocked. Even though the clerk wasn't much older than Qiana, she had skin that was large-pored and speckled as if polka-dotted with a black magic marker. It wasn't blackheads. It was flat moles that looked like dug-in ticks.

Qiana felt sorry for the girl who looked embarrassed as if she'd been caught in the middle of a crime: Not wearing make-up.

But no time to worry about that. Qiana needed to get away—right this minute, before the evil man woke up. Tears swam in her eyes, infringing on her vision. "Call the police! I've been kidnapped and hurt bad and—"

Polka-dots pointed her dust rag at the window. "There's a cop right there."

Qiana looked out the window. "In the room next to mine? No, that can't be..."

"Sorry," Polka-dots said. "Just about every room's rented out and most of them younger than you."

"WHAT?" Qiana was crest-fallen. "There's other little girls...?"

"And boys."

"But how can you stand it, working here?"

"Gotta eat, right? Can only go so many days without—"

"I know, that's what got me here," Qiana whimpered, her stomach knotting. Cold sweat ran down her face, mixing with her tears. No more feeling sorry for the clerk. Her ugly skin probably saved her from what Qiana was forced to do. Which would go on forever if she didn't get away—now. Every second counted.

"But there's gotta be a way out. PLEASE!" She hung her head, breaking down into wrenching sobs. If this girl didn't help her, she was doomed.

Cowboy boots came strutting in her direction, so Polka-dots had a heart. She put her arms around Qiana. "Hush up, you pretty little thing. I'm gonna help you, okay? Get you a cab to the train station, then turn them all in. Your guy first. He's the most evil—"

Hope infusing her, mixed with a bitter joy—revenge was coming!—Qiana rubbed her face dry. "What's gonna happen to him?"

"Bastard's going to prison. He's a dead man."

"Good, I want him to get the death penalty."

Polka-dots patted Qiana on the back. "One day I heard him talking. Believe me, imprisonment would be much worse for him than death. Me, I feel the same way. Being locked away is the worst punishment you can get. It stretches the punishment out. You die ten million times, not just once. Just shoot me, I say. How much money you got?"

"Money?"

"Yeah, running away ain't free. Cab fare, train ticket to the Carolinas. That's where I'd disappear to. Change my looks completely and blend in nice and easy, you know? Ever notice how many real bad crooks end up in that state? They're pretty lax down there. Halfway between New York and Miami, it's the perfect hideout. Oh yeah, you can fade away into the countryside there, sure you can... Well, anyway, pretty little girl like you? You'll raise that cash quicker than a wink."

276

"H-h-how m-m-much?"

Hearing "five hundred dollars," Qiana felt like she'd received a death blow. In agony she slunk back to her room. The Devil was still snoring. Good. She picked through his pockets. He wouldn't notice if she peeled a few bills off his wad. Every day a few more was her plan but it took so long. So when he was drunk again, she hung around outside her door, hoping to entice some other sleazebag into asking her to his room, then she'd filch a few dollars from him.

Afterwards she always threw up, but her stack of cash grew. Took a lot longer than she anticipated, but one day she burst into the office: "Got it."

Polka-dots smiled and tucked the money into her boots. "Told you, didn't I, you pretty little thing? I'm so proud of you. You didn't let on, did you?"

"Sure didn't." Qiana was hopping up and down, euphoric. Today was the day she was going to escape. Freedom. *No more abuse and pain. "Hurry, hurry! How long's it take for a cab?"*

Polka-dots was already dialing: "Just a few minutes."

Seconds later, the door burst open and the Devil stormed in. "Thanks for the tip, honey," he flung at Polka-dots, grabbed Qiana and slapped her. "Ungrateful little bitch. Wait till I get you back in the room."

Shocked, Qiana wrenched away from him. She felt crushed over the betrayal and was angry enough to scream until her vocal chords snapped. Later. *First she had to wrest herself free. She did and ran faster than she thought possible. Was almost out on the street when a noose came flying in her direction. Polka dots lassoed her in, yanked her back to the Kozee Inn, and with a big smile handed her over to the Devil. Qiana screamed again and bit and fought like crazy to escape. Next thing, blackness.*

When she came to, she had a big bump on her head which throbbed. She was trussed up in the rope, her hands knotted behind her back, her feet tied similarly. From the many bruises, abrasions, contusions and from the pain she knew the man had beaten the crap out of her. Probably would every day from now on. Amazing she was still alive.

She huddled suffering in a corner in the motel room, wishing she'd die because besides being brutally roped into a package, the end of the dirty rope was looped over a beam in the ceiling and around her neck. If she lowered her head more than an inch, her arms were jerked almost out of her shoulders. If she dropped her arms, she got choked.

If I could only cut that rope.

But she didn't have anything sharp. So no way out, not even room enough to move so she could get a little more comfortable. But sooner or later he had to let her use the bathroom. When he did, she broke a water glass.

"Damn you, clumsy idiot." He back-handed her before tying her up again. "Don't even think you're gonna cut me." He forced her fists open, poked and prodded and examined her everywhere until he was satisfied she hadn't kept back a shard. "Just look at the mess you made." She was bleeding from the many cuts the splintering glass made.

When he fell on the bed, exhausted from beating her almost to death again, she contorted herself. Whimpering from the horrible pain, she inched her foot up to her mouth. Bit off the scabs beginning to form between her toes and dug out the glass sliver she'd buried there. Holding it between her teeth, she started sawing at the rope. It was a slow process, a laborious process during which she cut her mouth and tongue. Many times she gave up, but by morning she was free and limped out of the room.

And then—

A guttural scream from Honee brought Qiana back to where she was: the wolf's lair in the Stefford Elementary School where the children had staked them out as bait. The wolf must've decided

278

Qiana was dead and turned its attention to Honee. It sniffed her up and down, taking its time. Suddenly it ripped a piece of skin off her calf, about the size of a fingertip.

That's why Honee screamed. The pain was incredible. It felt as if a muscle had been ripped out of her leg. She screamed again, gnashed her teeth and made more loud sounds. Sounding like howls, the noises distracted the wolf cub away from her leg. It leapt up to Honee's face, maybe deciding her unprotected neck was a better target. Sensing what was coming, Honee quaked in fear. She smelled the feral odor, heard the excited panting and saw the blood-streaked animal head. *Oh no, that's my blood but that won't be the end of it.* The wolf's razor-sharp teeth would plunge down shortly and rip out her throat. Oh Lord, what could she do to save herself?

Nothing.

Narrowing its eyes, the wolf bared its fangs, ready to attack Honee again and this time seriously and deadly. She reacted a split second before the sharp teeth sank into her. Rearing up as much as she could, she bit into the throat of the wolf. Bit down as hard as she could, making her teeth shred the matted fur. She bit deeper and deeper still while clenching her jaws. Clenching them hard until blood flowed—this time the wolf cub's blood.

She heard a deep-throated barking from the animal and similar sounds issue from herself but didn't let up. She chomped down until she thought her jaw bones would crack while above her, the animal thrashed and scratched at the air. It jerked in tremors on and on until it was twitching in death throes.

Just when Honee thought she'd drown in the profusion of wolf blood, the cub gave a last spasm, then no more. Honee fell back, feeling dead herself.

Finally Qiana managed to look over and had a revulsive reaction. What a horrible sight: Honee looking like a corpse, blood bathing her face and neck, the wolf lying on top of her.

"Honee," she screeched so loud her vocal chords burned. She bucked and fought against her nylon restraints. "Honee! Honee!"

"Shut up, girl." Honee's voice was hoarse. "The wolf's dead."

"Gee. I can't imagine doing what you just did, biting that— tasting that—" Qiana said, shivering, her mind wandering again. "But you know what? It just dawned on me. That wasn't any dirt on that big lasso, that rope, that was blood. That disgusting evil bitch!" She felt long-repressed anger and hate roiling through her, along with a horrible realization.

"Never knew it but seeing you with all that blood, Honee... Other kids bled on that rope, you know, lots of them. Oh yeah, she was the gatekeeper of hell."

"Who you talking about, girl?"

"Somebody from eons ago. Never could get my revenge on her and that's the biggest regret I have. Hurts like hell every time I think about her. But nothing I can do about it now. The main thing is you're okay. So let's get out of here. Rescue Logan, all those other kids, those poor animals."

Straining with every muscle, Qiana inched her fingers over to the dead wolf that draped Honee's chest. She managed to grab the tail of the animal and yanked until it was close. The fangs really were razor sharp. She rubbed the nylon strings binding her arms against them until first one strand, then another snapped and kept at it until she had freed herself. Then she liberated Honee.

Who had a violent vomit attack. It only stopped when Qiana filled a dog bowl with fresh water from a spigot and gave it to Honee who splashed it all over herself.

"Girl, that was horrible but didn't know what else to do. C'mon, let's turn the doghouse on its end."

"First I've got to bandage your leg." Ripping a piece of cloth off her overalls, Qiana wrapped it around Honee's calf that now wasn't bleeding much. Then helping each other, they managed to climb to the roof of the porch, where glass panes opened, wide enough to squeeze through. They jumped to the floor—but outside the patio.

"Wonder how much time we lost," Qiana said and flew through the empty classrooms. In passing, she snatched up some pretzel sticks in the snack area. Running back to the entrance of the elementary school, she sidetracked to an almost hidden room with a sign: The Executioners' Office.

CHAPTER 35

It was a large space in the middle of which rose a gallows. Next to it sat a table with blood-crusted medical instruments: a Stryker saw, scalpels, rib cutters, a hammer with a hook for lifting human tissue. On the floor that was slippery with blood lay a headless young woman who had been gutted and chopped into pieces, along some black Magic Marker lines. And on one side ran a row of pickets, one of which had the head of a pretty young female stuck on—

How horrible, how sickening, how ghastly. Qiana recoiled violently. She could hardly see the poster that screamed in big bold letters: *Remember the Stefford Code.*

Tattling is High Treason. The punishment is being hanged, drawn and quartered.

Qiana's mind was spinning dizzily. Obviously Ms. Hill had discovered the gruesome science labs and for that she'd been killed in a most horrific way. Poor teacher did so much good and this is how she ended up? It happened recently from the way the bloody stump of her neck looked. Strips of skin had also been peeled from the teacher's thighs and some of her fingers were missing. No telling what had happened to her organs.

There were signs this wasn't the first gruesome execution. In an alcove hunkered a walk-in freezer with a glass door that was blood-splattered. Qiana retched as she noticed several more corpses that had been chopped to pieces demarcated by Black Magic Marker lines. Rosario was probably among those victims.

Qiana felt her jaw dropping, her eyes beginning to roll back, her body becoming slack but Honee shook her hard and brought her back. "No time to faint, girl. Not now."

"Okay." Qiana's voice sounded dead but she impelled herself forward. *Logan, please hold on.* So back to the original ladder, the two women hurtled like exhausted track stars. All quiet so far— whew. They scrambled up to another floor. Finally back in one of the main corridors of the upper school, they looked down the hall.

Nobody around yet, thank goodness. All the older kids and teachers must still be outside, and the little ones were in their separate wing. What seemed like days must've taken less than an hour or two. Outraged and sick to their stomachs, the two women stumbled to the nearest classroom, lunged for the phone on the teacher's desk like it was home base. No dial tone.

"C'mon." Using whatever little bit of adrenaline she could muster, Qiana shot-gunned down the hall, Honee neck and neck with her. They ducked into the drama department, dived into a wardrobe closet and dug out some costumes.

"Gee, I stink," Qiana said. A spritz-spritz from an old Chanel No.5 bottle. With a groan, she slipped on some clogs. *I miss my Manolos.*

Qiana felt ashamed of that thought and hung her head. She was a mess. But now from the distance, the two young women could pass for teachers, which was important. Nobody could suspect they'd discovered the horrible secrets. So back out into the hallway with its polished floor and beautiful potted ferns making Stefford School so perfect—on the surface.

Underneath, it was worse than hell.

Fortunately the main building was still quiet, except for the workers' sledge-hammering in the distance. Sounds of plaster pieces falling, saws whirring and screws being drilled. Qiana hoped the men wouldn't miss their buddy for a while yet. If the two substitutes could only have a few more minutes alone before the bell—

Too late.

A boy strolled toward them from the office, a freshman, all preppy and hair cut just so. *Did he know anything about those horrors? Did he suspect anything?*

Acting as if on hall duty, Honee folded her arms and assumed an authoritarian stance. "Let's see your pass, young man."

The boy waved a freshly printed-out schedule like a diploma from Harvard. "Don't got one, ma'am. Counselor dude just enrolled me."

"You're one of the kids we saw in Guidance yesterday?"

"Yep, I mean, yes ma'am." The boy ran his hand around his belt to make sure his polo shirt was tucked in. "Remember you two hot teacher chicks."

"Beg your pardon, Jamar?" Shaking inside from tension, frustration and utter outrage over all those horrible goings-on, Honee speared the boy with a stern look. She was at the boiling point. All this insanity, this brutality, these senseless vicious murders. And right here in front of her was another ghost kid, just another piece of human garbage for that crook Ricky to funnel over to his crook brothers. Meanwhile nobody kept an eye on the little kids which allowed them to go totally crazy too.

So the two women had to get to a phone in secrecy right away, but how?

Eyes bugging out, Jamar sniffed the air. "Wha-what happen? You ladies was movie stars yesterday. Everybody was like, 'See those chickies yon?' And now—?"

"Jamar," Qiana cut him off, "we're new here just like you. So we have to pick up chewing gum, check for skippers and smokers. Do all the dirty work. But you're lucky. Every week a new student gets picked for a special assignment. And today that's you."

Feeling Honee's questioning look, she raced on, "You heard about everyone here making straight A's?"

"Yep, gonna try so hard. Make Obama proud."

"Well, let me help you." Grabbing his schedule, Qiana scribbled on it: *Give this student triple extra credit.* "Here you go. All you have to do is get us a phone."

"Like from the office, ma'am?"

"No, go out there," Qiana directed him to the rear campus, "and get Dr. Davis' cell. He's with the other kids behind the gym. Now let's see what you're made of."

"Okay, right back." Jamar fast-broke down the hall like on the basketball court, Qiana and Honee following at a distance. Minutes later, they peeked around the gym. To their relief, the clusters of students were still absorbed in their studies, with Jamar weaving between them like a motorcycle in traffic. When he found Ricky, he flashed his schedule with one hand while the other one snuck under the counselor's jacket. Then he came prancing back. "Anything else I can do for you slammin' chicks?"

***

"Just a matter of time now," Honee said. "Let's be nonwaverious."

"O-k-a-y." Qiana was trying her best to fidget less in their hiding place behind the gym. Earlier they had called the sheriff of Red Mill. Before she could finish telling him what hellish things she and Honee had discovered in the Jacks' hangout, the girls' club, the Spa basement, the tunnel, and the wing for the early

286

grades, he sprang into action. She could hear him dispatching several patrol cars even before she ended her call on Ricky's i-phone. The sheriff would also notify whoever was in charge in Stephen County, plus the SBI, maybe even the FBI.

After that, Honee connected with the press, the locals and the AP office in Raleigh. Squads of cop cars were now bleating toward Stefford School while more patrol vehicles and dozens of ambulances would speed to the Spa. And a platoon of reporters and TV crews would descend on both places shortly.

The most important job now was making sure none of the guilty people would escape. Ricky and his cohorts, his brothers included, and the kids should all be arrested. Well, quite a few students were probably innocent. But maybe they heard rumors about the outrageous goings-on and kept mum, which was bad too. As for the little kids, they probably didn't even understand what they did. They just followed the directions of the older kids, specifically Ian, who must think it was hilarious to have little kids re-enact the most gruesome medieval punishments and become cold-blooded executioners.

The workers were a different story. A few of them were definitely thugs of the first order but they wouldn't get far if they tried to run. Qiana had mentioned their involvement to the sheriff, plus the break-in and theft at the antique store. As a result, he immediately ordered road blocks set up to and from the school and the Spa, and promised to come by the Q Store later.

Thinking about all the things that had to be done, Qiana kept squirming like an anthill, her stomach rumbling. She dug out the pretzel stick, stuck it in her mouth. Something to chew on while waiting. The salty crust was delicious but the bread part was hard as a rock. "Honee, have you ever bitten into a piece of chocolate, expecting milk chocolate? Then found out it was meant for baking?"

When Honee stared at her uncomprehendingly, she went on, "Look, I almost broke a tooth. What is that?"

"Let's see." Honee scraped the outer layer of the bread stick until she held a little pale thing in her hand. It turned out to be a small bone, a human one.

"Oh God, no," Qiana choked out, spitting out everything in her mouth and whatever was left in her stomach. Then she kept retching and retching.

"You didn't know, okay?" Honee patted her on the shoulder. "But this is the absolute worst. They taught the little kids real killer lessons. Made cannibals out of them."

Qiana kept coughing and spitting, trying to get the horrible taste out of her mouth. She remembered Ms. Hill's mutilated body, her missing organs, her cut-up hands. "Oh no. All those crafts, those cute hand-made items? You think that wasn't any leather...? They... used... human... skin?"

"Who knows." Honee rubbed her forehead, not knowing what to say. It was all such a horrible nightmare, total insanity. While the faculty looked the other way, the oldest students abused the most magnificent animals. Then their cruelty spread, causing the middle schoolers to experiment on human beings. And to outdo the older kids, the little children resorted to outright executions and to devouring people.

Qiana was thinking along the same lines. How outrageous. While the country was preoccupied with terrorists, the economy and jobs-jobs-jobs, the schools were completely neglected. Of course she'd heard of failing schools before but this was the worst. Stefford School had been turned over to the criminals. They grabbed as much cash as they could while the upper-school kids developed no moral code except that of silence. And anyone who broke it faced the most horrible consequences. Not to be outdone, the younger kids heightened the immorality and the severity of criminal acts. And the youngest ones? They became so brutalized they thought nothing of becoming the executioners for the older kids. Then they used the body parts as crafts material or for food.

But how could something so incredibly deprave and insane go on in this elite private school that was supposed to set an example for other schools? Qiana didn't know how a horror of this magnitude could go unreported. The only explanation was that the Stefford Code had been perverted from "Act nobly" to "Don't tattle." The threat of punishment for being a whistle blower was so enormous that nobody, except for Rosario, Ms. Hill and a few students, dared open their mouths.

Qiana didn't have time to think through everything. She was still in such a state of shock. Yet strange as it sounded, there was some good news too. Finding Logan was a saving grace. "Sure hope some of those kids can be reprogrammed, especially the little—"

She stopped. In the distance, what she'd been feverishly hoping for.

At first the sound of the fleet of police cars was barely audible. None of the students and teachers seemed to hear anything unusual, but Ricky flinched like he'd been pricked with a straight pin. His eyes shifted around to see if anybody else had heard something. No one appeared to.

Reassured, he beamed back at the picturesque tableau: Fresh-faced kids studying for their exams, dedicated teachers monitoring their students. And right in the middle, Mrs. Taylor holding forth with dramatic gestures. She wore an elaborate Shakespearean costume.

As the police car noises grew, Ricky shot a panicked look at the trailer. Yet all was quiet over there and he had no reason to suspect Qiana and Honee had escaped. The approaching automobile noises grew louder. Still no sirens. Only the rumbling of many rolling tires as several black sedans zoomed past the buildings, with a dozen local and state police cars right behind.

The first car, a stuffed crocodile dangling from its rearview mirror, was chauffeured by Coach, with Dr. Reinholt sitting ramrod straight in the passenger seat. Before the car stopped, he jumped out. Using a megaphone, as numerous cops unfolded themselves from their Crown Victorias and formed a phalanx, he shouted:

"Attention, all students. Report to the auditorium. Roll will be taken. Anyone who doesn't show up will lose all their points."

"What about our exams?" Dressed in a sexy toga like a cheerleader in ancient Rome might've been—as portrayed in a Hollywood movie—Gibson back-flipped over to Dr. Reinholt. "Ave Stefford.,yay Julius Caesar, right?"

"Later, young lady. At the moment we have more serious—"

"What's more serious than exams?"

"I stayed up all night studying."

"There's the alkali metals, earth metals, transitional metals, nonmetals and all the *noble* gases. Helium, neon, argon, krypton, xenon, radon. But why aren't they called Duke or Earl like that old Earl of Granville?"

"Anyone want to know the 47 differences between the *glaucomys sabrinus coloratus* and the *macropus giganteus tasmaniense*?" a boy asked as more students spoke up: "Don't cancel our exams. We're whizzes on quizzes. Tests are the best."

"Quiet!" Ricky yelled. Grumbling, the kids calmed down and lined up, but Ricky didn't calm down. "What's going on, Dr. R.? We have five more min—"

"No, time's up, especially for you." Mopping his face with a crocodile-print handkerchief, the headmaster closed in on the counselor. "Stop. Right. There."

Watching this confrontation, Honee felt some better. Clearly the headmaster wasn't involved in any of the horrible goings-on. He was so into his image—that of a super successful education CEO—that he had no idea what was happening right under his nose. Until the police showed up with a stack of search and arrest warrants, at which time he fully cooperated. He had to, to keep his high-paying job.

Yeah right. He'd get his fool ass fired fast. Honee would see to it.

"Listen up, everybody." Mrs. Taylor gathered a few seniors around her like a hen her chicks. "Let's get back to Shakespeare later, okay?" Clutching her teacher's edition with dozens of Post-it notes sticking out, she turned to Dr. Reinholt. "Dr. Davis does have a point. We didn't even wrap up Act V. In the future could you please give us advance notice of any schedule changes?"

She slung a protective arm around the boy who played Brutus the night before. "Don't worry, we'll rehearse again at the end of lunch. Let me just mark this page." She took a pencil from behind her ear, underlined a word here, a footnote there, her lips moving silently. Nothing could ruffle her in her teaching duties.

Watching from a distance, Qiana and Honee were relieved none of the kids even tried to sneak off as a chain of policemen, with the help of the football coach and his assistants, surrounded them.

"Looks like Coach is off the hook too," Honee whispered.

Qiana nodded. "Right. So with Reinholt and Coach out of it, that leaves who?"

"The counselor, that loony secretary and—" Honee stopped. Dr. Reinholt had cornered Ricky, whose bald spot was dripping sweat beads the size of pearl onions.

"What's going on?" he yelled but had to know the answer. Cops everywhere.

That's when Qiana and Honee stepped into view. "Hello, Dr. Davis."

Stunned, the counselor stared at the two young women. He glanced at the trailer, his eyes darting like a trapped rat, and fumbled along his belt for his cell phone that was gone. Stunned even more, he knocked Dr. Reinholt aside and exploded across the lawn. Seconds later, the red Porsche roared into view, Ricky at the wheel.

Seeing this, Honee felt horrible. *Oh, Lord!* She could already picture his next move, a quick escape to a secret hide-out planned for long ago. *Bermuda or the Caribbean?* Ricky would never to be seen again. She was livid.

Qiana felt the same way. "Somebody stop him," she screamed. Otherwise this terrible criminal would circle the pond and head out the back way. There had to be another gate and a secret path to I-40. Or to a strip of land with a private jet where he'd meet his brothers, then all of them would be up and away.

She tried to focus on something positive. Surely by now the ambulances, escorted by many more police cars, had arrived at the Spa and rescued Logan, Josh, Angelo, and all those other poor kids. At least they were safe and on their way to the hospital in Red Mill. The animals were bound to be getting help too and most likely the little kids were in lock-down. But in the interim the horrible brothers and their accomplices would escape, maybe through those same tunnels and hook up with Ricky.

She couldn't let that happen. "Why don't you do something?" she screamed at the young, smooth-faced cops who just stood there. Feet planted apart, they remained stoic even as the Porsche roared around the barricades.

Frustrated, Qiana ran over to Mrs. Taylor who was so engrossed in her textbook she hadn't paid attention to what was happening. Now she noticed Qiana. "Excuse me?"

"You letting Ricky get away?" Qiana screamed, glad to see a few cops finally kneeling on the grass, aiming at the Porsche but still waiting for a clear shot. "C'mon, don't act so innocent. I saw your picture at the Spa. Down in that horror basement."

"Wha--what?" Mrs. Taylor looked shell-shocked. Turning around, she finally took in the pond, at whose rim her oldest son was driving erratically. He'd seen the sharpshooters get into position and was trying to give them an impossible target. "Son, wait up!"

Ricky kept driving around in an even more serpentine pattern as two men zipped along the creek in a flatboat, crossed the pond, and piled in with him. Mrs. Taylor's two other sons, both armed with what looked like Uzis.

"Good job, boys." Mrs. Taylor clapped, allowing the book to slip out of her grasp. Then unencumbered, she ripped off her brocade gown and wig. Wearing a track suit underneath, she jumped at Honee. Amazing how agile the teacher's lumpy body could be. She flung an arm around Honee's neck, tightened it into a strangle-hold, and hissed at the students like a bus door closing, "Hand it over. Quadruple extra credit."

Without the police interfering, a boy was able to lob over a pistol. She caught it and pressed it brutally against Honee's temple. "Back up, everybody. Don't shoot or she gets it."

As she was talking, she dragged Honee, whose face creased with pain, to the Porsche that had come to a halt, its motor continuing to rev. Meanwhile all three brothers trained their powerful guns on the rows of students. Mowing down a huge number of them would be like fishing in a commercial trout pond for them.

Death would have a field day.

The moment Honee was taken hostage, Qiana felt overcome by nausea. Her legs went numb as if they'd been chopped off at the knee. Trying to avoid falling, she attempted to marshal her thoughts, but nothing but questions came.

Is Honee getting kidnapped?
Are the crooks getting away scot-free?
Will all those kids get shot?

Of course many kids were guilty, at least to some degree, but if any of them got shot, Honee would always blame herself. And if Honee got shot, nothing would ever be okay.

293

Evil will not win out again. Not this time!

Mrs. Taylor had to be caught. Of course her sons had helped her but she was the diabolical mastermind.

"Wait!" Qiana chased after Mrs. Taylor who, walking backwards, was still dragging Honee to the Porsche, her pistol aimed at the students and finding its first target—Jamar. If her gun went off now, he'd get hit. Worse, Mrs. Taylor's shot would be the signal for her sons to mow down dozens of kids like weeds.

That's what Honee was most afraid of, not her own situation, but what might happen to the kids. Innocent or not, most likely all of them needed help in the form of a psychiatric evaluation, talk therapy, medicine, or with a combination of everything. For that to happen they first had to live.

"Stay back, Jamar," she screamed at the freshman, who was crawling between the legs of a cop, determined to be a hero, a dead one most likely.

"Wait!" Qiana screamed again, still trying to catch up with Mrs. Taylor. The policemen stayed frozen, still waiting for the best opportunity to take a shot.

At last Qiana reached the teacher. "Please take me and let her go."

"Why? Both of you are garbage," Mrs. Taylor cackled. "But you can run back and get my book. Once we trip the wire—"

"You're going to blow up Stefford School?"

"Well, don't we need a little diversion?" Mrs. Taylor clucked, a malicious expression unfurling on her face.

Horrified, Qiana imagined the whole campus soon looking like a London tube bombing. She raced back for the textbook and caught up with Mrs. Taylor and Honee again. "Okay, here's your little diversion." Using the book like a tennis racket, she whacked the teacher on the shoulder as hard as she could.

The impact made the pistol arc from Mrs. Taylor's hand. As she scrabbled for it, Qiana whipped the pencil from behind the

294

teacher's ear and drove it into her cheek like an ice pick into a can of cranberry juice. Blood spurted into Mrs. Taylor's eyes. Screaming, she released Honee from her stranglehold.

That's what Honee had been waiting for. Like a loosened coil, she kicked the teacher in the shin so hard Mrs. Taylor lurched around, limping and pawing at her face to find out how hurt she was. Holding her head like a glass bowl, she then managed to collect herself, vaulted to the Porsche, and piled on top of her Uzi-brandishing sons. "Let's go, boys. Out the back way."

Nope, not gonna happen. Honee didn't know how to detain the criminals. Without thinking, she sprinted after the car but stumbled and fell. After that, she and Qiana could only watch as the Porsche shot around the barricades for the last time.

But finally the cops had a clear shot. A gun went off and one of the car's back tires burst like a soap bubble. Because of its speed, the vehicle spun left. That's when the other back tire was shot out, making the Porsche veer right. Then uncontrollable, it roared ahead on tire rims, crashed through the barricades and cannon-balled into the middle of the pond where it smashed the remains of the platform to kindling.

"Let's book 'em," one of the cops ordered, waiting for the crime family to come slogging out of the muddy water. Instead, a horrible scream rose, then more screams. At the same time violent splashing ensued, even though the car had come to a stop. It settled deeper into the slime as another series of screams and more splashing followed.

Hearing the commotion, the students tried to rush to the pond but the police held them in check: "Don't anybody move!"

Only one person ignored the order.

Coach sprinted over to Honee, picked her up and carried her to the gym where he placed her on a wrestling mat. In silence, he examined her temple that still bore the imprint of the pistol's muzzle and her throat that had strangling marks like tattoos. When he was satisfied no medical attention was needed, except for a butterfly bandage on her calf, he brushed her off like a porcelain doll.

She was 5'10", slim—okay, thin—but strong as an ox. Yet this dude was carrying on like he'd stomp on anything daring to mar her exquisite beauty. Honee never thought those words had anything to do with her. Meantime his eyes seemed to run over with love like oil from a new Iraqi well. Honee could feel it.

"You okay?" he said and tugged at his beard that, from up close, was the latest manly-man style, soul patch and all, adding, "You sure?" when she nodded.

"Sure I'm sure," Honee whispered, awe-struck by how this dude's skin was molded to his muscular body. She didn't know guys could come this way—big bears on the outside but so different inside. "Thanks."

She was about to hop up when he knelt in front of her and bent his shaved and oiled head in prayer. After that he took her grimy, scratched-up hand with the ragged, dirty nails and kissed it like a Viennese count.

Shocking how the kiss sparked in Honee and whizzed all over her. Wasn't it the plum oddest feeling, needles pricking her toes one moment, the nape of her neck the next? Then her elbows, the back of her knees, her scalp. Prickle-prickle. A powerful force was stirring in her. Never had she felt anything like it. *Thank the Lord, nobody's around to see it.*

Embarrassed over her body's reaction, she jumped up, amazed she could do it. Her whole being seemed to melt in nooks and crannies she didn't even know she had. Everything in her was loose and perspiring to beat the band. *Even my soles feel liquidacious.* Honee looked down: Just sweat. She'd expected molten gold to pour from her gross Adidas. *Am I catching something?* Sure, this was a delayed reaction from the awful night in the pond, from seeing all those mutilated kids, those horrible corpses, those poor animals, that wolf, poor old Henry, that little bone...

But why did it feel like a bath in something sweet? *Honee with the honey-colored skin bathing in honey?*

She giggled like a baby and then stopped. *I've gone bonkers.*

Coach was staring at her, mesmerized. "Hello," he said, "I'm Emir al-Said and just as sorry as can be for what's happened. Believe me, I never suspected anything like it. I only work in the Upper School. Still I should've noticed something was off."

Man-oh-man-oh-man. Wasn't his voice wonderful? Not a hint of leering, nothing sleaze-like. Still shocked over her body going so crazy, Honee yanked her hand away and felt a sense of loss. Looney, how much she missed his touch already. What if he had kissed her on the lips?

Forget it, girl. Love's out of the question. I'm such a piece of— Condemned my own Momma to a horrible death.

At that moment Qiana waltzed up, clutching a stack of notes she'd raked up off the lawn. "Look guys. That's Mrs. Taylor's papers. Florida Islands Bank," she read out loud, "First International of Bermuda, Miami Holding Company... It's nothing but financial statements, stock reports and—"

"That's mighty interesting," Honee cut her off, momentarily caring lima beans about Mrs. Taylor's hidden millions. She had emerged from her haze of amazing feelings. "C'mon, guys, let's move the kids to the auditorium."

"You go, super substitutes." The old secretary clapped like crazy when the two young women entered the office half an hour later. That was tough for her because she had to use her rotating hand. Now she was alone, her assistants and all parents having been sent home. Damage control. Other changes were evident as well. For example, Dr. Reinholt's inner sanctum had been commandeered as headquarters by the sheriffs of Stephen County

297

and Red Mill County and other law enforcement personnel, with the crocodile collection banished to cardboard boxes.

First the police saw to every dangerous area, including the back gate where they dismantled a tripwire with many complex components and attachments in the tunnels. Then they transported the kindergarten and elementary school children to an institution staffed with child psychologists and pediatricians.

The older kids were in lock-down until things could be sorted out. The police had already found Rosario's, Henry's and Ms. Hill's bodies and the dead kids. All of them were being transported to the coroner's office. Plus, they collected all evidence of cannibalism, hauled the trussed-up worker off to jail, and did whatever else was needed to ensure Stefford School and the whole campus, including the pond, were completely secured.

"Just got to look for the platinum lining, you know," the secretary said, after filling Qiana and Honee in on the latest developments. She was counting reams of printer paper and toner cartridges. "Actually there's good news too. I went ahead and wrote you both up for the Stefford Medal. I'm afraid I was kind of ill to you yesterday. I'd like to take a moment to apologize."

"That's quite all right," Qiana said. "We owe you an apology too. We really thought you were mixed up in—"

"Me? For heavens' sake! Way too busy for any shenani—"

"Yep, we realized that, Miss—" Honee cut in. "Sorry, we don't even know your name."

"It's Mrs. Mercer but you two are special. Call me Mercy Me."

"Mercy me, Mercy Me." Qiana grinned. It felt good and sounded good, saying the word *mercy*. God had had mercy on her.

"Oncet—once again, please accept our apologies." Suddenly Honee felt so tired she could hardly keep her eyes peeled. And her belly was rumbling worse that a volcano. She'd picked up a chunk of clay when she hit the ground after Qiana sprang her from Mrs.

Taylor's grip. Looked appetizing, but the expression on Coach's face made her pitch it.

Noticing Honee's near-starvation, Mercy Me whipped out a Pizza Hut box. "Here you go, ladies, leftovers from last night. Really, who would've believed it? You two gals salvaged Stefford School."

"Not yet, I'm afraid," Qiana said, popping a curled slice of pepperoni into her mouth.

Honee chimed in, "Yup. Ain't—isn't over till all the crooks are nabbed, each and everyone one."

"You know what's disturbing to me?" Qiana asked with a frown. "I thought for sure it was *two* evil masterminds like that two-headed monster in the pond."

"Right, girl. The three brothers, they were just Mrs. Taylor's puppets. She planned everything and they jumped on it. And most of the kids had no idea what was going on. They got so wrapped up in that foolish competition, they didn't realize they were just being used. Their incredibly high GPA's and the top college admissions rates attracted slews of parents, waving their checkbooks. So the crooks could generate millions for themselves. And the pitiful mixed-up little kids, well, they just did stuff to outdo the older ones."

Honee ripped a strip of cardboard off the pizza box and chomped on it. "Maybe some kids considered themselves some kind of Columbine heroes, you know, and got sucked into those grisly experiments and brutal murders. But I believe, except for a few rotten apples, most of them were out of the loop."

More chomping. "So only Mrs. Taylor? Doesn't make sense to me either. *One* person could never... How could she get it all done—run the whole gruesome kitsch and caboodle-do with her teaching all day?"

"Well," again the secretary's hand was making those rolling motions, "it probably went down like this. Mrs. Taylor gets Ricky to pick out the most suggestible kids, the weakest ones, and a few junior mafia punks and bullies that you can find anywhere. Then she programs them to be devil robots or maybe—," she dabbed her face with a tissue, clearly shaken, "—she makes them just not care. But somehow she has them all develop an attitude of vicious indifference, even the babies. Oh, this is just terrible. But trust me, ladies. Each and every criminal's been nabbed. Yes indeedy. And I just called a PTA meeting, tada."

"And?" Honee, reaching for more cardboard.

"They asked Dr. Reinholt for a moratorium on tests. So all the good kids will get a break."

"A long vacation?"

"No, Ms. Money. C'mon, this is Stefford School. Just a couple days. But that means I get to take off too for a change and visit— Well, no need to advertise one's personal life, right? Of course, it's going to take time to sort out what all happened in the Science Labs and with the early grades and their sick deeds, their secret room. Who instigated everything, who lured the little kids in, who cashed in big. Mercy me, there were so many layers of secrecy, like a twelve-layer coconut cake."

"What's going to happen to the little young'uns?"

"Social Services already took charge of them, Ms. Money. After they're questioned and evaluated, most likely some are going to be placed in long-term—"

Qiana broke in, "What about Gibson and her—?"

"Those poor little chicks? For the moment, they and the ringleader boys are in a locked psych ward."

"What about Ian?"

"Well, he's older, so they took him straight to jail. He seems to be a real psycho. But confidential, Ms. Llove? It's quite a coup."

"A *coup*, Mercy Me?"

"Sure. Phone's been ringing off the wall. We're getting huge amounts of publicity. Dr. Phil's coming, Greta's doing a special, something called "A School for Killers." Anyway, could you take me shopping? Before they led Allie off, she told me about a hot new shoe store. I don't want to mess up my TV debut."

"Call us." Which reminded Qiana. She held out her hand and the secretary returned her cell phone along with the watches.

"More good news, ladies. Don't tell anyone but I just rushed the lateral-entry program through for both of you. Dr. Reinholt's golden with the state department of education. He signed off on all the forms and I already faxed everything over to Raleigh. You're going to get your emergency teaching certificates in nothing flat. Bet you'll be the next National Teachers of the Year. Which is just great because the country needs you two. Yes, you're going to straighten out the horrible mess education is in. Trust me, I'll follow you, if not in person then through TV or the pap—"

"But I don't want to teach," Qiana cut in with an expression that was a mixture of horror and disgust. "Not after this."

"Might need you again, girlfriend," Honee said in a soft tone.

"Well, in that case, count me in." Besides, helping out Honee would mean hanging around schools and that was probably the quickest way for Qiana to find kids who were abused. Her thumbs got busy checking her messages. "Can you believe it, Honee? Not one text or voice mail or email from Gunner. Wonder if he's been in an accident?"

Honee patted Qiana on the arm.

"There's probably bad reception over in Bermuda, girl. Or Gunner's tied up or something. But I bet he's gonna call you at the house. So-o-o," Honee yawned until her jaws almost separated, "can we scram, Mercy Me? Otherwise I'm gonna crash right here."

"Oh no, you don't. This is one of the finest learning institutions in the country, if not the finest. What're you thinking?"

"I'm thinking you better schedule another PTA meeting and make sure all the trustees show. 'Cause we're gonna make a full report. Believe me, none of those ghost kids will have suffered or

301

died in vain, nor those poor animals. There's gonna be inquiries out of the fanny. Plus scholarships in Ms. Hill's, Rosario's and Henry's name. We're after justice with a capital J and we're gonna get it." Honee made a sizzling sound. "Yep, we're on fire."

"Love your passion," the secretary said. "But now go home, both of you. Buh-bye."

As soon as the door shut behind the two women, she stilled her nervous hand. Grabbed a floral spray can and fumigated everything. "Substitutes these days? *Peeeuw.* Can't have Geraldo get a whiff of this but finally I'm getting some attention."

People never realized just how neglected school secretaries were. They did all the drudgery. Worse was, they got paid squat while year after year, waves of kids washed through, presenting ever more challenges. Then they left for college and made it big.

And the teachers? They breezed in and sat on their behinds. Played Solitaire on the computer, Words with Friends on their iPhones, or they gossiped. Still the whole country pitied them. Poor school teachers, boo-hoo. So they got all the praise while the secretaries were forever stuck at the bottom rung. Yet they knew about all the usual misdeeds, the secret affairs, the grade fixing, the cheating on finals, the forged transcripts, and the monies coming up short. All the underhanded business involving kids and faculty.

At Stefford the usual misdeeds had escalated to unimaginable crimes. But if caught early, they might've been preventable. If she'd only been asked her opinion years ago, she could have voiced her suspicions then.

But no, being a school secretary meant you were *nothing.* She was just a fixture and the butt of jokes. Mercy Me often thought she was at a bus depot, seeing the buses stop and leave and never having a chance to hop on. Her whole life meant fading into the supply closet, getting sprinkled with chalk dust and pencil sharpener debris, and picking up ink stains.

This was the sore spot in Mercy Me's life. Cinderella thought she had it bad? Well, what about her? She was wasting her life, doing all this menial work. Making copies, taking textbook orders, counting out locks for the lockers. Every day calling computer tech support and getting put on hold for eons. Issuing admit slips for kids who forged their parents' written excuses, not that anyone cared.

All of it was nothing a ten-year old couldn't do blind-folded, with hands tied. But no more. Starting today, she'd ride the express train—first class. Yippee! Rooting around in her hoodie, Mercy Me dug between her breasts and produced a printed-out email. "A limo picking me up? That's neat," she whispered to herself.

She rubbed her fingers to relax them. All that hand rotating took its toll but worked like a charm. People thought she was off her rocker. Meant they didn't take her seriously.

They have no idea.

CHAPTER 36

The Stefford School lobby was jam-packed again. Now instead of eager-beaver parents, print and TV reporters were wall-to-wall, trying to interview anyone who knew a smidge of what had happened. Leaning against a trophy case, Honee heaved out a breath. "Can't you picture tomorrow's headlines, girl? *Stefford Students Savages.*"

That wasn't true. Sure, a few kids were savages or criminally insane and had given in to their worst impulses. Yet she suspected most of them only acted like savages because they'd been remote-controlled by evil people. Of course, the groundwork for their being so docile and robot-like had been laid by the horrible education they received, with their parents being the enablers. Teaching kids tests, extra credit and blind obedience were the most important things had them failing at life.

Next to Honee, Qiana wobbled so bad she had to steady herself against a wall. She was trying to figure out how to sneak out of the lobby without being button-holed like that well-known psychologist at the other end who was being interviewed by a gaggle of TV reporters. A colorful silk scarf veiling her neck, she wore a black suit.

"These days emotional damage can occur so easily to our fragile youth," she said with a soft European accent.

"What makes them so fragile, Doctor?"

"One reason is their drive for perfection that's fueled by parents who push their kids beyond the limit. Another reason is what all that stress does to them. And from there it's just a tiny step to mental illness."

"Are you're saying the kids are innocent, Doctor?"

"No, a lot of them are guilty but not to the degree of their parents and teachers."

"But what can parents and teachers do, Doctor?"

"First, they have to realize unrelenting stress can dehumanize children. Besides that, kids brought up on a diet of video games, YouTube, FaceBook, and Twitter can forget what's real. And of course whatever goes wrong in high school seeps down to middle school, elementary school, even kindergarten. Little kids always try to one-up the older ones. So they crank up any bad behavior they see and worsen it to the nth degree. Unless we step in. If you study recent school killers, you'll find most of them went wrong in the early grades."

"Are you blaming the national testing craze, Doctor?"

"No, but when testing becomes God, character suffers. Do you know several states are now giving writing assessments in kinder—"

"Excuse me." Dr. Reinholt, who had been cleared of all wrong-doings other than total cluelessness, marched to the bank of mikes. Still looking like the CEO of a big-bonus dispensing Wall Street company, he wore another Armani suit, this one paired with a bright-yellow shirt, tie, and belt.

"Trust me, girl," Honee whispered to Qiana, "this is the last hurrah for that yellow-bellied sap sucker."

"Uh-hum," the headmaster cleared his throat. "The biggest problem is that everybody wants trophy kids. Moms and dads just do not parent like they used to and that has detrimental consequences. Under-parenting can make youngsters easy prey for the crooks. Sad to say, in our case a horribly corrupt woman and her criminal sons were behind a scheme of unbelievable greed and cruelty. But fortunately, and I cannot emphasize this enough, Stefford School had a most crucial *factor,* Ms. Money and her teacher aide Ms. Llove. You will meet them both in a just a min—"

In your dreams. Qiana laughed. "Is he crazy? The way I look, I mean feel?"

After the two young women stealth-walked outside as fast as their tired legs permitted, she said, "You know what, Honee? I figured it out. We really are substitutes."

"Sure, girl, our teaching license is in the mail."

"No, we're substitute sisters."

"Yep, Qi, we're like sisters."

"Not *like.* We really are sisters, Honee—chosen sisters. As soon as my parents get back, I'll ask them to adopt you."

"Are you out of your gourd, girl? I'm too old for that."

"Well, that's your decision, girlfriend. But if you want, you're going to have Jewish parents." They hugged, tears spilling down their faces. Qiana wiped her cheeks and Honee's. It was incredible but her emptiness had been filled *twice* in one day.

"This is... beyond my wildest... Bless you, Qiana. Always wanted a sister and a family. And now I got me one."

But how can that be, me being so rotten? Honee extricated herself from Qiana's embrace, hoping Qiana wouldn't detect the deep dark shame she felt and always would. But there was nothing to be done about it. So on to something that wasn't so filled with

307

sorrow, pain, and guilt. "Girl, can we make a stop on the way home?" she asked. "Just gotta see that little chick with my own eyes, you know, and check on the status of the other kids."

"Sure, sure." Qiana nodded like a bobble-head doll on speed but stayed rooted to one spot, her eyes flooding again. *Just hope and pray I'm strong enough.*

"Wasn't for Logan, I wouldn't have dragged you along," Honee went on. "Then who knows what could've— For sure wouldn't get to be your sister now. Man-oh-man, my brain still can't comprehend it all..." Her voice fizzled because she really didn't know what might've happened. Maybe if she'd gone to the school alone, the crazy kids would've overpowered and killed her like Ms. Hill. But maybe with Qiana there, their plans changed.

Filled with such relief, Honee hugged Qiana again and Qiana hugged her back, trying not to gag. "Peeuw," they chorused, their noses pleating like accordions.

Fortunately Coach al-Said had arranged for some transportation. After folding herself into the passenger seat of a cop car, Honee made sure the windows were down and the fan on max. She leaned back, reflecting on the past events: *Miracles do happen.* Why else had she just met a dude brimming over with love for her? Wonder what he looks like naked? Does he have a big hairy chest tapering down to a small waist, flat stomach, and muscular thighs?

Honee felt her neck blazing like a match was struck to it. She fanned herself, hoping Qiana, who had slid into the back seat, couldn't read her thoughts. *Don't deserve nobody loving me.*

Qiana was busy with her own thoughts. *Miracles do happen.* She knew all the terrible events were over. Still deep inside, she had a lingering fear. Didn't the horrible Stefford School tragedies prove that even the nicest veneer could veil the monsters? So had they done overlooked something?

308

Done overlooked? She smiled. *Gee, I'm sounding like a local... because I am a local. I'm going home.*

As the car curved around the gym, Honee's lips moved. Qiana leaned forward to hear what Honee was saying.

CHAPTER 37

"America, wake up. You call this the *American Ideal*? While the politicians impregnate their mistresses and run dirty elections, our kids are left to their own devices. No one watching out for them, you know, they feel abandoned. As a consequentiality, they turn into cold-blooded little Nazis. So let's straighten out education. It's the most important thing. Or do we want to be a nation that feeds on our young?"

"What're you doing, Honee?"

"Rehearsing what all I'm gonna tell the PTA and the trustees. Believe me, girl, I'm gonna check on Stefford many times."

"And I'm going to fight for abused kids. Get justice for them." Qiana sat back, planning her next steps. As the police car circled the main building, she noticed a woman standing by her car in the faculty parking lot. "Stop! Stop!"

There it was, what she'd been so worried about.

The second head of the Hydra.

As Qiana and Honee ran to the faculty parking lot, the woman kept loading up boxes in a hurry. Meanwhile their driver, a fresh-faced policeman, followed on foot.

"What do you want from me?" The woman sounded irritated over being interrupted.

"Some answers." Honee said. "Why're you in such a rush to get out of here?"

"Yes, where's the fire?" Qiana.

"Are you kidding?" The woman lifted another carton into her car. "You can't possibly be thinking I'm in cahoots with those horrible crooks." She turned to the cop who pulled out a notebook. "Don't listen to this floozy," indicating Qiana. "Or I'll file a complaint, count on it."

Honee folded her arms. "Watch your mouth, lady. That's my sister."

"That's quite all right," Qiana said. "I'd be furious too if there were all kinds of photos of me with Ricky Davis and his brothers." Riding in the police car, she had suddenly remembered the photo albums hidden on top of the closet in the bedroom of Ricky's trailer.

"Of course, there's lots of pictures of me with Dr. Davis. C'mon, we work together. Have for years. Look," the woman flipped through a yearbook that she lifted off a stack of annuals on the passenger seat of her BMW, "here he is next to me at the senior class picnic. And here he and his brothers are helping out with graduation practice. But I had no idea they had a dark side, and neither did most of the staff. So what're you going to do?" she asked the cop. "Arrest each and everyone who works at Stefford School? All the volunteers, the cafeteria ladies, the janitorial workers, the delivery folks, the yard crew? Get real."

Her outraged tone seemed to be netting results. The policeman squirmed, maybe getting more and more convinced she wasn't involved in any wrong-doings. Besides, there were so many aspects of this mind-boggling school tragedy, that he hadn't had time to process everything. His lieutenant would have to make the call. He certainly didn't want a "prone to making false arrests" notation in his file, no sir. He wasn't a rookie who jumped to rash conclusions, even though he had a baby face.

While he scratched his head and thought the situation over, the woman had a smile creep on her face. *Nice.* Wasn't that greenhorn policeman gullible, just like 90 percent of the Stefford kids? When she first hatched the plan to have the students go crazy with their fund-raising, they'd taken to it like ducks to water. So it was easy—day-by-day and behind the scenes—to fuel their over-the-edge creative projects with more and more incentives. Rewarding them for every wild scheme and plying them with alcohol, drugs, bling, and sex orgies did the trick. And of course the leaders drew an allowance.

These days inciting kids, even the littlest ones, to go crazy was simple. Without their parents being truly involved in their lives, she had big pool of willing accomplices. Of course, a few were junior Satans to start with. Even a few of the youngest kids had a vicious streak nowadays. All she had to do was to identify it and turn the worst of the worst over to Juditha Taylor and her sons.

That part was easy too. The Taylor clan was thrilled to have a chance to skim a portion off all the monies coming in. But even they didn't know *everything.*

Only she did. She smiled, reveling in being so smart. Oh yes, there was a lot more going on and all of it dealing with major cash, for the *real* profit lay in something else entirely—the organs-on-demand business. What made this so lucrative was today's lifestyle was so hyped up that many teenagers craved cash. Girls needed it for breast implants and nose jobs, boys for growth hormones and steroids. Even preteens wanted their own BlackBerrys, iPads, iPhones, debit cards, and who knows what else.

313

And this trend started early. Even four-year olds wanted grown-up gadgets now. Therefore quite a few kids could be paid to participate in organ harvesting—under the guise of carrying out the punishment for anyone breaking their silly Code of Silence.

The great thing was all of it was a natural outcome of the way things were. Since no school staff member ever got a million-dollar bonus, the smartest ones among them had to generate a windfall by themselves. Best of all, her plan fit in perfectly with the latest medical trend. Rather than waiting around for an organ to give out, it was now fashionable for millionaires and billionaires to have a transplant *before* their heart was severely damaged, their kidneys gave out, or their liver was too scarred.

Yes, among the super well-off, *prophylactic transplants*— before the necessity for them arose—were the latest craze. And she—with no education, a piss-poor background and a dreadful early life—was the visionary who discovered a never-ending supply of healthy organs from any tattlers and those street kids that made her sick. While the Science Club went crazy with their experiments, it was easy for her to grab a few trash kids for herself.Her brilliant scheme had started small and picked up steam.

And now it was about to make her super rich.

All she needed was a couple of weeks. That was easy too because a perfect solution presented itself—those two trashy gals standing right in front of her. After reading a newspaper article about two very pretty, but totally broke, young women, all she did was insert Honee's name into the substitute teachers list, hoping Qiana would tag along. Then while the whole school focused on their looks, she could quietly go about her business for a few more bonus-producing days.

Meanwhile those ditzy chicks had no clue they'd been hand-picked. Even now, they didn't know more than 10% of what was going on because there was an even more sinister scheme in the works. That was long-range, with nation-wide, perhaps even international, implications. It had to do with home-grown terrorism but not to worry. *That's the domain of the old guy in Florida. Earl Granville's got big plans...*

The young cop stopped scratching his head. Tucking his note pad away, he apologized: "Sorry, ma'am. With all what's been going on, we've got to check out every report of something irregular. You understand, don't you? But don't fret. All staff's going to be interviewed in depth anyway. We've already got everybody's address, phone numbers, email address, and so forth. So for the time being, you're free to go."

"Good deal," she said, shooting annoyed glances at the two substitutes who'd caused her this little delay. "Thank you, sir. I'll make a contribution to the Police Benevolent Society as soon as I can but right now I've got to run. These boxes here? It's my job to deliver annuals to all the kids who didn't pick theirs up last semester. And after that, with Stefford School being closed for the moment, I'm going to take a few days off."

"You can forget about that." Still suspicious, Qiana blocked her from climbing into her navy BMW, with Honee, arms still folded, standing beside her.

The woman patted her hair, touched her perfectly made-up face and turned to the young policeman. "Officer, would you move these pathetic chicks out of my way? Just look at them. Who needs more Marilyn Monroe and Halle Berry look-alikes? My goodness, those outfits."

"Don't change the subject," Honee said. "You got some major explaining to do."

The woman stomped her foot. "Would you stop with the crazy accusations? It's insane. Where's your proof?"

"Right here." Honee dug in the heel of her left Adidas, produced a small water-proof container and clicked it open. "That's Ricky Davis's thumb drive. I found it in his jacket in his trailer. Want to bet everything's on it, including your up-to-your-neck involvement?"

The young cop's face turned scarlet. "Hey, let's have that. Now y'all wait right here." He grabbed the external file and trotted off toward to the command center in the main office.

As soon as he disappeared, JoBelle Edwards said, "Dammit, that's nothing to do with me. I'm not hanging around." She stalked around her car, opened the passenger door and shifted the stack of yearbooks on the passenger seat out of the way, since Qiana still barred the driver's side door. Then the guidance secretary hopped into the car, intending to climb behind the wheel that way. As she scrambled over the annuals, they fell to the floorboard and opened. Except for the top one, all of them had been hollowed out like Easter eggs some people decorate the trees in their yard with. And in place of the copy and pictures nestled bundles of $100 bills.

"What's this?" Honee asked as Qiana calculated just how much money it might be. Thousands, maybe hundreds of thousands.

"Tsk, tsk. Can you believe it?" JoBelle said in a shocked tone. "Right under my nose those crazy kids cleaned out the safe and hid the cash. Real knuckleheads, getting me to hand deliver it to their crew, what nerve. Look, there's dirty little fingerprints all over. Well, that's what we get for taking in trash. Tell you what. I'll drive straight to the police department and hand over—" She cranked the motor.

"Stay put, didn't you hear that cop?" Reaching into the BMW, Honee turned the motor off and extricated the woman out of the car which wasn't easy. JoBelle fought like a bobcat, screaming, "Get your damn hands off me, crazy black bitch."

In the process of struggling to get out of Honee's grasp, the woman's page boy hair-cut got messed up and her perfect make-up developed cracks like a patch of earth that's parched.

Qiana decided to go for the car keys and reached between the tussling bodies. As she did, she noticed JoBelle's make-up disintegrating more and more and was stunned as recognition slammed into her. "No... no...no...That's... impossible," she whispered.

But it wasn't Qiana's imagination. The guidance secretary's makeup mask had developed deep lines, like a windshield with cracks that ran, revealing more and more skin, her real skin. It was pale, with large pores, and had lots... of... flat... black... dots...

"*You?*... Is... it... really... *you?*" Qiana nudged Honee out of the way and wrapped her arms around the woman in an iron grip, her vision clouding from a flashback.

CHAPTER 38

After Qiana had sawed at the rope all night with a sliver of glass and run away again, Polka-dots caught her again and trapped her in a bear hug. "Didn't think you'd break easy. So before I went to bed, I alarmed your door. You can't make a move that I don't know."

Qiana was sobbing uncontrollably. She had tried so hard to escape from the Kozee Inn. So hard.

"Not such a pretty little thing any more, are you? Snot running down your face, eyes sunk in, scabby and smelly—yuck. Don't know what my husband sees in you."

From then on the man shackled Qiana's feet, undoing them only when he wanted to. As a result, her spirit was broken. She didn't know what in the world to do except scribble in her notebook whenever she could:

Hurting real bad all the time. Day 'n' nite. The Devil hurts my body but his wife hurts me the worst. She kills my heart, my soul.

My everithing. Hate hate hate her. I forget about him now 'n' then, look out the window. Pretend im just a little girl waiting to grow up, thats all. But ill never eva forget her killing me inside. Long shes not punished ill neva eva be happy.

Will this pain ever end?

Now, many years later, Qiana yelled: "I can't believe it... but... I... think... you're... the woman... that... ran... that club... for pedophiles... at the Kozee Inn... in London, dammit."

"Pah. The only Kozee Inn I ever knew about was in Chicago. I've never been overseas."

"Aha, tricked you. Well, I was one of those little girls. You sentenced me to death, over and over. You lied to me, tortured me trying to make me fat. You took all my money and—" Qiana dug in her Louis Vuitton bag that had been returned to her. Unfurling the wad of notebook paper her Manolos were wrapped in when she had dug them out of her trunk the previous day, she read out loud, "*'Every time I try 'n' run away that bitch catch me & take me back. Its like she got a camra and waits 4 me. I fight her every time but shes 2 strong. Much worse than the devil. She murder me each 'n' every day—'*"

The woman shook her head. "That's absurd. I don't even know what you're talking about. Let's just wait for that policeman, okay?" He was still in the main building where all the other cops had assembled.

"Okay." After waiting for so many years to bring this horrible woman to justice, Qiana was willing to wait a few more minutes. But as she crammed the notebook papers back into her purse, JoBelle pushed Honee to the ground and took off running. Shocked, Qiana gulped the deepest breath in her life and charged after her like a mama grisly bear. "Stay back, Honee, that's my fight."

When she caught up with JoBelle, she slung her around. Rammed her head into the woman's mid-section and made her bend over. She pounded her with her fists again and again until the guidance secretary was sprawling on the ground, spitting up blood and sputtering: "Impossible—no... not you again... Who... would've... thought—?"

Filled with rage that kept escalating, Qiana kept kicking the woman, beating her, slamming into her and screaming, "You disgusting bitch. Three little boys committed suicide over what you did. That's when I finally sneaked away... during all that commotion..."

When JoBelle tried to scramble back up on her feet, Qiana kicked and punched the woman even harder, and with each hammer-like punch she drove her farther back until she fell against the old well. That was a decorative structure with wooden columns and a small dome, dating back to when Stefford School was first built. It shifted to the side from the impact and revealed an old well shaft.

Heaving in another Herculean breath, Qiana pushed the woman another foot until she tumbled down into the well. But before Honee, who had recovered and came running, could intervene, JoBelle managed to clutch Qiana's ankle and started dragging her down into the deep shaft too. Honee lunged for Qiana's arms and yanked her in the opposite direction—away from the deep hole and to safety. Which meant Qiana was balancing on the rim of the opening, with both JoBelle and Honee pulling on her from different directions. Desperately she pumped her leg like a piston, trying to dislodge the guidance secretary's grip on her.

Unfortunately JoBelle was like a bull dog and didn't let go.

But help was coming. "Ms. Money! Ms. Llove!"

A golf cart careened up, driven by Jefferson, with Chrissie sitting next to him. Obviously both students had been cleared of any wrong-doings. "What's up?" they shouted. But as soon as they understood the situation, they got Qiana safely away from the old well.

Relieved, she knelt on the ground and caught her breath while Honee ran off to find something with which to pull JoBelle out of the well and tie her up.

The kids were a great help. Without being told what to do, they assisted Ms. Edwards as she climbed out of the well shaft, after which she thanked them profusely. Her face a mask of fury, she then brushed herself off and looked around, calculating her chances. That stupid cop was still in the building, Qiana still on the ground, trying to recover. And Honee was still poking through the trunk of the police car, looking for a rope. Otherwise the front of the school was deserted.

Oblivious to JoBelle's inquisitive glances, Qiana stretched. Thank goodness, this scare was over and most importantly, justice was finally at hand. With the kids' assistance, they'd easily be able to detain JoBelle until—

Suddenly Qiana realized she couldn't count on the kids' allegiance. They clustered around JoBelle who screeched, "Hard to kill some vermin, isn't it? But not impossible." She whispered something to Jefferson and Chrissie.

And before Qiana could stop them, they yanked Honee away from the trunk and rushed her to the well where they pushed her in. At the same time JoBelle, some of her strength resurfacing, jumped Qiana and with the help of the students threw her in too. Then working together, the three of them heaved the old well structure back on top of the shaft, making it unlikely the substitutes' cries for help could be heard by anyone.

Now deep down in the earth and completely shut off from the outside world, the two substitutes wouldn't be found for days.

If then.

CHAPTER 39

Qiana screamed as she fell. She dreaded the thought of landing on top of Honee and hurting her. Fortunately the well shaft was wide enough for Honee to press herself against the wall and be out of the way. It was about thirteen feet deep, with a bottom so muddy, it acted like a cushion. So neither of the two women got hurt but now they were stuck in this dark hole, with no way out.

In the struggle they lost Ricky's iPhone and Qiana's cell wasn't charged. How horrible. At once Honee tried to scale the walls, hoping to push the boards that were the underside of the old well house out of the way, even just a few inches, and climb out.

No luck.

"Didn't think we'd have to do something tough like this again." She hunched down so Qiana could get on her shoulders, then straightened up. They had to do this in almost-darkness, by feeling around with their hands.

Standing on Honee's shoulders, Qiana could barely touch the boards but wasn't able to shove them out of the way with just her fingers. She gritted her teeth, stood on tiptoes, groaned and strained with whatever little strength she could muster, but in vain. "If I only had something, maybe I could scrape along the edge, Honee. Make a hole or something."

Honee handed her her metal necklace that she had bent straight.

Still standing on Honee's shoulders and scratching away like crazy, Qiana attacked the dirt rim at the top of the shaft, making clumps of dirt rain down. "Sorry."

"Hurry up, girl. I'm about to drop."

Finally Qiana chiseled out a hole big enough to let some light in, air too—the shaft was suffocating. "Now what? I'm hitting rock everywhere."

Only about the size of a baseball, this was as big an opening as she could make. They would never get out of here. Honee collapsed with a groan, taking Qiana down to the well bottom with her.

In silence, Qiana crawled to a corner and withdrew into a stupor. She was stuck in a deep dark hole with no way out. A dreadful feeling enveloped her as she remembered the time when she was four. Oh, her poor mother. On the run from a psychopath, she had tucked her sleepy little girl into what looked like a storage container to keep her safe. Mutti couldn't know the huge box was a shipping container but the psychopath did. Using a front-end loader, he pushed it into the Elbe River where it floated to the North Sea. Hours later, little Qiana woke up in fetid blackness, felt a moving sensation, and screamed, "Mutti! Mutti! Komm her!"

Because she was alone in a big dark box—but not all alone. There were little animals all over. She cried and screamed and when she was out of tears, she whimpered, "Mutti, Mutti, komm her. *Bitte bitte bitte*."

What bad thing had she done for her mother to abandon her?

She knew. *I was naughty*. Left the basement room, went into the fresh air and made sun angels in the red flowers. But was that bad enough for her mother to leave her forever? *Mutti, Mutti, Mutti.*

Even later, after she was rescued by a ship, she kept screaming for her mother.

That's when her life got even worse. At the Canadian orphanage where she was dropped off, she was punished for not being quiet and hustled out to the garden shed. The understaffed nuns thought the stillness out there would calm the girl down. More importantly, she wouldn't be able to disturb the other orphans with her incessant screaming: "Mutti! Mutti! Mutti!"

The garden shed was dark and musty-smelling. The cots had thin, hard mattresses, and the food was plain but okay. Not that Qiana ever slept on a cot or ate the meals that were delivered. As soon as the nuns dropped off the plates and left, the gardener locked Qiana and any other misbehaving child in one of his planting boxes. These were flat boxes with wire mesh covers that seedlings were put in before being carried into the sunshine to grow. The wire mesh kept the deer from eating the delicate shoots. In the case of the children, the strong mesh kept them from running away.

Then the gardener would take their allotted meals and sell them for whiskey. Whenever he felt so inclined he'd push crusts of bread through the chicken wire. But to get something to drink, the children had to wait until he dragged the boxes out in the yard and hosed them down. And whenever a child gave the slightest sound of protest, he sealed their box almost completely with slatted wooden covers that he fastened over the chicken wire mesh. If that didn't do the trick, he sank his scary teeth into their toes.

Usually it took only a one bite before a child learned his lesson. Not so in Qiana's case. She couldn't help it—she screamed and screamed. So she became "the girl in the box."

After six months her outbursts lessened but she still had them now and then—on purpose, whenever she managed to find a treasure: a smooth pebble, a shiny chestnut, a handful of golden leaves, a sprig of clover in bloom, or a lump of sugar. These she managed to sneak to the one girl who was a permanent resident of the garden shed. Her parents had beaten her so savagely that she lost her mind and was never released.

But giving that girl a gift was tough. It meant tossing over something small enough to fit through the holes in her chicken-wire confinement box. Which meant Qiana first had to scream again uncontrollably. And of course, to voluntarily get locked into a box was much worse than being locked in it involuntarily. Because she never knew if the nuns would ever let her out again.

That crazy girl never forgot Qiana's kindness. And decades later when the convent closed and the girl was finally released, she bequeathed Qiana the junky antique store in the South.

By that time Qiana had run away to Chicago where she ended up at the Kozee Inn. From there she moved on to a lifestyle in NYC that was deluxe and lavish but revolved around the same thing she'd been forced to do in Chicago except it paid more.

A bitter taste filled Qiana's mouth now as she realized again she never had a normal life, starting with her childhood. Even that first big box her mother hid her in was a nightmare. It was filled with rats. Qiana had to strangle as many of the little animals as she could, then she scrabbled to the top of the box to a small gap, the size of her hand.

"Rats, rats," Qiana shrieked now, returning to the present but still remembering, her hands flying all over to fend off imaginary rodents.

"Nope, girl. It's just us and the worms," Honee said, sounding hopeless as she felt around the well shaft for a dry piece of clay to chew on.

Suddenly Qiana remembered how back then she finally

managed to attract the attention of a passing ship by poking her hand out. She crept up the wall in the well shaft until she stood shakily erect. "C'mon, Honee. Let's try it one more time."

CHAPTER 40

Rolling around the other side of the main building was a rickety yellow cab, with the old secretary perching in the back seat. After changing into a low-cut tiger-print romper suit, Mercy Me had exited by a side door and hopped directly into the waiting taxi. Jubilant, she rolled the windows down a little, her hand rotating like in a speed contest. She felt like at the start of Christmas vacation.

"I'm off to see my hot new boyfriend," she said, talking to herself and thrusting out her chest. Folks never realized she had sex appeal in bushels. The older women got, the more they ripened into lush fruit, as her new boyfriend would soon find out. "Too bad he's got macular degeneration," she went on. "Still and all, he's rich enough to stay at Palm Island, the most luxurious retirement home in the world. Old Earl Granville's supposed to stay there too. Tada and yippee. I get to hobnob with the rich and famous. Hey, wait a minute. What's that... over there... by that old well?"

The driver couldn't help but hear her and slowed down.

"Huh? What? A plastic hand sticking out of the ground and waving? Mercy me, the kids're early this year with their Halloween pranks, aren't they? Tsk-tsk. Bet they got something spooky rigged up too with ghostly shrieks..." She lowered the window all the way and listened. "Mm-hm, just like I was saying... Huh, what's that?... A crippled little finger?... Stop. *Stop!*"

Fortunately the burly taxi driver had no trouble shoving the old well house aside and hauling out the two mud-covered substitutes who must've lost their minds. Instead of thanking the driver and Mercy Me, they jumped in the cab and took off.

"Faster," Qiana screamed at Honee who barreled across the manicured lawns and flower beds as if she were in the Indy 500. She sped to the guard house, shot through the open gate. "We've got to catch them."

As they raced along the winding country road back to Red Mill, Qiana glanced out the window at the beautiful sky. Puffy clouds strolled across it like grazing lambs. Oh, and those thick woods. They were just as pretty and unspoiled as the day before. Except this time long stretches of the road were lined with people brandishing placards: "Save Stefford School. We want Stefford Kids!"

Little did they know, Honee thought. Education was at an all-time low in this country because criminal elements had taken over the schools. Used to be Reading, Writing, and 'Rithmetic. Now the three R's were Robot-ing, Robbing, and Rubbing out folks.

But not any longer.

At that moment, traffic was getting to be impossible, with all kinds of vehicles chasing to Stefford School, trying to pass and obstructing Honee's way. It looked like a caravan of ambulances and lawyers. Finally in the distance a moving white speck. "Look, girl. I think that's them."

She swooped the cab up to the golf cart so fast that with all the traffic noises JoBelle didn't hear them until Honee screeched to a stop right behind her in the middle of the narrow bridge. Shocked, JoBelle looked back. She was even more shocked when she recognized who jumped out of the taxi—those two substitutes. Not again. She was so distracted she lost control of the cart. It veered right and smashed into the rickety railing.

Honee and Qiana lunged at the golf cart. At the last moment they were able to grab the two kids and keep them from plunging down into the river but they couldn't stop JoBelle, nor the cart. Both crashed through and fell. They landed with a splash, with the cart ending up on top of JoBelle and squashing her legs.

"Oh no, Ms. Edwards," Chrissie cried, looking down, "are you okay?"

JoBelle waved weakly. She was alive but just barely. Most likely her legs were gone and she'd be in a wheelchair during her trial. But finally justice would prevail.

Being locked away's the worst punishment you can get. Stretches the punishment out, you die ten thousand times.

Jefferson called 911 on his cell phone which wasn't necessary. One of the emergency vehicles coming from Red Mill had witnessed the accident and bleated up.

"Oh my God." Chrissie kept crying. "Who's going to sponsor our club now? We got the most important meeting of the year coming up and—"

"You mean the Inter Team Club?"

"No, Ms. Money, the Inter Terrorist Club. There's chapters in every high school."

First Abu Graib, now a terrorist club? Oh man, those poor befuddled kids. What's wrong with them?

Honee decided to check into it later. For now she had a new problem. Both lanes were completely blocked. "That won't stop us," she told Qiana. "I got something real urgent to do." She remembered a dirt path through the woods, which she barely managed to get to by veering onto the shoulder of the road before the other cars had the same idea.

CHAPTER 41

"Sweetheart, let me tell you. I was out of my fricking mind when I couldn't find you," Josh said, kissing Logan's palm. She was recuperating in a private room at Red Mill Hospital, one of the finest small medical facilities in the country. The police had already been by to take her statement. When she mentioned the flesh-eating monster, they said, "Don't worry, miss. It's all taken care of."

"I thought I was dead," Logan said, clutching a floppy doll.

"Did someone swing by your house and pick that up?"

"No, Josh. Ms. Money, she came to see me and she brought her friend who gave me this. And you know what's weird? Ms. Llove, that's her name, cried like you wouldn't believe, like I was dead or something. Never even sat down, just bounced around like a rubber ball.

"But they were both real nice but gross. Reeking yuck filthy but I shouldn't complain, 'specially not about Ms. Money. Wasn't for her, I would've died in the shed but she kept staying on my

333

mind. Gave me hope and stuff. Wonder why they didn't get me a teddy bear?"

"Maybe the gift shop was out of them." Josh looked at the rag doll with its woolly braids and blue eyes. "Or maybe they thought it looks a little like you."

"Silly Vanilli. Anyway, Josh, I heard your voice yesterday afternoon."

"Right. That's when Coach gave me that talking to. Sorry, I had no idea you were in that old shed. They grabbed me too, you know."

"Who?"

"Some of the JV football players. They've all gone bananas."

"Bet it was the same guys that locked me up. All I remember is getting in Mrs. Taylor's car for a ride home. She asked me to. Then I got knocked out or something. When I woke up, I was duct-taped to an old desk and so thirsty I thought I'd die. Plus there was this copperhead and gross spiders and rats."

"Don't worry, I'm gonna find those critters and whack them. I'm so sorry, Logan. Didn't know where you were but I never stopped looking. First I went crazy trying to figure out where you could be. I cornered every student and started in on the teachers. Thought maybe one of them gave you a B and you freaked out and—"

"Josh! You know I'd never go *that* far."

"Anyway, I jimmied your locker. Nothing. But when I poked around in the trashcans, I found a bunch of papers in the workroom. You know, where the teachers open their mail, but they were all torn up. So I spent all night putting the pieces together and then I knew.

"I mean all those bank statements with a gazillion zeroes? All in Ms. Juditha Taylor's name? When I asked Dr. Davis about it, he said it must be a mistake. Next thing I know I get jumped and—"

334

He stopped because the doctor came in, a distinguished gray-haired man who had known Logan and her family for years. He had a terrific reputation and was connected to many benevolent societies, including the adoption agencies in the big cities. He liked the Adams couple who had tried by every means possible to get pregnant, but without any luck. That's why he volunteered to pick up Logan's brother personally when he became available, and later baby Logan, a preemie. Ever since, the doctor had taken special care of her. "Hello, princess. How're you feeling?"

"Much better."

"I have good news. From a purely medical standpoint, nothing bad happened to you. You'll be able to have children."

"Not now!"

"Of course not now. I just wanted to fill you in on your future outlook. But now you must rest, all right?" The doctor cocked an eye at Josh.

"Just a few more minutes. Please? And about our future? We're not going to make another mistake. First we'll go to UNC—"

Logan cut in, "Yep, I'm gonna be a teacher like my role model."

"After that we'll get married," Josh said. "Then after a few more years, we're gonna start thinking about you know—"

"Yes, take your time."

After the doctor left, tears trickled down Logan's face. She remembered again the horrible experiences she'd been through. "I want to call Mommy."

"Just say the word, sweetheart. You can't call long-distance from your room. So let me get my cell from the car."

"No wait, Josh. Don't leave me, I'm still so scared. Wonder what happened to Angelo?"

"He's doing good. He's right down the hall."

335

CHAPTER 42

After the hospital visit, the two young women pulled over at a lane leading to a charred place deep in the woods where a trailer had burned to a black hull.

"You mind one more stop?" Honee asked.

"No, but make it quick," Qiana said. "I still haven't heard from Gunner."

They found a little spade and rake in the trunk of the cab. Each of them grabbing a tool, they traipsed in silence down the lane until Honee stopped. "Didn't tell you everything, Qi, sorry. Long time ago when Momma burned my Daddy tree, I got back at her."

"What did you do?"

"Burned her to death."

"Honee, c'mon. She just died last week."

"Yup but see, the dude that cut down my Daddy tree sawed it in slabs. You know, round wooden slices meant for table tops or

337

steps. I stole one and painted Momma's face on it with crayons. Glued on some Q-tips too."

"Wow, you were an artist even back then?"

"Not really, girl. Anyway, I squirted liquor on it, whatever I collected from the bottles Momma threw out. Stole some matches and burned her up good—whoosh. Dead, Qi. I made my own Momma dead."

"That was nothing, Honee. Just a drawing on a slab of wood. You were just an angry little kid that struck a match to a piece of—"

"But don't you know what happened later on? Momma died in a fire."

"There's no connection, okay? You think your little childhood act unleashed something evil down the road? It couldn't. So delete it from your mind once and for all. But with me it's different. I did unleash something evil."

"Girl, what'd you do?"

"I deliberately disobeyed my single mom. She told me never to go outside alone but I did anyway."

"You couldn't help it, girl. You'd been cooped up in that basement for so long you were going stir-crazy."

"But I shouldn't have sneaked under those sheets hanging from the clothes line. Still, if I'd only done that, it would've been okay. But I was selfish and stubborn, a real brat. I saw a flower field that should've been enough but no, I was greedy. Dived in the blooming clover. Still remember how it hummed with happiness. Didn't know it was some bees."

"Lord, girl, they sting you bad?"

"No, but how I drank it all in, that color, that sweet smell. The sky so cloudless and blue I felt like I could soar, touch the sky and make the world all better. Later I got on the sleazy path, as you know, but back then, if I'd only stopped at that point—But no, I danced and made sun angels. Just like snow angels but in a flower field. And that's what allowed that psychopath that was stalking us to catch up to my mother and me."

Qiana caught her breath. "Because I danced—almost like on my mother's grave. Next thing I know, Mutti comes running, trying to hide me. In her panic she picks the wrong spot and puts me in a big box that gets swept out to sea. I end up in a Canadian orphanage and you know the rest. Chicago was just a flash point. My tragic and sleazy past was really caused by me. *I ruined my life all by myself."*

She covered her face with her hands. "Worse is what my poor mother had to go through. She cried every day because she lost me. In her grief she married a slave driver, real SOB. She had to work herself to the bone and he drank and beat her. And my biological my father? How he suffered for decades too. Both felt worse than dead every day. Oh sure, I was recently reunited with them but you should've seen their faces when they saw what I had turned into. All their suffering over losing me was for nothing, for worse that nothing. Let's face it; they spent their whole lives mourning the loss of a daughter that was a disgusting prostitute. It was like I killed them again. How can I ever make up for that?"

Honee peeled Qiana's hands off her face. "Girl, you didn't mean to hurt nobody. You were just a spunky young'un starved for some fresh air and something pretty. And then you fell into the clutches of some horrible folks. But now you've turned your life around."

"But don't you understand? I can never ever let myself be *really* happy. First I don't deserve it, being a bad apple. And second, I'm always so scared I'll set another horrible series of events in motion."

"Nope, sis, that won't happen. You're gonna do good from now on. We're the Q Chicks, remember?"

"Will you help me, Honee? I really want to be a good person."

"Yep, sure, if you help me. But first I gotta tie up some loose ends. Can you stay *right here* and wait for me?"

"Sure." As soon as Honee disappeared around the bend of the path, Qiana started looking for a suitable spot. She found one and attacked it like a dachshund digging in a flower bed, while trembling so hard her body shook. But these were just the after-tremors. Because earlier she'd done it. Didn't let on what *really* happened when she was 13.

One time the man had to go out of town for two weeks. He told her, "Don't leave this room or I'll beat you to a pulp. I got spies everywhere." He paid his wife to bring Qiana something to eat every day.

She didn't try to leave. Where would she go? She had already tried to escape several times without any luck. Besides, it was a winter like in Siberia, and the Devil took her clothes and shoes. Next morning, she woke up with cramps, the worst ever. She cried and cried but nobody was around to help her, except for that hateful Polka-dots.

The cramps intensified. After a few more hours, something looking like a big blood clot worked its way out between Qiana's legs. It hurt like her heart was coming out. She watched TV enough to know about tying off the umbilical cord with a piece of string. Then she lay in bed wishing to die, for both of them to die. But not for long, because it wiggled and screamed, this tiny baby that so desperately struggled out of her.

Qiana panicked. What to do? She cleaned up the squirmy little thing, wrapped it in a towel, and cooed to it. The baby was cute with a tuft of hair and those big eyes, like a doll, a live one. Annie, my Annie. Qiana never had a doll before, now she had one. But—must get her away from here, far away. The Devil will kill me if he finds her. He might have been suspicious these past few weeks, but this would confirm his suspicions.

Then he'd take the baby, raise her and do to her what he does to me. Then his wife would kill her slowly every day, like she's done me.

Neva!!! *Qiana scribbled on a sheet of paper.* I ratha kill miself 'n' my baby.

But she couldn't because Annie was so pretty and innocent and dear to her heart. Annie was her life.

So I must get her out of here. Save her somehow, some way. Qiana worried about how to do it. And after a horrible night of pacing with the screaming bundle, she knew she was losing her mind. Quickly she made a shoulder bag out of towels and slung it around her neck. Tucked the baby in it, cracked the window. Just a sheet wrapped around her, she climbed barefoot outside.

Through some thick woods she stumbled, on and on, before that hungry pack of Dumpster dogs that always hung around the back of the Kozee Inn could spot her. But they did. Saw her trail, smelled the rawness of the birth and the odor of the blood still seeping out of her. She picked up the pace and ran like crazy, ran and ran until she fell into a hole filled with glass. And the bloodhounds were on her.

Somehow Qiana managed to beat the dogs back and keep going. Down a snow-covered embankment she stumbled on her bleeding feet, quick-quick, again being trailed by the dogs. The embankment was littered with more broken glass that sliced Qiana's soles to ribbons but she didn't care. At the bottom was a highway with cars rocketing past. Holding the baby up high with one hand, Qiana waited in agony for a break in traffic, waving and waving for help.

Nobody stopped. She made it across the road, the dogs still at her heels. Every step felt like she was raw hamburger meat down there. Blood leaked from between her legs but her bare feet were the worst. They were beet-red stumps.

Someday I'll buy myself the fanciest shoes in the world!

Qiana hustled on, her feet turning purple from the beginnings of frostbite. But the dogs stayed with her, barking and trying to get at the bundle. Tear it out of her hands, rip it to pieces. Devour Annie.

No! In a panic, Qiana stumbled up the embankment on the other side of the road. At the top, she hesitated. Now what? The dogs were momentarily busy sniffing the trail of blood. So okay, head for that church over there, with that brick building attached to it. Qiana knew what it was—another convent. Oh no, not the same nuns as in Canada, but they were. She remembered how negligent they'd been, turning her over to the gardener, but the vicious dogs were howling behind her again. And she knew she had to be back in the motel before Polka-dots came with the food.

The horrible beating she'd get if she wasn't back. Plus, she really didn't want to leave the Kozee Inn without first getting back at Polka-dots. So quick-quick, hurry. But no! Can't hand Annie over to those nuns. But what other place was there besides that ledge near the black forbidding door? There were no other houses, there was nothing. Can't put Annie on the frozen ground. Can't hide her in the snow either.

The wind roared, ripping the sheet from Qiana's shoulders. Crying hysterically, she tottered around, waiting to freeze to death. But Annie's whimpers roused her. No, can't let my baby die.

She prayed and prayed but no sign, no help from anyone. God must be on vacation. She cowered naked in the bloody snow.

Working feverishly, she tried to scrape out a hollow, some little opening where she could hide her baby until she could figure out what to do. But the ground was worse that granite. Her nails broke. She raked the hard dirt with her fingertips until the skin split. Raked her face until it was covered with bloody ribbons. Beat the ground and her head with a rock. The ground didn't open up, she didn't crack her skull. Wimp. Weakling. Coward.

What to do?

Defeated, she eased the little bundle on the ledge of the cloister. She pounded on the nuns' door so hard her hand felt broken. Then she walked away like a sleepwalker, trailing the sheet, but backwards, hoping and praying harder than before: Please God, let Annie be safe. Let the nuns be good to her and protect her. Make sure she has a good life. Don't let her end up in the dregs of existence like me.

All I want is for Annie to live and have a normal life.

That's all she ever wanted—just be normal. *Breathe in and out and just live.*

Back to the motel room, Qiana hustled. Hurry, hurry. Dig the glass out of her feet. Pull the bloody strips of skin back in place. Wrap her cuts with towels. Doctor her face with the bottle of lotion the motel provided. When a knock on the door came, she screamed, "Go away. I'm not hungry."

Then she lay in bed shivering and hoping Annie would live. That the nuns would take her in and look after her, but they didn't. She watched TV nonstop for the next days and nights, for weeks, for months, all the channels. Every hour she flipped from station to station, but never any mention of a baby found. Never a word of an abandoned newborn and a search for who—

Oh God, no. It was those bloodhounds that looked like skeletons. They pulled the bundle off the shelf and down in the snow. Unwrapped Annie and sunk their teeth into her. Ripped her little body to pieces and chewed her up.

And I abandoned her and put her within their reach. I'm a baby killer!

Qiana was mute when the man finally came back. The only thing she'd done was change sheets and throw the towels out with the trash. The wounds on her feet were healing, her face hidden by her hair. Dreading what would come, she stared at the wall.

"Good job, gal," the Devil told her. "The wife says you never once left the room." Qiana continued to stare at the fish, silently

343

counting, "...12... 45...98... 153..." She'd never say another word to him. How could she? Her life was over. It hated who she was so much it fled. Annie was her heart and she had killed her, so she was dead too.

The Devil walked around the bed until he stood directly in her line of vision. She stared through him but couldn't help notice his grin. "Here you go," he said. "That's for being such a good little gal." He gave her a rag doll.

CHAPTER 43

A hundred yards away, Honee was digging in the dirt too. She was overcome with that horrible guilt feeling again that had stayed with her ever since it happened—Momma burning to death.

All because Honee was so stubborn and haughty. She'd refused to listen to her mother's desperate pleas. Now it was too late. She'd always carry the weight of being responsible for the loss of her own mother's life. What's it called—mattericide?

Honee really didn't want to dig in the dirt but had to face what she'd buried here the night before last. After a few seconds she raked out a silver object that she hated with every fiber of her being—her cell phone with three new voicemails.

She had listened to them only long enough to know they were from Momma. Then she'd flung her cell phone from her like a tarantula. Finally she decided to bury it. But now? Now she had to confront the past just like her sister did. Honee sensed there was a story behind Qiana's rag doll but was willing to wait until Qiana felt like talking about it.

Taking a deep breath, Honee blew the dirt off the flip phone and opened it. "Press 1 for your messages," a mechanical voice said. Shaking like in an earthquake worse than the one that almost wiped out Haiti, she did. Didn't know if she could bear it—hearing Momma plead for Honee to come and rescue her: *Please please help me, Honee. Get me out of this trailer. Now!*

The rambling message was in a slurry voice.

First: "Hey, Honee. It's me, your Momma. Just want to tell you, I'm so proud of you for getting away from here. From me. And please stay away. See, that's the only thing I'm proud of, you know, that I made you strong. Strong as an ox. Strong enough to strike out on your own and have plenty ambition and sure to make it in this cruel world— Now don't worry, I'm all right. Doing good really but I caught cancer 'bout 15 years ago. The slow kind. Never told you, why should I? But yesterday the doctor come to see me. Says it's all over. Wants me to go to some hospice place but no. I don't wanna drag out nothing. I want to stay here and die quick-like. But don't you dare come back here or I'll kill you. I mean it."

The second message: "Only thing that would upset me real bad is seeing you again cause it would mean I failed. Would mean you're not as strong as I tried to make you. The world's a shitty place, you know, and during my last hour on this earth it makes me mighty happy to know you got away. And made something out of yourself. Heard somebody say you're a teacher now. Wow, my little Honee done good. So please don't prove me wrong and come back, you hear? There's nothing here for you. But I'm so proud of you, Honee. You made me so damn proud. Of course always did. You the only thing gave my life meaning. Everybody got a purpose, you know? Mine was to be a *con-doo-it*, that the right word? You're into words, not me. But yeah, I was a *con-doo-it* to you. That's why I lived. So don't worry, be happy. See, I got me some powerful sleeping pills. Just took them all with a little nip.

Well, a right big one, know what I mean? Just about there now. I want to be liquored up good, go to sleep and feel no pain."

The last message: "But before all them pills kick in and take me out, I want to say this to you. I was wrong, so damn wrong! Thought I couldn't make you strong lessen I treated you rotten. See, they took my first baby from me at the hospital, a boy. Said I won't fit, so I had you at home out of sight and was gonna raise you right. Now I know this wasn't the best way. Should've been good to you, girl. Sorry, sorry. Did me a few good things though, like when you went through that *phrase*—that the word?—of dressing up like a boy. Did pay off some real bad guys that was always after you. See, they knew you was a girl and was after you something fierce. Tracked you down like a K-9 squad. The worst scumbag was their top dog Hades Pym. All the time following you like an evil shadow. Claimed he *owned* you, being you used to work for his drug ring way on down the line but still. Anyhow I paid and paid. And paid some more, outrageous sums. Just about all my money—"

Honee flashed back to what happened in Luke Forest.

The attack was so brutal she prayed for her death and had completely given up when the torture suddenly stopped. An older man had come up, swinging a baseball bat and offering bribes, wads of hundred dollar bills. Earlier she'd offered Hades the 20-dollar bill she always carried in the hollowed-out heel of her Adidas. That was her "show" money, meant for anybody wanting to rob her. But he just laughed.

But this big money here now—that's what got his attention. One whistle and the out-of-control teens grabbed fistfuls and scattered like roaches when the kitchen light's turned on.

She scurried away like a mole that's been chopped with a hoe, tears of relief blinding her. She upchucked bile for an hour when she was far away and safe. Some of her wounds got infected and left ugly scars but she lived.

347

Until now she always thought it was just dumb luck.

"—I paid and paid. Year after year after year the price shot up, but I kept paying till Hades Pym and his posse left you alone. So I could never get out of that sleaze life, you know. Anyway, please forgive me. Just want you to always know how proud you made me. Never could break you, you know that? You're something mighty rare like the bluest-ribbon pony at the State Fair. Always was so much stronger than me you was, my—my—my *Honee Treasure*!... Always loved you, you know that?... As much as a train wreck of a person can love and more... See, my love for you made me more than a dumb animal. That's why I dropped one "o" out of my last name. Changed *Mooney* to *Money* to give you a goal—to make money, but the honest way. 'Twas the only good thing I ever did my whole life... So listen... I love you... my Honee Treasure.... Love you... forever... my... Ho...nee... Trea...sure—"

The voice mail stopped. Honee hung her head, her face soppy wet. *Oh, my poor fat confused bedraggled drunk old Momma. What a terrible ending she had, more than likely caused by a burning cigarette.*

Honee's head jerked up. *But she loved me, didn't she? Poor thing tried the best she could. Even fixed my last name to give me a goal. Even paid some scum to leave me alone, to not rape me, to not mutilate me, to not kill me. Momma tried hard to make up for her failings. And she called me her treasure. So that's what I am— not Honee Trash. I'm Honee Treasure!*

Overcome by emotion, Honee kissed the dirty cell phone all over. Rubbed it like a lamp with a genie in it and tucked it in her pocket. She'd never erase these voice mails. She raised her arms as high to the sky as she could. *Thank you, Lord. Thank you, Momma. I love you both.*

A few feet away, a wild rosebush beckoned. She stripped it of its pink blossoms, using her fingers like the tines of a fork, never

348

mind the thorns. She piled the petals in the hole. *That's gonna have to do till I can plant a beautiful bush for you, Momma. Many bushes, a garden, a little park with a bench where I can sit and think of you.*

Not far away Qiana was still digging in the dirt, now deep enough for a little grave. She pulled out some rags and buried them. Smoothed the dirt over ever so gentle, stood up and raised her arms as far as she could, reaching for the sky. *Thank you, God. Thank you, nuns. I'm not a baby killer.*

Because the nuns did find the little bundle and treat Annie well. No locking her away in a chicken-wire box. Oh no. They made sure she got a good home, not in Chicago but far away, with a nice mom and dad and brother. No question about it, Annie didn't die. She'd been adopted and had her name changed: *Logan.*

Finished with the little grave, Qiana looked around. And there it was not far away, the size of a big puddle. Somehow out of the hard beige Southern earth it had pushed: a field of red flowers, still in bloom this late in the year. Not clover, these blossoms were bigger and had opened all the way. Maybe some sort of pansies? She stared at this gift the world offered her and felt good. Her best childhood vision was still there. Of course over the years she had changed, but in her, like in everyone, there was still a child wanting to touch the sky and make the world better. She would do it by helping abused kids, those that had no voice. She'd speak for them. Fight for them. Get justice for them. This was another perfect moment, so she did it—flopped down in the flowers and made sun angels.

CHAPTER 44

When the two young women finally dragged their weary butts into the antique store a day later than they'd planned, they raced to the bathroom but only in their minds. In reality they crawled. They had to come in the front of the store. The back alley was clogged with building supplies and trucks but no workers. Of course not.

Inching through what used to be the show room that reeked of dust and mildew, Qiana ran her hands over the stained dressers and three-legged tables, with ugly chairs piled on top. She crept past worm-eaten armoires, water-stained bookcases, and a sway-backed sofa with its bug-infested guts spilling out.

"Pretty," she said, touching the pathetic inventory. Everything did look pretty, and if not, then, well, promising. All but one of the light bulbs in the dusty chandelier had burned out, turning the antique collection into a spooky cave reminiscent of a graveyard. No, she decided, not spooky and not a graveyard. It gave the place character.

Anyway, this was it—a new beginning. The Q Chicks would open the Q Store shortly. Qiana punched the air in a weak gesture. Yes, as soon as they had some money, they'd make a difference. *I'll show them*— Whoever hurts kids better watch out.

As the women continued to wend their way through the old furniture, Honee felt so sapped all of a sudden that she had sit down—on the bottom step of the circular staircase. That allowed Qiana to squeeze past her. She dragged herself up and into the bathroom, shedding her outfit piece by piece. The clogs she sailed out a back window.

In the shower, she reviewed the past 33 hours that seemed like years. Unbelievable, what horrible things she and Honee had been through, what tragic things they had uncovered, and what long-overdue act of revenge she'd finally carried out on Polka Dots.

She let the tepid water spill over her, hoping and praying it would wash away the worst aches and pains and the most gruesome images, along with all the grime and stench.

She couldn't wait to tell Gunner about everything. Oh, so many shocking discoveries. She had decided not to mention Logan to anyone but Gunner and Honee. The girl had such a wonderful life and her parents were on their way back from New Zealand. Besides, the doctor, who she confided to, said some day when the girl had a child of her own, she'd get curious about her birth mother. Then would be time to reveal—

Not now, though Qiana would never forget what happened.

She started scrubbing her hair furiously because she was puzzled. *Why hasn't Gunner called?* She didn't have an answering machine. So maybe he had called a dozen times on her land line with the old-fashioned phone that didn't record the caller's number. But nothing showed up on her cell which was charging. When she called him, his cell phone always switched immediately to voice mail. Maybe it was broken.

She mentally switched gears. Thank goodness, Logan didn't need anything. Her parents were comfortable middle class. But Qiana was broke and most likely Honee wouldn't get paid for her substituting job for some time, what with Stefford School being embroiled in all those horrific things that would take a long time to sort out and fix.

As for the money, Gunner would spring for the small wedding, but much more cash was needed. Maybe some of the antiques downstairs might bring a few bucks. Even more financial obligations came to Qiana: How much would those damaged wedding gowns set them back? Allie's new shoes? And how much would the caps and gowns for the underprivileged kids cost?

Plus, they'd have to pay the cab driver a fortune for "borrowing" his car, in addition to a hefty fine to the police, most likely. Oh, so much to think about.

From the back of her mind, it assailed her again, the vision of red flashes.

Got it, she thought. These flashes weren't warning signs, they were reminders. Since all of us face death in the end, we should live full-throttle. Go after our goals full-steam.

"Almost done, Honee," she yelled downstairs.

"Take your time, girl." Honee had woken up from a brief nap on the staircase, feeling more exhausted than ever and strangely troubled. Had they *really* taken care of all loose ends? But she couldn't think straight right now, so disgusted was she with her filthy outfit, her matted mop of hair, her sewer smell and—

Knock-knock!

Oh no, that cab driver already? With a bunch of cops waving handcuffs?

Groaning she peeked through a gray gauze curtain.

Nope, can't be. She must be seeing things.

Honee raced her hands over herself, her pulse revving up like a Camaro in a drag race on a country road. But no doubt about it. It

353

was Coach, the big huggy-feely-kissy guy she'd always dreamed of.

She looked for a place to hide, her mind chiding her: Quit being such a scared chickadee. Remember Momma loved you. *I'm Honee Treasure.*

"Just a second," she called, scrabbling out from behind the camel-backed sofa.

Man-oh-man-oh-man-oh-man. Wouldn't it be cool for the four of them to hit town together, soon as Gunner gets home? Take a stroll in Duke Gardens or zip down to Wrightsville Beach. Bikini time or skinny dipping but only on a night with no moon...

"One more second, okay?"

°EPILOGUE°

A mile away from the luxurious Fairmont Hotel in Bermuda, an old hut hid in a patch of overgrown shrubbery that lapped out on the beach. Every day the hut sank deeper into itself. Soon it would look just like another pile of driftwood swept over by the white sand. Nobody had used the hut in years.

Today the hut bustled with activity. Four men crowded in it, three of them wearing uniforms from a North Carolina company and high-fiving, and one slumping on a cot, tied up and handcuffed. His face was bruised, his nose broken. Blood streaked his forearms where he'd been cut and choke marks ringed his neck. It looked as if some security guards had caught their man and were just waiting around for a police van to trundle down the beach and haul off their dangerous captive.

"'Twas like taking candy out of a baby's mouth," one of the uniformed men said, grinning. He folded his switchblade and tucked it out of sight.

"Now all you gotta do is sound convincing on the phone." The second man grinned too and kicked the prisoner in the shin. "Say you just got an even bigger gig."

The captured man had his head between his shoulders in a gesture of defeat.

"Then put on the same act a couple more times. By then the trail will be cold. See, nobody's ever gonna hear from you again until the time's right. Nothing personal, buddy. Just following orders from Miami. Earl Granville's got major plans for you."

"And you know the best thing?" the third guard sneered, studying a copy of a bit photo that showed the captive, flanked by two beautiful young women, that had been over-nighted to him. "Nobody's gonna give a damn about you being gone. Your trash sister and your main broad—"

Gunner surged up with a roar that another kick cut off.

"—got nobody, with your chopper down in the ocean and no sign of it. So we're gonna party with them good. And that's before you get to star in that White House drama. Nothing's been happening since the World Trade Center but that's about to change."

Gunner made a sound that was interpreted as a question.

"All got to do with your looks, pretty boy. The National Teacher of the Year contest, you know. Winner gets invited to the White House. This year some Latina won but won't be around for long so the runner-up's gonna fill in. That's where you come in. You're the spitting image of the runner-up. Yup, old Earl's gonna deliver death and destruction via the schools."

He laughed. "Meantime your two chicks will be all alone, right? Nobody looking out for them, right? Now make that call or else."

**

Honee inched the front door of the antique shop open. Emir stood there, all clean and nice smelling, a hand behind his back. His eyes sparkled with excitement at the sight of her—the miserable stinking human being she was, barely hanging on, but his face showed nothing but joy.

"Hey." What's he got there? She thought, clamping her arms to her sides to hold in the sweaty stink. *Oh, man, is he gonna give me a rose?* Her heart was beating like trip hammer. Beat-beat-beat.

"Sorry, couldn't wait," he said.

356

"That's okay," she said, her voice trembling. Even though she looked like the nastiest scarecrow, she felt so alive, so in tune with everything around her. So happy being Honee.

"Just had to bring you this," he went on, his eyes softening. And while she waited breathlessly, his hand came from behind his back and reached toward her, offering her—

"*A biscuit?* Are you crazy, man?"

"Baked it myself...on a wood stove."

"Big deal, you can cook." She was fuming. Only some fool jerk would think of giving a chick a biscuit.

"Overbaked it on purpose."

"Do I give a gosh durn darn?" she snapped sarcastically, ready to slam the door in his face.

"Please let me explain. I can make the best biscuits. Ham, cheese, sausage, you name it. This isn't my best effort." The biscuit was still sitting on his open palm like an egg.

Filled with such disappointment, she grabbed it and pelted him with it. "That's what you can do with it. Now get the heck out of here."

"But haven't told you... My Gran, she's amazing. Uses grits for everything."

"*Grits?*"

"Yep, she scrubs with grits, eats them with mushrooms. But whenever she fidgets out, when she's on pins and needles. Worried out of her mind, you know? When everything's wrecked, she chews on something hard like a piece of wood or—"

"Didn't you hear me?" Honee screamed, her feelings hurt bone-marrow deep. "I said, get the hell—"

He still wasn't deterred. "So when I see you grab that clump of dirt I think— Well, maybe you...got the same... hankering like... my Gran... So therefore—"

"Hm, you thought..." Honee brushed the biscuit off, took a nibble. It was harder than granite but not bad. Actually it was

357

pretty good. Her anger gone in a flash, she felt flooded with happiness. She had changed, not only because now she had a place to stay, a store to run, plus a substitute teaching job but also because she had a sister and a brother. And man, now a first-rate buck was bringing her a present? Oooh, this was *so* important. She couldn't mess it up, getting some liking from a buck. No sirree, she had to do and say just the right thing. Act ladylike like Michelle Obama. Make no mistakes. *This is the new and improved Honee.*

"Well then," she smiled, her arms sweeping out in a graceful welcoming gesture, scattering dirt specks like crumbs and releasing an eye-watering cloud of body odor, "won't you step into our humble abodegia?"

***

Upstairs, Qiana was dancing around like crazy, wearing only towels and another pair of Manolos, this one a gold, velvet and snake, buckled, cap-toed slingback. She didn't regret tossing out her slutty clothes but couldn't part with her shoes. She heard the knock-knock. Let Honee handle it. She had too much on her mind. Most important, make her parents proud from now on. They'd be thrilled over what she and Honee had managed to do.

She fanned herself because besides being dead-tired, she felt so hot, so exhilarated. Oh, so many things to think about. How much would it cost to feed all the homeless on Thanksgiving? And how far in advance did Luke Chapel have to be reserved?

Qiana shoved as many trunks and boxes under the bed as she could, making a path, and pretend-walked down the "aisle." Envisioning herself almost at the altar, she stopped in her tracks, stunned by the view she'd see soon—Gunner in a tuxedo!

Oh wow, just wow. Words couldn't express the happiness she'd feel. The corners of her eyes teared up. Already it felt so real. She felt real. *Even big mistakes don't have to be forever.* Maybe God made people like artists do their work—first make a pencil sketch and if need be, erase it and start over. She felt the wonderful change in herself. She had turned her life around. *Gee, why doesn't Gunner call?*

The phone rang.

Miles away in a posh Miami rest home Earl Granville who was surprisingly spry but always pretended to be at death's door grinned from ear to ear. He was clutching a big picture that showed three people that were close.

"Swell," he said to himself, "three for the price of one. My chances for success just tripled."

~ The End

ABOUT THE AUTHOR

Erika Shearin Karres was born in Magdeburg, Germany at the start of WWII. When she was old enough to realize that one reason for the Holocaust was the terrible education German children received during the Nazi regime, she decided to devote herself to education.

She came to the US at age 21 and obtained a BA in Education, a Master's in Education, and a Doctor of Education degree from the University of North Carolina at Chapel Hill, NC.

She taught in the public schools and at the college level for 35 years.

For her outstanding work in education, she was honored by the Governor of North Carolina with the Order of the Long Leaf Pine award. The Governor of Kentucky honored her by naming her a Kentucky Colonel.

She wrote more than a dozen non-fiction books on educational topics, among them the best-selling "Mean Chicks, Cliques, and Dirty Tricks." Several of her books have been translated into foreign languages and are used as teaching materials.

She divides her time between Chapel Hill, NC and Wilmington, NC.

"Killer Lessons" is her first book of fiction, but definitely not her last one.

www.ingramcontent.com/pod-product-compliance
Lightning Source LLC
Chambersburg PA
CBHW051228260626
47162CB00002B/317